THE BEACON AND THE BRINE
KATHERINE MCINTYRE

Copyright © 2026 Katherine McIntyre All rights reserved.

The characters and events portrayed in this book are fictitious. Any similarity to real persons, living or dead, is coincidental and not intended by the author.

No part of this book may be reproduced, or stored in a retrieval system, or transmitted in any form or by any means, electronic, mechanical, photocopying, recording, or otherwise, without express written permission of the publisher.

Cover typography by: Cormar Covers

Illustration by: Linda Noeran

Editing: SJ Buckley

Printed in the United States of America

NO AI TRAINING: Without in any way limiting the author's exclusive rights under copyright, any use of this publication to "train" generative artificial intelligence (AI) technologies to generate text is expressly prohibited.

To those who continue speaking out against hate and injustice.

Acknowledgements

I didn't realize how much I'd fall in love with the yearning in this book, but I've been craving these forbidden vibes and this dynamic for a long, long while, so I'm thrilled I got the chance to write it.

For The Beacon and the Brine, I owe the biggest thanks to Molly, Jacqueline, and Katrina for beta reading this book and making sure Elrich and Ursuline's story was everything it needed to be. Also, huge thank you to Molly for letting me rebound questions and coming up with Elrich's name. I'm so grateful!

I also owe a large shout out to my reader group for sharing their love for the Monstrous Cravings universe with me. Your enthusiasm helps inspire even more stories! A huge thanks as well to Yoly from Cormar Covers for the typography and Linda Noeran for the art illustration, both of which I adore, and to SJ Buckley for her sharp editorial skills.

I'm so grateful to my wonderful readers. Every review, every message, every comment helps encourage me to keep writing, to keep creating stories, and I appreciate you all so much.

And as always, a thank you to my caring friends and family for the support and encouragement—I wouldn't be able to do any of this without you.

Content Warnings

This book includes mention of sexual assault (off-page and not main character), parental neglect, chastity cage, tentacle bondage, double penetration, and discovery of death of a relative.

Contents

1. Chapter 1 — 1
2. Chapter 2 — 9
3. Chapter 3 — 16
4. Chapter 4 — 23
5. Chapter 5 — 35
6. Chapter 6 — 46
7. Chapter 7 — 54
8. Chapter 8 — 63
9. Chapter 9 — 71
10. Chapter 10 — 82
11. Chapter 11 — 92
12. Chapter 12 — 104
13. Chapter 13 — 111
14. Chapter 14 — 120
15. Chapter 15 — 128
16. Chapter 16 — 142
17. Chapter 17 — 150
18. Chapter 18 — 162

19.	Chapter 19	169
20.	Chapter 20	175
21.	Chapter 21	190
22.	Chapter 22	201
23.	Chapter 23	209
24.	Chapter 24	216
25.	Chapter 25	230
26.	Chapter 26	247
27.	Chapter 27	258
28.	Chapter 28	277
29.	Chapter 29	290
30.	Chapter 30	303
31.	Chapter 31	316
32.	Chapter 32	324
Epilogue		330
Afterword		334
Also by		336
Also by		337
Also by		338
About the author		339

Chapter 1

If only life were brush strokes on a canvas.

Those, I knew.

Those, I understood like an exhale.

However, when it came to the rest of my life, I couldn't seem to get anything right.

Evidenced by...well, this.

I stared at the mess in the board room, which was now empty of people. Stacks of stapled papers were covered by the coffee that had spilled all over everything, and the room full of prestigious board members had raced out en masse after they were splattered with it too. I rubbed at the paint stain on my wrist, right where the long sleeve almost covered it. My father wanted a business shark for his eldest and only son, someone who would take over Albatross Industries. The communication empire was one that had passed down through our family for generations.

And the Durand family would not tolerate anything less than perfection. Particularly my father.

Clearly, I was excelling.

I heaved a sigh and began to collect the sopping papers off the table. My father had ushered everyone out of the board room, guaranteed to start smoothing ruffled feathers. He'd tried me in role after role in this company, but usually something ended up on fire. And then my mother and father would heave their collective sigh, one filled with a soul-weary disappointment.

Which made it clear that was all I'd ever amount to.

I tossed wads of sopping paper into the nearby trash can, which only held sundry things like toothpicks or tissues. Looked like it'd be pulling double duty today. Shame prickled across my skin, the feeling creeping in like always. When my father came back in, guaranteed I'd be informed I was being transferred out of yet another job in this company.

Who knew where they'd put me next.

The puddle of coffee on the table formed a swirl, and I dipped my finger in it, extending the swirl further, like ink crawling across parchment. I wasn't accident-prone, per se. More like...absentminded, I guess.

Colors, lines, shapes commanded my focus, but art wasn't a pursuit for a Durand.

No, board meetings were my future, in some incarnation.

I snapped to attention, realizing I'd been swirling the coffee into patterns on the table. Right. I rushed over to the cabinets and pulled out the paper towels from their hiding spot in the back. Watching them soak up the coffee only marginally distracted me from the fact I'd failed to live up to the Durand name again. I wiped up the rest of the table, needing to atone in some way. I already knew I'd be getting the silent treatment from my family for a spell after this stunt.

That was how it always went. I'd been ignored so much growing up that I sometimes wondered if I had the power to turn invisible.

A cough sounded at the doorway, and I froze.

My father, Angus Durand, stood there, looming like a specter.

His features were firm, proud, forbidding, every bit the figurehead he wanted me to become. And his dark eyes flashed, not with the disappointment I'd expected, but something else. Something that made my stomach churn.

"Elrich, it's time we had a talk," Angus stated, his tone like night-chilled granite. I often imagined him like a statue carved from ice, one brought to life. The reality wasn't far off for him and my mother.

"You're no longer a fresh teenager," my father said, resting his fingertips on the surface of the table. He lifted them up and grimaced. Some coffee residue remained.

"It'd be sort of odd if I was," I commented. "Just hit pause on the whole aging thing."

My father glowered back. Right, my flippant remarks weren't welcome here.

"Take a seat," he said, gesturing to the plethora of empty ones, since the board members had all fled from the great and terrible foe, coffee. "Natalie took everyone to the conference room down the hall, and they're going to chat amongst themselves for a bit while we recollect."

My stomach flip-flopped. Twenty-three years, and I still hadn't managed to find a way to garner my parents' approval. At this point, the prospect looked grim.

I took the nearest seat, because I had the feeling whatever my father was going to say would knock me square in the sternum. Even though they were all padded leather, top-of-the-line chairs, the cushion beneath me felt like a rock.

Angus Durand didn't take a seat. No, he stood, looming over me, the way he had my entire life.

"I hoped we could find you a position in Albatross Industries, but I don't think that's going to work," he said, crossing his arms.

Did that mean...I could pursue something else? My heart skipped a beat, hope bubbling to the surface. I'd wanted to be an artist my whole life, and at every turn my parents, my extended family, had stonewalled me from that dream. Durands didn't engage in "frivolous wastes of time."

Except nothing about painting was frivolous to me. I'd take any canvas—from stretched panels to building walls. Anywhere to let the explosion brimming inside me escape.

"Frederick Triton contacted me awhile ago," he started, and I tensed. I knew the name, albeit a newer one, because families like ours ran in similar circles. Most days, I loathed the wealth we had. And then guilt flushed through me all over again, because so many would kill for the hoard we'd accumulated. I wished we could give so much of it away, live more modestly. We didn't need most of what we had, while so many people in Peregrine City struggled to find housing or a warm meal.

I stared at my hand. I'd missed another paint spot when I'd scrubbed down last night.

"I told him no back then. It was clear he wanted a tie to our family, a bridge of sorts."

My brow wrinkled. Had I missed something my father said? It wouldn't be the first time.

"He has a daughter about your age," Angus continued. "I don't think there's going to be a position for you here at Albatross. Not one where I feel confident handing the reins over. I believe we should entertain Frederick's proposal."

Ice slithered down my veins. "His proposal would be...?"

"A permanent connection between our families. You might not be an asset to Albatross Industries, but securing some of Triton's wealth would help the Durand name," Angus continued.

My stomach sank. I didn't like the direction this was going. "Might not be an asset" drove a stake through my chest too. "I'm sure if I tried a different position, I'd be better at it. What about answering phones? Some sort of customer service role?"

Angus's lip curled in a sneer. "No son of mine will be answering phones. We've tried you in a variety of management positions, but every time, we end up in situations like this." He gestured at the emptied out board room. "No, I think meeting Triton's daughter would be a good idea. Arielle's a beautiful girl, and it's not like you're seeing anyone."

That was what I feared.

"What are you implying?" I asked, drumming my fingers on my thigh. The resolve in my father's gaze, as if his will would always be adhered to, sent a frisson of cold through me. Because truth be told, I'd been chasing his approval for so long that I didn't know another path. They'd made sure my assets were tied to theirs, so I wouldn't have the freedom to start over as an artist. Not the resources or the know-how.

Yet I was tempted.

"I'm stating that we'll set up a meeting between you and Triton's daughter. And by the end of it, hopefully we'll have a new, happy union on the horizon." Angus lifted his chin, as if daring me to rebel.

I swallowed hard. "So an arranged marriage."

The words landed stark in the air, a reality I'd never considered. My whole life, I'd been told I was following in my father's footsteps. That I'd take over Albatross Industries once I was old enough. I'd seen other marriages of convenience in the society we mingled in. Peregrine City's wealthiest. Well, wealthiest humans, at least. My parents had consorted with Human First on a regular basis, and they made their dislike of monsters clear.

I couldn't understand why.

The most beautiful paintings and pictures had variety—shapes and colors of all types. And the hate Human First preached had never settled well with me. Just another reason I didn't fit in with my parents and their peers.

I scrubbed my face with my palms, which smelled like the coffee I'd been cleaning up. The sharp scent wasn't enough to break through the haze that settled over me, though, like I waded through a dream that would soon turn into a nightmare.

"All we're asking is for you to meet Arielle," my father said, his voice insidiously light. "She's a beauty. I'm sure sparks will fly."

I licked my lips, swallowing back the questions bubbling up inside me. Rebellion on my part would be met with consequences. That was the way my efforts always ended up. The earliest time that stood out was when I'd pushed back on etiquette lessons, and they'd fired my favorite housekeeper as a result. The one who'd snuck me chocolates, who'd sung me lullabies when I was younger.

As I aged, the consequences grew sharper and more severe.

"Fine," I said. "A meeting."

Even agreeing to as much tasted like ash on my tongue. Guaranteed, we wouldn't be given an option. Our fathers were clearly planning our arrangement like we were pawns on a chessboard. Since I'd failed at following in Angus's footsteps at Albatross, he'd decided I'd be of better use sold off.

A lump formed in my throat, one he wouldn't approve of. I'd always been too sensitive for him. Too emotional.

Men don't cry.

"You can head home for the rest of the day," he said. "I'll bring the cleaning staff in to finish up here. We can discuss more about your future tonight."

My future.

Which I had no part of. No say in.

I pushed up from my seat and bobbed my head in a nod, shocked my legs could hold me upright. My hands balled into fists as I strode away, the melancholy settling inside me, a black void that some days I worried would swallow me whole.

He didn't say goodbye, and I didn't either as I exited the room. The hallway ached with a pristine silence that filtered in through my veins right now. The gold cage I'd been trapped in my entire life wouldn't be opened.

No, if I agreed to this arranged marriage, I'd be stepping into another one.

I strode through the halls, all paste walls and fluorescent lights and a sterility that seeped inside my skin more and more every day I spent inside it. My footsteps echoed as I headed to the elevator, and thankfully no one else was in there with me for the ride down. I leaned my head against the wall and looked up at the gold accents, the polished black of the rest of the elevator cab. The *ding, ding, ding* echoed in my ears as I descended to the ground floor.

When it opened, I stepped into the polished foyer, filled with artificial plants, cold marble, and more soul-soaking whiteness in varying shades. The receptionists remained busy at the desk, but I wouldn't stop and chat. Not while this anguish crept up inside me, begging for release.

I pushed the glass doors open and stepped outside. The sweet breeze beckoned me in one direction.

If I couldn't lose myself in a painting, there was one other place I could find blissful surrender.

I hopped in my car and headed for the sea.

Chapter 2

The music blared in my car so loud it ached through my bones as I sailed down the highway.

The Sentient Sea was an hour away from Peregrine City, renamed after the Awakening a century ago when the monsters emerged. Many had come from those subterranean depths, which was another reason why Peregrine City was such a locus. I'd loved swimming there from an early age, and I couldn't resist the constant pull to the sea, an inexplicable draw. While more monsters swam at Breakneck Beach, my preferred one, I liked being around them. I felt safer knowing those who could navigate the waters best were swimming alongside me. Out in that sea, I found a freedom I dreamed about every night when I lay down to rest.

A freedom I might never experience if I followed Angus Durand's orders.

What else could he leverage against me at this point?

Well, I still held onto a few things. My stomach soured, and I clutched the steering wheel tighter. I didn't know why I bothered forming any attachments. Too often, my family weaponized them against me, and Angus had the reach to ensure his orders were followed through.

I rolled down the window and sucked in a lungful of the salt air.

It soothed a part of me that was always broken, a balm to those jagged pieces. I let the golden sunlight wash over me, as if the rays were absolution, clearing away my troubles. And once I dove into the sea, the rest of my worries would drip away as well. The familiar signs for Breakneck Beach flashed into view, and my heart thumped a little harder.

I made the turn off the highway and caught the first glittering glimpse of the sea. The upset that had been plaguing me since the board room, since the conversation with my father, felt light-years away. Maybe I could swim as far out as possible and find an uninhabited island. Though I'd be far too lonely. Maybe a character flaw, but I'd always had a compulsory need for others.

Of course, I'd been starving for company, attention, my whole life.

The beach grew closer and closer, and I basked in the scent of the salt of the sea, the crisp wind whipping through the open window and sending strands of my hair flying in all different directions.

Breakneck Beach looked pristine, with the perfect blue sky dotted by puffy white clouds above, the calm, undulating waves of the sparkling cerulean water below. Why this cove was bluer than the rest of the area was a bit of a mystery, but most associated the color intensity with the monsters who preferred to swim there.

I might not have packed a bathing suit, but I wouldn't pass up the opportunity to dive in. After I found parking in the lot, I made quick work of getting out and then slipped off my woolen socks, my expensive cap-toe shoes. I carried them in my hand as I strode down the walkway, the slight sand dunes obscuring patches of the beach. The second my toes sank into sand, I let out an audible exhale.

I meandered up the travel-worn path between the dunes that led right to the shore. When I stepped into view of the sea, the crash of the waves filtered in, soothing me more. Already, a few monsters lounged on the beach. A kraken sprawled beneath a bright blue umbrella, their tentacles splayed out. A shifted kelpie—similar to a black horse, but with coal-red eyes— strode along the shoreline where the waves lapped in. A mermaid splashed around farther out, their bright red hair standing out amid all that blue.

The soft granules of sand bathed my feet in warmth, and I bent down to roll my pant legs up as I strode along to find a patch of empty sand where I could leave my belongings. My parents always hated that I came here, so over the years I'd stopped telling them. They didn't approve of a Durand associating with monsters, but they also didn't approve of anything I did, and this was the beach where I felt safest.

I began to strip off my shirt, button by button, as if I could shed this skin and become someone else. Someone who wasn't born with the Durand name. Someone who was free. The sun warmed my skin, and I soaked in every bit of it I could muster. I tackled my pants, kicking them off and leaving them with my discarded shirt, socks, and shoes. Down to my boxer briefs, I basked in the comfort of the beach and headed toward the water's embrace. The sea beckoned me, glittering perfection, and I wasn't immune to the lure.

The waves rolled up over my feet, and the burst of cool water sent a shock through me. I waded a little farther in, loving the ebb and sway, the tug at my heels every time the waves receded. This was the place I needed to be after that hellish morning.

The idea of going from my current prison to another...a shiver ran down my spine. Maybe I should run away from it all, detonate my current life and try to start over somewhere where no one knew me. The ache spread through me with an intense yearning. I waded deeper, the ocean swirling around my knees now. The cold had lessened, my body acclimating. In the distance, a few mermaids swam together, splashing, moving with an effortless grace. If only I'd been born there, in the sea. I wouldn't be as trapped as I was on land.

I strode deeper into the water, up to my chest, the brine churning around me. The waves lifted me up with each rise, and I loved the bob out here, how I could surrender to the rhythmic motions of the water. The buoyancy made me feel for those brief, precious moments like I could be free. Like I wasn't trapped in the prison of my birth.

If only.

I dove under the water and exulted in the feel of it surrounding me. If I had gills like some of the monsters out here, I could swim for hours and never tire, breathe without having to come up.

I kicked off and emerged above the water again, my arms moving automatically to carry me farther out. The waves rolled past me, the tug gentling as I swam past the shoreline. Three or four mermaids frolicked out here, ducking under the water then popping above it. Their giggles were buoyant, life-giving, capturing the sheer joy of being in the deeper water. I swam with the smoothness of practice, even though I didn't have the natural grace of those around me who were attuned to the sea.

Still, I continued to propel myself out into the brine, needing to escape everything I was leaving behind on shore. The disappointment to my family. The threat of an arranged marriage. The feeling of being trapped that had plagued me from birth.

Out here, it was me and the roar of the waves, the salty, swirling crests, the comfort the depths offered.

I plunged down below again, far enough out that I couldn't touch the ground anymore. The shore was a good swim away, but I needed to be farther, to bob and sway with the currents. My body moved automatically, with the practice of thousands of swims over the years, and I raced forward, as if I could escape all the problems barreling my way.

When I emerged from below the surface of the water, the sky above caught my attention. It had been blue and cloudless when I'd arrived, but scorched clouds reigned now, casting a darkness over the water. Already a few of the people on shore had started to pack up. My heart thumped a little harder, and I pivoted my direction. I needed to head back to land.

Thunder boomed, followed by the brilliant, blinding flash of lightning.

Oh, fuck.

I needed to get out of the ocean now.

The rain started pattering a few drops as I knifed through the water, making my way to the shore. Within a few seconds, though, those several drops turned into a deluge. The water churned all around me, the peaks getting taller, the waves more perilous. Shit. I plunged beneath the water, focusing on my movements rather than the dangerous storm that had rolled in. Otherwise I'd be freaking out. Even beneath the water, the turbulence affected me, though, the currents stronger.

I faced resistance with each stroke, even as my arms moved in automatic arcs, my legs slashing through the water behind me. I popped above for breath, but the storm had conquered the horizon. Rain pelted my face as I gasped noisily. Black stretched as far as the eye could see on the skyline, and the water reflected that as well, an inky churn to it that hadn't been there before. The lightning flashed again, the crest of the waves turning a brilliant white for a few moments, and then the sea-trembling boom of the thunder followed.

I continued moving toward the shore, the churning waves growing higher. The current yanked me to the right, and I kicked out, trying to stay on task. Yet the resistance increased by the second, and my stomach bottomed out.

The water dragged me to the side, no matter how hard I attempted to swim forward in the direction of the shore.

A rip current.

Fuck, fuck, fuck.

Normally, you flowed with a riptide, and I'd floated along with some of them before to swim back once it had carried me a bit farther out—however, this was in the middle of a storm.

If the lightning strikes weren't dangerous enough, the wild waves and currents were even worse.

I resisted the tug, trying to swim out of it with all my might, but the water dragged me to the right with a pull I couldn't fight. I was one small person against the wild, capricious sea.

I didn't wonder who would win.

Terror rushed through me in a fierce sweep.

The thunder boomed again, an omen, the scorched skies an active threat. The rain poured down from the skies in sheets now, and each time I bobbed up for breath, the water threatened to drown me on the surface too. My lungs strained, and my limbs were on fire, but I kept moving.

I tried to search for the shore, but everything had grown impossibly dark.

Rain obscured my vision with every blink, and I focused on slicing my arms through the water to keep myself aloft.

A wave dragged me up, up, up, and dread shot through me.

Because I knew what would follow.

For a singular moment, I was on top of the wave.

The shore formed a dark line that seemed farther away than before. Impossibly far.

Then the wave dropped, and so did I.

I plunged under the water with a threatening force, plummeting beneath.

And out here in the middle of the ocean, the depths were a different beast.

I tried to swim, tried to push my way forward, but water was above, around, beneath. The darkness threatened to consume me as I thrashed my way through, trying to find any sort of bearings, shunted beneath the surface.

My lungs spasmed, and the panic formed a second heartbeat. My chest burned, that tightness increasing by the second.

Oh gods. I attempted to look up, to lunge ahead, but no matter what, I couldn't seem to find the surface.

And I was running out of breath.

The current tugged at my heels, and I resisted all I could.

Yet it yanked me forward.

The last thing I caught in my shaky vision was a blackened blur rushing toward me at top speed.

Then everything turned dark.

Chapter 3

My body ached.

I was pretty sure my soul ached too.

Brightness hurt, even with my eyes closed, and each ragged breath that passed my throat sliced like swallowing shards of glass.

Solidness lay beneath me.

The last thing I remembered was getting battered around from the waves and the sea swallowing me whole. Was I dead? Was this the afterlife?

A low, sonorous hum sounded, a sweet melody that resonated inside me. Heat warmed through me from inside and out, and I didn't try to move, didn't try to open my eyes, just listened to the song that awakened me.

The richness of the voice, the precision, the firmness of the tones sent a thrill up my spine as the melody cast a spell over me. I existed in a nebulous sphere of reality and imagination, like a waking dream.

When the song ended, my heart ached.

My breath hitched, and I tried to open my eyes. They felt crusted shut, and when I managed to force them open, the bright, blinding sunlight made me shut them again. Ouch.

"Ah, he stirs." That voice again.

Fingers carded through my hair, and my body sparked to life, like the ignition of a car. I tried to open my eyes again, catching a glimpse. Someone hovered over me—a flash of paleness, light blue, silver—and the shift of something around me caused a pleasant, comforting reaction. The scent of brine overwhelmed me, though I caught threads of darkly sweet as well.

I sucked in a ragged breath, and those fingers continued to coax me into a sense of calm as I shut my eyes again, the sunlight too harsh and disorienting.

My mind dizzied, like I'd stepped into a centrifuge, and I didn't try to open my eyes again. I couldn't explain the implicit trust I felt, the safety here, but the fingers through my hair were sure, and the melody filtered through the air again, their low, resonant voice lulling me back to oblivion.

"Hey, are you okay?" a voice sounded. This one was different from before.

I blinked again, my whole body aching, but this time nothing braced me except the warm sand beneath me. The loss hit me acutely, the comfort gone. I pushed up, my bones creaking, my body stiff from being battered around in the ocean. The sun wasn't as bright, which must've meant it was late afternoon. I wiped the crust out of my eyes and looked over at who had spoken.

A redhead stood only feet away in her bathing suit, staring at me. Two guys trailed a bit behind her, as if they were keeping an eye out.

"Uh," I murmured, wiping my face to see if I could make myself function. My throat was wrecked, and it hurt as much too, corroded by the gallons of salt water I must've chugged down. "Got stuck in the storm."

"Wow, how lucky to get washed up on shore," she said, shaking her head. "Normally if you get stuck out there, you're a goner."

I didn't think my survival was luck, though. Whoever had been there when I first stirred...I had a feeling they'd saved me. With how far out I'd been, how strong those currents had become, the ocean would've dragged me to its depths.

One of the monsters lurking in the waters had to have been my savior.

I only wished I could thank them.

"Yeah, some sort of luck," I muttered. "What time is it?"

"Early evening," she said. "The storm raged for maybe half an hour but then rolled away. It was a fast and furious one." The woman who stood in front of me had flowing red hair that glittered in the sun, a bright infectious smile, and looked polished in a way I was familiar with, given my family's pedigree.

"Tell me about it." I scrubbed at my face. The idea of returning home wasn't a comfort, but I didn't have another place I belonged. At least I could talk to Jason about the whole ordeal, fill him in. Maybe I'd stop by his business before going to the Durand estate.

Chances were, if my parents caught sight of me now, looking like the ocean had spat me out, they'd send me back out and let the elements finish the job.

"Thanks for checking in," I offered, appreciating that this woman had stopped and asked.

"Of course," she trilled and offered a small wave before strolling in the other direction with the two men in tow, who had to be guards.

I scanned the shoreline, realizing I was still at Breakneck Beach. Far up on the sand lay a pile of clothes that looked familiar. How they hadn't been swept away in the wind and rain was another small miracle. I peeled myself off the ground, my bones creaking, my muscles screaming. Fuck. I needed water, first and foremost. My mouth was so parched, like I'd decided to eat spoonfuls of cinnamon.

My legs were shaky as I staggered over to the pile of clothes that were soaked through. My wallet was sodden, the bills wrecked, but at least my cards were intact. Same with my keys. Relief shuddered through me, and I dropped to my knees again. I wrung out my shirt and slipped my arms through the soggy sleeves. They were damp and felt disgusting, but if I was going to visit Jason, I needed to put on something. I slipped my legs through the gross pants but didn't bother with socks or shoes. Those could wait a little longer.

I took slow, steady steps toward the parking lot. Coming here felt a lifetime ago, after my brush with near death.

I could barely fathom how I'd survived that. However, I'd need a bit more time before I swam in the ocean again. I'd stick to the pools for a while.

I sank into the driver's seat of my car and turned on the ignition. The hum of the engine settled me a little, and I pulled out of the parking lot, heading in a direction I'd traveled a thousand times.

Jason's studio was my respite, somewhere I'd snuck away to for years now. My parents had never supported art lessons, or my pursuing the craft in any sense, and they'd cut off any of my teachers who didn't step into line with their vision for me. But once I grew old enough, I'd sought them out on my own. Jason was a talented artist who lived in Oak Hollow, a suburb of Peregrine City, and I'd begged him to teach me.

At first, he'd turned me away.

The kraken was reclusive and not prone to visitors, even though his art was on display in some of the best art museums in the world.

However, I'd visited every day after, and he'd eventually let me in one day for tea.

I'd been learning from him ever since. Oil, watercolor, sketch, charcoal, any medium I could get my hands on. And he'd been the one steadfast friendship I'd maintained, difficult to do with the circles my parents thrust me into.

By the time I reached Jason's small house in Oak Hollow, my frayed nerves had somewhat calmed down. However, I was thirstier than ever, my throat impossibly dry, and my whole body felt like I'd been tossed inside a washing machine and spat out.

As unobtrusive as Jason tried to be in his personal life, he couldn't help the expressiveness that leaked out of him, and his house was a testament. It was all cerulean blues for the exterior, and black trim with a black roof and black accents, from the shutters to the door. The sight of it filled me with relief, and I pulled to a park in front of the house. I bypassed the main house, which he rarely spent time in anyway, and headed for the studio behind it, a smaller cottage that had been a safe space for me for years.

I tested the doorknob—it was open. Even if it hadn't been, I had the key. Jason had granted me access to his studio years ago, since I had no place in the Durand estate where it'd be permissible to explore my art.

Angus and Mina Durand had made that clear years ago when they rampaged through the house destroying everything I'd created.

"Hello?" I asked, my voice raspy as I walked in.

"In the other room," Jason called, his tenor rich and quiet. The studio had three rooms, one as you entered with couches and flat, wide tables, as well as a small, functional kitchen for tea and fixing light snacks, and the other two had more windows, better lighting, and moon and sun panes in the ceiling. Those were the rooms he stored his art and supplies in as well, even though he had a whole warehouse of his own, which held countless priceless works.

Instead of walking straight in to greet him, I stopped to grab a cup of water, filling it up from the tap. I took a sip, and bliss coursed through me at the reprieve on my dried and salted tongue. As much as I wanted to chug back as much as possible, I restrained myself to slow sips, making sure I didn't vomit it up again.

After a few minutes, I refilled the cup and walked with it into the other studio space where he was working.

Jason had a humanoid upper torso, his skin a deep greenish blue, and his tentacles that flooded out beneath him were the same. His longer forehead formed a point, and he had two elongations where the ears would be, reminiscent of a hammerhead. His eyes were on either side of his face, black and sharklike. One tentacle held a paintbrush poised in front of his canvas, another holding the palette aloft while he balanced on the others.

I leaned against the wall, not wanting to interrupt him while he was zoned in his own world. A lot of his seascapes offered a glimpse at what lay beneath, that normal humans might never get to see with their own eyes. At least not see and live to tell the tale. A shiver rolled through me at how close I'd come to my end today.

"Why do you reek of brine?" Jason asked, pausing to glance my way.

"Got caught in the storm," I murmured. "I think someone must've saved me."

He stilled for a moment, his paintbrush poised, and he brought his focus back to the canvas in front of him. "The storm at sea is beautiful but deadly." The gentleness in his tone told me everything I needed to know. The old man didn't show much outward emotion or speak it to life, but he was a master class in body language. That from Jason equated genuine concern. Which honestly, was far more than I'd get from my own parents. "You should make yourself a cup of tea. The warmth will do you good."

I nodded, craving that. As much as the sun had helped, the wet clothes I wore, the remaining memories of the currents dragging me under, all of it chilled me to the bone. "Thanks," I said, knowing he'd understand the deeper meaning.

Because Jason was the closest thing I had to a parent, even though I'd spent a lifetime trying to please my own.

I walked back into the entry room and fixed myself a cup of tea, watching as the vapors chugged from the electric kettle as the water boiled. Once I poured, the fragrant fumes settled me in a way little could, and instead of returning to the studio where Jason worked, I settled back on the couch with my cup, on solid ground.

In a solid place.

For these moments, I'd claim what safety I could. I'd cling to the comfort I found.

Once I left here, I'd have to return to reality, and the fact that my future would soon change trajectory. Yet my near run-in with death had shaken me to the point I imagined other possibilities.

Maybe, just maybe, I could run away from it all. Leave my family and everything behind.

Maybe, just maybe, I could find my freedom.

Chapter 4

Several days passed before I was summoned for a dinner at the Triton family estate.

My parents hadn't asked about my bedraggled state upon my return from being spat out by the sea, and that was for the best. However, both Mina and Angus had reiterated that we'd be having dinner with the Triton family soon to see if an arrangement could be met.

The thought made me sick.

Just dinner. The visit was just dinner tonight—nothing binding.

I hadn't mentioned the arrangement to Jason—hadn't wanted to bring it up there—but if I needed somewhere safe to fall, he'd offer.

My plans had begun to thread themselves together.

I slid into the stiff, starched material of the button-down, of the fine tailored suit, like I settled armor into place. Unfortunately, I never quite managed to avoid the blows, even if I pretended like the vipers in high society didn't bother me. My room was sterile, as always, filled with books on business, and the stuffy, expensive paintings my parents deemed appropriate rather than the surrealism or art deco I gravitated toward. I could appreciate the mastery in the pieces, but they didn't call to me, not like other works.

"Are you ready, Elrich?" My mother's voice sounded from the other side of the door.

"Coming," I said, slipping on my cuff links and then heading for the door. We'd all be arriving together of course, our driver, Anthony, taking us there. My parents disapproved of my preference to drive myself places when we had drivers, but I'd claim every inch of independence I could.

My mother stood in the hallway, dressed to the nines like always. She wore a tea-length dress with hand-painted flowers across the cream fabric. She rarely donned the same outfit twice, and the sheer waste of her wardrobe bothered me more with every passing day. The jewelry she wore sparkled, delicate yet costly, and guaranteed my father would be wearing his own displays of wealth, from his designer watch to his handcrafted cuff links. I minimized updating my own wardrobe, even when they insisted.

"Are you ready to meet Arielle?" my mother said. "She's a lovely girl."

"You've met?" I asked. As much as I'd tried to research a bit on the family, a lot about them remained elusive. They were old wealth but secretive, and of course my parents would be drawn to that like flies to honey. Triton Industries was a unique purveyor of orichalcum, a rare metal zealously guarded by the underwater dwellers. How they'd established a foothold in New Atlantis remained a mystery, yet the lucky few they did business with ended up wealthy beyond measure.

Guaranteed that was what my father searched for in selling me off. As if he wasn't surrounded by enough money.

My stomach curdled at the thought, but nothing could be set in stone without my permission. I was an adult, as much as they still attempted to control my actions, and I planned on walking away the first chance I got.

"Of course we've met," Mina said with a light laugh. Her black hair was pulled back into a low chignon, and a coldness reigned in her eyes, similar to my father's. "I've been to the Triton Estate before."

"Right," I murmured, not wanting to engage my mother more than needed. "Let's go."

We hustled to the car outside with nary a word, my father waiting for us. Our mansion was a sterile environment I'd hated growing up in, and I continued to hate it now. Nothing like the coziness of Jason's studio, where streaks of paint were on the floor, cobwebs in some of the corners. It was real in a way I craved.

The drive to the Triton Estate was filled with my father making the occasional comment on an upcoming business proposal and my mother humming along as if she had a part to play in any of this beyond faux-doting wife. I closed my eyes and tried to follow the threads of an image that had been coalescing in my mind ever since I'd almost drowned at sea.

Of my mysterious savior.

The low, dulcet tones of their voice felt like blue and white brushstrokes on canvas, an idle flowing brook and dappled sunshine, and I needed to get that out onto canvas.

"We're here," my father announced, snapping me out of my daydreams. This was probably why I made so many mistakes in his line of work. Whenever images took root in my brain, I struggled to dispel them. The itch to get them out on paper, on canvas, on any possible surface, grew stronger and stronger until I succumbed.

Anthony drove us past a wicked wrought-iron gate with a trident adorning the center peak. A winding road led up to the silhouette of a mansion at the top, darkened by the surrounding night. Delicate globe lights dotted the way, as if fairies beckoned us deeper into the forest.

Once we wound around the staggered curves up to the top of the hill, the lights illuminating the Triton Estate cast it into magnificent view. The estate was vast, the mansion itself featuring arched display windows, decorated cornices, regal columns at the front entrance, and sharp steeples on the domes of the shorter spires. It made our storied estate look paltry in comparison, and I guaranteed my father was seething with envy as he often did around his peers.

Anthony pulled to a stop in front of the entryway, where my father stepped out first, then my mother and me. My skin had begun to crawl like the onset of the flu at the idea of being here. Maybe I'd made a huge mistake in indulging them this much.

I should've run while I had the chance.

When I stepped up to the entrance, the chill from the stone exterior settled over me. Guaranteed, this was another sterile prison, like the one I'd come from.

A butler strode up to us, clad in all black. He had a distinguished air about him, like he'd been with the family for ages. "The Durands?"

"Yes," Angus said, giving a sniff.

"Follow me," he said, holding the door open and gesturing us inside.

My father escorted my mother, and I trailed behind them, the butler taking the rear. Upon entry, splendor sprawled out in every direction, a marble staircase to the right, a seafoam bluish-green color to the walls with white accents. The chandeliers were made of sea glass that cast glimmering deep blue and green patterns on the tiled white floor, with veins of silver and black.

Two figures emerged from an anteroom. One was a tall man with a crisp black and gray beard and similar hair, dressed in a formal suit like my father. The other, though...

They weren't human. I'd seen cecaelia before, but never any as striking as the one before me. They stood at an equal height to the other man, but instead of legs were eight dark tentacles. Their short silver hair was carefully coiffed, and their skin gleamed like a moonstone in the light with a pale-blue hue. The suit jacket they wore had longer tails, and they had a maroon vest on underneath, the whole look complementing their broad shoulders and solid frame. Their dark eyes held a sharpness that fascinated me, and the severity of their pursed lips made them seem dangerous.

My mother bristled. Of course she'd take offense to being in the presence of a monster.

"Ah, my esteemed guests," the man said, stepping forward. Frederick, I presumed. "I was just finishing business with my lawyer here. Ursuline, this is the Durand family."

They gave my father and mother a quick scan over and arched their brow, as if they found them wanting. Then their gaze landed on me, and I froze. The intensity there was something I'd never experienced before. A whole-body shiver traveled through me, as if I'd been plugged in, and the hum of electricity zipped to life.

Ursuline tipped their head in a nod and then shuffled past us on their tentacles. I glanced behind to watch them go, wishing they didn't have to. They were the first bit of unexpected since the moment we'd headed out for the night. Everything else felt like the same old-wealth circles I was accustomed to—and loathed.

"Come, dinner will be set out for us soon," Frederick said, sweeping his arm to the right. "Arielle is waiting, as well as my wife, Darla, and our two other daughters, Olivia and Pearl."

"Right," my father stated, heading in the gestured direction. My mother quickened her pace, as if she could escape having been in the same room as a monster. Much of my family involved themselves in Human First far too much for my liking.

We stepped into the dining room, where four women were seated around a massive table, the cherrywood seats polished to perfection, and a cream tablecloth and pale-blue table runner across the length. The chandeliers in this room mimicked candles with their tremulous false flames glittering. The older woman with her hair in a low bun must've been Darla, and two women who appeared to be in their twenties sat beside her.

My gaze landed on a familiar redhead. "You're from the beach."

She glanced at me, and her smile brightened. "And you're the one the sea spat out. Funny seeing you here."

"You've already met Arielle?" my mother asked, stepping beside me.

"Apparently so," I said, taking the steps to go sit beside her. I'd rather her company than my parents'. I'd rather most company to theirs.

She flashed me another grin when I sat. "Who knew you'd be the esteemed Durand heir?"

I shook my head. "Nothing esteemed about me. Just happened to be born into a rich family."

My father coughed into his napkin, and when I looked up, his glare burrowed deep into me. Clearly, that had been the wrong answer. Though I never knew how to navigate these conversations, not truly. I wasn't interested in business or fluffing my ego, and my real passions were off the table for discussion.

"Do you go swimming often?" Arielle asked, and I leapt onto the question, grateful for one I could answer.

"I love it," I responded. "I've been swimming in the ocean for as long as I can remember."

"Same," Arielle said, a glimmer to her eyes. She glanced over at her mother, who glared as well. Apparently we could both garner parental disapproval.

Frederick entered the room at last and took a seat at the head of the table, something that probably had my father prickling. For as much as my father had always scolded me for being sensitive, he was a hypocrite given the amount of small things that hurt his feelings on a daily basis. Like not getting to sit at the head of the table.

"Dinner will be served in a moment," Frederick said with a smile, "but I'd love to talk with you, Angus, on how business has been as of late."

My mind started drifting at the mere mention. All around the room, more of the trident motif threaded through the decorations, as well as a lot of oceanic details. One room might be a style choice, but the exterior, the main foyer, and now the dining hall felt more like this was tied to the Triton family themselves.

"Have they filled you in on their plans?" Arielle asked in a stage whisper.

"They have," I mentioned, my heart sinking at the reminder this wasn't just a normal dinner. "What do you think about it?"

She shrugged. "As a woman in this society? I'm lucky if I find someone who's kind, not cold. I never expected love from a marriage, nor even fidelity."

Her words break my heart.

"But hey, if I'm married to the right man, I'll be free to do what I want." She flashed a smile. Damn, I wish I had her cavalier attitude about all this. Though maybe she donned a mask, like the most of the people in this society.

Staff wearing all black slipped in with the first course, a salad with what looked like tentacles in it. My mother wrinkled her nose, but I took a bite into one, which crunched. The taste wasn't bad, just a little lemony due to how they'd cooked it.

"Any reason for the aquatic theme?" I asked Arielle, since she seemed the friendliest here.

Her lips twitched with a grin. "The sea is how we made our wealth, isn't it? Orichalcum is found deep in the ocean."

"Look how well our children are already getting along," Frederick said, his tone booming through the room. Darla offered a wan smile, while Pearl and Olivia whispered to each other. My parents offered their normal pinched smiles, edged with a hint of desperation, because this was their last resort.

Arielle seemed resigned to her fate, but I hated the idea of marrying someone because my parents told me to. Maybe it was the romantic in me, but I'd always hoped for the all-consuming love I'd only witnessed in movies and books or on canvas—never in real life. Even the handful of relationships I'd had fizzled out fast, because once the people I'd dated realized I wasn't interested in the social climb, they had no more use for me.

The next course was a type of fish that probably cost an obscene amount, cooked in a delicate orange sauce, along with sweet potato mash and asparagus. I focused on my food, as conversation petered out. I wanted to escape from this dinner with everything in me, just step outside for a breath of fresh air. Arielle poked around at her plate, giving the occasional sour look up at her father, which at least made me appreciate her more. Perhaps that was something we both had in common.

I'd get through this dinner, and then I'd pack my bags and leave. It was beyond time I struck out on my own. Even if I made a mess of myself out in the real world, at least I'd be free.

"What did you think of Carina's new hats this season?" my mother asked Darla, who murmured a response.

The pressure inside me increased the longer the dinner wore on, to the point I had to swallow back a scream.

I rose from my seat. "Where are the facilities?"

"I'll accompany you," my father said. "They were pointed out on the way in."

Right, because I hadn't been paying attention. My father joining me was the last thing that would help the pressure. More likely, he'd make it pop.

I strode out the door, and my shoulders eased an inch at being out of the spotlight in the dining hall. Until footsteps followed a moment later, and my shoulders tensed all over again.

"The Triton family will make a good alliance," my father murmured, walking in time with me.

"Why don't you just do a business trade with them?" I asked.

"That's what this is," he responded, and my chest sank. No matter how often they spoke to me like I was nothing, like I was a problem, those barbs always stung. "And you'll make your proposal tonight."

Ice flooded my veins. No. No I fucking wouldn't. For once, I would stand up to my parents, even if they tossed me out of the estate. I didn't want to live there any longer anyway.

I whirled to face my father, my hands balled into fists.

He stared down at me, his brow arched, an arrogant cast to his features that seemed permanent. "We know about Jason."

I stilled, the words dying on my tongue.

"All it would take would be a single call," my father continued, as if he talked about the weather. "And your friend Jason would...disappear. Peregrine City's a bit treacherous like that. So many dark corners that it's easy to get lost."

My shoulders squared. "You couldn't. He's a famous artist. You try to make him vanish, and you'll draw far too much attention."

My father arched his brow, his eyes dead and cold. "A monster artist. Do you truly think the people in power in this city will search for him?"

Oh gods. My eyes heated, and I clenched my jaw to force the tears back, the shame and rage overtaking me in a fierce sweep. I should've known. I should've fucking known they'd been monitoring me. That no aspect of my life they could manipulate would remain a secret. I was going to be sick.

Jason didn't deserve that. He'd offered me everything—a safe place when I needed one the most, the chance to explore art in a way I'd only dreamed of. I couldn't put him through whatever hell my father planned on doling out. Bile rose in my throat, and I swallowed hard to keep from spewing right here.

"I'm heading back to the dining hall," my father said, his chin lifted, a smug look on his face. Because he knew, like every other time, he'd gotten the upper hand. All because I'd been careless. All because I wore my heart on my sleeve. My father turned on his heel, and the echo of his footsteps reverberated through me.

I tugged open the ornate knob on the restroom door and made a beeline to the sink. Cold water sprayed from the faucet, and I splashed it on my face, not giving a damn if it messed up my appearance. The icy blast didn't do much to quell the panic circulating through my veins. Fuck. Fuck. Fuck.

There went every plan of escape. Of leaving this hellish life behind and chasing something real. A life I truly wanted.

My heart thumped so hard I was surprised they couldn't hear it in the dining hall. I splashed more water, hoping to stop my mind from spinning, spinning, spinning, but the effort didn't work. I couldn't find a way out of this, not without hurting the only person I cared deeply about. I hated, *hated* how my parents always managed to be one step ahead.

I wiped my face on one of the plush wash towels left out, probably there for decoration more than anything. Fuck it. I needed to pull myself together before heading back into the room.

I sucked in a shaky breath and turned the knob, not feeling braver or more composed when I stepped into the hallway. As I approached the dining hall again, conversation trickled my way, but with the buzzing in my ears, I couldn't focus on the specifics.

All I knew was that the window to my future was quickly closing, and I wasn't doing anything to stop it.

Fuck. If only I were cleverer, if I had the skills to navigate out of these situations—but instead, I ended up duped every time.

I stepped into the dining hall, where dessert had been served based on the delicate confections in blues and purples with streaks of cream on small plates. Arielle tucked into hers, not looking up. However, my father's stare bored into me.

He'd set his expectation, and defiance would cost me.

No, Jason would be the one punished.

I walked over to Arielle, who still hadn't looked up at me, and my heart *thump, thump, thumped* so hard I could scream. I swallowed it back.

So much for the dreams of walking down the aisle with someone who brought me to life like a paintbrush on canvas. Who made me feel safe, secure, loved.

I hadn't been born for that.

No, I'd been born in a gilded cage, and I'd head to a new one.

Frederick's brows lifted as I sank to one knee.

Arielle looked over at me then, and her hand clapped over her mouth with a gasp.

"Will you..."

The words came out of my mouth, but my mind abandoned me as I sold the rest of my soul.

Chapter 5

One proposal, and my entire life was shifting at a rapid speed.

The house I'd grown up in would no longer be my home. A week from the fateful dinner, and I would move to the Triton Estate, since I'd been handed off to them like a prizewinning cow, all for a share in the orichalcum trade. My father and mother were thrilled, but not for me. Simply that their income would increase.

I packed up the rest of the things I wanted to take with me, which was less than I'd believed given that I'd grown up in this estate my entire life. Some clothes I'd grown attached to, a handful of comics I'd been gifted, my collection of notebooks with drawings that hadn't been confiscated. However, my parents had chosen and restricted so many of my belongings, of my life, that I didn't have the same attachment to the paintings on the walls I hadn't chosen, the wardrobe they'd curated, the books on my shelf they'd deemed worthy.

No, more of my soul remained at Jason's house, where he stored my art in his studio alongside his own.

I'd packed the basics into boxes over the past week, and they were to be delivered separately. However, today, someone was coming to pick me up to take me to the Triton Estate.

Arielle had seemed thrilled—at least based on the show she put on during the engagement—yet I couldn't shake the dread that followed me like a cloak. The Triton family didn't feel like they'd be drastically different from my parents. Just more cool, reserved distance from a society I'd never melded with.

"Your chauffeur is here," my mother stated at the entrance of my room. Like always, her dark hair was pinned back, her attire pressed and neat. Her lips were pressed together in a firm, unyielding line.

My stomach dropped. Right. "I guess this is goodbye?"

She lifted a hand to her mouth and lightly laughed. "How dramatic, Elrich. We'll be over for dinners, and likewise, the Triton family will attend ours."

I swallowed hard, trying to ignore the stinging in my eyes. I'd shed enough tears for a lifetime hoping and wishing for their love. And yet, part of me still hoped. Still wished this might be an emotional parting on her end. That she might show some shred of caring for me.

My mother gestured toward the hall. "We can't leave them waiting."

"Is Angus around?" I asked, my chest tight.

My mother shook her head. "He had a business meeting that couldn't be avoided. You know how busy it gets over at Albatross."

Boot to the gut. Not only did my mother not care, but my father hadn't given enough of a damn to even be here. Maybe I wouldn't be as invisible somewhere else. Maybe this would be a good move.

Right.

"I'll miss you," I offered, even though those words tangled with confusing emotions. I missed parents I didn't think ever existed—not in Angus and Mina.

My mother's pinched lips formed a quasi-smile, and she nodded. No touch, no reaching out. Simply a nod. "Do us proud."

I strode down the stairs, faster, as if I could run past the feelings trying to tug me under like the tide. At the bottom of the steps waited the last person I expected.

The cecaelia from the night of the dinner.

Today, they wore another trimmed vest along with arm wraps, their pale, smooth skin on clear display. Their silver hair was coiffed, their jawline sharp, the ridge of their nose the noble sort that demanded attention. They had magnetic, compelling eyes that made me shiver. I stopped mid-stride.

"I've been relegated to fetching you," they said dryly, arching an elegant brow. Their lips twisted into a wry grin.

"I'm guessing you have better things on your agenda?" I asked, even though my limbs trembled. This was it.

I was leaving.

"I'm one of the top lawyers in Peregrine City, so you tell me." A cool competence to their words belied what they said, and I couldn't help but be intrigued. Why were they the one picking me up, then? Ursuline tipped their head in the direction of the door. "We need to get moving along, though."

"Right." I turned around to say goodbye to my mother.

She wasn't there anymore.

Her disappearance slammed into me. Bad enough my father couldn't be bothered, but my mother was here, and she wouldn't even see me off in the end. That parting...well, that had been it.

I swallowed the lump in my throat and strode up to where Ursuline waited for me. Their sharp gaze skimmed over me, and they cast an errant glance toward the steps, as if they thought I might have a soul to say goodbye to. If only. When silence responded, they took their cue.

They shuffled outside, and I followed, bringing the door closed behind me.

Leaving my old life behind.

Bitterness corroded my insides at what awaited me, at what I'd been forced into. Arielle wasn't repulsive by any means, and I'd enjoyed talking to her at dinner before my father pushed my hand. However, I wasn't in love with her. No chemistry existed between us, none of the elusive sparks I'd always longed for.

Ursuline strolled up to a sleek silver car with a wider frame and unlocked it. They settled into the driver's seat, which fascinated me, since a lot of the cars weren't designed to cater to monster specifications. At least none I was aware of.

I sank into the passenger's seat and heaved out a sigh as I stared up at the ceiling. Gods, my heart hurt.

And I'd have to plaster on a false face, pretend everything was okay the second I stepped into the Triton Estate.

"Have you eaten today?" Ursuline asked, the low timbre of their voice snapping me out of my thoughts.

My stomach rumbled on cue, because I hadn't. Between nerves and a forever daydreaming mind, food had been the last thing on my agenda.

"Right, we're going to make a stop before we show up at the estate." They turned to the right and hopped onto one of the main streets leading deeper into Peregrine City.

Gratitude flushed through me. I hadn't been sure how the hell I'd compose myself before arriving at my new home, and the fact Ursuline was buying me extra time meant a lot right now. Considering they'd just mentioned how busy they were, I had the feeling they extended a kindness, one I'd willingly take.

"How long have you worked with the Triton Estate?" I asked.

"Long enough," they answered, a darkness to their tone. The elegant arch of their nose, those firm lips held a solidness I craved right now, with how out to sea I felt. They turned on music, and deep, pulsing synth poured from the speakers, which seemed to fit them. In close proximity like this, I caught their scent, a slight hint of brine and cedar, like being on a ship in the middle of the ocean, with the undercurrent of something sweet.

"Do you like being a lawyer?" The second the question left my lips, I wanted to swallow it back. They didn't seem to be the conversation type, yet here I was bothering them.

Their lips twitched, a flash of humor that surprised me. "Are you always this chatty?"

"Personality flaw, I suppose," I said, heat flushing through me.

"I never said I minded," they responded in the same calm tone, a spark in their eyes. Comfort rushed through me at the acceptance. I was so used to apologizing for every misstep, everything that didn't live up to the Durand name, that finding someone who didn't mind gave me such relief. "As to being a lawyer, I'm certain no one enters the field unwittingly. I like detail work, and I like puzzles, and this career allows me to indulge in both."

"I've never heard of being a lawyer described like that," I responded, curiosity sweeping in. A livelihood like that existed so far out of my skill set, though most careers in the business sector had been. My parents had tried and tried and tried until they finally sold me off in exchange for shares in orichalcum, I presumed. The truth settled sour in my gut, ruining my appetite.

"And what do you do, Elrich?" The rich, low way they said my name sent a shiver through me.

I licked my lips, trying to focus on their question rather than how my body perked up. "Nothing of use." Shame, an old familiar friend, filtered over me.

"I'm not asking for your job or title," they responded. "In your free time, what do you like to do?"

They slowed down in front of Haven Diner, the neon sign in view. My heart sped up a little. I'd never been to this part of the city before. While monsters and humans coexisted in Peregrine City, both tended to dwell in different sectors. Haven Diner had a reputation for being a sanctuary, particularly for monsters of all walks.

Though, Ursuline was a cecaelia, so of course they wouldn't think twice about going here.

"Art," I burst out, realizing I'd never answered. "Uh, painting, drawing, murals, that sort of thing."

"The world needs more artists," Ursuline said, passing me a wan smile. The curve of their generous lips, how their dark eyes soaked in every detail—I couldn't stop watching them. And those words—my heart bloomed over them. I'd grown so used to the usual condemnation of the arts the Durand family delivered.

"I'm glad you think so," was all I managed to say, my mind whirling. My fingers itched to sketch out a few lines. Maybe I could ask for a pen or pencil and get the impulse out on a napkin.

"Come on," Ursuline said, cracking the car door open. "Haven's got the best food in town."

My legs trembled as I rose, the weight of these changes crashing over me. Heading into a new life, away from everything I knew. Marrying someone I'd just met. Everything about this situation made my stomach churn, but when I glanced up, Ursuline's steady gaze remained on me. They stared, a quiet solidity to them that I couldn't help but be drawn to.

I swallowed hard and followed them up the walkway to Haven.

A burnt sugar scent filtered through my nose as we approached the door. Probably magical. I'd heard this place was spelled for safety, run by a witch? Witches? The slightest bit of excitement pumped through my veins. All my life, I'd been craving something different from the society I'd been born into—rigid, confining, restricted.

I stepped into Haven, and my senses launched into overload. The place smelled like cinnamon and other spices, sharp and alluring, and the colors sparked my inspiration. Black and white checkerboard tiles on the flooring, purple and green vinyl on the booth seating. Purple velvet curtains that I itched to paint. And that was only the décor—the patrons were just as varied, just as fascinating.

A massive horned minotaur sat with a dainty human, deep in conversation, while three satyrs took up another booth, their cloven hooves nudging against each other beneath the table. A vampire applied her makeup from a compact in another booth, in professional business attire. A group of humanish people sat around a table, but the bright colors, the tattoos, the flash of their accessories drew me in. Somehow, I had the feeling they weren't all humans, despite their appearance, but even if they were, their presentation was far more fascinating than I was used to.

Unexpected comfort filtered through me, despite this place being new, being different.

A woman at the host stand strode up to us, her hips swinging like a pendulum. She was tall and gorgeous with dark wavy hair and a sanguine smile.

"Sofia," Ursuline said, their voice a seductive purr. Was this a partner of theirs? They were both so impossibly attractive.

"And who's this you've brought?" Sofia asked, a wicked sparkle in her gaze as it turned on me.

I stood a little straighter under her perusal, even though it didn't seem flirtatious—more curious.

"Elrich," Ursuline said. "Another addition to the Triton family collection."

Sofia's lip curled into a sneer. "Frederick hasn't stopped his acquisitions?"

Ursuline's jaw tensed, making it razor sharp. "Why would he do that?"

Sofia gave a knowing nod and swept an arm out before she directed us over to one of the nearest open booths. Maybe they weren't partners, but they were definitely familiar with each other. Curiosity burned through me—both at their intimacy and their comments. Even though Ursuline worked for Triton, they didn't seem to have a strong care for their employer. And the reach of their job seemed a bit...more than that of a regular lawyer.

"Here are the menus," Sofia said, her intense gaze landing on me. "You look like you could use something sweet."

"Don't you have a wife to attend to, Sofia?" Ursuline arched their brow.

Sofia's canines flashed with her grin, her gaze wicked. "Doesn't mean I can't tell the truth. Just look at him."

Heat flushed through me, my cheeks burning. Both of their gazes landed on me, and I squirmed in my seat. The perusal did something surprising to my insides, waking up my libido. I hated when my folks talked about me like I wasn't in the room, but this wasn't registering negatively. No, this felt...positive in the way it pinged my senses, in how they stared at me like I was the only one here.

Far from invisible.

"You're not wrong," Ursuline said, a smirk on their lips. "Want me to order for you? In case it wasn't obvious, I've been here plenty."

"That works for me," I said, relief prickling through me. I could barely focus on the menu let alone make a choice right now. Not with all the changes coming up.

"Cinnamon roll pancakes," Ursuline said. "A club sandwich for me as well as a coffee." They paused to look at me. "Coffee or tea drinker?"

"Tea," I stated. "Coffee makes me too jittery."

"I've got you," Sofia said, passing me a kind look. "We've got a great tea selection." With that, Sofia whirled around and headed for the kitchen. Her skirts swirled around her legs as she moved with a mesmerizing fluidity.

"She's quite a woman, isn't she?" Ursuline said, a low mirth to their tone.

I blinked, realizing I gawked, and another blush colored my cheeks. "Does she work here?"

"She's the owner," Ursuline said. "As well as a formidable witch."

I nodded. "That makes a lot of sense."

"You don't seem twitchy to be in Haven," Ursuline commented. "Unlike most of the humans I've met in your sphere."

I shrugged. "I don't share their perspectives. A kraken is the one who taught me art, and he's probably the closest person in my life."

Ursuline arched a brow. "How well known is this kraken in the art community?"

"Fairly," I said, a hint of a grin on my lips. In the moments where despair crept in, I held those memories with Jason close to my chest.

Maybe I'd still be able to see him. To go visit his home and find the escape I'd need.

"It wouldn't be Jason VanStaten, would it?" Ursuline asked.

I blinked. I forgot I was around monsters here, not in my parents' world, where only human artists and creators were lauded. "He was the best teacher I could've asked for."

"If he deemed you worthy of teaching, I now want to see your work," Ursuline said. "Jason is a close friend of mine."

"Really?" I asked, excitement prickling through me. "What are the odds?"

"Mm, undersea monsters band together a little more than you'd think. The ocean might be vast, but the ones who traverse between this stretch of the sea and Peregrine City are limited."

"What's it like?" I asked, fascinated. "Being able to go to the depths like that?"

"For me, swimming is as natural as breathing, so the sea feels more like home than the land often does," they said, one of their tentacles giving a lazy twirl. "Curious?"

"More than anything," I breathed out.

"Sofia's right," Ursuline said, their voice low and decadent. "You're sweet."

A shiver rolled through me. "Why do you say that like it's a bad thing?"

They shook their head, a wan smile on their face, one that didn't reach the shadows in their eyes. "In Peregrine City? You'll get eaten alive."

I swallowed hard. The warning in their voice, the seriousness, settled in my bones.

Those dreams of escape, of running free in the city felt so laughable when faced with parts I'd never even explored before.

Maybe I really was destined for nothing more than a gilded cage.

CHAPTER 6

When Ursuline finally dropped me off at the estate, I'd been tempted to beg them to stay.

Odd, seeing as they were a total stranger, but their formidableness filled me with the first bit of comfort I could latch onto.

However, once I entered the Triton Estate and the butler escorted me to my room, I felt like I'd been sent to another posh prison. The Triton Estate might have different décor than the Durand Estate, but it was cold and forbidding in a way I struggled to settle into.

I lay down on the plush bed in my new room, all ocean blues with sea glass décor. At least this felt a little more comfortable than the room I'd left behind. To be honest, I was surprised they'd put me in a separate wing from Arielle, since we were betrothed. Although, from the understanding I'd gotten from her, she also viewed this as a transaction, not anything…real.

A knock sounded at the door, and I sat up.

Arielle stood in the doorway, a smile on her lips. Her long, coppery orange hair traveled to her waist, twined back in a braid today, and she wore a winsome yellow dress that cinched at the waist to flow out in a larger skirt. She was stunning, with wide, curious eyes and delicate features, but my body didn't respond in the slightest.

"When did you arrive?" she asked.

"An hour ago," I said, running my fingers through my hair. I attempted to paste on a smile, but it wobbled.

"Don't look so tortured," she teased. "I'm well aware of what this is—a marriage we've both been pushed into. I'm not under any delusions I'm your one. We played the parts, did our duties, and now we can enjoy our lives and our own pursuits."

That should comfort me—that Arielle wasn't trying to force a romance on me, but instead the words knifed at my heart a little more. That I'd never have the love I'd longed for. That I'd only get trysts in the dark while we put up a facade.

"You're as free as you want to be while you're here, apart from the appearances we'll need to make at balls. What do you like to do, besides getting spat out by the ocean?" Arielle asked, coming over to plop down on the mattress beside me.

"Do I have to stay here?" I asked. "In the estate?"

Arielle's laugh was light, tinkling. "You're not a prisoner." She gave me a light push, and I fought the urge to lean into the contact—any contact—after being touch starved my whole life. "You might need to let us know where you go so you've got guards with you, but of course you can go where you like."

The idea of heading to Jason's with guards felt ridiculous, but maybe they'd allow me to go in by myself and wait outside. The first fluttering of hope burst in my chest. That even though I'd been sold to a rich family, I might not be as trapped as I'd imagined.

"What do you like to do?" I asked, even though I never answered her question.

"Dance," she said with a wink. "Papa wanted me married off as fast as possible because he was tired of finding me at the clubs in Peregrine City. He said I partied too much. Thought it gave our family a bad name."

"If you want to dance, that's great," I offered, appreciating her openness. "I'll forewarn you, though, I've got no coordination."

"Our parents will probably require us to take lessons before the wedding," she said. "Something formal. Definitely not anything slutty." Another laugh spilled out of her. "This is weird, right?"

A laugh burst out of me, and some of the pressure that had been weighing me down lightened. "So damn weird. I spent so long with my father hounding me to take on the family business after him, and now that those responsibilities aren't mine anymore, I have no idea what my future looks like."

"This is about freedom." Arielle passed me a glance. "I don't know about you, but I'm not feeling any sparks, no offense. But I also didn't enter into this expecting some romantic whirlwind."

"You don't hold back, do you?" I said, more knots loosening. "I'm not offended, though I can admit I never wanted an arranged marriage."

"Then why did you propose?" she asked, curiosity dancing in her eyes.

"My father is excellent at coercion," I responded. "He's always had methods of getting what he wanted."

"Mine's...complicated," Arielle said, the light dimming from her expression for the first time. "But he's loyal to our family."

Loyalty to our families was what got us into this in the first place, but I swallowed the words back. She already knew. "Would you mind showing me around the estate? It feels odd to poke around on my own."

Arielle rolled her eyes. "You realize you're living here, right? You're free to go anywhere you like—just respect people's privacy. Don't rummage around in bedrooms." She tugged at the opalescent blue pendant hanging down by her breasts.

"Let's start with the kitchen," I said, even though I ate recently. "I've seen the entrance and dining hall, but this place is massive. It'll take a while to explore."

"Sorry you had to deal with Ursuline bringing you over," Arielle said. "They're so serious and pissy all the time."

My brow wrinkled. They hadn't come across like that in the slightest. If anything, they'd been sharp, attentive, and kind. I'd felt comfortable in their presence in a way that was rare, and I liked that they'd taken me to their monster hangout rather than some stuffy human place. "They made the transition more bearable."

"Are you a saint or something?" Arielle said with a laugh. Their comment prickled under my skin, even though I had no reason for allegiance. Maybe more because I didn't have reason to condemn them when they'd done nothing wrong. "Anyway," she said, pushing up from her seat on the bed. "Let's go to the kitchen first. I'll show you the best places in the house."

She traipsed forward, all lightness, with an upbeat nature I envied. I wasn't mired in misery, but I waded more through a palette of emotions, splashing different ones on the page every waking hour. To be that carefree wasn't in my nature.

We strode down the staircase on the opposite side of the hallway, this one leading to what looked like an entertaining area, with flatscreens mounted, couches scattered about, and a grand fireplace on the far wall. The entire wall along the back was glass, two doors carved in the middle. It showcased a breathtaking view of Hawk Bay, which lay directly behind the Triton Estate.

"How often do you swim in there?" I asked. Even after my last experience with the ocean, the itch to swim hadn't been knocked out of me. And in the bay, it'd be far safer than facing the riptides in the sea.

"Daily," Arielle said without turning around. "Why else do you think we chose this property?"

"Does your whole family like to swim?" I asked.

"You could say that," she said, a hint of a tease in her voice, like some secret danced beneath the surface. "The kitchen is right through here."

She strolled through the archway into an open kitchen, also with an oceanic motif, the breezy, beachside feel present through the entire house. White latticed windows spread out across the back of the kitchen, displaying more of the stunning view. The bay sparkled, beckoning me to take a dip. The tan furniture arranged by the windows complemented the pale sand-colored flooring and the cream walls. The blue accents were purposeful, symbols I recognized as belonging to the settlements in New Atlantis.

The blue tiles shimmered along the back of the burners and framed the kitchen counters. The multiple ovens and extensive ranges made it clear some of the cooking was done here, even though I had the feeling they also had a private kitchen as well. Most places like this did.

"You never answered my question, you know," she called over to me from where she stood by the window. "If you don't have hobbies, you're going to go insane here. Unless you want to give dancing another try and hit the clubs with me."

"Do you have anywhere I can paint?" I'd bought some basic supplies this week, since I was no longer in my parents' estate where they'd forbidden it. If I could do that...maybe I'd survive this after all.

"We've got studio space," she said. "It's by the music room. Our parents always encouraged pursuits in the arts, but none of us had much talent or interest."

My mouth dropped. "Studio space?"

Arielle wrinkled her nose. "Yeah, a whole messload of brushes, paints, whatever artists use. Is that your thing? My father will be thrilled. He purchases a lot of art."

"Do you mind showing me over there?" I asked, the itch to create prickling along my fingertips. The glitter of the bay under the late afternoon sun caught my attention, the sight sparking inspiration like nothing else. Water had always lured me in, a constant font of creativity flowing when I was near it. If I could take a canvas down by the bay to paint, I'd be able to tap into that.

"If you want to," Arielle said. "I think painting's boring as hell. It's the sort of stuff I was forced to do as a kid, and since the second I didn't have to anymore, I haven't picked up a paintbrush again."

"If it's not your passion, I understand that," I said. "Doesn't mean you can't appreciate the end result."

She wrinkled her nose. "Like galleries? Gag."

I shook my head, even though I didn't take her dislike personally. She'd stated from the outset we weren't compatible. "Or just a painting that strikes you. Art can hit people in so many different ways."

"Maybe if I got drunk enough," she commented, leading out of the kitchen. She led me through a few different hallways, turns I memorized as I'd be heading to this area the most.

When Arielle stopped outside the open studio door, I strode past her.

The space smelled like paint and turpentine, and I savored the inhale, a hint of familiarity I'd craved. Unlike Jason's cozy studio space, this aimed for cool yet functional, and the white walls, the extra lighting on the ceiling, the countless drawers lining the side wall, all suggested this was designed for an artist.

"If you need to romance the canvas or whatever you plan on doing, go ahead," Arielle said. "I'm going out for dinner and drinks tonight with my friend Sandra."

My chest twisted at that. Not like I'd expected an invitation, but part of me had hoped Arielle and I would at least find solace in companionship through this. But she seemed to have her own agenda that she didn't plan to stop just because she was engaged.

"Yeah, I think I'll work on something in here," I said, rooting through some of the cabinets. I tugged out a fresh blank canvas, the sort of pure white that begged for splashes of color. Already the swirls of water in the glittering bay flashed in my mind. I found a palette, as well as acrylics and paintbrushes, neatly organized.

"Enjoy," Arielle called to me, heading for the door. Her easy dismissal stung a little, but I didn't fault her. She had her own life here, and I'd disrupted it, all because our parents deemed our marriage beneficial. I hadn't heard what my father got out of the deal, but guaranteed he'd sell out a lot more than me to get a piece of the orichalcum trade Triton possessed.

As her footsteps faded, I set up a canvas on the easel and smeared some paint on the palette, the practice second nature. The motions soothed me, the measured preparation that came before setting color to the canvas.

I dipped the paintbrush into the dark blue, stepped up to the canvas, and placed the first stroke.

Comfort filtered through me like the first sip of hot tea on a winter morning.

The colors burst in my mind, my body taking over as I painted.

The blacks, the darker blues emerged, the splash of red from the ember of fury rising inside me amid the deep sadness. That I'd been pawned off, that my parents had never truly loved me, that the care I'd been searching for my entire life wouldn't be found here. The strokes transformed into oceanic sprays, into wild waves and angry horizons. Into a truth and wildness boiling inside me that could only be unleashed here.

I surrendered to the feelings rushing through me, pouring onto the page, to the reprieve from the loneliness.

Even if it was temporary.

Chapter 7

I f Arielle had ever come back last night, I wasn't sure.

I'd wandered into the kitchen and met Jacques, the chef, as well as Maribella, one of the maids. They were both receptive to my chatter, though I found the staff in these sorts of families often were, since their employers ignored them. The Triton family probably roamed somewhere in this gigantic place, but I hadn't seen hide nor hair of Frederick and Darla or Pearl and Olivia. Though if I had run into them, I wasn't sure what I'd have said anyway, since they were essentially strangers.

And then I'd walked along the bay for awhile, aimlessness seeping into my bones. After being groomed to take over Albatross Industries my whole life, my days crammed with work or lessons, this openness was foreign to me. My parents had tried to keep me in a cattle chute of what they wanted from me, so the escapes to Jason's to create were the only outlets I'd had.

The brine clung to me, even though night had fallen and I'd come in a while ago. I wandered into the kitchen.

"For you," Jacques said from the kitchen island. The middle-aged man wore all black, a kitchen uniform, and his long silver hair was braided down his back. He lifted a plate of lemon salmon, jasmine rice, and roasted asparagus my way. My mouth watered at the gift, and I walked a little faster to claim it.

"Thank you," I said. "Does this family do...dinner or something? Did I miss it?"

Jacques's lips lifted, and he cast a glance out the window to the water. "They're often indisposed. Tonight, Frederick and Darla are meeting with a different contingent."

My brows drew together. Something felt off here, from the fact that the Tritons never seemed to be in their house to certain other details that stood out. The hint of brine that existed in the place, no matter what. How I'd found shimmering scales in one of the bathrooms earlier today. Even the staff had been evasive with most questions I asked about the Triton family, which made my curiosity multiply.

"Well, thank you for this," I said and took the first bite. The lemony taste of the salmon exploded on my tongue. Delicious. "It's amazing."

"A friendly face like yours is welcome," Jacques said, giving a gentle tip of his head. "A rarity."

My chest twisted tight. The Tritons didn't seem as callous as my parents, at least from the interactions I'd had with Arielle, but they clearly followed the pattern of neglecting their staff. "You say that now. Just wait until you get sick of me pestering you."

Jacques snorted. I settled onto a stool at the island and made quick work of the food. Apparently, I'd been starving. Jacques busied himself with the dishes while I finished up and wiped my face with a napkin.

"Thanks again," I said. "I appreciate the consideration."

Jacques glanced at me, his eyes softening. "You don't belong in a place like this. Surely it's not too late to go a different route?"

I wrinkled my nose, not sure if he was joking or not. His tone sounded too serious for a joke, but if that were true...his words caused my stomach to sink. "Can't be worse than the estate I left."

Sympathy flashed in his eyes. "Don't hesitate to call me if you need food. You'll be able to find me in the private kitchen, anytime."

I nodded, confusion churning through me. Jacques finished washing up, offered a wave, and slipped down one of the hallways like an apparition. Still, his warning lingered in the room, consuming the space until I needed to move.

Instead of heading to my room, I strode in the direction of the studio.

The subtle strains of a melody caught my ear. I bypassed the room where I'd painted the night before, this time heading in the direction of the music. The closer I got, the clearer the sounds of the piano grew.

My heart squeezed tight at the strength and power behind the melody, at the contained fury and fervor of the keystrokes. Music and art were so intertwined for me that I couldn't help the inexorable draw. This wasn't someone's hesitant or careful learning of the piano—no, it was the force and finesse of a maestro.

I stepped into the entryway of the music room. The space was massive, like most of the rooms in this estate, with polished pine floors and high ceilings for better acoustics. Instruments hung up on the walls, also polished—brassy tubas, silver flutes and clarinets, as well as some items I'd never seen before, like shells with holes along the ridges, and pieces of coral, polished with a few slits along the side.

However, a grand piano stole center stage in the room, along with the person who sat at the keys.

I recognized Ursuline by profile alone, even though they faced away from me. They sat at the bench, the low curve of another vest of theirs exposing their muscular back, the lines and form there mesmerizing as they played. Their fingers raced along the keys, but their tentacles swept in as well, catching high and low notes with a fluidity I couldn't look away from. The contrast of the black piano bench to their pale blue skin imprinted in my mind, their silver hair slicked back.

As much as I wanted to watch from a closer vantage point, I didn't want to interrupt the flow of the music. I leaned against the doorframe and simply watched. Their shoulders shook from the force of the way they played the keys, the intensity of the melody washing over me. It reminded me of my ferocious attack on the canvas last night, pouring out everything I'd locked away onto that space.

They manipulated the keys with a precision I was enthralled by, not a single off note, not a moment's pause as the music echoed through the room in a booming crescendo, like the fury of the waves amid a storm.

I clutched the doorframe a little harder as they slowed in the aftermath, the denouement settling deep in my bones. They trailed to a close and...stopped, those resonant notes lingering in the air.

"Not often I have listeners." Ursuline's voice sliced through the quiet, startling me.

"I couldn't help it," I said, taking my first step into the room. "That was a beautiful melody. A memorized piece?"

"No, one of my own," they said as they rose from the piano bench, moving forward on their tentacles. When they faced me, the breath snagged in my throat. Ursuline towered over me, a natural height that should've made me feel threatened. Instead, I was transfixed. They cocked one of their careful brows, a smirk on their lips. "Do you play?"

I shook my head. "No, just appreciate."

"You seem to be talented at showing that," they said, a husky note to their voice that sent a shudder through me. Something about Ursuline made me stand up a little straighter, made my whole body hum with attention in a way I hadn't experienced before. "I don't mind if you listen."

I licked my lips, my mouth dry. Their dark eyes zeroed in on the motion, intense and searing. My cock stirred with interest at a look like that.

No one looked at me like that.

Like I was the only thing in existence. I was used to being set aside, invisible, discarded.

However, whenever I was in their presence, they treated me like nothing else mattered. I remained their sole focus, and my chest strained, a desperation to experience more of that broiling inside me.

"Where's your betrothed?" Ursuline asked, shifting back.

The tension between us snapped, and I ran fingers through my hair. Guilt bubbled through me at the emotions churning inside me, even though Arielle had made it clear she didn't plan on loyalty from either of us.

"I'm not sure," I admitted. "She stopped by to show me around yesterday, but went out after. I haven't heard from her since."

Ursuline's lips thinned. "Frederick's attempts to rein her in have clearly failed."

"Is that why he wanted to marry her off?" I asked. So much of this situation was a mystery to me.

"One of the reasons," Ursuline said, not clarifying. They tilted their head and led me over to one of the plush benches that lined the music room. I took a seat first, and they reclined right next to me, one of their tentacles lingering a mere inch away from my leg. If I shifted the slightest bit, I'd brush right against it, and tension percolated through me, the urge for touch turning into such a roar. "Why did you offer your hand?"

I swallowed hard. The truth or a lie? When I looked up, Ursuline's stare bored into me, like they'd know if I attempted any falsehoods.

I never liked putting on a mask anyway.

"My father's good at coercion," I stated. "I'd planned on escaping. Trying to make a go on my own after he told me I was of no use to the company." My heart clenched tight at the admission, the shame filtering over me. I didn't glance up at Ursuline, but I could feel their steady gaze pressing into me, urging me to continue. "He'd somehow found out I was getting lessons from Jason. He threatened him."

A low growl came from Ursuline's throat, drawing my attention upward. Their eyes glittered with anger, their jaw clenched. "Despicable."

I shifted in my seat, their intensity surprising me. Their tentacle brushed against my leg.

Electricity rippled through me at the mere touch, and I had to swallow back my gasp. That simple brush had felt so good I melted, so tempted to move again just to chase the sensation. My loneliness had reached a fever pitch, but even still, I'd fallen into bed with strangers who I had less of a reaction to than a mere touch from Ursuline.

Ursuline studied me with a solemnity that made me shiver.

"What about you?" I asked, needing to distract myself. "How long have you worked for the Triton family?"

"My whole life," they said, their tone as dark and lacquered as a coffin, as if it contained death and decay inside.

I assumed they meant since they started their work as a lawyer, but something in their tone unsettled me. "Did you live on the surface growing up or in the sea?"

"So curious, sunshine," they purred. "Do you ask everyone these questions?"

The nickname sent a thrill through me. The intimacy in the way they spoke, like they peeled back my layers with each conversation, had me craving more and more time around them.

I shrugged. "I've always been curious."

"I lived in the sea," they responded, one of their tentacles curling and brushing my leg again.

This time my breath hitched, a full-body shiver running through me. Their eyes widened but then grew voracious, dark and consuming. Their full, lush lips were pursed in an analyzing, assessing way. When their tentacle slid back against my leg, they rested it there. A sob rose in my throat, one I hadn't realized bubbled inside me, and I swallowed it back.

I'd been craving touch for so long that this filtered into me like the sunrise after an ageless night.

Ursuline didn't realize what a gift they offered with such a simple gesture, but I remained still in my seat, not wanting to break this moment.

"Down in one of the settlements near New Atlantis," Ursuline continued, their voice low and sonorous. "I came from a mining family."

"Do you ever visit them?" I asked. Maybe all families weren't flawed and fragmented like mine. Maybe parents actually cared for their children.

"I can't," Ursuline said, their voice flat, even though their tentacle brushed along my leg, as if offering comfort.

I blinked, sadness spreading through me, though more questions bubbled up as well. "Sorry" dried on my tongue, feeling paltry. "And you came to the surface?"

Their gaze softened a fraction, their expressions so minute they fascinated me. To anyone catching a glimpse, Ursuline would seem stonefaced, uncaring, but their responses were so small, so fascinating, as if they kept an ironclad control over themselves at all times. "Let's just say I'm familiar with arrangements like yours."

Forced.

I swallowed hard, my fingers twitching. The temptation to reach out and rest a hand on one of their tentacles rose in a real way, but I wasn't sure if the touch would be welcome. When I looked up at them, their serious gaze stripped me bare.

"Did you have dreams?" The words escaped my lips as we treaded into deeper territory than I'd expected for someone I'd only met twice. And yet, something was familiar about them, their voice. Something that screamed safety.

"Waking nightmares mostly," they commented in a wan tone. "Though when I do dream, I dream of freedom."

Their words struck me square in the chest.

I'd never connected with another person this deeply, and their steadfast touch on my leg amplified that all the more. I gripped the edge of the bench. "When I feel that way, I swim," I murmured.

"Lucky for you, the whole bay is available," Ursuline responded.

"Do you swim here?" I asked, assuming since they were cecaelia they frequented the water.

"Here, the Sentient Sea, wherever I can find water. I need a certain amount of time in it or I start to feel withered, desiccated." Ursuline leaned back a bit, tipping their head against the wall. Their flat chest was on display, wide planes of muscle, their shoulders broad. My mouth watered at the smoothness of their skin, at the lingering scent of currants and salt air around them.

"Do you miss living under the sea?" I asked, curiosity bubbling to the surface again.

They shook their head. "Not solely. Peregrine City's become a home, and I've carved out my friendships here too. The Tritons might own my contract, but they don't own my soul."

Those words resonated within me, a reminder I needed. Because I was going to be marrying a woman I barely knew, who had no interest in me back.

"There you are." Arielle's voice rang through the room, startling me out of whatever spell I'd been under. I shot upright, and Ursuline's tentacle slid away from my leg. I missed the touch at once, craved it with a fierceness that surprised me.

"I was sleeping off a hangover all day," Arielle said, flouncing into the room without a care in the world. She flashed a grin at me but then gave Ursuline a sour look. "Were you playing your depressing music again?"

"I was just heading out for the day," Ursuline stated, rising to full height. Awe filtered through me at the regality of their movements, at the lift of their chin. They didn't strike me as the sharing sort, and yet they'd sat here with me and done as much. They'd offered a safety raft when I'd been adrift in a loneliness that threatened to wash me under. Ursuline's gaze landed on mine. "Thanks for the chat."

I swallowed hard and bobbed my head, words escaping me for a moment. Before I could push them out, Ursuline slunk toward the door in those fluid movements. Arielle strode up to me in their wake. She'd begun to chatter about something she'd drunk last night and a guy who'd hit on her in the club, but my gaze was fixated on Ursuline's departure.

I watched until they vanished through the doorway, taking the brief glimpse of comfort and safety along with them.

Chapter 8

A week had passed in the Triton Estate, and I had yet to run into Frederick or Darla, even though I'd seen Olivia and Pearl on two different occasions. The sisters gave me a nod and little more, clearly uninterested in getting to know me. Ursuline appeared and disappeared like the tides, at the oddest times, and I couldn't piece together why the lawyer would be appearing like this. Arielle was the person I saw more regularly, but only when she came to find me.

In the interim, I'd gotten to know more of the staff, and I'd put more time in on a multitude of different pieces I was painting in the studio in oils, in watercolors, in acrylics. I planned on asking to leave soon, maybe to visit Jason, as Arielle had assured me I wasn't trapped here. Yet after spending so long painting in secret, I found relief in being able to go to the studio whenever the mood struck me, no constraints, nothing forbidden.

My parents hadn't messaged once.

Clearly, I was no longer their problem.

Harsh voices came from the foyer, where I'd not so long ago entered this place, and I found myself drifting in that direction.

"He deserves to know." Ursuline's voice rang loud and clear, full of unerring command. "You can't keep him in the dark forever."

"That is our choice, Ursuline, not yours." Frederick's booming voice echoed through the corridor.

"Amusing you'd defend your right to choose while denying so many others theirs," Ursuline retorted, a tension in their words like a dam threatening to burst.

"Enough," Frederick shouted, and I froze. I shouldn't have walked into this conversation. Fuck, where could I go?

Frederick and Ursuline stepped into view of the doorway.

Their gazes landed on me, and Ursuline's lips curled upward in triumph.

Frederick's eyes burned, and he huffed out in anger. "How much did you hear?"

I swallowed hard, stepping back a pace, except the sight of Ursuline standing there in challenge gave me the courage to ask. "What do I deserve to know?"

Frederick's jaw set, his gaze stony as he scanned between Ursuline and me. Tension stretched between us all, like the threat of an oncoming storm. I squared my shoulders, prepared to run if needed. Hell knew, I'd never been a fighter.

Frederick let out a sigh and gestured. "Follow me." He strode past me, his steps echoing through the hallway. I pivoted on my heel and heeded his direction, aware of Ursuline's presence at my back. They were close enough that I could feel them there, and I didn't want them to leave.

He made a left turn into a sitting room filled with plush cerulean couches and gilt trim. Crystal lamps glittered on every stand, casting the room in a soft amber glow. Frederick sprawled out on one of the couches, a grimness to his features that unsettled me. The man was massive, with slick black hair threaded with grays, and the same salt and pepper mustache and beard. His features were precise, along with his appearance as well.

Everything about this family remained a mystery, no matter how much I'd tried to look for information. Any hint of what I'd stumbled into would help.

"Given that you'll be marrying my daughter, I will let you in on a family secret. I suppose living here, there's no way to avoid the truth," Frederick said. "However, if word of this spreads to anyone—your parents included—I don't care if you're her fiancé. You'll end up dragged to the depths of the Sentient Sea."

A chill spread through me, and I took a seat on the opposite couch, not trusting my knees to keep me upright. Ursuline sank onto the couch beside me, their tentacles mere inches away from me. Why hadn't they sat with Frederick? Granted, they didn't seem to share much fondness for their employer.

"I understand," I croaked out.

Frederick let out a low rumble that echoed through the room. "Our family isn't human. We're merpeople."

The hints whirred together, everything I'd questioned since I'd entered this place. The disappearances, the proximity to the bay, the iridescent scales in the bathroom. I should've figured them out from the start. All those hints felt glaringly obvious now.

"So the reason no one is ever here..."

"This isn't the only home we own," Frederick confirmed. "Oftentimes, we go to our estate in New Atlantis. Arielle does have a preference for the surface, though, which was why we believed she was the best daughter to marry a human."

"So the alliance was for a foothold," I clarified.

"In the human communities, businesses, yes. While we're treated politely, since we're relative newcomers, we've garnished a fair amount of hesitation and distrust. The Durand family has a longstanding reputation in Peregrine City."

My stomach churned. Of course I'd been used as a pawn between both the families. I knew it, yet hearing the words aloud sliced into me.

"How are you walking up here?" I asked. The mermaids I'd encountered in the water all had fins—they weren't capable of walking around on two legs, or shifting, that I was aware of. When they did visit the land, they were conveyed around in mobile water tanks to make sure they could easily move rather than flopping on the ground, or in altered scooters, unlike kraken or cecaelia who had the tentacles to shift around.

Frederick's lips quirked. "Let's just say arrangements with witches have their benefits."

So, a spell. And for it to transform something like that, it had to be a powerful and costly spell, one that only a family as rich as the Tritons could afford.

"I'm aware your family flirts with the Human First delegations..." Frederick started.

"I don't share those allegiances," I said. "I have no issues with monsters."

"So you'll keep our secrets," Frederick said, the underlying threat simmering in his tone.

What choice did I have? This was the family I'd been sold to, their daughter the woman I was supposed to marry. "Of course," I reassured him, even though I shrank at the way he glowered.

"Papa, I'm home," Arielle said, striding through the entryway. She paused and glanced between us. "Did I miss something?"

Frederick heaved out a sigh. "No, sweetheart. Your fiancé is aware of what we are now, that's all."

She let out a tinkling laugh. "Thank the gods. I was so tired of making excuses. Plus, Olivia has the bad habit of shedding a few scales in the main bathroom when she scrubs off after a swim."

"I wondered what those were," I offered, appreciating how she lightened the mood. Being in a room with Ursuline and Frederick was like standing between two titans about to wage war.

"He would've figured it out sooner rather than later," Ursuline reaffirmed, their voice like granite. When I'd first met them, I'd believed they were just aloof, a professional. But the more I got to understand them, the more I noticed the subtleties to their body language, their movements, the more I realized they loathed the Triton family. Why they stayed employed with them was a mystery to me, but I'd just cracked the surface of this place.

The Tritons being a monster family made far more sense. How they'd amassed their orichalcum fortune when no humans had a reliable source, why oceanic motifs were everywhere throughout the house. The place also had an inordinate amount of bathrooms with tubs, which had seemed a bit of an extravagance.

Now I understood it was a way to connect to the water if they couldn't dive into the bay.

"Can I go swimming with you sometime?" I asked Arielle, even though I'd been tempted to ask the cecaelia right beside me. Still, Arielle was my fiancée, and I should at least be making an attempt.

Arielle shrugged. "Whenever. I usually need to take a dive a few times a week, though the urges don't hit me like they do the rest of the family."

"This one blends with the landwalkers better than the rest of the family," Frederick said, pride emanating in his tone. "Your marriage will be ushering in a new era for the Triton family."

I sat close enough to Ursuline to feel them tense beside me. Questions bubbled up at once, ones I swallowed down. They wouldn't answer anything in our current company.

"When is the engagement party going to be?" Arielle asked, resting a hand on her father's shoulder. He glanced up at her, affection gleaming in his eyes. My heart squeezed tight with envy. I'd always wanted parents who'd look at me like that, not with the disappointment I'd received at every turn. "I'll have to commission a new dress for the affair."

"In a week," Frederick said, switching his gaze to me. "I'd warn you on expectations, but you've grown up in this society."

I bobbed my head. "Yes, sir."

"The invitations have already been sent," he continued. "Your parents will be there, as well as many of your family friends."

The pronouncement made my gut twist. I should be excited about seeing my family again, yet the thought filled me with dread. Just another opportunity to let Angus and Mina down.

"I don't suppose you'll be matchmaking for Olivia anytime soon," Arielle said, swaying back and forth where she stood. "She's pouting that I'm the youngest and getting married first."

"She'll marry a good merman," Frederick said. "There are a few potential suitors from prominent New Atlantis families."

"Does the chef have dinner ready yet?" Arielle said, switching topics at lightning speed. "I'm starving."

"I'll go check," Frederick said, rising and giving her an affectionate peck on the head. "Elrich, you'll join us."

Question wasn't in his tone, which meant I was in for the first family dinner since the one that had landed me in this house in the first place. I didn't feel comfortable, but surprisingly, I wasn't as on edge as I was when dining with the Durands.

"See you up there," Arielle called, not waiting for me as she swept off. Frederick strode out after her, already making the turn in the direction of the staff kitchen.

Ursuline sat beside me, and neither of us moved away. Truthfully, I didn't want to.

"Thank you," I said. "For fighting for me."

"You got dragged into this as a pawn," they said, their tone simmering. "It's the least I could do."

"I still made the choice," I said.

A low growl emerged from them. "Some choice. You marry her or they disappear your friend?"

My chest squeezed tight. I wasn't used to someone caring like that. Jason had for years, in his own way, but the flash of protectiveness from Ursuline, seeing them stand up for me... I couldn't stop the flutter inside me, the way I yearned to lean closer again, to feel their touch. I'd never experienced electricity like that before—not with flings, not with the transitory partners I'd had.

"If you want to swim..." Ursuline started, then stopped.

I clutched the edge of the seat, waiting for them to continue. Arielle's response had been a blow off—I was aware—and I wanted to dive out there again. But after getting swept away in that storm, nerves held me back.

"I usually dive in the bay at midnight," Ursuline said, their voice cool, unassuming, even though they proposed the very thing I'd hoped for. "I'll be there tonight."

The invitation rang clear between us.

"I'll be there," I said, my voice soft, as if the offer would be retracted at any moment. As if they were a hermit crab needing to be coaxed out of their shell.

"You'd better be getting to dinner," Ursuline said, rising from their seat. Their tentacles shifted around them, moving with a mesmerizing fluidity. And tonight, I'd get to see how they coasted through the water. My heart sped. "Frederick doesn't take kindly to lateness."

"Where are you going?" I asked.

"Home," they said, their eyes twinkling. "You didn't think I lived here, did you?"

"With the frequency you visit, I sometimes wondered," I admitted, squeezing my nape.

They headed toward the exit, but before they left, they cast a glance back. "I'll see you, Elrich."

"Tonight," I promised.

Their lips quirked, and they disappeared past the door.

Tonight, I'd take my first dip in the water since the storm; however, spending more time around Ursuline?

Those were much more dangerous waters, indeed.

Chapter 9

The bay looked entirely different at night.

The moon was full, its pale luminescence cast over the land and water. I stepped out of the estate and a shiver ran down my spine. I'd tossed on a pair of sweats and a light tee and slipped into sneakers, but most of that would be coming off for my swim. The temperatures had been warm enough today that I didn't worry about the water being too cold, but I'd never been much of a night swimmer before.

However, after Ursuline had extended the invitation, I found myself drawn from my room and heading out of the estate at quarter to midnight.

The sand sloping down to the water was pale and purplish in the dark of night, and the moonlit waves glimmered with a mesmerizing rhythm. My heart thumped a little harder at the sight. Memories of the tug beneath, of struggling for breath, of fighting against the wicked storm that had reigned flashed through me like rapid-fire, and sweat broke out on my skin.

When I reached the sand, I kicked off my shoes, stripped off my sweats, and then tugged my tee over my head. The cool breeze caused a shiver, since I was down to my boxer briefs, and goose bumps pebbled across my skin. Had Ursuline skipped out tonight? They didn't seem the type, but I'd also believed in people more than they deserved for a good part of my life, particularly my parents.

I walked up to the edge of the water, where the gentle waves lapped at the shore. The scent of brine tripped my wires, a familiar comfort and now a caution as well. The water lapped at my toes, the icy kiss shocking my system.

This was an unfamiliar shore, but the waves greeted me like a friend all the same.

As much as my nerves fluttered in the background, I couldn't stay away from the water.

I strode another pace in, the cold water wrapping around my ankles. Some of my fear dissipated, but I couldn't seem to move any farther. I'd been hoping for...well, companionship, I supposed. Arielle seemed to be uninterested, which was fine, but Ursuline had captivated me from the moment I met them.

I'd been longing for more time with them, if I were being honest.

A splash drew my attention.

Farther in, drops of water sparkled in the air, and a dark shape blurred right beneath the surface, just visible. I tensed, watching, waiting.

Then, in another burst of water, the dark form breached the surface again.

Ursuline tossed their head back, droplets glittering as they emerged and turned to face me. Their pale-blue skin glowed like the moonlight itself as they swam in my direction. They moved with easy strokes of their arms, most of the power generated by the tentacles beneath the water. I took a few more tentative steps forward, until my calves were submerged, and they continued to slice through the surface, heading in my direction.

"Punctual, I see," they said, their voice a low purr as they slowed a distance away, remaining in the depths rather than the shallows where I lingered. "I like that quality in a person."

I squeezed the back of my neck as I waded a little farther in. "Then you'll be sorely disappointed. I'm usually too lost in my head to be punctual...or effective at anything."

Ursuline swam back and forth, the liquidity of their movements something I envied. There was a stark difference between a human swimmer and the monsters who emerged from the depths, like we were paltry imitators, reaching for the stars out of grasp.

"Which sounds like any artist I've ever met," they said. "Just because you're focused on the art you create doesn't mean you're ineffective."

My heart squeezed tight. Their statement was the opposite of what my parents had drilled into me for years. That my daydreaming meant I wasn't focused, that my lack of skills in the business world meant I was a failure. I waded deeper, the water settling around my waist now. It was cool but not ice-cold, warm from the earlier sun. And the waves were gentler here in the bay, without the power or intensity of the ones at Breakneck Beach.

Besides, Ursuline's presence filled me with an undeniable calm.

"Nervous?" they asked.

"A little," I admitted. "Last time I was in the water wasn't a great swim. Got caught up in the storm a few weeks back."

"And yet you're still coming out here," they said, swimming a little closer. I waded deeper, wanting to get near enough to feel the buoyancy of a swim. To get close enough for another casual brush, another casual touch.

I played with fire here. Ursuline wasn't the person I was engaged to marry. In fact, they were bound to this family.

And yet, I couldn't seem to keep away from them. Each scrap of attention offered a balm to my battered soul. I hadn't realized how touch starved, how attention starved I'd been until they delivered those careful brushes, those long, intent looks. Under their gaze, I bloomed in a way I hadn't understood was possible.

Ursuline shifted nearer, their movements so fast I almost didn't catch them. The moonlight accentuated their pale skin, their defined muscles. Their pecs were solid, their nipples a darker shade than the rest of their skin, and heat roared through me. They weren't even wearing a scrap of clothing.

My cock perked to attention, even with the cold water I waded through, and I chewed on my lower lip until I tasted blood, trying to keep a hold of myself. Having this sort of reaction to Ursuline wasn't right. I was engaged to be married to Arielle. However, Arielle didn't seem to care in the slightest about getting to know me more. And since Ursuline had first picked me up, they'd offered solace, comfort, things I'd been craving for so long.

The water reached my shoulders at this point, and I floated in place, enjoying the bob and sway from the gentler currents that came into the bay. This was a better return to the water than facing Breakneck Beach again, after my near brush with death.

"Do you always swim out in the bay?" I asked, my feet lifting off the ground with a bigger wave.

"The ocean too," Ursuline said, so close now that their tentacles could easily brush me. Fuck, I wanted them to. The urge to feel their touch raged through me, stronger than even the clutch of the water surrounding me. "But I've taken to nightly swims out here for a long while."

"Why the night?" I asked. I'd always been more of a sunshine person, craving the warmth of the sand, the feel of the sun pulsing at my back.

"It's quieter," Ursuline said. "A peace exists at night that I could never find during the day."

They weren't wrong. A sense of the forbidden had filtered through me approaching the beach at night, and it only amplified as I swam beside Ursuline in the water. And yet, despite the velvet darkness surrounding us, when I stared up at the sky, those stars glittered like the orichalcum beneath the sea, with an unearthly glow.

"I can see that," I said, lifting my arm for a lazy stroke through the water. I dunked my head under, and the caress of the water around me caused some of the pressure of the thoughts and worries circulating through my brain to ease. When I emerged again, I'd moved even closer to Ursuline, mere feet from them. Their tentacle brushed along my leg, and rather than jumping away, I stayed still. The sensation sent a silent thrill through me, an endorphin rush I craved with all my might.

I bobbed in place, trying not to stare at them, even though the pressure of their gaze made me shiver. When I glanced up, they watched me carefully, their dark eyes gleaming in the moonlight. Their silver hair was plastered to their head from the water, and the sharp angles of their jaw, the noble arch of their nose lent them an air of regality that made me want to fall to my knees. Their hungry stare kept me pinned in place, and the breath snagged in my throat.

Then they brushed their tentacle across my leg again, on purpose this time.

Electricity pulsed through my veins, and I sucked in a sharp breath. The salt-soaked air was heavy, charged, and I floated in the water, craving more, more, more.

"You don't flinch," they noted.

I tilted my head to the side. "Why would I?"

"Most humans do," they said. "Even if they're tolerant of monsters, they're startled by the differences between us, uncertain about them. Yet you don't react the same way."

"Differences are beautiful," I said. "If I painted the life my parents wanted of me, it'd be a muted palette and a dry and stark picture, void of emotion. However, capturing Peregrine City itself? The riot of color, of shapes, of contrasts create such a breathtaking composition."

They brushed their tentacle around my arm this time, and they rested it there. The solid feel, even as I bobbed in the water, calmed me like little else did, all while setting my blood afire.

"You've got a beautiful mind," they said, their voice low, throaty. They shifted a little closer so mere inches separated us, their tentacle resting on my arm still. The urge to run my fingers across it, to touch them in return, rose up ferociously. A wan smile danced upon their lips and glittered in their eyes as they glanced between my face and where their tentacle and my arm met. "I can see the curiosity in your gaze. You're free to touch back."

Heat flooded through me in a fierce sweep, and even the chill of the surrounding water couldn't dampen it. The Triton Estate was illuminated in the distance by a few spotlights, some cozy glows emanating from certain rooms, but Arielle had headed out after dinner to the clubs in Peregrine City. Again, I hadn't been invited.

Touching Ursuline back felt like crossing a line, and yet, I couldn't help but reach out.

My fingertips brushed against the cool tentacle that wrapped around my wrist. They gave it a light squeeze, and lust rocketed through me. The idea of being trapped by them, at their mercy... I closed my eyes and ran my fingers along the slick surface of their tentacle, surprisingly smooth but a different texture than human skin.

Already, I could pick out the types of brushes I'd want to use, the paint to convey it on canvas.

The suckers on the underside twitched at my perusal, just as smooth but perfect circles I couldn't help but trace. A hitched breath sounded, and I opened my eyes to see Ursuline mere inches before me. They loomed in a way that thrilled me, and their dark gaze blazed with a raw, unrestrained hunger. They looked like they wanted to devour, to consume, and being their focus was an undeniably new feeling.

I'd grown so used to being invisible or a disappointment to my parents, and even when I'd taken lovers they'd been tepid affairs, most more concerned with a quick lay—whether they fucked me or I fucked them. My whole body hummed as I continued to trace the circles of each sucker along the tentacle they'd offered me. Ursuline's breath came out more rapidly, choppier, and a powerful creature like them giving me this much free rein of their body filled me with a bubbling, heady feeling.

"You keep doing that, and you'll land yourself in trouble," Ursuline said, their voice harsh, ragged, and low.

I paused mid-stroke. "Sorry," I apologized, letting go of their tentacle. Still, they didn't unwrap it from my wrist, and relief flushed through me. I could imagine my limbs being restrained like this, bound at their mercy. Lust heated me up from the inside out.

"No need for apology, sunshine," they stated, a spark in their gaze that held me captive. "Just a warning not to bite off more than you're prepared for." The sensual purr to their words stroked at my skin, and between that and the hold they had on my wrist, I launched into overdrive. All too easily I could imagine surrendering to them in every way, letting them take me over, consume me.

Feeling the tensile strength of their tentacle wrapped around me, I couldn't help but wonder what it'd be like in other places, probing deep inside me, stretching me wide. Ursuline was precise, methodical, and steady. Surrendering to control like that was beyond any fantasy I'd had before. And here in the water, this was their terrain. I couldn't be safer than swimming out with a cecaelia.

"How does it feel to be able to swim like you can?" I asked. Year after year, as I'd visited the Sentient Sea, I'd always wondered what diving underwater like the merfolk and other oceanic monsters felt like. To be able to exist down there without fear of drowning.

Ursuline's tentacle stroked my arm, and a shudder rolled through me. Their eyes crinkled at the edges with their soft smile. "What does it feel like to walk on two legs?"

I nodded, understanding trickling through me. Some things were incomprehensible unless experienced. "I always wished I could swim like that. The water's been a second home to me from an early age."

"To think, you're going to marry a girl who wants the opposite," Ursuline stated. Their features grew tight, and they withdrew the tentacle from around my arm. I bit back a cry at the loss of touch. I didn't blame them, though. I was betrothed to a mermaid who at most offered a bright smile and tinkling laugh before going her own way. At first, I'd been charmed by her lightness, but the more I got to know her, the more I understood she accepted her place in this society. She was comfortable with her role, not mourning it.

Unlike me.

"The irony," I said, arcing my arms through the water as I swam around Ursuline. The air between us was charged, as if we could generate a storm ourselves, all lightning and thunder and a torrent of sheer energy and passion I'd always longed for.

Nothing like the marriage I was about to enter.

My stomach soured at the thought, but I didn't want to waste my time with those. I was beginning to hoard the minutes we spent together, collect each and every second and tuck them away in my mind.

"Can I watch you swim?" I asked. I wanted to see the fluidity as they wove above and beneath the waves, the naturalness of someone in their true element. They were graceful on land, but in the sea, they'd be magnificent.

Ursuline scanned me over, their gaze dark and measured. For a moment, I thought they'd say no. We'd already danced around forbidden territory tonight, pushed a little too much. Then their full lips quirked, and they shook their head. "Or you could swim with me," they said. Ursuline swirled around in the water so their back was to me, and I couldn't help but soak in the sight of those defined muscles, the broad, sturdy frame. "Hold on to my shoulders."

My mouth dried. Oh. That was far beyond what I'd hoped for, and even though I should, I couldn't say no. Instead, I bobbed my head and swam forward until I bumped against their back. I rested my palms on their shoulders, and the breath snagged in my throat. My chest plastered against their back, and the heat that bloomed between us created an inferno. The cold waters around me no longer mattered.

"Grip me tight, sunshine," they said. "Do you want me to stay above water?"

The fact they asked meant more than I could express. I wasn't sure if I could handle going under right now, not after the way I'd been dragged to the depths at Breakneck Beach. However, if they were the one controlling this, I knew I'd be safe.

I chewed on my lower lip. "Above water for now."

"You might want to wrap your legs around my torso," Ursuline warned. "Once we start moving, it'll be fast."

I followed direction, but then realized what a mistake that was. The moment my groin pressed against their lower back, my cock woke the hell up. I kept my legs around them and prayed it would deflate during this swim. "Are you sure I won't be weighing you down?"

Ursuline let out a low laugh, one that left a resonant mark in the air. "You weigh nothing in the water. Are you ready?"

"Yes," I said, even though my heart thrummed a mile a minute. I clung tight to their shoulders, and my legs wrapped around their midsection. With my whole front plastered against them, I couldn't ignore how their proximity awakened my body like nothing else. This close, their scent of salt and black currants cast its spell over me.

Without another warning, Ursuline surged forward.

The breeze whipped my hair around with the speed they sliced through the water, the spray of droplets and smaller waves churning up around us. They sailed like a boat through the bay, leaving a foamy trail in their wake. I clutched them tight as their arms sailed in lazy arcs to direct them, all while the power of their tentacles propelled them forward in powerful surges.

This wasn't anything as simple as a swim. No, we soared across the water, waves forming around us from Ursuline's speed. My soul grew as buoyant as I was right now, the worries and concerns about my future shedding away. All that existed was Ursuline, me, and the water.

I pressed against their back, their muscles moving against mine, and lust pumped through me, hot, undulating, and inexorable. Yet I didn't dare unlatch myself with how fast we raced across the water in big bursts as their tentacles pushed us forward. They circled around the bay, the crystalline water glimmering in the moonlight. This was what I'd always envied when I'd watched the monsters swim in the ocean. The speed, the way they zipped by with an ease of familiarity I'd never know as a human.

And yet Ursuline gifted me with a taste tonight.

Fierce appreciation trickled through me, the heady warmth spreading through my limbs even as the winds grew icy from their speeds, and combined with the spray of water, my cheeks stung. I squinted, the droplets blurring my vision temporarily, but then Ursuline surged forward again, and we flew.

A *whoop* escaped me, exultant and unencumbered. In this moment, I wasn't trapped here in an arranged marriage. For this brief swim, I was free.

I clutched tight to them, our bodies melding together, and I couldn't think of another time I'd ever felt this close to anyone. They pushed through the bay again, the salty taste of droplets of brine landing on my tongue, the sting in my eyes. My heart hammered hard, and I clung with all my might since they moved with a grace and speed I was unused to.

The moon glowed down on us, the bluish, lavender light coasting across the bay, turning the sand pale as well. With Ursuline zipping us through the water, I wasn't afraid of anything. Not the waves, not the currents, not anything else that might be lurking in the water. A safety existed with them that I'd craved my whole life—a safety, and a comfort.

It would be far too easy to fall for them.

My heart twisted hard. Except I was engaged to another.

And not just anyone—the people they worked for.

I clutched them a little tighter and stared up at the night sky, the wavelets of brine splashing around us. The velvet dark held the stars hostage, so far away I'd never be able to reach. But as I soared through the water on Ursuline's back, for a few transitory moments, they grew closer.

Chapter 10

The day of our engagement party had arrived, and I'd been dreading it.

Social affairs in high society were something I loathed, and this time I had a whole different family with their own set of expectations—plus my parents. The fact the Durand family would be there was far from a comfort. Angus and Mina would be analyzing my every move, making sure I upheld our family's reputation, or else.

A knock sounded on my door, startling me out of the whopping nothing I'd been doing apart from absently staring at my pressed and hung-up attire for the evening.

"What're you doing there?" Arielle said, sweeping into my room. She wore a gauzy pink dress that swished when she walked, and her eyes sparkled like she held a secret. "Meditating?"

I snorted. "I was never very good at meditation. Your mind is supposed to be blank, and mine always wandered."

She plonked down next to me on the bed, with a casual familiarity I wished we actually had. But no matter how hard I tried to get to know her, she remained a bit guarded and elusive beneath that sunny exterior. It'd be easy to chalk her up as superficial, but I didn't believe that about people. Everyone had emotions, cares, fears—some people just chose to ignore or hide theirs away from the world.

"I've tried it a few times, but same," she said. "Meditation class is boring as sin. Just like this engagement party is going to be, unfortunately."

"Not looking forward to your debut as my fiancée?" I joked, even though the words tasted like ash on my tongue. The more we talked about our engagement, the more my soul rioted. When our arrangement was in the abstract, I could ignore it, but moments like this where we would set the date we'd be bound together by marriage...they shredded the dreams I'd held from an early age.

Of finding something real. Someone who'd love me with a depth that rivaled the ocean.

Not this farce of a role I'd been forced to play by our families.

Arielle let out another tinkling laugh. "Papa and Mama have gotten off my back ever since you proposed, so I have to thank you for that. I don't mind being married, so long as I'm free to do as I like."

That was where we differed, I supposed. I hated the constraints of the society I was born into.

"We'll enjoy the food tonight, the fanfare, and ignore the catty bitches who'll have comments on my hair, dress, whatever," Arielle said, swishing her legs back and forth. "They're all jealous anyway."

"What if I hate the fanfare?" I responded, my mouth drying at the thought of the spotlight. When it came to our society, that spotlight meant more focus on my mistakes, my inadequacies.

"Then you can stick to the food," Arielle said. "I'll navigate you through the rest."

I offered a genuine smile at that. Even though she'd barely been around since I arrived here, the idea we'd be in this together tonight gave me a bit of solace. I'd been hoping for a bigger connection with the person I was going to marry, but for now, I'd accept a temporary alliance.

Hell knew I'd need it tonight.

"I suppose I'd better start the process of getting ready," Arielle said, swinging her legs back and forth along the side of the bed. "I've got a lovely seafoam-green affair for the party."

"Sounds beautiful," I said, and she preened. Arielle had a wild effervescence that felt impossible to pin down, impossible to know. However, out of the Triton family, she was the only one willing to give me any acknowledgement. Olivia and Pearl spent most of their time beneath the sea in New Atlantis, evidenced by the occasional glimpses I caught of them returning to land. And whatever affairs Frederick and Darla got up to kept them far away from here.

Arielle hopped up from the seat she'd taken and strode to the door. "See you at the engagement party."

With that, she vanished.

I made quick work of putting on my suit for the party tonight, the fabric form-fitting and well tailored in a way only money could buy. Of course, I hadn't gotten to choose it. The colors were a deep navy with the insignia of the Triton family, since that was who I'd been bartered to. My stomach churned, the suit a restrictive reminder of the society we were a part of.

However, I wasn't about to bide the rest of the time until the party cloistered in my room. I stepped out and strode down the hallway. The estate hummed with an energy that had been lacking since I'd been here—probably because more people occupied the place.

Maribella strode in my direction, carrying a teetering stack of folded laundry. The top few towels shifted precariously, and I quickened my pace to nab them before they fell.

"Oh, no," she said, shaking her head. "You don't need to take those."

"I've got nothing better to do," I said, matching pace with her. A few strands of her practical bun had slipped out of place, and the sheen of sweat hinted at how hard she'd been working. The staff operated in full swing right now, and Jacques was probably cursing up a storm in the kitchen with the rest of his sous chefs.

"The party is in your honor, sir," Maribella said, a hint of a stern note in her voice. She was barely older than me, though, and she had a sunny disposition that didn't confuse me the same way Arielle's did. "I can handle these."

"Consider it a favor," I said as we wound down the grand staircase and into a room I'd only peered into before. The ballroom was tucked away on the far right side of the estate, and I hadn't much use for an empty, lavish place like that. The marble floors glittered, and sea glass and silver chandeliers created a beautiful juxtaposition to the black tables and chairs surrounding the main dance floor. Wide windows showcased the sprawling emerald meadows with hints of the crystalline bay creeping into view.

The preparation was underway, and other staff drifted by, all of them moving with a calm sort of precision given their expertise.

Maribella strode over to the nearest round table and placed the stack of cream linens down. "Now, you go. Get prepared for tonight. This whole party is in your honor."

"Would it be terrible if I skipped out?" I teased, even though I sorely wanted to. My stomach flip-flopped at taking the step to making this engagement that much more real.

Maribella shook her head, an impish grin on her lips. "You won't want to. Jacques snuck in your favorite crab soup, just for you."

"Oh, the guilt card," I said. "How did you know my weakness?"

"You're too kind, Elrich," Maribella said, her eyes softening. "Don't think we aren't aware of how you've made an effort to get to know each of us. It's appreciated."

My chest squeezed tight. I'd tried to form connections back at the Durand Estate, but whenever I got attached, my parents would use the person as a bargaining chip when I didn't conform to what they wanted. However, the Tritons didn't seem to need the same ironclad control over me. Maybe here, I could make the friends I'd always wanted.

"Thank you," I said, skimming my fingers through my hair. "I suppose I'll see you at the engagement party."

"We'll be watching out for you," she said with a wink, and then she began to place the tablecloths over the rounds. I sucked in a breath and took my leave, heading over to the doorway.

The nervous energy inside me hadn't abated, but I had no outlet, so I strode into the kitchen and stepped out to the balcony. The bay glittered before me, but all I could see was those moonlight waves as Ursuline and I had soared through the water the other night. My heart thrummed at the reminder, and the reality that in a few short hours I'd be publicly pledging myself to another twisted my gut.

I hadn't seen Ursuline around all day. Would they even show up to this? The Triton family didn't need their lawyer to bear witness to our engagement party. I wasn't sure if I'd rather they attend or prefer they didn't.

The idea of seeing them while celebrating my engagement sent a sharp shard through my chest.

The salt-soaked air offered a small comfort, and I basked in it for a little longer, the sun seeping through the layers of my clothing, all the way to my skin. I wasn't sure how long I stood there, staring out at the bay, but I lost myself in the dreamy blue.

A rap on the glass behind me snapped me to attention. I whirled around to see the last two people I wanted to face.

My gut sank.

The door opened, and my father and mother stood in view. I could feel their criticism from here.

"What are you doing?" Angus asked, his voice sharp. "You look disheveled."

My mother tutted and beckoned me into the house.

"You showed up early," I said, disappointed. I'd been hoping for a little more time, hoping the party would be underway once they arrived and I could avoid them more easily.

The coolness of the estate slithered over me, along with the unease. My parents hadn't reached out once since they'd bartered me off. Not a single call. Not even a message. And now I'd have to face them alone.

The silence between us spoke volumes. Of blood that had never formed a family. Of a discomfort we shared.

"Am I interrupting anything?" Arielle asked, stepping into the kitchen. Unlike before, she now wore a seafoam-green chiffon dress that looked ethereal but sparkled with gemstones in the beading of the bodice. Her copper hair was in glossy waves down her back, and the makeup she'd applied made her features pop, her skin flawless. She had a natural beauty that was guaranteed to make admirers flock to her, and she transformed into elegance and class with ease.

"Oh, of course not," my mother tittered, slipping her mask on in front of one of the Triton family. The tension lessened since Arielle was here, and I grasped onto the lifeline she offered with all my might.

"Are you ready to head into the ballroom?" I asked, hoping this wouldn't be another point where she jetted off on her own agenda.

Arielle swept into an effortless curtsy, the epitome of grace. If I were someone who'd ever fit into society, she'd be the perfect wife. Pretty, affable, and content with living the rest of her life in secret, she blended with this lifestyle more than I'd first realized.

Unlike me.

I offered my arm, and she accepted. We gave my parents a nod before I escorted her down the hallway to take the long route to the ballroom.

The second we were out of earshot, she leaned in. "They're dreadful, aren't they?"

A laugh escaped me. Maybe this wouldn't be the end of the world. As much as I hated the situation, Arielle wasn't cruel, and she at least had a lighter spirit that could pull me out of these tense situations. Even if I craved more. "There's no love lost there."

"Well, we only have to bear most of these people for the occasional soiree," Arielle said. "I don't know about you, but I have no plans of getting heavily involved in the politics of either New Atlantis or Peregrine City."

"My talents don't lie in that realm," I teased.

"Oh, and where do they lie?" Arielle responded, the flirt clear in her tone.

I swallowed in discomfort. This was my fiancée, and I should be able to respond to her advances. However, I'd always needed a connection, a comfort and depth for attraction that was difficult to find.

I'd only ever met one who sparked that to life, and they were forbidden territory.

"Not in business," I responded, realizing I'd waited too long to respond.

"Thankfully, my father doesn't need assistance there," Arielle said cheerfully. "He likes to keep his pursuits private. Despite the human contacts he has here, most of his upper echelon are merfolk in New Atlantis."

"What's it like down there?" I asked as we meandered along the corridor that led to the ballroom. Bustle and noise filtered from our destination, but I wanted to claim a few moments of peace before we faced everyone.

"Terribly dull," Arielle said. "And a bit depressing. The orichalcum miners are a morose lot. They live below in the Pockets."

Ursuline's family was from down in New Atlantis, and I couldn't help but remember the distance in their expression, the flash of sorrow there.

"Please tell me you can at least formal dance?" she said as we neared the entrance. "My father's going to be glowering at us the whole night. Reputation among his human peers and all that."

"I'm trained in the basics," I said. "Enough that I won't embarrass us."

We stepped up to the entrance. Already murmurs reached me, the genteel sort that came from others of our station rather than the comforting kind from the staff. I straightened my spine, mentally donning my armor.

"Come on," Arielle said as she took the lead into the ballroom. "A glass or two of champagne and things won't feel as dull."

The room had been transformed in the hour I'd been away from it. The staff had set out the crisp cream tablecloths and well-lined place settings, and the chandelier lighting had been dimmed for better effect, as if the whole place flickered with tiny flames, and those wide windows showcased the sprawling yard. A few families that I unfortunately recognized milled around the dance floor, chatting amongst each other. A four-piece quartet had set up on a platform in the corner, and a light melody threaded through the room, as formal and prosaic as these gatherings always managed to be.

"Oh, look," Arielle said, yanking me in the direction of Theodore, one of the staff who walked around with a tray of champagne. We stepped in front of him, and he offered me a soft smile. Arielle didn't even acknowledge him as she snagged a glass. I took one as well and mouthed "Thank you." He bobbed his head in a nod. Before I could ask him how he fared during this, Arielle pulled me away.

Before the Vandergorns could intercept us, Arielle made another abrupt turn, and we were face-to-face with her family. Frederick, Darla, Olivia, and Pearl entered the room together, bringing with them a sort of hush. My parents clung on close behind the Triton family like barnacles, as if they could absorb wealth and stature just by proximity. Behind them were a few others who had similar sharp noses, taller height, and the pale and smooth skin of the Tritons I'd met. I assumed they were part of the family, even though many of the Triton connections wouldn't be showing up tonight.

And I was one of the few humans who knew why.

The secret simmered under the surface, and when Frederick glanced in my direction, warning flashed in his gaze.

Understood.

I took a sip of my champagne, focusing on the fizz of the bubbles, the mixture of dry and sweet on my tongue. Better than focusing on most of the people here. Maybe once the events of tonight concluded, I could continue on my latest piece in the studio. The ability to regularly put paint to canvas without having to sneak to Jason's soothed something in my soul, and it was the one good change that had occurred in the past month.

"Elrich?" Arielle said, tugging at my arm. "Let's go mingle. I think I see the Friedrichs over there, and I abhor their oldest."

"So we're steering clear?" I asked, following her stare over to the four individuals who huddled together on the opposite side of the dance floor.

Arielle beamed at me at let out a peal of a laugh. "Oh, definitely not. I'm going over to gloat."

I heaved a sigh.

This was going to be a long, excruciating night.

Chapter 11

An hour in, and I was begging for an exit.

My parents hadn't said more than two words to me, and despite Arielle's promise to stay by my side through this, her company had lasted all of fifteen minutes. When Darryl Gershwin started flirting with her, making eyes, she responded in kind, and they'd been glued to each other the entire night.

My stomach churned as I sat at a table, searching for an avenue out. A few, I think from the Jessenthal family, clustered on the other side, but no one engaged with me other than passing judgmental looks, which was fine. I wasn't sure what to say to them anyway. Arielle spun around on the dance floor with Darryl, and I couldn't help but feel like even more of a failure. This was the one thing I'd been required to do—marry the woman—and I couldn't even hold her attention. My parents kept shooting me glares from a few tables over, as if they expected me to storm in, break Gershwin's nose, and start dancing with Arielle. However, I couldn't fake attraction there, and chances were, I'd only annoy her in the process.

Altogether, this was nothing close to what I'd imagined getting engaged to someone might feel like.

I loathed it.

When I glanced at the main entrance of the ballroom, my heart lodged in my throat.

Ursuline stepped into view. Their silver hair was styled back, the sheen reflecting under the dim lighting, and their pale-blue skin glowed. They wore a black poet blouse that hung low on their hips and lay open in the center, showcasing their broad, smooth chest. Silver dangled on their ears, the cuffs around their biceps, and the choker around their throat. Their eyes held a predatory gleam as they surveyed the room, as if they were picking out their prey.

I swallowed hard, trying to squash down the thoughts that emerged.

Because I very badly wanted to be their prey.

Their dark gaze landed on me, and they glided forward. Darla stepped up to them and placed a hand on their shoulder, her lips pursed in irritation. They jerked out of her grasp, and I almost rose from my seat on impulse. I tried to plead with my eyes, beg for Ursuline to head my way, to spare me from this solitude. I was at a party, technically in my honor, and I not only didn't know most of the people here, but I also didn't have the slightest thing in common with any of them.

Ursuline's eyes met mine again, and they headed in my direction.

Darla glowered at them, but I wasn't sure why. Due to their appearance or something else? Much of what Ursuline did for them remained a mystery, same as much of what the Triton family did for their wealth. I'd asked a few light questions around with the staff, but everyone had snapped up tight on the subject, and I could take the hint.

They closed in on my table, and I rose from my seat, not caring if I seemed eager. The glares from my parents grew more intense from their corner, but I ignored them. They'd sold me to the Triton family, and my fiancée didn't even want to spend time with me. Arielle was getting up close and personal with Darryl on the dance floor, and I could do nothing about that situation without causing a scene.

"You showed up," I said, my tone a little breathless.

Ursuline stopped in front of me, and they quirked a brow. "Uninvited, at that."

Anger rushed through me. "What do you mean?" Ursuline had been the one person who'd made me feel welcome from the moment I'd arrived here. And given their loyalty to the Triton family, I couldn't fathom why they wouldn't be included in such a large event, even if I had conflicting feelings for more personal reasons.

They glanced down to their tentacles. "Do you happen to see any other monsters, sunshine?"

I glanced around the room, so similar to the frequent parties my parents threw. All homogenous, all in muted tones, everyone looking a certain way. The conformity made my skin crawl. Embarrassment flushed through me, first that I'd be associating with people who'd behave like this, but that fast burned into a steady prickle across my skin at the knowledge that the Triton family would forsake their own kind with this pretense.

That trying to woo the upper echelons of Peregrine City would cause them to cast off Ursuline.

"Well, I'm glad you're here," I said, a little more heatedly than necessary.

"You might be the only one," they said wryly, casting a glance across the room. I followed their gaze to where Frederick and Darla whisper-hissed at each other and shot glares toward Ursuline. Their lips quirked, and they lifted their hand to offer a wave to both Frederick and Darla. I didn't need to look in my parents' direction to know they were aghast. Not like I was their problem now, though.

Arielle hadn't broken away from the dance floor. Darryl's hands roamed all over her body in its flowing chiffon dress, and she ate up the attention.

"Want a drink?" Ursuline asked, their low, rich voice sending shivers through me. Time and time again they kept extending a hand, a lifeboat when I needed one the most.

"Gods yes," I said. "The champagne I had feels like hours ago."

They tilted their head in the direction of the bar set up on the far side of the ballroom, the one less frequented. I stepped forth, ready to be away from this table of people I'd barely talked to.

"What prompted you to come?" I asked as we strolled across the room, maneuvering around throngs of partygoers deep in discussion. "I can hardly imagine part of your retainer involves attending many of these events."

"I wasn't going to," Ursuline said. "Truth be told, these affairs are insufferable. But Jacques was making his crab soup." Their gaze lingered on me a little too long, a little too knowingly.

My heart sped a bit faster. They hadn't come here for me, had they? Jacques, Maribella, and others on the staff had done little things to make this night less hellish for me, swinging by with hors d'oeuvres when I was alone, making my favorite dishes, and offering a few whispered check-ins. However, Ursuline showing up when they weren't invited, when they weren't welcome by their own employers—my stomach swooped.

One of their tentacles brushed against my leg, and a shudder racked through me. Fuck, I'd grown so lonely tonight, and this kindness they extended had my emotions brimming close to the surface.

We stepped up to the bar, where a hook-nosed bartender I hadn't met before stood wearing the traditional all-black attire.

"What do you recommend?" I asked.

"Want me to order for you?" They arched a brow.

I bobbed my head. Truthfully, handing them the reins would be a little too easy. In the short amount of time I'd known them, they'd already earned my trust.

"Two Tidewakers," Ursuline said.

The bartender's brows lifted in surprise, but he set forth to pull out a few bottles, including one I didn't recognize. It was a shimmering blue, as if glitter swirled inside it, though the iridescence seemed too natural to be that. He shook the concoction and poured it into two glasses. Ursuline thanked him, nabbed them both, and passed one my way. I clutched the cool surface, letting the calm filter through me. Together, we headed for a small alcove by the window where no one loitered.

"What's in this?" I asked, glancing at the swirling depths of the drink.

"Sour cherry cordial and jessamine," Ursuline said. "It's a liquor from a type of kelp that's distilled and sweetened."

I tipped the glass back and took a sip. The sweetness mixed with an addictive tang, and I savored the flavors on my tongue. "It's good. From New Atlantis, I suppose?"

"The Triton family has access to all sorts of things the other families here are unaware of," they murmured, a darker note to their tone. I couldn't help but wonder the secrets they hid, the mysteries they contained. My fingers itched to sketch, to paint them out on paper, splashes of purples, dark blues, and black in swirling strokes.

"How do you deal with this?" I asked, my voice low. No one stood nearby, but that didn't mean people weren't watching. Weren't attempting to listen in. "The hypocrisy."

Ursuline's lips pressed tight, and then they heaved out a slow sigh. As they leaned back against the wall, they took a sip from their drink, and at first, I wasn't sure if they'd answer my question or not. Granted, this wasn't the place to ask—not surrounded by the Triton family in their finest and their human peers.

"I wear who I am as a badge," they said, lifting their chin. They stared out at the dance floor, where dozens swirled across the surface like unfurled flowers. "I can stand it because I'd never choose to be like them—not for all the riches both land and sea could offer me."

My heart twisted hard. I resonated with that more than I could express in words. And I wanted to become like that more than anything as I stood here in my sham of a future marriage, both my fiancée and I playing in the farce.

I was so achingly tired of being a pawn, a toy.

I wanted to matter.

Ursuline's eyes met mine, and my stomach squeezed. Would they ask my question back? Expose me for the fraud I was? Except their gaze softened, and they took another sip of their drink.

I clutched the glass in my hand so hard I worried it'd break, yet there weren't any easy escapes, unless I wanted to exit the party and head back to my room. I'd considered the prospect a dozen or more times tonight.

"Have you seen the private gallery attachment to the ballroom?" they asked, tapping a nail on their glass.

I shook my head. "Can we go?" If the words came out a little pleading, I was beyond caring.

Their wicked smile set my insides aflame. "Follow me, sunshine."

That name on their lips was indulgent, holding an intimacy I craved with my whole soul. I'd follow them off a cliff just to hear them call me sunshine in those dulcet, husky tones.

Ursuline swept along the far wall and back to the corner, past the bartender setup. He didn't even blink as we traveled by, too busy fixing glasses of wine for a couple who I should probably be getting to know right now. Instead, I was hiding away, and I couldn't find it in myself to care about abandoning this farce of an engagement party. It had been organized to show off Frederick and the Triton family. Beyond Frederick's initial mention that his daughter Arielle was getting married to me and a nod to the Durand family, the rest of his speech had been focused on the future expansion of his business.

We stepped out of the ballroom and into the hidden gallery.

The quiet here ached around me, a stark contrast to the steady noise throughout the engagement party. No music in the background, no thrum of conversation. And then I looked around the room. The walls were a deep blue, and the sea-glass chandeliers shimmered on the pale white marble floors, casting gorgeous oceanic patterns. Yet what drew my attention were the pieces hung on the walls. This wasn't art curated for wealth, though the pieces were priceless. No, it held a theme that bled with a longing for the sea.

One I resonated with deeply.

Ursuline stood beside me as I soaked in the staged pictures staggered across the walls, interspersed by the occasional shelf that displayed crafted pottery pieces behind glass. The room here exploded with more color and creativity than the entire ballroom we'd stepped out of, and even though the gallery was quiet and still, I found more peace here than I did out there.

A few of the pieces along the far wall were familiar, and I wandered in their direction.

"You can spot Jason's work anywhere, can't you," Ursuline said, their voice rich with amusement.

"I studied under him for a while. Enough that I'd always recognize it," I said, reaching up to stroke my fingers along the ridged frame of "Terror," splashes of blacks, reds, and swirling blue. He'd told me a long time ago it had been inspired by where he'd grown up in the depths. In the Pockets. Of the pain and torment his family went through under the rulers down below. The haunted expression he sometimes wore felt so similar to Ursuline's.

"Do you miss him?" Ursuline asked. They stood beside me, close enough that my body hummed with awareness.

I took another sip of my drink before responding, letting the flavors roll around on my tongue and settle there. "I do. I'd love to see him again, but..." My stomach bottomed out. Jason had messaged me a few times to check in, but he wasn't a chatty sort to begin with. I hadn't told him everything that had changed. And I was terrified to reach out.

"You don't want any potential harm to come his way." Ursuline finished my statement.

I swallowed hard. "How did you know?"

"I'm no stranger to coercion." They stared at the piece before us, their dark eyes a little lost, a little haunted, as if their own ghosts dwelled there. The elegant arch of their nose, the firm press of their well-defined lips, the hollow of their throat created such perfect lines that I wanted to trace them on paper. "But I also know Jason would rather see you, risks be damned."

My eyes stung at that, and my chest squeezed tight. Learning that someone out there still cared was all that kept me going. If he found out my parents had almost disappeared him, would he ever want to see me again?

Ursuline's tentacle stroked against my side, sending a shiver through my body. "Monsters know the dangers of existing here among the humans. For all the equality Peregrine City proclaims, the law is rarely in our favor."

They weren't wrong. I'd attended enough of these parties, seen enough of the anti-monster rhetoric from the people with some of the most money, the most power in the city. Their attitudes disgusted me deeply.

"Contact him," Ursuline said. "We can arrange something."

Gratitude thrummed inside me on a bone-deep level. "Thank you."

Being in this place, with the gallery devoted to the sea, just made me want to escape to the bay. To feel the sand between my toes, to experience the exultant thrills from the other night when Ursuline had taken me swimming with them.

"Do you think it's too early to escape?" I asked, glancing toward the door again.

"Where do you have in mind?" they asked, their lips quirking. They took another long sip of their drink, finishing it.

"The deck, maybe?" I asked. I couldn't very well run off into the bay right now, but at least if I could stay away from the pressure of my parents' disappointed gazes, I might survive tonight. "Let me just find a restroom first."

"I'll wait for you on the deck," Ursuline said, gliding toward the door again. "There isn't anyone I care to speak to at a gathering like that."

Which only confirmed they'd come here for me.

Heat rushed through me, tangling with gratefulness. That they'd cared enough to show up, despite the confusing situation. Shame tugged on my heels a moment later. Because no matter how I felt, I'd pledged myself to another.

When we stepped back out into the ballroom, the music threaded over me again, the conversations crashing in a moment later. My parents sat at the same table as before, looking as dour as always. I kept my distance, going toward the exit to the private bathrooms I knew about, rather than the adjoining ones to the ballroom.

Besides, this route would make my detour to the deck far easier.

I trailed down the long, empty hall before I spotted the door to the left.

The door to the bathroom was shut, which meant someone else had ended up here. I leaned on the opposite wall and waited. A few thumps and muffled noises were coming from inside, ones I recognized fast—looked like the privacy had been sought out on purpose.

I rolled my eyes and knocked. As much as I didn't want to interrupt their fun, I didn't want to return to the ballroom more. A few more sounds came from inside, some moans and a shout. I took the final few sips of my drink, savoring the sweetness of the jessamine. Anticipation roiled inside me, that in mere moments I'd escape this garbage engagement party I'd never wanted.

Away from all the scrutiny.

The door creaked open.

Darryl stepped out, his black hair rumpled and a satisfied grin on his face. It was clear what he'd been up to, as evidenced by the lingering scent of sweat and sex in the air. My skin prickled with unease, as if with a premonition. As if I'd known what would happen all night.

My gaze landed on the next figure.

Arielle emerged from the bathroom, her copper strands mussed, her eyes sparkling with a freshly fucked glow. Her cheeks were rosy red, and her skirts still askew, the fabric a mess. She glanced up at me, and recognition flashed in her eyes. She delivered me a bright smile. "Fancy meeting you here."

Completely unconcerned. Not the slightest hint of guilt or turmoil, even though she'd fucked another guy during our engagement party.

My stomach bottomed out.

Any hopes of us finding common ground, of finding companionship and camaraderie out of this arrangement disintegrated. I pasted on a false smile, one I'd worn for my parents time and again. One I'd mastered over years and years of soirees just like this.

"Did we miss the cake?" Arielle asked airily. Her blue eyes were cloudless, free from anything but enjoyment. If only I could live life that unburdened. My chest squeezed tight.

"Let's get back," Darryl said, placing a hand on her shoulder. He glanced up at me and offered a nod. "See you around."

Acid churned in my gut as Arielle and Darryl strolled away from me. I froze in the hallway, watching their casual touches, the way they laughed together. The intimacy that I craved. Arielle had said she didn't expect me to be loyal. I had processed her words cerebrally, but my heart...my heart still hadn't perceived that I wouldn't be marrying for love.

That the person I would promise my life to wasn't my soulmate.

When they disappeared around the corner, I snapped into action. I used the restroom, numbly washing my hands in the sink after, far too aware of the lingering stench of Arielle's floral perfume in here.

I stepped out, and my feet moved automatically, carrying me toward the deck. I couldn't possibly return to the ballroom, not after witnessing that.

What bothered me the most wasn't that Arielle had fucked Darryl.

It was that after promising to stick by my side through this, she'd abandoned me. That she showed none of the guilt or confusion that

I faced with my blooming feelings toward Ursuline. That Arielle was enmeshed in this society and comfortable with her role in it.

I pulled on the handles of the double doors that led out to the deck that overlooked the bay, accessible from both the kitchen and an entrance closer to the ballroom. This was a gorgeous place to watch the sunset, and I'd taken advantage of the view as often as possible.

Adirondack chairs and fairy lights decorated the space here, meant to be enjoyed, and a propane fire pit graced the center area, which rarely got used. My gaze traveled to the lonely figure standing by the railing.

Ursuline waited for me, staring out at the sea.

A gravity settled over me, as heavy as the salt-soaked air.

And I traveled to them, like my path was predestined.

Chapter 12

The night sky stretched before me in an array of soft blues, blacks, and purples, studded by starlight.

I wanted to reach out and touch it, as if the surface would be as velvety as it looked. I wanted something soft to soothe the ache in my chest.

I stepped up beside Ursuline by the deck railing, and their shoulders relaxed, even if they didn't verbally acknowledge me. I'd spent enough time around Jason to learn to read the signals. The breeze was heady and cool, swirling around my limbs, dizzying my mind. The distant susurration of the water lapping the shore formed a sweet melody, one I needed to hear in the moment.

I clutched at the railing, the grain of the weathered wood imprinting in my palms. "I can't do this." The words escaped me, even though I'd tried to restrain them. "Following their rules...marrying when I don't love her...it's killing me."

It was the first time I'd admitted the truth out loud, and something tight inside me unspooled.

Ursuline turned toward me, and I faced them.

They stood inches away from me, towering above. The elegant arch of their nose, those imperious brows, their firm lips—everything about them mesmerized me. And with the way their dark eyes glittered, with the same intensity as the stars above, I couldn't look away. The tension broiled between us, growing stronger and stronger with every second.

Denying myself felt foolish when the woman I was promised to marry had fucked another man in the bathroom during our engagement party.

No love would be lost between us.

Mere inches separated me from Ursuline, and the ache in my chest expanded, a longing so ferocious I could barely breathe. One that promised to consume me body and soul. Just the smallest taste, and I could die happy.

I needed to know what it felt like to be possessed by them, to be theirs, even if only for a few stolen moments.

"I just want to be able to choose," I murmured, the words barely audible. Because I hadn't chosen this engagement. I hadn't chosen to come here. I hadn't chosen my path in life. And the truth left an indelible mark on my soul.

One moment, I was staring up at Ursuline, my whole soul pleading for them to close that distance.

The next, they succumbed.

Ursuline stepped forward, wrapped their hand around my nape, and they leaned in.

The moment their lips pressed against mine, my soul soared.

A thrill rose inside me, tentative and trembling at first, but it fast rose to the power and fury of the tide. This kiss was my early sketches, pencil scratching on paper, the expansion of my chest as my soul poured out of me onto the pad. The prickle of the forbidden across my shoulders, because if my parents caught on to what I was doing, they'd be furious. I'd frequented quiet corners, abandoned rooms, anywhere I might not get caught.

Because a Durand didn't indulge in whimsy.

Except my art had never been whimsy, just as this kiss was anything but pale or fleeting.

Living on the surface, refusing to dive beneath, had never been for me. I craved the colors, the depths, the thrills, the spark of creativity, the pulse, the pulse, the pulse of the blood pumping inside me.

No, this was what made a life not just survivable, but the exultant joy that made it memorable.

Ursuline's lips memorized mine at first, quick brushes as they tasted me. However, then their tongue delved into my mouth, and they *claimed*.

Their hand wrapped around my nape, and the other pressed against my lower back, keeping me in place. My whole body trembled from the sensations crashing through me. Their kiss held the same silent intensity that they did, more powerful than I ever could've imagined. And I surrendered to it at once. The dam inside me burst open, everything I'd been containing from the moment we first met. We kissed and kissed and kissed until I floated above with the stars themselves.

Their tentacles roamed around me, lightly caressing, keeping me on edge. The brush at my hip, the one around my leg, my arm, stabilized me. I sank into the feel of their lips as they devoured me, the way their touches consumed me. I'd never been kissed like this before, like I was something of value. Like I was worthwhile. Ursuline's scent wrapped around me, the deep sweetness of currants mixing with the salty brine. My heart thrummed, and I gasped for breath between kisses, not hesitating to dive back in.

In this pristine moment with them, every other worry faded away.

Every fear, every bit of guilt and shame and sorrow.

I just existed, the sea in the distance, the moon steady and incandescent overhead. The nighttime breezes swept by, but they did little to cool the rising inferno inside me. Ursuline's tentacles tightened around my wrist, around my ankle, and a silent thrill rippled through me. The sensation of being bound, the bit of helplessness, sent a shot of lust through my system. Rampant fantasies of them pinning me down, of them using those tentacles to pump inside me, all while I was bound by them circled through my mind. My cock woke up, testing the confines of my dress slacks.

The fantasies I'd had in the past were similar but always with someone faceless. I'd never met anyone I even hoped could give me what I needed. Who I'd even trust to hand control over to. Except with Ursuline, that came effortlessly.

Because from the moment we met, they'd proven themselves to me over and over again.

They broke the kiss to nip at my neck, my ear, and I panted, the touches making me delirious. I'd never felt this electricity before, never experienced the charge that ignited between us. The emptiness in me ached now, but not from being alone. From finding a connection I never believed I'd have. From the way each kiss of theirs, each stroke, each touch made my soul shine brighter and brighter, until I could turn this night to day.

Ursuline nipped at my ear, then licked at my neck, and a shiver ran through me. They kept their hand braced on my lower back, the other around my nape, but their tentacles roamed, caressing down my sides, twining around my arms, my legs. The sensations coming from all directions made my head spin. I was delirious with desire, drunk on lust, and I didn't want to stop.

My limbs trembled, but I didn't need to hold myself up. Not with the way Ursuline kept me braced right now. With them, I was free to fall into their embrace. To lose myself to pleasure.

They kissed me on the lips again, drinking me in with each claiming stroke of their mouth on mine. The thrills burst through me like fireworks, again and again and again. The contrast of the wild capriciousness between us and the sheer safety was everything I loved about the sea, and I felt it here with them. Ursuline dominated me with ease, their command as effortless as their competence. I kissed back, greedy for every taste, every touch they gifted me. My cock was hard, and my balls ached, my whole body sensitized from how they consumed me, from how their touches lit me up from the inside out.

I wasn't sure how long we kissed, whether minutes or hours melted away, but the gentle lapping of water in the distance created a lullaby beyond, the cool moonlight gliding over us, and the crisp nighttime breeze a caress. I lost myself in every second, never wanting to break away, never wanting this to end.

Eventually, Ursuline pulled back, even though their grip on me remained solid, reassuring. We stared at each other, our breaths mingling, our shoulders heaving from the force of how we'd crashed together. This was everything that had brewed for weeks in this place, every stolen glance, every stolen touch.

We'd crossed the forbidden line we'd been flirting with all this time. Because deep down, I'd recognized the tension between us and what it meant, even if I hadn't been able to fully acknowledge it. However, seeing Arielle's lack of concern tonight gave me the impetus to grab for what I'd wanted all along.

What I'd craved from the day Ursuline came to pick me up.

Their dark eyes were mesmerizing, intense and heated, and the light flush on their face lit me up inside. Their lips were even fuller from the way we'd kissed, and I longed to taste them again. The distant sounds of the water and the softness on their features soothed something inside me that was raw and ragged. Like they'd begun to knit my damaged pieces together.

"This..." They let go of me. Pain flashed across their features, and my stomach turned. "We shouldn't have done this."

"Don't say that," I blurted out, panic rising inside me. The loss of their touch on me brought reality crashing in, cold and stark and so, so lonely. I loathed it.

"You're promised to the Triton family," Ursuline said, the softness bleeding away. Their features shuttered, and they slipped back a few paces. "Something like this...we can't."

Anger flared up inside me.

I was so sick of being told what to do. How to live my life. That I should take the high road when no one else around me did.

My hands bunched into fists at my side. "You're promised to them too," I said, the words tumbling out. "Just in a different way. So don't pretend like we're so different."

Ursuline blanched and slid back farther. The anguish on their features socked me in the stomach. I regretted my words at once, but I couldn't swallow them.

"I'm sorry," I said, taking a step toward them. "Please, wait—"

They lifted their chin up, the imperious mask sliding into place, the same one I'd seen the first night I'd glimpsed them. As if they were cold, unaffected by the world around them. That couldn't be less true.

"I've got to go," Ursuline said, and they didn't offer me a second glance. No, they pivoted around and slunk toward the double doors to escape the deck. I watched them leave, frozen by the railing, even though everything inside me yearned to rush after them, to stop them.

I'd soared to the highest heights only to stumble and careen back down.

They disappeared through the door, and it clicked shut behind them.

I sagged against the railing, my heart aching, aching, aching. Fuck.

I'd received the kiss I'd dreamed of my whole life on the night I announced my engagement to someone else.

Maybe I could fling myself into the bay. Let the water carry me away. I knew they were guarded about their past, their association with the Tritons. I never should've tossed that in their face. Yet I longed for what we'd experienced right here with my whole soul. I wanted more, not this brief moment in time. These were the type of sparks I'd begun to believe I'd never experience. The sense of fate playing a winning hand for once.

I turned to stare out at the bay, the darkened waters glimmering. Some days, when I looked out at those depths, they were inviting. Others, they were as distant as the stars above.

I clutched tight to the rail, the events of tonight threatening to bring me to my knees. From encountering my nightmarish parents, from Arielle's dashed promises, from the brief, tremulous hope that unfurled while kissing Ursuline—only to have it dashed away.

When my parents had first broken the news to me that I'd be marrying Frederick's daughter, I thought I'd been desolate.

But that didn't compare to the reality.

Tonight, I'd tasted what true bliss could be, and in the aftermath, I'd gotten a taste of ruin.

Chapter 13

I hadn't seen Ursuline since the night of the engagement party.

In fact, as if spending that much time with surface dwellers had exhausted the Tritons, I hadn't seen a single one of them since either. Not even my fiancée, which struck me as odd, considering Arielle liked living on land. If it weren't for the members of the staff, I'd have thought they'd all but abandoned this place. Even still, I'd started out lonely, and ever since that night, the ache had grown in intensity.

I applied a few more brush strokes to the canvas, reveling in the feel of those perfect colors meshing on the canvas. This piece I'd started the night Ursuline had kissed me. The silhouette of a kiss, but inside the darkness formed, an array of reds, blues, and purples, all competing for dominance, threatened by the splashes of black on the space. Even though I'd poured those emotions out into the piece, they still dwelled in me, as ever present as a heartbeat.

I finished the last stroke I was working on and pulled away from the canvas. I'd been here the whole day, focusing on the things I could control rather than everything that spiraled beyond me.

At least through this pain, I'd created more art than ever. Though that could also be because I had unhindered access to supplies for the first time in my life. No painting in secret or stealing away to Jason's.

I wiped my hands on my ratty, paint-splattered jeans and then brought the brushes and palette over to the sink to wash. The usual scents of cleaner bloomed in the air as I washed my brushes off, the paint bleeding into the sink.

A thunk sounded from the upper floor, which drew my attention. It might've been Jacques or Maribella or Kendra. I'd made friends with Reiliana this week too, as well as Gerald, both of them on the serving staff. They'd all been overwhelmingly kind, which surprised me given the lukewarm reception I'd received from the Triton family.

Maybe because their employers were only here on occasion. The job probably wouldn't be as unbearable as working for people like my mother and father, who lobbied a different complaint against a different staff member each day of the week.

I finished washing my brushes and stepped out of the room to investigate. My stomach rumbled in response, in a reminder that I hadn't eaten anything yet today. And a fair amount of the day had passed.

Maybe that was what my parents had meant when they told me I needed to focus on reality. But when I sank into a piece, everything else melted away. Time grew immaterial.

I strode out of the room, making sure my footsteps were quiet. I wanted to see what I was walking into rather than diving in. Everyone was so secretive in this place, and I thirsted for any scrap of knowledge. When I stepped closer to the kitchen, the voices drifted my way.

"He's escalating." Jacques's voice rang out loud and clear, and I slowed to ensure I didn't give myself away. "The bay's been busier than normal."

My stomach flip-flopped as I crept to the edge of the doorframe.

"Shh, we don't talk about that," Maribella hissed at him.

"They're down below for the week," Jacques said. "Cleanup needed in their kingdom."

"I don't know how they can keep that contained," Kendra said. Everyone had congregated in the kitchen. My palms sweated. I wanted to ask what they were talking about, but the second I appeared, they'd clam up. Even though they were friendly and kind with me, I was attached to the Triton family, whether I liked it or not.

"They won't," Jacques said. "Not for long."

"Are you thinking of leaving?" Maribella asked.

"I've looked around," he said darkly. My blood chilled. What was the Triton family involved in? All I knew was that they made their riches in the orichalcum business, but I'd never be able to visit New Atlantis to investigate. Only sparing and carefully crafted information reached the surface.

Maybe I shouldn't be complacently painting in this estate while I knew nothing about the family I'd be marrying into. Arielle had made it clear she put loyalty to her family first and foremost, and she didn't seem to care to dig. What I'd mistaken as a similar parental disapproval between us at first, I'd fast realized wasn't the case. Frederick adored her, and she didn't seem dissatisfied with her lot in life. She was plenty happy to skate upon the surface.

I lost my grip on the doorframe, and a second later, I plunged into view.

A gasp escaped Kendra, and the cluster of her, Maribella, and Jacques by the kitchen island separated at once as they all put distance between each other.

"Sorry," I said. "Just popping up to raid the pantry."

Jacques plastered on a bright smile, even though his dark eyes were wary. His hair was slicked back and pulled into a ponytail today, and he was dressed down, the way he often did when the Triton family flitted off to New Atlantis. "Please, I can prepare something."

Kendra and Maribella vibrated with tension, passing each other worried glances. Clearly, they wondered what I'd overheard. Not enough.

The sense of being a trespasser had followed me around in this place wherever I went, never being able to settle. Even in the house I'd grown up in, I'd never felt a sense of ease, a mythical idea of home. The one person I'd experienced comfort around, I'd scared off.

And I missed their presence more and more with each passing day.

"I don't want to put you out," I commented, heading to the cabinet.

"Not a problem," Jacques said. "I'm here, and quite frankly, I'm bored."

"Well, I need to get back to the laundry," Maribella said, taking the first steps in the opposite direction. Her expression was shuttered—to be expected, I supposed.

"Me too." Kendra followed close on her heels, eager to escape the awkwardness.

I settled on one of the stools at the island, and Jacques pulled out several containers from the fridge. I'd tried to help before, and he'd smacked my hand with his spoon, so I no longer attempted it. Slight tension remained, buzzing between us, growing louder by the second.

He turned on the stove range and set a pan there, then doused it with a drizzle of oil. The sizzle of garlic hitting the hot pan echoed in the quiet between us.

My nerves couldn't take it anymore.

"I won't say anything," I blurted out.

"Call me naïve, but I didn't think you would," he said, even though his shoulders relaxed. "I know you're marrying into the family, but you don't seem close to any of the Tritons." He glanced back at me. "A certain cecaelia, on the other hand..."

A furious blush heated my cheeks. He wasn't wrong. And Jacques was far more observant than anyone gave him credit for. "I couldn't even tell you where any of the Tritons are this week. They've been keeping me in the dark."

Jacques shook his head, letting out a low hum. "That's their modus operandi. It's not personal, but I can imagine you're feeling a bit adrift."

I scrubbed at my face. "Tell me about it. I went from a household where I was micromanaged to one where I'm essentially abandoned."

The scent of garlic and tomato filtered through the air, and my stomach rumbled. He seemed to be whipping up a sort of pasta dish, if the bubbling pot of water beside the pan was any indication. Everything Jacques made turned out lovely, and I had never been a picky eater. My mouth watered.

"You know, it's not too late to escape," Jacques mentioned. This hadn't been the first time he'd warned me away from this place, and my body hummed with a sense of danger at his words. The comment might've been delivered simply, but the seriousness that dwelled behind the statement wasn't lost on me.

"Where would I go?" I said. "Some spoiled rich kid with no access to funds? I don't have any useful skills."

He shook his head. "That what they'd have you believe? I've seen your paintings. That sort of talent belongs in a gallery."

"Which takes time to build," I replied. "Not like I can chew on some canvas when I'm hungry."

Still, the idea of running off sparked in my brain, burning brighter than ever. What was to stop me? The Tritons were rarely here, and they didn't seem concerned about keeping a leash on me.

Jacques didn't respond at first, plating the meal he'd worked on with the panache and speed of a professional. My stomach rumbled, the hunger I'd ignored for hours taking precedence as he brought over the decadent pasta dish, bright tomatoes and zucchini giving it color.

"Thank you," I said, gratitude burning in my gut. Not just for the meal, but also for the fact he encouraged me to leave. That he was willing to be as honest as he could with me, even though it came with risk. Maybe because he planned on leaving himself, but I appreciated the concern nonetheless.

"Careful with the contracts," Jacques said as he leaned against the kitchen island. "That's a slippery slope you can ask Ursuline about."

My gut simmered. Marriage was a binding contract, but guaranteed I'd also be required to sign a prenup. And I doubted they'd let me use an independent lawyer to make sure my best interests were taken care of. What did Jacques mean about Ursuline? They were the main family lawyer for the Tritons, but was a contract involved in why they worked for them? Ursuline had always danced around the subject, and now that we'd kissed, I wasn't sure they'd even entertain a conversation, let alone a personal one.

My chest throbbed at the thought. I'd been squirreling away moments with them, savoring each one like a glass of ice water in the middle of the desert. The idea of not having any more sent a spike of pain through me. I speared a few pieces of pasta with my fork and chewed a bite in an effort to distract myself. The richness of tomato and garlic burst on my tongue, and I savored the flavors for a moment.

"So what you're saying is that my window is quickly closing," I murmured. Because we'd begin talking wedding dates soon, and guaranteed the prenup would come next. Frederick had made veiled threats due to my knowing their secret, and once I was tied to the family for good, I was sure there'd be more to carry. The prospect made my stomach roil.

"I—" Jacques started to say, when he stood ramrod straight.

"What are the two of you doing in here?" Arielle asked, a tinkling laugh escaping her. "Secret dinners?"

I froze. We'd just been talking about escape, because I thought the estate was empty of Tritons. However, if Arielle had been lurking in the halls, who knew what she'd heard? Who knew which other members of the Triton family were back as well. "I got caught up with painting," I blurted out, wanting to divert attention. "Jacques here was kind enough to make me a meal, since I'd forgotten to eat."

Arielle smiled at me, and when I'd first arrived here, I would've believed that glib laugh, her bright grin. However, after spending more time with her, I'd come to recognize a bit more of the false front. Her eyes might sparkle, but they were creeks not rivers. And her loyalty was to her family, even if she was aware of her limited role in this society.

"Did you want something to eat?" Jacques hurried to ask, seizing the moment as well. His shoulders were tense, and I didn't miss the slight flare of panic in his gaze.

Arielle shook her head. "No, I had a big meal down in New Atlantis earlier. Still stuffed. I'm looking forward to being back up on the surface for awhile now that Papa's business is wrapped up."

"Good to hear," I stated, plastering a smile on my face as surface level as hers. Maybe if I'd read her right from the start, I could've avoided this farce of an engagement somehow. Or maybe I'd always been destined to be a pawn for my family. I took another bite of the pasta, even though my appetite had vanished.

"I'll leave you to it," Jacques said with a quick bow before he departed. His eyes wouldn't meet mine, and guilt flushed through me. Hopefully, he'd tender his resignation sooner rather than later, even if that meant losing his friendly presence in the house. I'd rather he be safe.

Arielle plunked next to me in the seat, but I didn't feel comforted by her presence. Far from it.

Ever since the night of the engagement party, I'd been hesitant to trust her. I might be naïve, but even I could eventually see when someone didn't have my best interests at heart. Arielle cared for her own agenda and whatever allowed her to further it.

"Were you down there painting all week?" Arielle said, swishing her feet back and forth. "You know you're allowed to go out places. Just get a chauffeur to escort you."

Right. Because I couldn't drive off on my own. My best chance of escape would've been while the Triton family had been down in New Atlantis. Jacques was right. My window of opportunity was fast closing.

"I'll do that," I said. "I've been feeling a bit cooped up as of late."

Even though Arielle always broadcast charm and lightness in spades, for a brief moment, I caught it.

The slight draw of her brows. The coolness in her eyes.

She'd heard our conversation.

My insides chilled.

Just as fast as a storm in the summer rushed past, her expression brightened again, all sunshine and smiles. "You're always welcome to come dancing. Or hell, even go to brunch. Live a little, Elrich."

I forced another bite of the pasta down my throat, even though her appearance had soured my appetite. Something was going on with the Triton family, something I was unaware of. And I had the sinking feeling if I didn't get to the bottom of this mystery, I'd be sentencing myself to a fate worse than an arranged marriage.

The secrets that floated around in this society were deadly. One misstep, and I'd find myself a casualty.

Chapter 14

Jacques was missing.

I'd searched the past few days, trying to seek him out in his normal spots—the staff kitchen, the one out here—to no avail. I'd asked Maribella and a few of the others, but they'd given me tight-lipped answers and hurried away. None of which made me feel better about the circumstances.

My stomach churned as I raided the cabinet in the kitchen. The idea that he'd gotten in trouble lingered. Maybe Arielle had ratted him out to her father and he'd been fired.

Yet I couldn't shake the lingering dread that curled within me, like the scorched clouds that preceded a storm. I'd gone swimming in the bay today, by myself again, and the loneliness here threatened to undo me. If I didn't even have Jacques or the other staff to interact with, I wouldn't survive.

Maybe an escape plan wasn't a bad idea.

I'd spent my whole life trying to live up to my parents' approval only to fail, and the Triton family seemed just as disinterested.

I grabbed some crackers and sliced up some cheese, arranging it on a plate, though not with the panache Jacques would have. The sound of the front door slamming drew my attention, echoing all the way to here. I carried my snack with me, taking a few absent bites as I wandered in that direction. A shuffling sounded, and the creaking of footsteps trailed after.

I followed the source until I stepped in through the doorway of one of the entertaining rooms, this one featuring a comfortable arrangement of sofas and sitting chairs as well as a large wooden bar in the corner. The copper furnishings gleamed under the low light.

Frederick paced in the middle of the room, his shoulders tight and his brows drawn.

I paused. Was there a way to get out of this unnoticed?

His gaze zeroed in on me, a darkness percolating there that froze me to the bone. "What are you doing?" he growled.

"I just heard the clamor," I stammered and lifted my plate. "I came up to get a snack."

Frederick towered over me and crossed his arms over his chest. "And where is Arielle?"

I shook my head. "You know she's a free spirit as much as I do."

He glowered. "Except I told her she needed to spend time with you. You're to be her husband, and if she's out at the club by herself constantly, it could look bad for our families. You wouldn't want that, would you?"

I swallowed hard. Was this his attempt at pushing me to rein her in? If so, he'd chosen the wrong fiancé for the task. Not only was Arielle the whimsical sort to do what she wanted, but I'd never been a domineering personality. If that were the case, I wouldn't have ended up in this predicament.

"No, sir," I responded, even if I didn't have the slightest idea what he wanted me to do about his daughter. If anyone would have sway with her, he would.

"Besides, too much time in this place will make you idle," he said, glancing over me. "You and Arielle need some excursions away from here."

My heart thudded harder. What had inspired his sudden concern? The conversation with Jacques lay heavy in my mind. If Frederick was breathing down my throat, my window of escape had minimized if not vanished. All those hours and days when the family had barely been around, squandered.

"I'll make sure it happens," Frederick said, an edge to his tone that I perceived as a threat. There was something about him, a darkness in his eyes, tension in the air in his presence, that had made me uneasy from the start. My stomach twisted, and all I could do was bob my head with a nod. I clutched my plate and took the silence as a cue to dismiss myself. Walking by him felt like striding by a crocodile in the wild, where you were aware that at any moment, they'd snap their jaws and devour you.

The moment I stepped into the hall, breath filled my lungs again. Shuffling had sounded earlier, implying someone else had been here. I'd heard voices.

But not another set of footsteps.

My heart thrummed as I stared down this corridor, one that had become achingly familiar in the past few months. One I'd traveled time and time again to go paint. I walked in that direction, looking to put some distance between Frederick and myself. Arielle had been around this morning, but after her phone rang, she'd flitted off to another social occasion, the same way she always did.

The closer I got to the studio, the slower my footsteps grew. A sound drew my attention at once, coming from the other room that Ursuline had showed me early on in my time here. From the music room.

A faint piano melody reached my ears, and excitement simmered through my veins. Only one person I knew played the piano in this house, and they were the one I'd been desperate to see for well over a week now. The one I'd dreamed of every night, who I ached for.

The familiarity of the melody stopped me in my paces. I'd heard it before. Somewhere.

Somewhere important.

Then they began to sing.

Their rich low voice swept through me like a caress, and with the steady saturation of a rainstorm, the realization rolled through me of where I'd heard that melody, that voice before.

I'd barely been conscious, but someone had held me. They'd sung the song while I ached all over, trying to recover, after somehow making it out of the storm at sea alive.

After someone had saved me.

My heart thrummed at a hummingbird's pace. Could it truly be?

I stopped in front of the doorway. Their back was to me, but they played the piano with a fervor that enthralled me, their voice seductive and so memorable it engraved itself on my very bones. They continued to sing, the lullaby I'd awoken to on the shore what felt like a lifetime ago.

The memories crashed into me—of being tossed around by the ocean, of the slow, sure drag to the depths, of the panic, the fear, the choking realization that this was the end.

And then of safety. Of the warm sunlight and the immense calm.

Of being in their arms.

No wonder they'd felt familiar from the moment we met.

"It was you," I murmured, unable to help myself. My heart expanded to the point it threatened to burst out of my chest. "You're the one who saved me."

The slight slipped key and hitch of their shoulders offered the only indication of their surprise as they continued to play and sing in their strong, steady voice. I leaned against the doorframe, the surprise cascading over me. Of course Ursuline would've been my savior. They'd been rescuing me over and over again, whether in large or small ways. Guilt prickled through me.

And I'd pushed back at them after we'd kissed.

They hadn't said they didn't want me. They'd said we couldn't do this.

Because I was betrothed to a Triton.

I swallowed hard, the lump forming in my throat. Even still, yearning bloomed within me anew, a desperate desire to be theirs.

They'd saved me from the sea. A sense of inevitability settled over me. Ursuline was the only reason I stood here today.

I didn't want to walk away from this.

Their voice trailed off, and they played the final notes of their melody. It resonated through the air, a steady hum elongated by the tension that bloomed between us. They'd been avoiding me for over a week now, but tonight, they were here. And the feelings and confusion that had percolated inside me bubbled up to overflow.

Ursuline pushed up from their seat at the piano bench, and they glided in my direction. Their eyes contained a hungry intensity as they looked me over, the sort I'd surrendered to. And with their broad shoulders, their height, they loomed over me, even from feet away.

"A guileless human had been swept away in a storm," they said. "What was I supposed to do? Let him drown?"

"Others would," I commented. Their kindness sparked in my chest, kindling that now burned. They'd shown that care and consideration with me every step of the way through my time with the Triton family, but knowing they were my mystery savior? I wanted them more than ever, with an unabating ache that carved into my chest.

"I've seen enough cruelty in this world to not want to contribute more," they murmured, averting their gaze.

Boldness gripped me, and I closed the space between us, step by tentative step. When I reached up, they didn't jerk away, even though I telegraphed my movements. I skated my fingertips along their jawline, sharp and undeniably sexy. heir demeanor, their features were cool, remote, distant. Yet gods, they were so warm. So real, when everything else in my life wasn't.

A shudder rolled through them, slight but undeniable. They opened their eyes, and pain shone in their dark gaze. "You have no idea what you do to me."

A lump formed in my throat. "I've never felt this way around anyone before. I can't..." I sucked in a sharp breath, my eyes stinging. "Please don't go away again."

They reached down and wrapped their hands around my hips. "You belong to the Triton family."

I stared up at them, heat blazing within me, a stubborn resistance born and bred from their resignation. "I belong to *myself*."

Their eyes widened, and their grip on my hips tightened. My heart thrummed at the closeness between us, at the feel of their hands on me. I'd craved this for so long, to the point I'd dreamt of it this week, whether in slumber or reality. I wanted them to take me apart piece by piece until I was screaming, with their mouth, their teeth, their tongue. I wanted their tentacles thrusting inside me until all I could feel was them.

I wanted them to claim me until I felt utterly possessed.

"The look on you, sunshine," they said, a hoarseness in their voice. "You'll be my undoing."

I dropped my hands to their chest, their heart *thump, thump, thumping* at an accelerated pace beneath my palm. Even with the fabric of their tunic separating our skin, I could feel the heat there, amplified by my own.

"Please," I begged, not sure what I even begged for at this point. For them to stay? For them to make my fantasies come true?

Truly, I just didn't want to be without them again. They were here with me in this room, and their hands on my hips settled the rising panic in my chest like nothing else. They were the calm in the wake of a storm—the one who'd saved me from the worst storm of my life. My heart squeezed hard. If they rejected me now, if they walked away—I couldn't bear it.

"Please, what?" they asked, bringing a thumb and gliding it slowly across my lower lip. The deliberateness of their action sent a violent shiver through me.

"Take me," I gasped. "However you want. Just make me yours."

Maybe the admission made me shameless, but I didn't care. I burned with need tonight, with pent-up desire I couldn't contain any longer.

Their eyes widened and then scorched. The blaze in them was the hottest inferno I'd seen, and I lit up from it. My whole body sparked with awareness, like it had awakened from a long slumber.

"Careful what you wish for, sunshine," they growled. Their hand traveled underneath my shirt, sliding up my side in a slow and sinuous movement, and their tentacle twined around my leg, climbing up to tease the inside of my thigh. I gasped from the burst of lust that coursed through me. My cock stiffened from the touch, from the sheer hunger in their eyes as they regarded me.

"Please." The word came out in a mewl, my body so sensitized from being near them. All my fears, my concerns with my current trajectory flew out the window when they were near, their presence scrambling my brain.

I wanted to be claimed by them with every ounce of my being.

Tonight, more than ever, I needed the reminder I wasn't alone. That I was more than some chip to be bargained with.

That I could still choose.

Ursuline withdrew from me, and disappointment swept over me in a fierce wave. That ache would go unabated, doomed to fester inside me, growing more agonizing by the day. I opened my mouth, but before I could say anything, they slid over to the door—and closed it.

They flipped the lock, the sound echoing through the room.

My heart lodged in my throat.

They leveled a voracious look in my direction. "I've tried," they admitted, their voice hoarse, wrecked. "I've tried to avoid you, to stay away, because I know you're betrothed to Arielle." Their gaze burned into me, setting me aflame. "But I can't any longer. I'll make you mine, until you're screaming my name, until you can't feel your legs.

"Even if it's only for tonight."

Chapter 15

Ursuline had always felt like safety to me, but when they fixed their gaze on me, a thrill rippled up my spine. The intensity in their eyes screamed danger for my heart, yet they'd won my trust through my time here, and even though they approached me slowly, as if I might get spooked, I held strong.

I wanted to be here with them tonight.

"Strip for me," they said, undeniable command in their tone. It sent a shiver through me. While I wasn't a hookup type, boyfriends and girlfriends were fleeting in this society. I'd fucked and been fucked by men and women before, but I'd never been with a monster. Despite what my parents tried to convince me of about monsterkind, out of everyone I'd been with, I'd never felt safer than with Ursuline.

I tugged my loose linen shirt over my head and tossed it to the floor. Ursuline stopped in front of me, a mere foot away.

The tip of their tentacle traced down my bare chest, slow and deliberate. A shudder racked my body, and then they teased the tip near my nipple. The slightest brush and a flare of pure lust rushed through me. They wrapped their tentacle around my nipple and gave a light tug. A gasp escaped me, and my cock strained with how hard I was.

"You're so responsive, sunshine," Ursuline purred as they continued to tug at my nipple. Each time, sparks flew through me. Another tentacle slithered up my other side and wrapped around that nipple. Holy fuck. Those sparks intensified, and my cock leaked pre-cum, enough to leave a stain. They tugged both at the same time, and electric pleasure coursed through me. A long, low moan escaped me. Their tentacles were soft and smooth, and the thickness wrapped around my nipples sent a shiver down my spine. They stood mere inches from me, their darkly sweet scent caressing me. They were a contrast of sharp angles and curves, from their broad shoulders to their sharp jaw to the curve of their hips and the undulating tentacles below.

I never believed I'd get this close, but I would savor every second I got with them.

They tugged at my nipples again, and I balled my hands into fists to keep in place. I'd never realized how sensitive they were, but the suction around them, the gentle tugs of their tentacles, vaulted me into euphoria.

"And how do you like being taken?" they asked, their voice deliberate, sinuous. Another of their tentacles slipped through my legs, and they brushed it right between my cheeks. Heat flooded through me fast and fierce.

"There," I gasped out. "Oh gods, there." Their tentacles wrapped around my nipples, another one gliding up and down my crack, and sweat broke out on my temple. My breaths came in ragged. They could overload me, make me forget that anything else existed but them. This close, I could see slight slits along the sides of their throat—gills? The urge to run my fingers along them struck me, but I could barely do anything but moan with the way they teased me right now. The wicked arch of their brows, the teasing smile on their lips vaulted me even higher.

"You're a bit overdressed for that," they said, gliding their tentacle between my cheeks again. The fabric of my pants and boxer briefs separated us, and I hated it. I wanted to be bare for them, stripped down at their mercy.

I fumbled for the button of my pants, and they gave my nipples another tug. A shudder racked through me, halting my progress as I paused on the zipper. Fuck, how was I supposed to pay attention? The pure electricity percolating through me was unreal, something I'd never felt with anyone I'd been with before. I managed to shunt the zipper down, and then I grabbed my waistband and shoved both my pants and my boxer briefs to the floor in one go. Ursuline drew their fingertip along the center of my chest, down, down, down until they reached the soft curls at the base of my cock.

My whole body trembled as I kicked my shoes, my pants, and my underwear off. I was in the middle of nudging at my socks when they glided their tentacle back between my cheeks. The slight suction of the tentacles against my skin sent a violent burst of pleasure through me. My hole ached, to be filled, to be fucked, to be stretched open. I stumbled a little but managed to divest myself of every scrap of clothing.

Completely bare in the middle of the music room, I should've felt exposed. However, with the way Ursuline surrounded me, their tentacles around my hard nipples, sliding against my hole, and their fingertip trailing up and down my chest, I incinerated. The sensations threatened to overwhelm me in the best way. My knees trembled. I wouldn't be able to keep myself upright for long.

Would they fuck me with a cock? With a tentacle? I wasn't sure of their anatomy at all. I just wanted anything Ursuline was willing to offer.

"You're thinking too much, sunshine," they teased, the wry note in their tone undeniably sexy. "You want to get taken by me?"

"Desperately," I gasped out.

"In every hole?" they asked.

Lust roared through me fast and fierce, and I bobbed my head.

"Words," they said. "I need your words."

"Yes, please," I begged again and thrust my ass back, as if I could somehow get their tentacle inside me. My cheeks heated at the shamelessness of it, but I didn't care. My whole body hummed with awareness, with a need desperate for satiation.

"Bend over on the bench," they said, drawing their tentacles away from me. "Expose that pretty hole for me."

Their dirty talk set me aflame, and I reached down to stroke my cock, the pulse of lust hitting me fast and fierce. I hadn't realized how much I wanted someone to command me like this, to tell me what to do every step of the way. To take me over and let me embrace blissful oblivion, even if only for a few moments.

My nipples were hardened nubs from the attention, distracting me as I walked over to the piano bench. I placed my palms flat on the surface and followed instructions, bending over and spreading my legs until the air from the room hit my exposed hole. Ursuline's stare burned into me the entire time. Maybe I slowed my movements a little more due to that attention. Maybe I thrust my ass out a little farther because of it too.

They let out a low rumble that echoed through the acoustics of the room.

"As much as I want to hear all your gorgeous sounds, this has to stay between us," they said as they approached, gliding forward. "Which means you'll have to be a good boy for me and suck."

They stopped behind me, their presence consuming the air between us. I glanced back, and the sight of them looming over me struck me with such intense desire that my legs trembled. Their silver hair was swept back, their jawline sharp, their pale blue skin a shade darker in the lighting of the room. They stood upright on their tentacles, but two slithered out from beneath, looking slicker and more defined than the others.

"Have you ever been with my kind, sunshine?" Ursuline asked, crooking a brow.

I shook my head and gulped. The idea of those pumping inside me...fuck. My cock dripped, pre-cum forming a puddle on the floor beneath me.

"Let me introduce you to my mating tentacles, then," they said, their gaze flashing with the sort of heat that threatened to undo me. "Be my good boy, and open your mouth."

I obeyed at once, desperate for whatever they'd give me. Ursuline stepped up behind me, close enough that their body brushed against my ass cheeks. One mating tentacle hovered in front of my open mouth. With the tip, they brushed against my lower lip, then my upper, teasing me. The slickness left a residue there, something that tasted a bit salty. I swallowed hard, my throat bobbing. The urge to lean forward and lick rose in a fierce way, but I wanted to follow their instructions more.

The tip of their tentacle probed into my mouth, gliding along my tongue.

"Suck," they commanded.

I eagerly obeyed. I wrapped my mouth around the appendage and sucked. It was thick and smooth, warmer than I'd expected. A small gush pumped into my mouth, salty and hot, and I swallowed it down.

"You're going to get more than a mouthful, sunshine," they said. "Your belly and your hole will be full of cum by the time I'm done with you."

My lashes fluttered, and I moaned around the tentacle in my mouth. They gave a slight thrust in and out, the tip diving down my throat. I choked on their tentacle, tears blossoming in my eyes, my throat convulsing. Except they stayed there, patiently waiting as I adjusted. I drew deep breaths from my nose as I got used to the length lodged in my throat, as their slickness lubed the way.

I continued to suck, and they began to fuck my throat with those light strokes. Heat brimmed in my eyes at how careful they were with me. At their consideration and communication with every step. I'd never felt safer, even as I free fell.

"Damn, that throat feels like sin," they said, their tone gruff. Their palm ran along my side, down and around my ass cheek as the caress sent a shudder through me. My hole ached to be filled. I couldn't imagine being consumed by them, wrecked and completely full. Yet I yearned for the sensation with every ounce of my being.

They gave those light thrusts inside my throat, the occasional gush from their mating tentacle traveling inside me. The slickness of their length, the suckers along it that rubbed against my tongue, my throat, all of it had me overwhelmed. Their fingers ran through my hair and tugged, and I moaned around their length. I closed my eyes and surrendered to them, wanting this more than my next breath.

"Looks like this hole is just as needy," they said, and the tip of their other mating tentacle slithered against my hole. The slickness there set it apart, and the feel of the suckers and wetness across the sensitive skin made me shiver. They continued to stroke along my pucker, slow and deliberate, while their mating tentacle fucked in and out of my throat. I sucked automatically, until it became as natural as breathing, and my mind started to grow fuzzy, like I waded through a dream.

"Gods, sunshine," they purred. "You're too good at this. Just begging to be bred."

A shudder ran through me at their words, pure pleasure traveling my veins. Fuck, I hadn't known how much I wanted this, but my palms burst into a sweat as my whole body trembled. And they hadn't even breached my hole yet. I sucked hard, and a ragged breath came from them. The fact I could do this to them too gave me a burst of power I'd sorely needed after feeling like I was tossed at sea.

Even now, Ursuline was still saving me.

The tip of their mating tentacle paused from stroking my hole, and it nudged inside. A whimper escaped me, muffled by the length pumping inside my throat. The occasional drip of their juices trickled inside me, and fuck, I wanted every drop they could give. I wanted to be slathered in their release inside and out.

They thrust their mating tentacle a little deeper inside my hole, the natural slickness there eliminating the need for lube. As it traveled deeper inside me, a slight sting zinged through me at the stretch. I tried to thrust my ass back to take more, but Ursuline retracted.

"Nuh-uh, sunshine," they said. "I'm in control here."

Ngh. My eyes rolled back at the words, at the smooth, rich competence in their voice and movements. Drool dribbled down my chin as I continued to choke on their mating tentacle, the little bumps of their suckers rubbing against my throat. The droplets splattered onto the piano bench, a few hitting my palms.

Their mating tentacle thrust inside my hole again, and this time I waited patiently. They pumped in and out shallowly, a few exploratory strokes inside me, even though I craved for them to thrust deep and hard, enough to steal my breath away. The feel of the suckers along my insides sent a violent shiver through me, and they pushed in a little farther, the thicker part of their mating tentacle probing me. They stroked with the tip against my inside walls, and bliss roared through me. I howled around the length lodged deep in my throat. Their breathing came a little faster as they teased me.

"Damn, you take me so well," they said, their voice hoarse, wrecked. "Like you were born for this."

Tears prickled at my eyes as I choked on their mating tentacle still thrusting inside me, another glob of spit dribbling down my chin. My legs trembled as their tentacle pushed even deeper inside my hole, until that thickness fully lodged inside me. Until I wasn't sure how much more I could take. A satisfied breath escaped Ursuline, and they combed their fingers through my hair, giving me another light tug.

"Good, good boy," they said. "You're being so perfect for me."

A few more tears slipped down my cheeks, but I wasn't sure if they were from the impact of their praise or how good I felt. Maybe both. I sucked and sucked and sucked, losing myself in the fullness in my throat, in how they filled me up inside my hole as well. A gush of their juices burst inside, and another shiver racked through me. I wasn't sure how I'd survive when they came. I hoped it was so much I dripped with it.

The glide between my cheeks made the most obscene noises, the amount of slickness amplifying the sheer bliss without the slightest bit of discomfort. They fucked into me with a steadiness that drove me insane, one that made my balls throb. My cock leaked onto the floor, the pool of pre-cum almost as bad as the pool of spit. I was a mess, trembling under their careful ministrations, yet I wanted more.

I wanted them to pin me down with their tentacles, to fuck inside me hard and desperate.

I writhed as they dragged their suckers along my prostate, the flares of pleasure enough that I was about to collapse. My body was coming apart at the seams, and the need for release formed a steady *thump, thump, thump* that grew by the second. They squirted another burst of fluid down my throat, and I gagged again, some of it gliding down my chin, along with more saliva. They fucked into me a little harder, and the sloppy sounds of how wet they'd made my hole sent a dose of adrenaline through me. I wanted to exist in this space forever, being overwhelmed and dominated by them.

Consumed.

Tears trickled down my cheeks, and I tried to blink them away.

"Fuck, your tears are so sexy," they swore. Their voice was gravel on silk, an addiction I needed more and more of. They thrust into my hole hard, and the pleasure burst fast and fierce.

I sobbed around their length, more tears streaming down. They tugged on my hair, the slight sting keeping me grounded in the moment, all while they fucked into me from both ends, this undulating loop I couldn't get enough of. Their length was the perfect thickness to split me open, the tapered end probing so deep inside me I could barely believe how much I'd taken. My thighs quaked, my arms trembled, and sweat burst across my body, pebbling my skin. My balls ached with the need to come, but I couldn't coordinate stroking myself off, not when it took every ounce inside me just to stay upright.

One of their tentacles wrapped around my legs, as if they sensed their imminent collapse, and I sagged forward onto the piano bench, my sensitive nipples pressed against the cool wood. I splayed out my arms, palms resting on the surface as they continued to fuck into my mouth as steadily as ever. Their mating tentacle in my hole thrust in harder, at a speed that would take my breath away—if my mouth wasn't full of them. Their tentacle wrapped around my leg, their grip in my hair vaulted me higher, the touch coming from every direction. They could dominate me with such ease, and fuck, that was so sexy.

They gushed with another burst from their mating tentacle, and I choked on it again, more tears streaming down my cheeks. Yet the glide was effortless, smooth from the slick pouring from them. The length in my hole shuttled faster and faster, with a finesse that made me lose what little remained of my mind. They tugged my hair again, and another whimper escaped me, muffled by how they fucked my throat. Sweat trickled down my back, and my legs at this point, the salty scent fragrant in the air.

Everything melted away. All that existed was their tentacles plunging inside my mouth, my hole. Their fingers in my hair. Their tentacle gripping my leg.

Short inhales burst through my nose. More saliva dripped from my mouth. The gush of their tentacle inside me smoothed the way. My balls ached with a steady pulse.

That thrust tagged my prostate with every stroke. Pure fireworks.

I could live in this moment forever.

Their breaths grew choppier. "Oh fuck, sunshine. Think you can take two loads for me?"

I bobbed my head. I wanted that so badly. My cock dripped so hard it throbbed, but I didn't even care, not while they fucked me so well.

Except then their hand wrapped around my length. They gave it one stroke, two. I sobbed around their length again, tears streaming down my cheeks. The tension, the ache was unbearable. My balls lifted. The third stroke sent me tumbling over the edge.

Pleasure rushed through me, fast and fierce, with the intensity and speed of a tornado. The cum rocketed out of me with an audible splat, and I almost blacked out from the force of my orgasm. For a few moments, my limbs seized. I let out a ragged, muffled moan, and the bliss radiated through me, sending me vaulting higher than I believed possible. I'd never come so hard in my life.

And they weren't even finished with me yet.

Ursuline continued to fondle my deflating cock, as I floated along in a dreamlike space. It was oversensitive, but I loved the feel of their hands on me so much that I didn't care.

They picked up speed again as they fucked into my mouth, my hole. The drool poured from my mouth like a faucet now. I was completely limp against the piano bench, there to be taken and defiled however they pleased.

"I'm so close," they gasped out, the thrusts fast and fierce now. The sensations as they slid against my prostate were agonizing after coming, so intense I could barely handle it, but I was also so fuck-drunk I didn't want to budge. "So. Damn. Close."

One moment I was sucking their length, and it was driving into my hole. The next, a deadly growl came from them, and their mating tentacles paused.

And then they emptied inside me.

Their cum flooded down my throat in a torrent, and I choked and spluttered on it at once as they withdrew. The rest of it sprayed across my face, hot and sticky and salty. At the same time, they filled up my insides, the gush so intense that even while they were still lodged inside me, the cum oozed from my hole, dribbling down my legs. I gulped down breaths, my face soaked with their release, and I licked my lips, just to taste more. Heat pulsed through me. That was so insanely hot.

"Fuck," they said, softer this time. "You took me so well, sunshine."

Their words filled me with a warmth I'd been craving, the praise like a balm on my cracked and splintered soul. They pumped into my hole a few more times, but when they began to withdraw, more cum came rushing out. It drenched my hole, the insides of my thighs, trickling all the way down to my calves. I was a sloppy mess, covered in them, and I couldn't be more elated.

In my wildest fantasies, I couldn't have imagined being dominated and taken like this.

And now that I'd experienced submitting to them, I wanted this bliss every day for the rest of my life.

"Stay put," they said as their grip on my leg released, their fingers in my hair slipped away. Their glide sounded through the room, followed by the click of a door. I rested my forehead on the wooden bench, so beyond wrecked it was a miracle my legs still kept me up. They trembled and quaked as I sucked in one slow breath after another. My head whirled. Every part of me felt used and sticky, and I loved it more than I could express.

The door clicked again. "I'm back," they said, announcing themself. They stepped beside me, their shadow rolling over, and their hands landed on my shoulders. "Come on," they said, giving a slight nudge as they helped me up from my slump. "Take a seat on the edge."

I obeyed, scooting to the edge of the seat, my legs lazily splayed open. Ursuline's tentacle was wrapped around a wet washcloth, and they stroked at my bared hole. Around my limp, deflated cock. They took their time, cleaning up the mess they'd made all over my body. They'd marked me with their cum, and I wanted to experience that again and again and again. Their dark, intense eyes tracked me as they cleaned me up, meticulous in their diligence. The feel of the washcloth between my cheeks, along the inside of my thighs made me shudder, and I was stripped down in a different way.

How they'd taken me tonight was lifechanging. I'd never felt so possessed or claimed in my life. I'd never experienced such elation or pleasure either. The quiet between us was the comfortable sort, their natural tendency just like mine, to daydream.

They'd been inside me in every way. I could feel their cum both filling my stomach and slick in my hole, even though so much of it had poured out. My heart soared.

They looked at me and ran their palm along my cheek. "I'd walk you up to your room…"

The unfinished sentence lingered in the air, dropping my mood slightly. But we couldn't get caught. Frederick, Arielle, and who knew which other Tritons lurked around the house tonight, and after what we'd gotten up to, our interlude would be too obvious if Ursuline escorted me back up.

"Right," I murmured, the disappointment rising up in me regardless.

Ursuline pressed a kiss to my forehead, and the mere touch, the mere act of tenderness banished the negative feelings. I basked in bliss once more.

"I won't stay away," they promised, their palm cupping my cheek as they stared into my eyes. I believed them. Ursuline lived by their word.

I swallowed hard and bobbed my head before pushing off from the bench. I took my time tugging my clothes back on, Ursuline helping the process along as they yanked my shirt down, buttoned my pants. The whole process felt intimate, their care shown through every motion, every lingering look.

With my clothes on, I was ready to return to my room—even if my heart wasn't. The exhaustion slammed into me something fierce, and my eyes kept trying to slide shut. I needed to sleep for a week after the way they'd fucked me. I turned toward them and met their gaze. Their lips were right there, so close, and I longed to reach out and taste them once more. I licked my own, and their eyes flared.

Ursuline let out a low curse and leaned in. They claimed my lips with a surety I'd sorely needed. They drove their tongue into my mouth, and I melted into them at once, kissing back for all I was worth. Not wanting to let go.

When I drew apart for breath, they let out a heavy sigh. "You need to get some rest."

I bobbed my head, even though a lump formed in my throat.

"I'm not going to disappear," they reassured me.

"Famous last words," I teased. The promise did help, though. Because even though they kept secrets like a shroud, they'd proved themselves trustworthy by their actions. I hated to do so, but I pulled away and strode toward the door. I didn't look back when I walked out, otherwise I'd never leave.

I believed I'd feel nothing but emptiness as I traveled up the stairs and down the corridor toward my room, but the twinge in my hole, the lingering sensation of their cum inside me, offered the reminder that this was real.

That Ursuline had taken me tonight and fulfilled me in every way I'd hoped.

A slow warmth spread through my body as I reached my bedroom and stepped inside. I collapsed onto my bed, the heat still glowing inside me, a small flicker of a candle for now, but one that promised to last throughout the night.

Chapter 16

My whole body ached like I'd swum an entire day in the sea.

I lay in the bed and rubbed my eyes, basking in the slight soreness in my hole, the lingering rasp in my throat too when I coughed. I wasn't sure what time it was, but the sun streamed brightly through the windows, suggesting it was a good way into the morning.

Not like anyone would be waiting for me, though.

After being locked into a corporate environment for years, this stark shift to joblessness had thrown me for a loop, but I'd burst at the seams with inspiration for new art pieces. After years of restraining it, the colors and strokes on the canvas exploded out of me.

I should get downstairs and make some tea.

Except that required moving.

I heaved a sigh. All I wanted was to see Ursuline right now. To get the reassurance that they didn't regret what we'd done last night.

A knock sounded on my door, and I popped upright. With a groan, I pushed myself up from the mattress.

Before I could reach the door, the knob twisted open, and the person I'd wanted to see most slipped inside.

Ursuline shut the door quietly behind them. I was a rumpled mess, my hair askew, my clothes half on, half off my body after falling asleep in them. Unlike me, they were pristinely put together, this time wearing a black tunic with a stiff collar that circled their neck. Their bare arms were exposed, the muscles defined and delicious, and they glided farther in on their tentacles. Saliva gushed in my mouth at the memory of their mating tentacles inside me, bringing me to completion.

"How are you feeling?" they asked, scanning over me. The sun highlighted the sharp angles of their chin, their long neck, their clavicles.

"Tired but so damn good," I responded, a grin rising to my lips. My heart thumped hard. They'd come to check in on me.

"Everyone's stepped out for the day," they said with a glance back to the door. "So it was safe for me to swing by." They stepped closer and ran their thumb along my cheek. "I promised I wouldn't stay away."

I swallowed hard, my eyes heating up. "Thank you."

They shook their head, a soft smile tilting their lips. "You're too genuine for this world, sunshine."

"Is that so bad?" I asked, leaning into their touch. Their tentacles wrapped idly around my legs, offering lazy caresses. A shiver ran through me at how much I loved the possessive touches. I'd been starved for so long that I soaked up every ounce of what they gave.

"Not at all," they said, their voice low. "You're rare, Elrich." They heaved a breath. "Are you serious about wanting this for as long as we can?"

"Yes," I said at once. "I...fuck, there's nothing between Arielle and me. Not like this. And I don't even want to get married to her."

Something complicated crossed Ursuline's features, but they smoothed out. "I have a request."

"Anything," I said, desperate for whatever they'd give me.

They shook their head and brushed their thumb over my lower lip. "None of that, sunshine. You need to listen to the request before you agree. You're allowed your own wants, your own dislikes, your own desires. You can always say no with me."

My eyes burned, and a few tears slipped down my cheeks.

They shook their head, their expression pained. "Your family never gave you options, did they?"

I hadn't realized how much their mandates had destroyed me over the years until Ursuline offered me choice. Until I started to claim what I wanted in turn.

They brushed away the tears on my cheeks, the touch firm and a balm to my battered soul.

"While I have you, I want you to be mine, and mine alone," they said. I opened my mouth, but they slipped their thumb inside, and I sucked automatically. A shiver raced through me at how even that made my mind fuzz over. "I want you knowing every second of the day who this belongs to." They reached down and cupped my cock, and lust pulsed through me fast and fierce. "I want to lock you up."

My brows drew together, even as I continued to suck their thumb, not wanting to let go of the comfort.

"With a cock cage, sunshine. So the only person who decides when you get to use it, when you get to come, is me."

Oh fuck.

Heat roared through me in such a blinding torrent I almost buckled. Thankfully their tentacles coiled around my legs, keeping me upright. I sucked even harder on their thumb, as if it could communicate how badly I wanted that. My cock stiffened, the length tenting the fabric of my pants.

They caressed it with their hand, and I continued to suck on their thumb, loving the way they teased me. How they instinctively seemed to understand what I needed most. One of their tentacles around my leg inched farther up, until it slid between my cheeks, the thin fabric of my pants the only barrier.

"Someone likes that idea, don't they?" Ursuline purred as they continued to rub their tentacle between my cheeks, the brush against my hole making me whimper. Saliva gushed into my mouth, and all too fast I vaulted back to yesterday, to being overtaken by them. And the idea of my cock being caged during that? Of being helpless to do anything while they penetrated me over and over again? I incinerated at the mere thought.

They withdrew their thumb and stopped stroking my cock. A second later, their tentacle slid back down around my thigh again. I sagged forward, my forehead resting on their chest. They carded their fingers through my hair, and another shiver coursed down my spine.

"Words, sunshine," they said.

"Yes, please." My words were muffled from where my face pressed against their chest, but I didn't care. "I want you to lock me up."

"How are you so perfect?" they wondered aloud. The praise filtered through me, like effervescent bubbles.

"When will you do it?" I asked, pulling my head up to face them.

A wicked grin transformed their features, and the breath snagged in my throat. "I brought a cage with me. I want you reminded every second of the day who you truly belong to."

My heart lodged in my throat. That was what I longed for. The idea of marrying Arielle at this point made me sick, but I wasn't sure how to get out of my predicament. Yet Ursuline was willing to be with me regardless. Was willing to make me theirs for whatever time we had.

They reached down and tugged at my cock. "This will be an issue, though. You need to be soft to fit into the cage." They brought out the cage they'd tucked in their pocket, a metal contraption that looked like it would be a tight fit. If anything, the sight made my cock harder. "Need some help, sunshine?"

I bobbed my head and wet my lower lip.

"Ditch the pants," they said, taking a step back. "And hands by your sides after."

I obeyed at once, tugging my pants down and kicking them off. My cock jutted out, hard, flushed, and red, a drop of pre-cum beading on the tip. My insides simmered with excitement at what was to come. I'd never even thought of anyone locking my cock away, but having a steady reminder it belonged to Ursuline? Heat roared through me.

One of their tentacles wrapped around my length, smooth and thick. Their mating tentacle hovered over it and squirted a bit of that slick. It twined around me, enveloping my cock entirely. They tugged at my cock with their tentacle, the suckers rubbing along the skin sending shivers through me. The slick started to disperse along my length, making the glide so delicious I was delirious. There was no way I'd last long, not with their tentacle strangling my cock like this. I was going to come, but after? I'd be locked away until they decided upon the next time.

I trembled, my hands balling into fists as they worked my cock over. The smoothness of their tentacles, their slick, made for an easy glide, sending a rush of bliss through me with each pass, and I closed my eyes. Ursuline handled my body with finesse, and their attention to detail led to an exquisite pleasure I'd never experienced before. Even now, they tightened each time they squeezed around my sensitive tip, and a moan escaped again and again.

The tension increased, my balls achy and heavy and ready to spill. They worked my cock faster, their tentacle squeezing around the length at a quickened pace.

"I'm going to come," I gasped out.

"Do it," they challenged. Their tone was pure silk and seduction.

The taut thread tightened more, more, more, until it finally snapped.

I tilted my head back, a sob erupting from me. My balls unloaded, the cum shooting from me, and my mind blanking with searing pleasure. Some splattered on the hardwood, and other drops squished between Ursuline's tentacles, which made sloppy sounds as they continued to squeeze, coaxing every drop from me. I coasted on the sensation, not wanting to come down from it. My breaths started to even out, and the tingles spread to my extremities, my cock quickly becoming sensitive.

Even still, I was voracious for more. My hole ached with the memory of the way they'd filled me, and saliva pooled in my mouth at the idea of sucking on them again.

"Good boy," they said, and their praise radiated through me, warm sunlight that pierced within.

The jingle of metal drew my attention, and I opened my eyes. Ursuline had glided in front of me, and they opened up the metal contraption before them. They reached down and fed my emptied sac through the large loop and secured it at the base, then they drew my cock through the small loops, which looked far too short to contain me. Once they settled my length inside, they clicked the lock on the cage shut.

My body reacted at once. Even though I'd just come, my cock swelled at the constraints, slightly uncomfortable but not problematic. The metal bars it pressed against excited me that much more. I loved the idea that I couldn't do anything to myself. That I had this reminder around me of Ursuline.

They lifted the key to the cage. "I'm going to give you my number. If there's any pain, any problems, message me at once. I'll keep a key here for you in case of emergencies. Otherwise, you've got to come to me to get unlocked."

I bobbed my head, thrilled at the idea. I was used to getting off on the regular, stroking myself when I was bored, but now I couldn't. The thrill intensified. "Can I play with my hole still?"

"I'd be disappointed if you weren't stretching yourself for me," they said. "Eventually, you're going to take both of my mating tentacles at the same time, sunshine."

Oh. My cock pulsed against the cage, and a dizzying wave of lust crashed through me. Oh fuck. I nodded. "I'll be good."

Ursuline's gaze softened, a gleam there that made me shiver. They stroked along my cheek. "I know you will." They heaved a sigh. "Unfortunately, I have a full docket today, so I've got to go. Will you be around tonight?"

"I believe so," I said. "The Triton family seems disinterested in what I do."

Except Frederick had demanded I spend more time around Arielle, something she would hate. My stomach roiled.

"Give me your phone," Ursuline said, reaching out with their palm.

I walked over to the bed, since moving with the cage around my cock was different. Each step reminded me about the weight there, the slight pressure keeping me contained. This would be the most delicious torture. I grabbed my phone and deposited it into their open palm.

"Here's my number," they said, typing it into my phone. "Message me if anything changes. Otherwise, I'll check on you later."

I bobbed my head and accepted my phone back.

They leaned in, and I pushed up on my toes to meet them in a kiss. It was searing and careful at the same time, and they placed a hand on my lower back in a possessive move that made me swoon.

When they pulled away, they reached down to cup my caged cock, a slight smirk on their lips. A thrill rose inside me.

"See you later."

With that, they slipped out of my bedroom with the quickness they'd entered. I stood there in the middle of the room, my hands clutched to my chest, my heart thrumming.

Tonight couldn't come soon enough.

Chapter 17

Of course Frederick decided today was the day I'd start keeping his daughter company.

My stomach churned as Arielle and I sat in the back seat of the black car we were being chauffeured around in. I'd texted Ursuline at once, and they'd told me to keep them updated if anything changed.

"I don't know why Papa sent you to chaperone," Arielle said with a huff. "I'm sure you'd rather be doing your artsy thing than going to the club."

"Would you hate me if I said yes?" I responded.

She let out another of those tinkling laughs. "Of course not. We're both aware this is just for convenience. Neither of us expected love."

The reminder made my heart ache. The pressure around my cock served as a reminder of who I truly wanted to belong to. I'd loved being caged for Ursuline so far. Even now their presence lingered because of this connection I carried with me.

"Probably due to the disloyalty from the help," Arielle continued, and I perked up. I'd wondered what happened to Jacques, and no one else on the staff was forthcoming.

"Who was a problem?" I asked carefully.

She glanced at me, a calculating flash in her expression that made me uneasy. Early on, it'd been easy to believe she was this carefree thing, unconcerned about whatever life threw at her. But no one with that many secrets could truly be carefree.

Then she shook her head, letting out another light laugh. "Who isn't the problem? Have you seen how much they all talk amongst each other? Ursuline's NDAs are ironclad, though. Somewhat makes up for having their gloomy presence around all the time. If any of the staff tried to reveal our secret, they'd be buried."

I wasn't sure what upset me more, the complete disrespect she had for Ursuline or the cheerful way she talked about eliminating the staff. A chill crawled through me. Arielle had been the one member of the Triton family I'd thought I could try to connect with, who I could trust. But she seemed to be as complicit as the rest of them, as comfortable with the same stilted society I wanted to escape from.

"Are we grabbing food before the club?" I asked. "I'm starving."

"Psh, you don't want to bloat before going dancing," Arielle said. "Rookie move, Elrich."

I rolled my eyes. "I don't think anyone's going to be checking me for bloat."

She shook her head, an ever-present smile on her lips. "Come on now. You're gorgeous. Of course you're going to get swarmed on the dance floor."

My stomach twisted. I didn't want that, though. And I hated that she wanted that for me. That she searched for any excuse to go pursue her own passions, even at my expense. All I wanted was Ursuline. The reminder of them was there around my cock, the cage they held the key to.

"What's your favorite thing about going dancing?" I asked.

"The attention," she said, preening. "I love having the spotlight on me."

"Do you not get enough at home?" I asked, the curiosity percolating inside me. I wanted to find depths, still sought them out, some way to relate to her.

She wrinkled her nose. "Don't be depressing, Elrich. You're going to kill my pre-club buzz."

The quickness of her reply told me everything I needed to know. As much as she was a daddy's girl, I hadn't missed how often her parents were busy with expanding their business. I'd experienced the same neglect.

The car jerked to a stop in front of a club, and the bodyguard in the passenger seat got up, clearly to join us.

Arielle cast a glance at him and heaved a sigh. I could echo the sentiment. At least when I'd lived with my parents, I'd traveled around without a chaperone. When I stepped out of the car, the sight of Velvet Noir greeted me. I'd heard of the club in the past, though it had never been on my radar. As much as I liked being around people, I felt claustrophobic crushed in at dance clubs, and there were too many groping hands.

I craved touch and sex, but I needed an emotional connection, something my peers had never been able to understand.

Something Ursuline seemed to get effortlessly.

The light button-down with rolled-up sleeves and black slacks felt a bit formal for the club compared to the flirty outfit Arielle wore—a tight green bodycon dress showcasing her sloping curves. However, I didn't want to flaunt anything on the dance floor. No matter what Arielle said, I didn't want strangers grinding up on me because they found me attractive.

The *boom, boom, boom* from inside the building traveled all the way out here, to the framework of what looked like used to be a warehouse. Which meant vaulted ceilings, echoing sounds, clusters of bodies. I'd liked my existence better when Frederick ignored what we both did.

I sucked in a shaky breath and glanced at Arielle. She flitted ahead of me, the bodyguard keeping pace in between us. I quickened my own steps, even though I wasn't eager to go to a dance club. I shot a quick text to Ursuline with the location and a sad emoji. After the way they'd given me release this morning and then caged me, I'd been looking forward to more time with them—whether they were fucking me filthy or swimming in the bay with me.

I craved their presence more than anything.

The moment we entered the club, I wanted to run out again. The heavy thump of the music reverberated in my bones, a chaos I didn't enjoy, and the air grew thick and tense from the volume of people inside. The place was all flashing lights and shadows, platforms and cages where dancers undulated to the beat of the music. A few people jostled by me, and Arielle plunged inside. The bodyguard went over to the bouncer and pointed to the two of us, clearly handling our entry to the place.

Arielle didn't even look back for me as she carved her way through the crowds, seeking the epicenter of the noise and bodies. I didn't want to be anywhere near that, so I gave up on trying to follow. Instead, I navigated toward one of the warehouse walls, where the throngs of people grew smaller. The bar might be a good spot to people-watch if it wasn't teeming with folks trying to get drinks.

I leaned against the wall, trying to absorb the coolness, and tipped my head back. The lights flashed in every direction, whites and reds that lit up the place. The noise came from so many directions it created a massive hum from all the voices. Maybe I should've mentioned to her that I got claustrophobic. That these sorts of places tended to trigger it.

However, the concern remained that at the end of the day, I wasn't sure she'd even care.

Arielle had made it clear she wouldn't be deterred from living the life she was accustomed to, whether or not she was engaged. I was just an inconvenience to be handled.

I scanned the crowd, though I'd lost sight of Arielle. Even the bodyguard seemed to have vanished, though he was competent, so I could guarantee he had an eye on both of us—particularly Arielle.

My skin began to crawl as a few other people brushed past me, even though I was mostly tucked out of the way. The glances back at me confirmed those had been intentional, along with a few winks from different guys and girls. When I skimmed over the crowd, one thing stuck out—tons of humans were in here, and very few monsters. I hated how we were forced into different boxes, how the society I'd grown up in continued to push separation, even though we lived in the same city, the same continent, shared the same air, the same water.

I didn't plan on going out to the dance floor—I'd be swallowed alive. And I didn't want the attention from people who only wanted me for my body, who would make me feel as small as I always had in my own family.

No, I'd rather give everything over to Ursuline.

Their singular attention lit me up like nothing I'd ever experienced.

I tugged my phone out of my pocket and shot them a text.

I hate it here.

Part of me needed them to know I'd rather be with them.

The *thump, thump, thump* of the music poured through the speakers, and I did my best to drown it out. I closed my eyes, trying to stave off the panic of feeling boxed in that this place brought to the surface.

The bodies undulated, so many unfamiliar faces, and trying to look at all of them made me feel like I was drowning all over again. Even with my eyes shut, the tension in the air, the heat brewing from the mass of bodies left a mark.

"What are you doing here by your lonesome?" a low voice asked.

I blinked my eyes open and frowned as the flashing lights attacked my vision again. A huge guy stood to my right, far too close for comfort. He leaned against the wall beside me, crowding in my space.

I opened my mouth and then realized I had an easy out. "My fiancée wanted to come dancing."

"And where are they at?" he asked, not moving in the slightest and scanning the crowd.

My stomach twisted like a wet rag. Apparently that wouldn't deter him. I searched the crowd again to see if I could find her quickly, to hide behind the excuse. She wasn't difficult to spot.

Arielle stood on one of the platforms, dancing her heart out. Guys swarmed around her on the pedestal, and she beamed up there, soaking in all the attention.

"Over there," I said, pointing her out.

The guy let out a laugh. "She looks occupied." He loomed over me, but not in a way that I liked. His blond hair was combed to the side, and he was muscular, like he spent an overabundance of time at the gym. When he flashed me a smile that came across sleazy, I wanted to back away. "You want to get a little busy too?"

"Pass," I said, gritting my teeth. Was this how the rest of my life would be? Following Arielle into clubs I hated, getting hit on and having to fend off strangers?

"Come on," the guy said, trailing a finger down my chest. "Don't be like that."

I jerked back and searched for the bodyguard. Maybe he'd let me wait in the car. "I've got to get out of here."

"What about your fiancée?" he said, moving in a few inches closer, until he was almost on top of me. This close, he reeked, the sweat and body odor mingling with whatever strong cologne he'd bathed in. The smell of alcohol poured off him too. Clearly, he'd drunk enough that his filters had gone by the wayside, if he even had them. "You don't want to leave her behind, do you? If both of you want to take a spin, I'm happy to oblige."

"What part of no don't you understand?" I said, thrusting my chin forward.

"That body's too hot to waste," he said, trailing a finger down my arm.

I stepped away from him another pace. He was drunk, which might give me an advantage if I bolted.

"What's the harm in just talking?" He stepped in closer again, and my stomach churned.

"Get the fuck away from him."

The familiar voice was one I'd been longing for, one I could barely believe I was hearing.

Except Ursuline glided in behind the drunken asshole, and they placed a hand on his shoulder.

"Who the hell let you in?" he stuttered, trying to scramble away from them. "Fucking freak."

Ursuline's lips twisted with the hint of a grin as they kept their arms crossed, staring him down until he slipped away into the crowd. Then their gaze landed on me. "Want to get out of here?"

I could cry with relief. It rushed through me in such a fierce torrent, but all I could do was bob my head. They tilted their head toward the back, to a different entrance than the one I'd arrived through with

Arielle and the bodyguard, and I followed. After dealing with the drunk asshole, I refused to stay in this hellhole any longer.

They reached back to offer a hand, and once I grabbed theirs, the touch soothed me in a way nothing else had. I could breathe again.

We stuck to the side walls, veering around a few throngs of people as we headed for the exit sign lit in neons. I didn't bother trying to call out to Ursuline, focusing on the *thump, thump, thump* of my heart from the adrenaline hit. I'd been prepared to bolt and hope for the best, but they'd swept in and chased away the asshole in seconds.

They pushed the back door open, and the moment I stepped through, I almost sagged forward. The crisp night air mingled with the pavement and some residual cigarette smoke from the groups that loitered out here, the glow of the cherries making their smokes obvious.

"If that was presumptuous—" Ursuline started, and I shook my head.

"Thank you," I said, my voice hoarse. "He wasn't taking no for an answer."

"Where was Arielle?" they asked, their gaze darkening as they glanced back. "I thought Frederick wanted you two to go out together."

"She left me the second we got here," I admitted. "She was dancing on one of the platforms for a crowd, last I saw."

A growl left Ursuline, one that soothed me. "Why Frederick's forcing this is beyond me."

I scrubbed at my face. "I think I know why."

They placed a hand on my shoulder and guided us toward a clear spot along the back wall. Out here didn't trigger my claustrophobia like the club, and I could finally relax. I leaned against the wall, and

Ursuline slipped their arm around my shoulder. I leaned in against them.

"I caught George on the way in," Ursuline said. "Told him I'd get you home."

"George?" My brows crinkled.

"One of Arielle's normal bodyguards," they said, a wry grin on their lips. "You're on a first-name basis with most of the staff in the house, yet you don't know the bodyguards?"

"I haven't left the estate enough." I shrugged. "And about the staff...did something happen to Jacques?" I chewed on my lower lip, the nerves percolating in me. "I feel like...we were talking, and now he's not here, and I'm worried."

Ursuline's lips pursed, their stormcloud expression not exactly reassuring. "Jacques is gone."

"Like, fired, right?" I asked, even though my stomach curdled.

They stared at me slow and steady. "Do you want the answer? Frederick Triton is a dangerous man. Trust me when I say you don't want to cross him."

And yet, here Ursuline was, risking everything for me.

I swallowed hard. Maybe I didn't want the answers, at least not if I wanted to hold onto the hope of escape. "He warned me to get out while I could."

"Jacques should've heeded his own advice," they said, a somberness in their gaze. "Though he's not wrong. They've started having me draft the prenup, and there are some clauses Frederick wants in there..."

I shuddered at the idea of signing anything that tied me permanently to this family. I couldn't imagine spending a lifetime in that house, with those cold people. And knowing something had happened to Jacques...ice filtered into my bloodstream. One of Ursuline's tentacles wrapped around my leg and squeezed, and I appreciated the comfort more than I could express.

"They own a contract on you, don't they?" I murmured, remembering an earlier conversation we'd had.

Ursuline swallowed hard enough the sound was audible. "Yeah. I wouldn't recommend it."

"If we're both tied to the family, maybe we can..." I started off and then paused, because I couldn't imagine keeping this secret for the rest of our lives. The enormity of it dizzied my mind.

"If you get the chance to run," they said, their voice ragged. "Run. Whether I can come with you or not."

I shook my head, loathing the idea of leaving them behind.

"Want to get out of here? Have a real night out on the town?" they asked.

I wrinkled my nose. "As long as it's not at another club. I get claustrophobic in clubs and concerts."

Ursuline let out a low swear. "And yet she dragged you out here."

I shrugged. "You've met Arielle. Try stopping her from doing what she wants."

"Frederick's about the only one who can rein her in, and barely," they said, urging me forward as they moved. "I promise we won't be heading anywhere like a club. They're not my scene either."

"What's your ideal night?" I asked as we made our way toward the parking lot along the side of the building.

"Apart from spending it fucking a pretty boy within an inch of his life?" they teased, the heat behind their words setting me on fire. My balls ached, and my cock throbbed, pushing against the cage they had me in. Throughout the day, the cage had been all I could think about, and if anything, I was even hornier than before. The lights lit up on a silver car I recognized—the one that had taken me to the Triton Estate on that first day. "My favorite types of nights are relatively boring," they said. "Going out for a dinner somewhere I've never tried before, the monthly game night at Cillian's, or swimming out in the sea. I'm easy to please."

My chest grew warm at their answers. I loved that they weren't flashy. That their ideal lined up with mine. "What's the monthly game night?"

"Sofia took me under her wing when I first arrived in Peregrine City," Ursuline said as we reached their car. They opened the doors, and then they slipped into the driver's seat. I hopped into the passenger side. The engine turned on, and away we went. "I'd never lived on the surface—not around so many humans either—and it was isolating. They introduced me to their collective of friends, and once a month we go to the Spires to play games in the upper levels."

My jaw dropped. It wasn't until they mentioned the Spires that I connected the dots between the Spires and Cillian. "You mean you're friends with Cillian Ashmore?"

Ursuline cocked a brow. "Sunshine, he's friends with *me*."

The attitude was hot, and I was turned on beyond belief just from being in their proximity. And the fact I couldn't do a damn thing for relief only fed into my state. I shifted back and forth in my seat, the ache inside me increasing.

"What's your ideal night?" they asked.

My heart twisted. I'd grown so used to asking questions and getting none in return. Of giving interest but never receiving any care. Yet Ursuline changed all that. "Honestly? Swim. Curl up with someone and watch the sunset. Maybe wander through some galleries and discover new art. My lifestyle isn't the flashy sort either."

"Mmm." Their hum resonated through the car, settling in my bones. "We're here."

When I looked up, my lips stretched into a grin.
Haven Diner.

Chapter 18

"I have a surprise for you," they said. "One that I think...hope...you'll like."

"More surprising than appearing at the club to whisk me away?" I asked, already in better spirits about where we were headed. Haven Diner had been a cozy spot the first time we'd come here, and I was happy to return.

"Yes, more surprising than that," they responded dryly. "You sent me a cry for help. What else was I supposed to do?"

I swallowed hard. They'd done more than anyone else in my life, and I didn't think they even realized how unique they were. Someone whose word was bond, who showed up when everyone else failed me.

"Come on," they said as they pushed open their door. "We've got a visitor waiting inside."

My brows drew together. A visitor? Who could want to see me?

Ursuline wouldn't bring my parents. More likely, my parents would never go somewhere with Ursuline. Yet that concern grew as I stepped out of the car, the crisp air coating my skin. Who could they mean?

They headed toward the door, sure, confident, and I sucked in a sharp breath. So far, they'd only had my best interests at heart. I'd trust them in this.

Haven Diner's neons glowed on the sign, and the chrome exterior caught the moonlight. The wide windows showcased the interior, which was filled with people this time of night. I strode up the walkway, and my stomach rumbled. I had been hungry before being tossed into the fray at the club, which had diminished it. Now my appetite started to return.

The slight scent of burnt sugar hit my nose as we approached, part of the spells that guarded this place. Ursuline swept the door open and gestured me in. I walked forward, and upon entering, the scent of cinnamon and safety greeted me. The place was warm, in a comfortable sort of way, and my shoulders sagged with relief, as if I could take a load off them.

"To the right," Ursuline said, close enough that the heat of their breath tickled my ear.

I glanced to the booths lining the righthand side, the eye-catching purple and green.

However, someone in them snagged my attention.

He sat there with a cup of coffee, as casual as anything, even though I hadn't seen him since the day I'd been spat up by the sea.

Jason.

His long forehead was creased, his skin a deeper greenish blue in the overhead lighting, and his tentacles spilled out of his side of the booth.

I whipped toward Ursuline. "You contacted Jason?"

"Hope that's okay," they said, their dark eyes scrutinizing me.

Joy burst inside me at the familiar face. I'd wanted to talk to him, explain where I'd disappeared to, but I also hadn't wanted him to know the threats my family had made.

He looked up, and those dark, sharklike eyes settled on me. A faint grin rose on his lips, which for him was the equivalent of beaming. "It's been a bit, Elrich."

"Can I have a hug?" I blurted out once we neared him, and he rose from his seat and outstretched his tentacles. They curled around my shoulders, brought me a few steps closer, and squeezed me tight to him. Heat burned in my eyes, tears of relief that my friend hadn't forgotten me. That he still cared.

My choice to protect him had been the right one. I'd known it back then, and I was reassured of it now.

"Ursuline contacted me," Jason said as he let go. The fact he'd offered a hug in the first place was nothing short of a miracle.

Ursuline slipped into the seat opposite Jason and patted the spot next to them. I slid in at once, and they curled their tentacle around my shoulders. The touch they so readily offered made me swoon. I'd never been on the receiving end of anything this constant in my life.

I met their eyes. "Thank you."

They offered a wan smile, so I leaned back into the seat, their tentacle securely around me. Jason stared between us, his expression unreadable, but he wouldn't judge.

"So, the Triton family?" Jason did ask, breaking the quiet.

I wrinkled my nose. I wanted to tell him the truth, but I didn't want him feeling guilty for my choice or what my family tried to do.

"Not by choice." Ursuline stepped in for me. "Society pulling their usual chess moves."

Jason let out a low grumble.

A waitress swung by, a brunette with a long braid and a sharp expression. "What can I get you to drink to start?"

"The Elixir for me," Ursuline said, then glanced to me. "Tea?"

I nodded, warmth spreading through me that they knew what I preferred. I shifted in my seat, the cock cage keeping my length tightly contained. The mere movement made my balls throb. Sitting beside them was a different sort of torture with this constant reminder—not only that my cock belonged to them but the memory of what their mating tentacles could do to me.

"The Elixir?" I asked, curiosity striking me as I skimmed over the menu. Like before, it fascinated me to see human menu items like meatloaf alongside seaweed and krill salad and blood and carrot soup.

"It's a specialty for oceanic folks," Ursuline said. "A brine smoothie filled with nutrients from the sea. It's the sort of thing we'd normally get from living in New Atlantis, but for those of us who spend more time on land now, it helps balance our diets."

"Can I try some?" I asked, curiosity filtering through me. All the differences between monsterkind and humans fascinated me.

"Sure, sunshine," they said, an amused smile on their face.

"A new development?" Jason asked, glancing between the two of us.

I swallowed hard and glanced to Ursuline. I wasn't sure how much they wanted to say, even though with their tentacle wrapped around my shoulders, they clearly didn't mind PDA.

"As much as it can be," Ursuline responded.

Jason nodded and sipped at his coffee. Like always, he wasn't chatty, but his presence was a solid weight I'd missed. He'd been a refuge when I needed one the most, the monster who'd taught me to unlock the passion for art that'd been brewing inside me my whole life.

"Have you worked on any new pieces?" I asked Jason.

His small smile hinted he had. "A few for an upcoming show. And you?"

"Yeah," I said, heat rising to my cheeks. Most of my latest pieces had been inspired by one person—the one sitting right beside me. Creativity had flowed, whether from moonlit swims to the melody of the music they played or from the sheer pleasure of their competence in the way they'd taken me apart. "It's about all I'm doing now that I'm stuck milling around the Triton residence."

Jason shook his head, his tentacles twitching in the process. He glanced to Ursuline. "There's no way to get him out of this?"

They blanched, and my stomach twisted. The more I learned about Frederick and his family, the more uneasy I grew to be attached to them. So much was a mystery still, especially what happened when the family went under the sea to New Atlantis.

"I'm trying to figure that out," they said, casting me an apologetic glance. I didn't mind learning more about the contract here, though. They had told me enough, and they didn't owe it to anyone to bear whatever past still burdened them. Even though I hoped one day they'd be able to open up to me. "Frederick wants a foothold with the wealthy humans, and he's going about securing that by marrying his youngest to Elrich."

Maybe if Jason was alerted, if he escaped now, then I could cancel the engagement. The idea began percolating in my mind, one to entertain before I signed anything.

"I'm going below in a week," Jason said, taking another sip of his coffee.

The waitress swung back over with my steaming mug of water with the tea bag on the side and Ursuline's Elixir, which was an oddish blue color. "Figured something to eat?" she asked, giving a nod to the menu.

"Uh, a burger for me," I said, since I'd gotten so caught up in conversation I'd barely given the menu a glance.

"Rassoul," Ursuline ordered. "With a side of rice."

"Good choice," Jason said with a grunt. "I'll do the same."

"Thanks," the waitress said with a quick bob of her head before she darted off. The place was hopping tonight, so no doubt she was running from patron to patron. To the right of us, a group of demons sat in a booth, deep in discussion, their black curled horns prominent. A human and an imp took up one of the other seats, sharing a root beer float, clearly on a date.

The diner was so colorful, same with the clientele. I loved how different Haven was from the staunch rigidity of the human functions in high society. This was an explosion of color and cultures, and I loved it with my whole heart.

"What's prompting the visit?" Ursuline asked.

"I haven't gone in five years," Jason said. "Going back...it invites pain."

Ursuline's lips flattened, and they bobbed their head. "If only I could."

"You can't go below?" I asked.

Ursuline shook their head. "Underwater, yes. To New Atlantis, no. I'm employed for Frederick's human relations."

"Part of your contract," Jason said, sympathy in his dark eyes.

What sort of terrible contract had they signed? They didn't hold any fondness for the Triton family, but the more I discovered, the more I was almost terrified to find out the extent of what they faced.

They licked their lips and let out a sigh. "Can I ask a favor?"

Jason nodded.

"No one I know has gone below in awhile. Could you check on them for me?"

"Of course."

The questions multiplied in my brain, but the tension in the air grew so dense I'd need a chainsaw to cut through. If I probed for more information here, Ursuline would shut me down.

"Here, try the Elixir," they said, nudging the drink in my direction.

I didn't hesitate, grabbing the glass and lifting it to my lips. The taste was a mixture of salty sweet, like a Bloody Mary. I didn't hate it. "Interesting."

"You can tell me if you don't like it," Ursuline said, amusement in their eyes.

"Just different," I said. "But I like different."

"I know." Their eyes glittered with approval, which I soaked up. "You're a rare sort, Elrich."

Heat flushed through me. Praise from them lit me on fire, and I shifted in my seat again, all too aware of the ache in my balls. Of the way my cock pushed against the confines of the metal cage. They gave me a long and slow glance, their gaze resting on my trapped cock. A slight smirk lifted their lips.

"How's your brushwork been?" Jason asked, cutting through the tension between Ursuline and me.

I blinked, trying to switch my focus back to normal conversation. "Less rigid. I've been trying to let things flow a little more, going a bit more into impressionism."

Jason bobbed his head, clearly approving. "You could do a lot with exploring that. Your passion is your greatest asset."

I swallowed hard. Jason had always said that about my art, but I'd always felt in life it had been my downfall.

Ursuline's tentacle brushed against my leg, the caress sending another shiver through me.

At least until lately.

Lately, passion had been the one thing I held onto.

Chapter 19

By the time we left the diner, we were late into the night hours. Except, I left feeling full of warmth, calm for the first time in a long time. And that was due to being in a safe place like Haven, in being with two people who showed me genuine care.

I'd never gotten that from family growing up, only from the staff members I'd formed attachments to, ones my father had inevitably ripped away. The brisk night air curled around me, the burnt sugar scent accompanying as we headed down the walkway. Tonight had started out terribly at the club, but it had ended in the best way.

"Thank you," I said as we reached Ursuline's car. They crooked a brow at me, so I continued. "For the rescue. For bringing Jason out. I missed him."

"I know," they said, an enigmatic smile on their face. "He missed you too."

They tugged open their car door and got into the expansive driver's seat, built to accommodate a monster. The prices for anything monster-modified were always jacked up by the larger companies, which seemed unfair, that human-based products were the status quo. However, the more and more I learned about monsterkind and their struggles, the more I realized how much unfairness they'd weathered the moment they stepped into human-dominated spaces.

I hopped into the car alongside them and settled into the seat. They turned on the ignition, rolled down the windows, and set off through Peregrine City. The scent of asphalt, diesel, and the night swept in, and I basked in it. I'd always been more of a sunshine person until meeting Ursuline. Now, I savored the night more than ever.

"Will Frederick be upset that I left Arielle?" I asked, the thought occurring now that we were heading back.

"Frederick's not around tonight, and Arielle's bodyguards were relieved to not have an extra body to watch," Ursuline stated. "I covered my bases."

Relief settled through me. My time there had almost been easier when none of the family cared what I did. Now that Frederick wanted me paying attention to Arielle, the concern of what might happen if I stepped out of line had begun a marching drum beat of fears. The idea Jacques had disappeared lingered stronger than ever since Ursuline had filled me in. My mind had been concocting worse and worse scenarios with all the unknowns.

"Are you heading home after?" I asked. "Where do you even live?"

Ursuline's lips twitched into a smile. "So, now you're asking me."

Heat flushed my cheeks. I'd wondered, but when I was with them, coherent thought tended to escape me.

"I live in an apartment not far from the Tritons' manor," they said. "But when I first came to the surface, I lived in the manor, which is why I'm so familiar with it. Frederick doesn't like to let his possessions stray far." Disgust rang clear in their voice.

"Is that why you can't visit New Atlantis?" I asked. Fuck, had that been too intrusive a question?

Ursuline's shoulders tightened, their expression granite. Then they let out a sigh, one heavy enough to contain years of anguish.

"You don't have to answer," I rushed to say, not wanting to push them.

Their grip on the wheel tightened. "I can," they said. "The reminder is with me all the time, though, so speaking it aloud is painful."

My throat tightened, but I didn't dare interrupt them.

"If you live in New Atlantis, you're either one of the few elite who can enjoy the city, or you're the poorest of the poor, working in the mines. It's nothing like Peregrine City. And the poor have no rights, no protections. If you can guess, I wasn't born with a silver spoon."

Shame flushed through me. I'd been born into high society, and I'd had issues for years with how we operated, with how we hoarded money that could help others. Yet even I was aware of how much more of a disparity there was in other areas of Westia, let alone the other continents.

Their eyebrow lifted. "Not a censure on you, sunshine. You're rare."

My eyes burned at their comment, and my chest squeezed tight, but I remained quiet, wanting to give them the space to talk. Still, the way they read me was incomprehensible sometimes. They understood me better than people who'd known me my entire life.

"My family was struggling, and I was the oldest of three siblings. The middle had a particularly...rough time." They swallowed hard, a stormy look back in their gaze. "I was adept with language, with contracts. I took courses, got ahead, and I offered Frederick a deal. My family's safety. In exchange, I'd come to the surface and work for him on retainer."

"How old were you?" I asked, my heart twisting.

"Seventeen," they replied.

"To have completed the education to be a lawyer?" I asked, awestruck. They weren't just smart, they were a godsdamn prodigy.

Ursuline shrugged as they zipped down streets that were fast becoming familiar. "Like I said, I had a knack for it. I finished formalized education after I moved to the surface."

A realization struck me. "Wait, so you haven't seen your family since then?"

Ursuline's lips flattened. "No. But I get letters from my family."

"Were you close?" I asked, my heart twisting. With the amount they'd given up for their family, I imagined they had to be.

"Very." They let out a slight breath. "But I'm made to endure. My younger siblings needed protection. Our parents suffered a lot with health complications from spending a lifetime in the mines. Injuries, gill issues are common."

"Jason never talked much about below either," I said. The brief bits he had were always filled with a grief that made me wonder.

"It's not a gentle place," Ursuline said. "I miss my family fiercely, but New Atlantis? No, I'm glad to be away from there."

"What standing does Frederick have down there?" I asked, almost afraid to know. I was shocked how little we were educated about a place that wasn't all that far away from us, even if the average human couldn't exist down in New Atlantis.

"Oh, he controls the whole thing," Ursuline said. "There's an appointed mayor, but she has little power. Frederick pulls all the strings."

My chest sank. Not only was I marrying into a terrible family, but they were one who'd caused suffering for so many. My own was complicit in their share of horrors, but they didn't have the same level of power and control as the Triton family to inflict so much harm.

I needed to get out.

"Does your contract have an end date?" I asked, even though I knew the answer.

"The exchange is my servitude up here for my family's safety down below. My parents and siblings were given positions outside of the mines, my siblings protected. If I step away, all of that is forfeit."

Fuck. That was terrible. I couldn't imagine what it was like carrying the weight they did. And yet, they still held such compassion, such kindness. No wonder they were remote, why they kept their feelings close to the cuff. Why they loathed the Triton family.

Did Arielle know about the underhanded things her father did? The idea she could be aware and overlook them slithered under my skin. It shaded her ignorance with complicity.

"Are you sure there isn't some escape clause in the contract?" I asked. Even if it meant they got to leave and I didn't, I wanted them to be free. More than anything, Ursuline deserved to live their own life.

Ursuline shook their head. "I've been studying ever since I came up here to find one. Frederick's other lawyers are competent, and he only hires the best of the best for a reason."

"So what you're saying is, once I'm handed the prenup..."

"Your window of escape will be gone," they said.

Fear chilled my bones.

They swallowed hard. "I won't let that happen, Elrich."

My heart hurt. They protected everyone but themself. And I wanted to save them too. To take the edge off their suffering with my whole soul. They seemed so resigned sometimes. As if they'd just accepted this was their lot in life, as if they had no hope for a future of their own, and I burned to show them differently.

They drove up the winding drive to the Triton Manor, which loomed ahead of us, the windows glowing. Yet I wasn't ready for our time together to end.

"Did you want—" I started and then hesitated.

"What do you want, sunshine?" The tenderness in their question gave me the push to continue.

"Did you want to go for a swim?" I asked, longing pumping through my veins.

"And that's all you want?" they teased, the underlying heat in their voice incinerating me.

I shifted in the passenger's seat, my cock cage snug. "Depends. I'm a bit compromised at the moment."

"Just because you can't ejaculate doesn't mean you can't orgasm," Ursuline said. "Especially when you've got a very responsive prostate."

Oh. *Oh*. Flames coursed through me. My body was sensitized from my cock being locked up, an awareness of the area more present than ever before. And the idea they could fuck into me over and over while my cock was trapped, that I existed there for their pleasure—my fantasies overflowed. My balls ached, feeling fuller than ever. My cock swelled, pressing against the confines of the cage, and I squirmed in my seat all over again.

"Let's go swim," Ursuline said, a wickedness in their tone. "I'll make sure it's one you never forget."

Chapter 20

Ursuline led the way down to the bay. With each step closer, my heart accelerated.

The water glittered invitingly, and yearning tugged me forward. To be in that vast expanse. To be closer to Ursuline. Now that we'd breached the tension between us, that we'd begun to explore it, I never wanted to stop.

The fantasies in my head alternated between filthy and sweet.

To being bent over and bound for them, both their mating tentacles fucking into me.

To wake up in their arms, to share space freely without fear of being found out.

I wanted, more than I ever thought possible, and that ache in my chest was as steady as a heartbeat.

"Strip down, Elrich," Ursuline said.

I startled, realizing the ground had transitioned to sand, that we were already at the shoreline. They'd divested themself of their tunic, and their pale skin shone under the moonlight. My mouth watered at the sight of their darker nipples against their pecs, the lean but strong arm muscles. At their dark, thick tentacles keeping them upright, smooth and strong. Their short silver strands glinted in the moonlight, and the shadows sharpened their jawline, the dip of their clavicles. When I met their eyes again, an amused grin played on their lips.

Right. I needed to undress.

I kicked off my shoes, then stripped off my socks and pants and shirt quickly. All that remained were my boxer briefs, but I hesitated on the waistband. Somehow, being out here naked with a cock cage felt far more vulnerable than normal.

Ursuline's tentacle slid up my leg, slow and sure, the touch making me tremble and melt in the same breath. They reached right to the fabric of my boxer briefs, and the tip of their tentacle teased around the bulge of my trapped cock. The sensation shocked me, my whole body attuned in the moment.

"Fuck," I groaned out, the ache in my balls intensifying. I needed them inside me something fierce. I tugged down on my waistband, and they removed their tentacle so I could shed the underwear. Once I kicked it off, the breeze curled around me, my skin so sensitized that any touch would make me react far more than normal. I reached down and squeezed my caged cock, the metal trapping the swollen flesh. I was so turned on I could barely breathe, and I needed whatever Ursuline could give me tonight.

"Follow me, sunshine," they said, gliding toward the sea.

I took the first steps into the water, the coldness bracing. I'd normally worry about my cock getting smaller, about the cage sliding off from how chilly these waters were, but my body was aflame with a desire that wouldn't abate. Ursuline had glided farther into the water, moving more naturally here than on land. The water was waist-deep for them, and I waded deeper into the bay. The waves were gentle here, spurred on by the wind more than anything, and they felt a lot calmer than the wild crashing waves of the Sentient Sea.

The Triton Manor overlooked the bay, looming ahead of us, and a shiver ran down my spine. All it would take was an errant glance from the wrong person to expose us. However, the staff kept to themselves, and the Triton family was gone from the manor tonight. I trusted Ursuline to be thorough because they had to be.

Now that I understood what was at risk for them, the fact they still pursued this with me drove a shard of longing deep into my heart. Because in being with me, defying Triton, they took a chance that could end terribly for not just them but their family. And yet they continued to show up for me time and time again.

"Closer, sunshine," they said, beckoning me a little deeper, higher up on their waist. I recognized that they stayed in the shallows due to me. Ursuline could breathe underwater, fuck underwater, do anything they liked beneath the ocean, but I wasn't in the same situation. The consideration sent another burst of warmth traveling through me.

I waded up to them, my heart slamming hard enough that the sound dominated everything else. Last night, when they'd taken me, had felt like the culmination of all the intensity that brewed between us, but tonight? Tonight was inevitable.

A claiming, another reminder that I belonged to them alone.

Instead of stopping when I came close, I waded until I bumped into them and looked up. They loomed over me, but their lips were right there, and I yearned for their kiss so badly.

Their tongue slipped out to wet their lower lip, and a moment later, they leaned down to claim my mouth. I moaned into their kiss, loving how euphoria swept through my veins. They tasted like the drink from Haven, like sex, like safety. I shuddered as I placed my palms on their chest, savoring this connection between us, more intense than any I'd experienced in my life.

The thump of their heart, the way their tongue snaked into my mouth to caress—everything about them made me reel.

I reached up, curiosity stoked, and ran my fingertips along the gills lining their neck. They shuddered in response, and I tried it again, enamored by their responsiveness. Ursuline's tentacles twined around my thighs, tightening there, even as they kissed me like there'd be no tomorrow. I loved their tendency to wrap their tentacles around me, the possessiveness making me swoon. With them I was safe, cared for, in a way I'd craved my entire life.

They pulled back for breath, their arms encircling me. "Think you can take both of my mating tentacles tonight?"

A shudder rolled through my entire body, an aching want. "Yes, please."

"So polite, sunshine," they teased as they swept their mating tentacle up my inner thigh. It felt distinctly different from the other ones, hidden from sight even as they roamed around on land. It was softer than the other tentacles, smaller than the thick ones they used like limbs. Yet the girth had been perfect thrusting into me last night. The idea of taking both at the same time made my cock swell in its confines. I craved the stretch, the claiming something fierce.

Could that imprint on me, make them linger even when we were apart?

Their mating tentacle caressed along my taint, sending sparks through me, and the tip slid along my hole. I clutched their shoulders, the pleasure racking my body from those strokes alone.

"Hold on tight to me," they said.

I squeezed their shoulders, my grip firm, and their tentacles tightened around my thighs as they hoisted me up out of the water. Held aloft by their strength, the water dripping off me, I was as vulnerable as I'd ever been, but in their arms, I loved it.

"I'm going to start with one," they said as their mating tentacle rubbed along my hole again. Being taken out in the bay by them, exposed completely, sated something in me I hadn't realized I'd needed. The public claiming, how even in this situation, I felt safe. I'd always longed for a relationship like this—the stuff of dreams—but couldn't have it in this life.

So tonight, I'd stay here with them.

Their gaze traveled down to my trapped cock, swollen and straining against the cage they'd locked me in. "You look gorgeous in that."

Heat roared through me at the compliment, and I preened.

"If I could, I'd keep you trapped all the time," Ursuline continued. "Let your cock out when I needed to ride it and then cage it back up while I fucked you senseless. Keep your hole dripping with cum day in and day out."

Fuck. I breathed in deep, trying to suppress the desire that raged inside me at those images parading through my head. "You have..." I asked, curious by what they'd said.

"A mating hole too," they said. "Most cecaelia have a mating hole and tentacles."

My cock strained even more in the cage. Imagining them riding me, strapped down by their tentacles, taking what they needed set me afire.

"However, you haven't spent enough time in the cage," they said. "That'll be your reward for when you're freed."

"Pretty sure taking you isn't a hardship either," I said a little breathlessly. They teased their mating tentacle along my crack again, the slickness slathering across it. Then, they thrust the tip inside. My breath snagged, and I was grateful for how their tentacles wrapped around my thighs kept me steady.

They squirted more of their slick inside me, easing the way as they thrust in a little deeper. When they brushed against my prostate,

I howled. My nails dug into their shoulders at the sudden flare of pleasure, so much more intense than before.

"Did I mention caging can make the prostate more responsive?" Ursuline teased.

I struggled to catch my breath, panting. "You...did...not."

They thrust in again, another stroke that robbed me of my senses. I keened backward, holding on to them with all my might. Fuck. I needed this more than my next breath. I needed their length thrusting inside me, making me complete. And after taking them yesterday, the thickness felt comfortable enough as they fucked into me where there wasn't any sting.

And I craved the sting, the stretch.

I wanted both of their mating tentacles tonight.

They lowered me back down into the water, even though their mating tentacle continued to fuck inside me. The sensation of the cool water around my body, of the slight floating feeling, of the way they held me secure—all of it threatened to overload my systems. My balls ached, my cock was trapped, and yet I didn't care. Not while they fucked me with their mating tentacle, each thrust inside me sending a shock of pleasure stronger than I'd ever experienced before.

"You're so good for me, sunshine," they purred, their palms running down my sides. I loved how they could pin me down with their tentacles, touch me with their hands, wholly consume me. And unlike yesterday, when they'd been behind me while they fucked me, today I could see their expression.

The dark desire brewing in their features threatened to consume me. Sheer hunger poured from their gaze, a concentration there that made me feel more naked than I already was. That made me feel seen.

Their jaw tensed, their brow furrowed, and they fucked into me harder than they had yesterday, as if they'd been holding back. I clutched hard with every thrust, the sensations rocking through me enough that I was so relieved I was suspended in the water at their mercy. The swish of the bay around me, the floating feeling sent a ripple of security through me, something I'd always yearned for but hadn't known I'd love this much.

Granted, no one had ever taken control of my body the way Ursuline had, or played it quite so well.

My feet barely skimmed the sandy ground, Ursuline's grip on my thighs ironclad. I hoped the suckers left marks. They fucked into my hole again, and I let out a keening cry. Sinful pleasure exploded through me, the suckers gliding against the sensitive skin, their brush against my prostate more intense than I could've imagined. The burning interest in their dark eyes snagged my soul, held me in rapture. I'd never felt so stripped down and seen before in my life.

So cherished. So claimed.

Their mating tentacle gushed more of their slick, and even though we were in the water, it was enough to keep the glide smooth.

"You feel so good," they rumbled out. "So perfect for me."

"I can..." I gasped out as they continued thrusting into me. "I can take more."

"Mm, my good boy wants to take everything, don't you?" they teased, the wicked glint in their gaze my undoing. My cheeks flushed. The greediness for more, more, more had been unlocked inside me, and where before I might've hesitated to ask, Ursuline made me want to be shameless.

"Please." I bobbed my head. The ache in my balls formed a steady thump, but I loved that I couldn't do anything to relieve it. I loved that I was a vessel for their length, as they claimed my hole again and again. The steady thrust of their mating tentacle, the swish of the water around me, the weightlessness I felt suspended in the bay and by their tentacles, everything elevated me higher and higher. A floaty cotton-ball sensation entered my brain like last night, just pure surrender.

"You're nice and easy tonight," they said. "Time for a bit more of a stretch. Cry all you need to, sunshine. Your moans are delicious."

The praise fluttered through me, a balm to my battered and bruised soul.

"Hold on tight to me," they commanded. I fixed my grip on their shoulders again, their hands steady around my waist, keeping me braced. Their other mating tentacle slithered up the inside of my thigh, and I gulped hard. Would I be able to take them? I wanted to so badly. The tip nudged against where their other tentacle was lodged deep inside my hole, teasing at the rim. The sensation sent a shiver through me, violent and fierce.

They lifted me out of the water again, and I reeled from the weightlessness.

The water dripped off me, tickling as it slid down my skin, my feet, my calves still submerged even if my hole was bared to the cool winds. The bracing chill of the breeze wrapped around my body, my caged cock, my aching balls, but I'd grown so feverish on lust, the desire pumped through me hot enough that it didn't matter.

They squirted more of their slick along my rim and then teased the tip in.

The breath snagged in my throat at the stretch, not quite a sting. Yet the sensation of it gliding in alongside the other one was new, curious, and turned me on more than I could've imagined. I wanted to feel both of them ramming into me at the same time, taking me apart, stretching me open until I was loose and sloppy. Until I could take the heavy volume of cum they'd dumped into me last night.

They teased their tip a little deeper, a little more, squirting plenty of slick along the way. The stretch grew intense, and I forced myself to suck in a sharp breath again.

I leaned against their chest, and the steady thump of their heartbeat soothed me even as they pumped the tip in and out, getting my hole used to the sting, the way they stretched me with both of their tentacles inside.

"Gods, sunshine, you're so snug, so perfect. You're doing so well." Their low voice had a cadence that compelled me, and as I clutched their shoulders, my cheek pressed against their chest, I'd never felt more secure. Even as they stretched me beyond anything I'd ever taken before.

They thrust their tip in deeper, and the stretch—fuck. I sucked in a breath and whimpered, even though my balls throbbed.

"Do you need me to stop?" they asked as they lowered me slightly, so I floated in the water again. The buoyancy there eased me, and they nudged in deeper. I kept my grip on their shoulders, even though my cheek now pressed lower on their chest.

"No, I want it," I said, meaning that with every ounce in me. My cock wasn't testing the confines of the cage right now, not with the sting from the stretch, but after experiencing them rubbing against my prostate with just one...the need to know what it'd feel like had reached a fever pitch.

"You're going to be dripping cum for days when I'm done with you," Ursuline murmured. Their words filled me with a delicious thrill. The idea of being caged for them and leaking their cum, of being marked and claimed like that—fuck, I loved it.

"Please," I begged again, clinging onto them for dear life. They pushed in deeper with their mating tentacle, the other holding still, and at first there was resistance, a sting that made my jaw clench automatically. I breathed through my nose and tried to relax as best as possible. For one tense moment, the pressure felt overwhelming, like I might never be able to take all of them.

Until they slid through the ring of resistance, and their length dragged against my prostate.

Pleasure flared so intensely that I half sobbed, half screamed as I clutched onto them with all my might.

"Good boy," they purred, and I pressed my cheek harder against their chest as they began to glide both of their lengths inside me. At the same time.

I wasn't going to survive.

I was so full, so godsdamn full I was about to burst, but I adored the sensation in the same breath. Like they could consume me this way, take me over. Fuck, I'd never been stretched like this, but I could fast see it becoming an addiction.

They slowly, excruciatingly, pumped their lengths inside me, one pushing in as the other pulled back. The contrast dragged against my walls, and I howled. Ursuline stroked their hand down my back, as if they were petting me, and they ran their fingers through my hair as well. I shuddered as they started to find a slow rhythm, a push and pull. The water sloshed around us. Sensations flooded me so strongly that I panted, I mewled, I screamed. My cock strained against the cage, but there was nowhere it could go.

They thrust their mating tentacles inside me, the movements sinuous and so intense my jaw ached. One brushed against my prostate, more sensitive than ever, and the pleasure that shuddered through me sent my whole body into spasms.

"You feel so damn good," they murmured, continuing to lightly pet me as they fucked into me, slow and steady, as they took me apart piece by piece. Above us, the sky was studded by stars, crystalline and glistening against the navy canvas, and the inky bay swelled around us, the gentle ebb and flow seductive. All while both their tentacles pumped in and pulled back at the same time. Another stroke to my prostate, and lightning sparked through me, my body seizing up. Oh gods.

"Fuck," I moaned out. "Fuck, fuck, fuck."

"That's right, sunshine," they said. "You take me so well." Their praise sent another shiver through me, barely competing with the pleasure that flushed through my body. Sweat broke out on my temple, despite the chill of the water we floated in. I registered the tight band of their tentacles around my legs, how they kept me stable, because the way they claimed me so fully stole my focus.

A gush of slick squirted inside me, but not the torrent that signaled they'd come. However, it smoothed the glide as I sagged against them, boneless in the wake of the bliss flooding through me with every move of their dueling lengths. The bumps of the suckers dragged against my walls, and I was grateful I wasn't standing, because I wouldn't have been able to keep myself upright.

Tears formed and stung as they slid down my cheeks, the intensity so great that I almost couldn't handle it. Except I also never wanted this to end. Being taken by them like this, filled and claimed, sated something deep inside my chest, a raw ache that I'd never thought would be healed.

"Beautiful," Ursuline said, wiping at the tears leaking down my cheeks. "You're absolutely beautiful."

Their eyes were fevered, and their breaths quickened as they continued to pump inside me the entire time. Seeing their responsiveness, how turned on they were as well, thrilled me beyond end. Their chest heaved, my cheek still pressed against it, and the heat there built by the second, sweat prickling as well. The water sloshed around us as they fucked me with a fluid grace that fit them far too well. Their competency made them that much hotter, and I surrendered to Ursuline in every way—body, mind, and soul.

My cock strained against the cage, but I didn't even care if I came. Not while their lengths wrung such intense pleasure from me with every sweep. Fuck. Shivers racked through my body, but not from the cool water around me. I was fast hitting overload point, and I wasn't sure how much more I could take.

Even if I never wanted this to end.

They stroked in again, and their suckers brushed against that spot.

Sheer, blinding ecstasy rolled through me. My whole body seized, and the crest of what felt like an orgasm spread throughout. I rolled along the waves, more pleasure than I thought humanly possible, and I howled, my nails digging into their shoulders. The tremors left in the wake were unreal, with a strength and fervor that would knock me down if I wasn't wrapped up in their tentacles, bobbing in the water.

The intensity of the sensations rolling through me were more than I'd ever experienced before, and I sagged against their chest, clutching onto them with all my might as they continued to alternate the thrusts of their mating tentacles. My balls throbbed, but in the wake of what I'd experienced, the desperate need for release had somewhat abated.

"Good boy," they murmured, their breaths coming in a little choppier. "Looks like someone had a prostate orgasm. It'll make you nice and lax to take my loads."

Ngh. I incinerated as I held on for the ride, as I leaned against them while their lengths shuttled in and out of my hole at a quicker pace. Ursuline's breathing grew faster, and sweat beaded on their chest.

"So close, sunshine," they warned me, but I could barely force my eyes open. I just wanted to float in this feeling.

"Fuck," they groaned out, and a second later, first one of their tentacles started to gush inside me, and then the other one thrust in again and throbbed, then released as well. The blast of cum flooded my insides, and a long, low groan came from me. The unholy amount of cum that soaked my insides sent a burst of adrenaline through me. I already sagged against their chest, so I rubbed my cheek against it, a sob leaving me. The way they claimed me, how they'd fucked me so thoroughly I almost couldn't believe it—the whole experience was transcendental.

Ursuline pressed a kiss to my forehead, and I shivered again.

"You were so good for me," they said, running their fingers through my hair. The soothing strokes sated something deep inside, and combined with the bob of the water around us, the cool breezes caressing my skin, I relaxed in a way I didn't realize was possible. I floated there, flew really, and with the steady *thump, thump, thump* of their heartbeat against my cheek, I never wanted this moment to end.

They continued to press slow kisses on my head, the tip of my ear, anywhere they could. The tender touches meant everything to me, and shudders overtook my body. The praise, the care they offered was everything I'd craved for so long.

They retracted one of their tentacles, and some of the cum gushed out, dissipating into the water. Already I missed the fullness, even with one of their mating tentacles still lodged inside me. Then they pulled the other from me, and I whimpered. My hole was so gaping that the water rushed right in, and I squirmed. I wanted to keep Ursuline's cum inside me for days, not have it swept away.

"We should get you inside," they said as they swept their arm beneath my legs and hoisted me up. I didn't try to fight it at all, just rested against their chest as they sliced through the water with ease, carrying me back toward the shore. The wind swept around me, caressing my bare skin, and once we trod out of the water, it began to grow chillier.

We reached the shore, and Ursuline lowered me down to the sand. The clothes we'd left behind remained in piles there, and they tugged their tunic back over their head. I snagged a shirt, but I didn't even have the energy to put my clothes on.

"I..." I opened my mouth and then closed it. What could I even ask them for? They couldn't spend the night with me. Not when the Tritons could return at any moment. The discovery would cost them too much. "I don't want to go back there."

The truth hung heavily in the air.

Ursuline lowered down behind me, relaxing their tentacles to an almost sitting position. Their tentacles wrapped around my arms, my legs, caressing them, and I sank back against Ursuline's chest. The steady thump of their heartbeat soothed me, and they wrapped their arms around my torso. Even though my hole ached, and I was bare and shivering, the heat from their body warmed me all the way through.

"That's how I feel every time," they murmured, pressing another idle kiss into my hair. "Except you...fuck, I can't let you become tied to this place too."

I clutched their arms tight, and my eyes stung. I wasn't sure if it was from exhaustion, from the emotions brewing inside me right now, or from the note of despair in their voice. However, I blinked away the glossiness, my chest torn open from tonight. From everything they'd shared with me.

From everything we'd shared.

"We'll stay on shore until you're ready to head in," Ursuline said. "That's all I can promise for tonight."

I pressed an idle kiss to their forearm, my heart thundering. The yearning inside me stretched as vast and consuming as the starry sky above us. Yet it felt as impossible and distant too. Like no matter how hard I tried to reach it, I'd never manage.

I knew what I wanted. I wanted Ursuline, but the hurdles between us were higher than I ever could've imagined.

If only we'd met each other in another world. In another lifetime.

"Stay with me a little. That's all I ask for."

Chapter 21

My whole body ached.

Late in the night, I'd dragged myself back up to the manor. Ursuline had parted ways with me by the shore, which I understood but hated all the same. I pressed against my hole, a zing rushing through me at the tenderness there from taking both of their tentacles last night. Their cum had washed away in the bay, but I'd longed to keep it inside me, to hold some part of them close.

Even better would be having them in bed with me, by my side, but that was one fantasy that couldn't come to life.

Not while I was promised to marry Arielle.

My heart twisted, and I shifted in the bed, trying to make the pain dissipate—even though it wouldn't.

I pushed up from the mattress, though exhaustion clung to me like a shroud. What time had Arielle even gotten back last night? If she'd decided to return. I should've been paying attention, and yet, my focus had been wholly on Ursuline. On the way they'd saved me. On the way they'd surprised me with my friend. On the way they'd fucked me so well no one else would compare.

I heaved a sigh and stood, my limbs a little shaky. So far, I'd been content to float to my usual spaces—the studio, the balcony, and the kitchen—but today, a newfound urgency thrummed within me.

Jacques's warning tolled in my head like a bell, sonorous and louder with every passing day. Yet if I ran, where would I go?

I needed to understand what the Triton family was about, behind the furtiveness, behind the charade. However, the staff continued to zip up around me since Jacques had left, so I couldn't ask them. If they were like my parents, they kept their secrets locked up tight.

I chewed on my lower lip. Rooting around in their private chambers would surely get me in a load of trouble, but if I started wandering around in more innocuous spots, I could always claim I got lost. I tugged on a loose pair of pants and a tight tank. My balls gave their steady throb, my cock still caged, and we'd had no discussion of when I'd be free. Yet I loved being caged up for Ursuline, loved being fucked until I cried.

The reminders of the way they'd taken me last night were all over my body, sucker prints and light bruising around my thighs, my hole puffy and tender. I pressed down on the spot along my thigh, and even over fabric the feeling sent a zing through me. When I glanced in the mirror, I almost burst into laughter. My hair was askew, and the dazed look on my face was fuck-drunk if I ever saw it. However, I didn't need to be presentable to roam the castle.

What I did need was to get an inkling of why Triton had presented the idea of marriage to my family in the first place.

The more I thought about the warnings, about Ursuline's history down in New Atlantis and the pain that lingered with both them and Jason, the more the urgency to know *something* burned through my veins.

Before I married into this family for good.

Because while Arielle might not care if I stepped out, I believed with my whole heart that Frederick would enforce whatever stipulations were in the contract he'd have me sign. And I was also sure he'd never let me out of the marriage—alive.

I stepped out into the hall, the hush a relief given my current intentions. Normally the quiet in this place crawled under my skin, even though it wasn't a far cry from what I'd grown up with. My parents had always made themselves as sparse as possible, but at least they'd had a robust staff who'd shown me care when my own blood hadn't.

I hadn't bothered with shoes, and I padded down the hall in my socks. The Tritons had stationed my room in the opposite wing from the family one, which was probably intentional. I didn't expect to find a "master plan" hanging around, but even a little more information of Frederick's business, who he employed down below, would help me get a clearer understanding of what was going on behind the scenes.

I'd tried to look the family up online countless times, but if any undersea monsters had posted anything, none of it surfaced. The idea that records could've been scrubbed sent a chill down my spine. And all that human businesses up here reported on was the Triton family as a newcomer into the business scene with unprecedented connections. Neither hide nor hair about them being monsterkind.

I passed the familiar rooms and skipped past the large reading room up here that always lay unused. None of the family seemed to be bookish, and if they spent time together, I hadn't seen it happen in this household, so the massive darkwood room with the polished furniture, huge oaken tables, and towering shelves filled with books went to waste.

To my right lay the staircase I traversed down to the kitchen, to the areas I spent most of my time in.

Today, I went straight ahead, down the hall into the Triton family's wing.

My nerves thrummed. They hadn't been home last night, but that didn't mean they were still in New Atlantis. And if Arielle had returned, she'd be here, sleeping off whatever hangover or wild night she'd entertained at the club. There should be camaraderie with my own fiancée, but if she caught me snooping around, I knew what would happen. My gut sank. She'd go right to her father.

Would I disappear like Jacques?

The silence grew louder in this hallway, as if amplified by the secrets trapped behind these walls. I took care to gentle each footstep, to keep them quiet and to listen for any errant noises.

Going into bedrooms felt too intrusive, and I didn't want to risk stumbling in on anyone, so I avoided closed doors. However, the silence lingered, thankfully, and I peered into the first open doorway I found. What looked like a large office spanned out, just as big as the reading room by the staircase. Yet this one contained a set of desks with computers on them, shelving on all the walls, and more ostentatious pieces—simple designs by curated artists, similar to the ones I grew up with that denoted wealth more than an awareness of the art world.

Maybe I'd find something in an office. If this were Frederick's personal one... Well, he would have things here he wouldn't put elsewhere.

I stepped inside and froze, waiting for some alarm to go off, for someone to jump out at me—from where, I had no clue. Sunlight streamed in through the window on the far side of the room, deceptively calm despite my erratic heartbeat. Dust motes drifted lazily through the room, as if there weren't a care in the world.

Except if I got caught in here, guaranteed it would invoke Frederick's wrath.

And he wasn't the type of person you crossed.

I sank into one of the computer chairs and pressed at the keyboard. The screen flickered on, but it was locked behind a passcode. I wrinkled my nose. My experience with computers was negligible, and I'd be more liable to set off an alarm if I tried. Somehow, I doubted Triton used "password" for his password. This whole idea was ridiculous. Jacques had been the only one willing to share anything with me, and Frederick wouldn't have left a paper trail. I had the feeling he was far too clever for that.

The fact he'd hidden so much of his family's history as well as the fact they were part of monsterkind from Peregrine City was proof positive.

Maybe I should run regardless. Listen to the warning flares setting off in my mind. And yet part of me needed the push, the impetus, the confirmation to make the final move. Because if I tried an escape…I could never return to this life.

Not only that, but I might spend the rest of my days on the run.

My stomach bottomed out, and I puddled into the computer chair, wishing I had some skills that would be useful here. That daydreams and brushstrokes weren't all I had to offer the world.

With Ursuline, I felt useful. I felt cherished. I felt wanted. And they were trapped here regardless, so why was I even poking around in here, borrowing trouble anyway?

The minutes ticked by in the room, and I kept my attention focused on the hall, but the responding silence didn't give me any solace. Not while I sat here in Frederick's office, clearly forbidden territory.

I gave the computer chair a spin, and a bright blue snagged my attention on one of the shelves behind me.

I stopped and stared. The blue glass triangle on the shelf featured a black circle in the center, a silver ridge around the edges. It was the size of a paperweight, enough that to most it would be nondescript.

However, I'd seen the same piece on my parents' shelves. It was the emblem of Alpha Blue, a "security" company everyone knew was a front for kidnappers for hire. The men worked in the underworld, and my parents had the same token in their possession my whole life, a reminder that anyone could easily disappear.

I'd dropped it once. I had picked the glass triangle up because the glass was pretty, and then it had slipped out of my hands. Yet another instance where I'd been klutzy. My parents had...well, overreacted was putting things mildly. They'd screamed and screamed and screamed, and I'd been locked in my room for days.

Hardly the response for a random paperweight, but I'd gauged over the years that Alpha Blue didn't give those tokens out freely.

I surged from my seat and walked over to it, a tug in my gut that I couldn't ignore. The sight of something so familiar here was a bit jarring, a bit disorienting. Almost as if...

I picked up the glass triangle and ran my fingers along the back.

My stomach bottomed out.

The same fracture was on this one. The fracture I'd caused when I'd dropped it as a child.

Somehow, Frederick Triton now had access to this token from Alpha Blue, the one that had lived in my parents' mansion since I was young. I didn't believe in coincidences—not with this. All this time, I'd been wondering what they could've wanted in a union between our two families. What Frederick Triton could need that my family had. Sure, we had money and access to the human side of the wealthy in Peregrine City, but so did many others.

Not everyone had access to Alpha Blue like the Durand family did, though.

I was going to be sick. Who was Triton trafficking? Who would he disappear? Too easily, answers emerged.

Anyone who'd escaped New Atlantis. People like Jason, who had left, searching for a better life on the surface than the pain he'd dealt with down below.

Oh, fuck.

I bit my lower lip and set the token down on the shelf again before I dropped it. The second I did, my hands started to tremble. If I married Arielle, I'd be complicit in this. I'd be enabling him to hurt more of the sea monsters up here. Did Ursuline know? They couldn't possibly. My throat tightened as panic rose with a steady *thump, thump, thump*.

I had to tell them. I didn't have concrete proof, but the pit in my gut was unerring. This was the confirmation I'd been waiting for, the signal.

And I needed to follow it.

Voices sounded from farther down the hall, and my heart jackknifed. Oh fuck.

If I was discovered here, I'd be buried.

I ducked beneath the desk, curling myself into the tight area. My knees pressed hard against the wooden sides, barely any space here. Yet I slowed my breath, focusing on quieting it as much as possible. The voices grew louder by the second.

Ones I recognized.

Arielle and her mother, Darla.

Adrenaline surged through me, tingling through my extremities, but I couldn't budge. There wasn't a secret exit here, and they were heading down the only hallway out. The footsteps pounded louder, and I tensed, not wanting to move an inch, to risk discovery. All it would take was for them to slow while they strolled past the office. Guaranteed, I could be seen beneath the desk if anyone looked hard enough.

And if they found me, I was in deep trouble.

I never should've been poking around back here. I should've listened to Jacques and got out the first chance I could. My palms began to sweat, but I didn't dare wipe them or make any movements.

The voices became clear enough to hear now, so I sucked in a slow, steady breath and closed my eyes, just listening.

"They've been here more than ever," Arielle complained. "And you can't claim it's because you have an overabundance of contracts for them to work on."

"If they're spending time around Elrich, does it matter?" Darla asked. "It's not as if you want to be saddled with him more than necessary."

"Tell that to Papa," Arielle grumbled. "He tried to send Elrich to the club with me last night." My stomach curdled at the disgust in her tone, so different from the perpetual cheeriness she usually delivered my way. It reaffirmed the decision that settled deep inside me.

I needed to leave.

"You know the importance of appearance," Darla chided her.

"Oh?" Arielle shot back. "Then tell that to Ursuline. How does public appearance view a cecaelia lurking around my fiancé all the time?"

"It's better they're occupied," Darla responded, the footsteps so close they had to be right near the door. I barely dared to breathe. "We don't want them asking questions. There's a reason they're prohibited from going back down to New Atlantis."

My blood chilled. Darla said the phrase so casually, but I knew why Ursuline had to stay up here. Why they'd been tied to the Triton family for so long.

What was the family hiding from them?

"Ugh," Arielle said. "I don't understand why you two have clung onto them for so long. With the money you have, there are a million and one lawyers out there."

"Even the highest sum can't beat contracted loyalty," Darla said as her voice sounded right outside the room. The breath caught in my throat, and I didn't dare expel it. My whole body froze as I tensed, waiting to get caught. For one of them to pause and sense that I hid here.

"Whatever," Arielle said. "I'm just saying other options are out there."

Their footsteps continued past the door, and their chat didn't pause, but my ears rang, my mind buzzing from the conversation. My hands were slick with sweat, my breath stuck in my throat, ready to burst out, and my muscles taut, as if I'd need to run any second now.

Their discussion grew quieter as they walked farther down the hall, and the creak of a door echoed before the sounds hushed.

I let out my held breath.

What were they hiding from Ursuline down in New Atlantis? My gut soured. Hearing Arielle talk like that in private had shown me more about her personality than I'd seen in the entire span of time I'd been here. And I couldn't marry someone like that, even if it were in name only.

I definitely couldn't further this despicable family's aims.

I couldn't stay.

But would Ursuline? I chewed on my lower lip until I tasted copper. The quiet remained for minutes, enough time that I dared to crawl out from where I'd stuffed myself under the desk. If they emerged again, I'd run into worse trouble. Better I try to escape now.

My limbs creaked as I rose to a stand and tiptoed over to the door. My heart thrummed. At any moment, if Arielle and her mother headed back this way, I was screwed. And neither of them held me in any sort of regard, based on their discussion. I swallowed hard and peeked past the doorframe.

The hall was clear to the left and clear to the right.

Before I could second-guess myself, I plunged back down to the right, traveling the way I came.

My shoulders prickled as I walked as quietly as possible along the corridor. *Please don't come back out. Please don't find me.*

My hands trembled, and my breaths were shallow and shaky. I bypassed the open rooms from before, along with the closed doors, trying to remain silent, wary of the floor beneath me. Sweat trickled down my back, tickling the whole way.

Up ahead lay the staircase leading down, along with the reading room. If I could just get there...

I quickened my pace—not quite a run, but a fast, silent stride.

I lunged forward, right in front of the doors leading to the reading room.

A creak sounded from farther down the hall I'd come from. My whole body tensed. Fuck.

Except I was clearly in sight. I whipped around to face that direction. Arielle poked her head out, her long ponytail swinging with the movement. I offered a wave, hoping she didn't notice how my limbs trembled. She gave a polite wave back before flouncing to another room in the hallway—probably hers.

The second her door shut, I sagged with relief. I reached for the railing of the staircase and gripped it tight, just to keep myself from swaying forward. I was drenched with sweat, my shirt plastering to my chest. Snooping in the area the Triton family inhabited hadn't been my brightest idea. And I'd come too close to being discovered.

However, I had more information than I'd started with today.

I needed to plan my escape. No other option existed. And yet, the idea of leaving Ursuline behind squeezed my chest hard, pain radiating through me. But if Darla's words held weight, staying wouldn't just be dangerous for me.

Ursuline was in trouble too.

Chapter 22

U rsuline wasn't able to come to the manor until that night.

I'd texted them at once and then done my best to avoid the Triton family by spending the rest of the day painting in the studio. Distraction was all I could do to keep from losing my mind. I didn't want to fake conversation with Arielle or Darla, not after what I'd overheard.

I splashed color onto the canvas in one furious brush stroke after another. I hadn't even come up to eat, because the kitchen served as a reminder that Jacques had vanished. That the Tritons were no different than my family in disposing of people who didn't reach their exacting standards.

And I couldn't tie myself to that for the rest of my life.

If I tried walking out of here, someone would catch me before I trekked halfway down the long, winding drive. If I asked to leave, a bodyguard would escort me, and I'd have to find a way to ditch them, which wasn't my strongest suit. I stabbed red onto the canvas, as if I could somehow unleash the frustration and desperation bubbling up inside me.

"What did that canvas ever do to you?" Ursuline's voice sounded behind me, their tone wry. I tensed and relaxed in the span of a breath as the surprise of their appearance faded away. Tension percolated inside me with the weight of what I needed to tell them, and my lips dried. Maybe they already knew. They were viciously intelligent, so I might be spiraling over information I'd been blind to.

Would they have hidden all of that from me? The idea made my gut churn.

I dipped my brush in the murky cup of water and stepped away from the canvas. When I turned around, the sight of Ursuline in the doorframe offered the first gasp of relief I could clutch onto, even though nerves still simmered through me.

They'd clearly come from work, wearing a high-collared black shirt, cut long like most of their tops to drift over their hips before the tentacles flared out beneath them. Their silver hair was slicked back, and the lighting of the room cast their light blue skin in a slightly different hue, deepening the dips of their muscles, the definition of their clavicle. They carried a plastic bag in one hand laden with foam containers, rich scents of food traveling my way.

"Figured you hadn't eaten," they said, holding up the takeout. "Here or upstairs?"

"Here," I said, casting a nervous glance to the door. At least the studio room was contained. I couldn't risk sitting up in the kitchen where anyone could overhear from another room or walk right in.

Ursuline's brows drew together, and they gave a tight nod as they found the nearest bench and sprawled over it. I took a seat on the floor beside them, not wanting to be farther away. They passed me one of the foam containers, and I popped it open—pancakes with strawberry topping, which I'd commented was my favorite the last time I'd looked over Haven's menu. My heart thrummed. Their consideration, the way they listened and saw me, touched a deep part of me.

Silence spread between us for a few moments, and I took the opportunity to cram a bit of pancake into my mouth, just to stave off my rioting stomach. I hadn't eaten much at all today—couldn't manage it with all the confusion churning around inside me.

"What's going on?" Ursuline asked, breaking through the quiet. They hadn't taken a bite of their food. "Based on your message, how jittery you are, something happened."

I swallowed the bite of pancakes and then sucked in a deep breath for bolstering. "I need to leave."

Ursuline lapsed into silence for a moment, but they bobbed their head. "I agree."

"You need to leave too," I said, daring to meet their gaze.

Their dark eyes flashed with pain, and their lips thinned. "If only I could, Elrich."

I shook my head. "Beyond what they have planned over the union between my family and theirs, I don't think they're being honest with you about your deal."

Ursuline sighed. "The contract is ironclad. I wrote it myself. If I violate it, my family is forfeit."

"If your family is safe..." I hedged my bets, even though my pulse thumped so rapidly I thought it'd take off. "Then why are they trying to keep you distracted? Why don't they want you to go to New Atlantis?"

Ursuline's eyes widened, which told me all I needed to know.

"And I stumbled upon what my family gave them in return for a chance at some of the orichalcum wealth," I continued, before they could argue with me or stop this train from moving forward. "Access to Alpha Blue."

Ursuline's expression darkened, and they let out a low swear. "How do you know?"

"I overheard Arielle and Darla talking about you earlier," I murmured, squeezing my nape. "They weren't aware I was there. As for Alpha Blue, I found my family's token in Frederick's office."

Ursuline's tentacle wrapped around my leg, and that broke the tension between us. I surged forward to lean against their strong, warm tentacles, just collapsing there. A moment later, their fingers threaded through my hair as they gave a tentative stroke. Relief shuddered through me at their touch, that they weren't angry at me for what I'd told them.

"I've been a fool," they said, their voice threadbare. "I...I get messages from my family. I'd taken those as enough all these years."

"No calls?" I asked, my brow furrowing.

"Not for a long while," they said. "Though calls between above and below the surface have never been too reliable." Still, their expression darkened with realization.

The truth dug in, deep and ugly. Because if Frederick was willing to commit all sorts of unconscionable acts, there was no guarantee those messages were either from the sender or done without coercion.

"Jason's going below," I stated, needing to reassure them in some way. "He'll be able to check in on your family."

Their tentacle tightened on my leg, their fingers stilling in my hair. "I've had a feeling in my gut for a while now. That something was wrong. Yet whenever I messaged my family, they'd reassured me they were fine. That everything was okay."

My stomach twisted in knots. I couldn't imagine the heartache they'd suffered all these years.

"But I've been cut off from everyone back in New Atlantis for so long," Ursuline said. "Most who escape to the surface...most of us don't want to return."

Their pain echoed Jason's, how he'd often shut down at mention of his past. How he'd avoided going back for so long. The relief and guilt they must feel at being away from what they'd left behind had to be so staggering. So complicated.

I stroked my fingers along the tentacle wrapped around my leg, and Ursuline let out a ragged sigh.

"Come with me," I murmured, my heartbeat thrumming.

They'd say no. I knew it, deep down. They couldn't throw away their family's safety for me. Even if I didn't trust the Tritons to honor a deal in the slightest.

"I want to," they admitted, their voice hoarse. My gaze drifted to the closed door, as if listening ears might be outside. I now understood for a fact we weren't safe anywhere inside this place. They might not be able to give me an answer now, but I'd just dropped this bomb on them.

Maybe, maybe they'd realize escape was their best option too.

I squeezed the tentacle wrapped around me and rubbed my cheek against the one I leaned against. "I'm going to figure a way out of here. I'm not sure where I'll land or how I'll do it, but I can't stay. Not knowing what my marriage to Arielle will do."

"No, you can't," they agreed.

They stroked the tip of their tentacle along my leg, and they began to run their fingers through my hair again. The motions soothed me unlike anything else, even though my heart still ached. We agreed that I had to escape, but the idea of leaving them behind tore my heart in two.

"Where would I even go?" I asked aloud. If anyone would know the inner workings of how to escape the Tritons, I was sure Ursuline had given the prospect plenty of thought over the years.

"Fuck," they swore, their voice as ragged as my heart. "Sunshine, I'll make sure you're taken care of."

Even if they couldn't be there.

Gods, the idea of a future without them hurt. In my time at the Triton household, I'd grown closer to them than anyone in my entire life. They'd shown me more care and consideration than I'd ever experienced growing up. And my soul called to them, like the tug toward the stars in the night sky, inexorable and inescapable.

"I knew from the moment we met that I couldn't keep you," they murmured, almost as if to themself. "I can't keep anyone. Not in this lifetime."

Their pain lay heavy in the air, a suffocating blanket that crushed my shoulders. My eyes stung, and I chewed on my lower lip, not sure what to say. I wanted them to come, but I understood the risk. They had family who they loved. Family who depended on them. And if my gut feeling was wrong, that their family was still safe and the Tritons were upholding their end of the deal, then running off with me would put them all in danger.

I couldn't imagine the weight they carried on a daily basis. The pain they shouldered.

"What if you could?" I asked, even though indulging in this would slice me open even more. I stared down at the floor, unable to look at them without breaking down. The warmth and smoothness of their tentacles at my side offered the solidity I craved right now, but if I looked up at them, I'd break.

The quiet in the room was laden with a thousand regrets.

"If I could keep you, we'd wake up in my apartment every day," they said, continuing to stroke their fingers through my hair. I shuddered from the touch, from the sheer imagining. "You'd be covered in flecks of paint like you are now, pursuing your craft. I'd be working for non-profits to help advance monsterkind and protect those in vulnerable situations. I'd come home and make you scream over every surface possible, take every hole until you were trembling." They let out a heavy sigh. "We'd go on trips to the ocean and swim and bask in your sunshine. I'd make you pancakes for breakfast on lazy mornings and take you to game nights with Cillian and the others. We'd...live. Every day and every moment belonging just to us."

The tears slipped down my cheeks. I wanted that future so badly I could feel it hovering in the air before me, just there to grab. My chest spasmed. It aligned with everything I'd longed for, and I didn't doubt for a moment this was the soul I'd waited for my entire life.

And now I'd be leaving them behind.

"What if we find a way to get you out too?" I asked. "The Tritons...they're distracting you for a reason."

Their fingers stilled in my hair again. "Leaving with you is all I've ever wanted. But without concrete proof, I'm tethered to them. I can't put you at risk of being hunted for the rest of your days. The Tritons are relentless."

It'd be worth living on the run if we could be together, but the words lodged in my throat. Ursuline seemed to be wavering, but if they left with me, it had to be their decision. I couldn't stand it if I'd pushed them and then retribution rained down on their family in response.

"By the end of this week," Ursuline said. "Get your most important belongings together. Pack a bag but keep it under your bed. I'll get you out of here."

My mind whirred at the shift. The reality brought up the main problem I'd been dancing around. "What about Jason?"

"He's on my list to contact. Given a heads-up, he can lay low. If..." They paused, the quiet laden as if they were deep in thought. "If my concerns are founded, we might have a much larger problem on our hands."

The gnawing in my gut emerged again, the same as when I'd found the Alpha Blue token in Triton's office. Something terrible brewed, and we were in the epicenter of it.

"You won't put yourself in danger?" I asked. If they wouldn't come with me, the idea of them staying behind to face repercussions for helping me...fuck, I couldn't bear the thought.

"Sunshine, I haven't been surviving up here for this many years without a few tricks up my sleeve," they said. "When I send you the text, you'll need to head to the back entrance where the staff deliveries happen. A car will be waiting for you."

Which implied they wouldn't be there too. My throat tightened.

"Please come with me," I begged again, needing to try one last time. I wouldn't push, but I couldn't fathom heading out of here without them. Knowing they were still trapped in this misery, a punishment without end.

Their tentacle stroked at my ankle again, but their silence gave me the answer.

When I escaped this place, it would be alone.

Chapter 23

"Are you down here again?" Arielle's voice sounded from the doorway of the studio. I'd been painting furiously, even though I'd known I would need to leave all these behind.

I almost jumped out of my skin. A week had passed since my conversation with Ursuline, and they hadn't returned to the manor. At least not that I was aware of. The Tritons had been more present this week, Frederick and Darla emerging at the beginning, appearing at random when I was painting or in the kitchen, but then they'd abruptly left yesterday. All three sisters had been in and out in regular occurrences, but with the weekend approaching, Arielle would want to head to the club every night.

"Yeah," I said, attempting a fake smile. "Just working on a piece." Trying to pretend I hadn't seen an uglier side of her exposed beneath the plastered, empty grins. After seeing that glimpse, I couldn't buy the superficial front any longer. The truth leaked out of every tiny twitch to her expression, every sharper edge to her words.

"I'm supposed to invite you to the club tonight," she said, leaning against the doorframe. "But you hated it, right? Papa isn't here, so we can claim you went with me."

"Definitely not my scene." I told the truth there. "Go ahead without me. I'll pretend I went."

"Oh, thank fuck," she said, flashing me another empty grin. "No offense, but I didn't feel like babysitting."

"None taken," I said, forcing a smile. The idea of being away from the manor now, when I could get a text at any moment, sent a spike of panic through me. I'd been existing on a perpetual state of adrenaline throughout the week, the readiness stamped into my bones. My go-bag waited for me beneath my bed. I'd even packed the key to the cage, the pressure around my cock a reminder of who I belonged to—and I didn't want to take it off.

My phone buzzed in my pocket, and said adrenaline shot through the roof.

Arielle lingered in the doorway, even though I itched to check.

"This week we'll be starting the preparations for the wedding," she said. "A whole lot of boring stuff and decisions. Plus a prenup, you know, the usual."

My grin faltered. The urgency filtered through my system stronger than ever. Once I signed those papers, the Tritons would own me. In the eyes of the city, in the eyes of society. Ursuline had already warned me the clauses worked in there were nasty, not the normal stuff included in a prenup, and out of everyone, they would know.

My legs trembled with the itch to run, to bolt to my bedroom and grab my bag, but Arielle was still in the doorway.

"Sounds good," I forced out, trying to keep my tone normal. "I like the details. I'm happy to do most of the work if you find it boring."

"Perfect," she said, her expression lightening. One of those tinkling laughs escaped her again, but everything had a phony edge in the wake of seeing her in a different light. "I'll see you around. Have fun with your art."

With that, she disappeared out of the doorway.

I let out a held breath and snagged my phone. The message was from Ursuline.

It's time.

Oh fuck. I needed to leave. Now.

I didn't bother cleaning up in the studio, which felt like sacrilege. No one ever visited down here anyway, and I could guarantee no one cared about losing a few brushes. Instead, I headed down the hallway and up the stairs, making sure to keep my steps slow and measured, even though my insides jittered like I'd mainlined an entire carafe of coffee. The silence hummed around me, but I kept my focus forward, passing the familiar rooms as I headed to the room that had become mine during my time here.

One that would fast become a memory.

My gut churned.

I was leaving.

I was escaping the Triton family, my own family, maybe even Peregrine City.

But I was also leaving Ursuline.

My chest spasmed, and pain sliced through me. The idea of going without them wounded me in a way that would scar. In a way I'd carry with me every waking moment. They'd somehow emblazoned themself on my soul. I didn't know when I'd fallen for them, but between midnight swims and diner trips, I had.

They owned a piece of my heart.

I reached my room and closed the door behind me as I grabbed the black bag I'd packed and left under the bed. As I slipped the straps over my shoulder, the weight of it settled heavily inside me.

I trusted Ursuline had let Jason know. I trusted they were sending me off to a better future.

However, they would remain in this hell.

I adjusted the bag on my shoulder as I stepped to the door. From here on out, I needed to be quick, and I needed to walk through these halls unseen. If the staff spotted me, my bulky bag could raise questions or sound alarms. If Arielle wandered through the halls, I'd be fucked before I even stepped foot out the door.

My hand rested on the doorknob, and I paused, staring around the room I had as little attachment to as the one I'd grown up in. For me, home hadn't been a refuge but the spaces I carved for myself around safe people.

I'd never experienced the idea of a home or felt the comfort deep in my bones the way I did around Ursuline.

Except now I was walking away. The sense of guilt tugged at my gut, sent my stomach roiling.

However, if I stayed, we'd not just be trapped in hiding, in agony, but Triton would use my family's connections for harm.

I opened the door and stepped into the hall. Ever since Ursuline had given me the instructions, I'd practiced the trek from here to the back entrance. I'd figured out the best pathway there, the one to avoid passing by most of the main areas. The one that bypassed the staff lounge space too. Oftentimes, they were the only people in this manor besides me, but ever since Jacques vanished, everyone who had been friendly before had grown colder.

Maybe I was at fault for his disappearance. If he hadn't been talking to me, if Arielle hadn't overheard...

I tightened my grip on the strap at my shoulder and slowed to peer around the first corner.

Clear.

I sucked in a breath and headed down the corridor. Instead of heading to the main staircases, I detoured to a smaller one that was used by the staff to navigate around with laundry, cleaning equipment, or whatever else they were involved in for the upkeep of this massive mansion. Even as I reached the stairwell, the idea still hadn't settled in that I wasn't going to be stuck under the constraints of a rich family. Or any rich family. My actions had been dictated by the society I'd been born into my whole life.

But I'd be free.

Except Ursuline wouldn't.

I kept my steps quiet as I descended the stairwell, one that would bring me close to the exit. Tension threaded through the air with my every move forward. Because the stakes at this point weren't disappointment or a slap on the wrist.

No, I'd seen the cruelty in Frederick's eyes. I was aware of what he was capable of, and betraying him would have consequences.

Shame flushed through me. How had I gotten myself into this situation in the first place? Maybe if I'd trusted Jason to be able to take care of himself, if I'd contacted him to run, I could've avoided all this.

Yet then I would never have met Ursuline.

And I couldn't regret a second of our time together.

I reached the bottom of the stairwell, my heart lodged in my throat. Sweat burst on my palms, and I kept forgetting to breathe. I pushed open the door leading to a corridor that led to the back entrance as well as the staff lounge.

The moment I walked through the door, I paused.

In the far distance, a laugh sounded, coming from the other end of the hall, tucked farther down in one of the rooms. From the lounge.

Someone was there. Or several someones. My throat grew drier than I believed possible. If any of the staff walked this way, I was fucked. My naivete had dripped away the longer I stayed in this place.

I took the first step forward. And then another.

The sounds at the other end of the corridor continued, and I paid close attention to them, to any minute shifts, all while I approached the door.

Feet lay between me and my freedom.

As long as the car Ursuline had mentioned waited for me outside the door.

My heart squeezed tight. I wanted to see them again to try to convince them to come. To tell them goodbye. To feel their tentacles wrapped around my limbs just one last time.

I reached the door.

The tinted glass was difficult to see through, obscured further by the darkness of night that awaited me. This was the final step. My heart lodged in my throat.

The sounds at the end of the hall quieted. My internal alarms rang. If they weren't talking anymore, they could be heading this way at any moment.

I yanked the door open and stepped out into the brisk night.

A black car thrummed before me, the engine on, ready to go.

Time to leave.

My back prickled with awareness, enough to nudge my feet forward. I stumbled up to the back seat of the car and tugged at the latch.

"Get in," a low voice barked at me.

My pulse thundered, but I dove inside, drawing the door shut behind me. The car jerked forward, and we set into motion.

I sank against the seat, the breath rushing out of me. To my left, I could feel someone there, watching me, but I hadn't caught up with the fact that I sat in a car, escaping the Triton manor.

That I was leaving my old life behind and heading into the unknown.

"You okay?"

That voice...no, it couldn't be.

Hope surged into an almost sickening swell.

I whipped my head to the left, and the person I'd wanted to see most was sitting beside me.

Ursuline reclined in the seat, their dark gaze glittering with concern. The air hummed with an undeniable electricity as one question emerged in my mind. Hope fluttered to the surface, too desperate and insistent to smother.

Their tentacle wrapped around my wrist, and they squeezed. Their gaze met mine, and I couldn't look away if I'd wanted to. My heart lodged in my throat.

"Why?" was all I managed to push out.

"I'm coming with you."

Chapter 24

Ursuline was coming with me.

Joy rushed through my veins fast and fierce, and I blinked, my eyes stinging from the sheer emotions rocketing through me.

I could barely process everything that had occurred in the last few minutes, but as the car wound down the long drive, I reached over and threaded my fingers through Ursuline's.

They were *here*.

That was all that mattered.

"Where to?" a low voice came from the driver's seat, causing me to look forward.

A handsome man sat in the front seat, lithe and humanoid, dark black hair and profile full of sharp edges. His brown skin held an unusual pallor, which made me wonder what kind of monster he was. Most of Ursuline's connections seemed to be other monsters. Given the frigid reception so many humans gave, it made sense they'd band together in communities.

"Sofia's house. At least for tonight," Ursuline responded, squeezing my hand again. "Then we'll most likely head to the Spires for a spell while we figure out where to go."

Questions swirled inside, ones begging to burst free. The car zipped onto the main road, and the Triton Manor disappeared in the rearview. A breath escaped me, relief saturating through me. Even though I didn't believe we'd escaped unscathed, that Triton would let us run off without pursuit, at least we'd pulled off the initial departure.

"What changed your mind?" I asked, glancing between Ursuline and the driver, unsure what they were willing to share around him.

"Jaffar is well aware of the goings-on in the city," they said with a wan smile. "And he's got a pulse on far more than I ever could. It's safe to talk about this around him."

I let out a small laugh. "Good to know."

Ursuline drew in a short breath before responding, their features growing dark. "After you mentioned Alpha Blue, I looked into what they've been up to lately. There's been a rash of monster disappearances related to them, all involving sea dwellers. I believe Frederick's using his newfound connections to round up anyone who's escaped New Atlantis. Anyone who isn't under his thumb."

Oh gods. My stomach rioted, and I swallowed hard to force the bile back down. Jason would've been under threat no matter what option I chose.

"Fucking asshole," Jaffar said from the front seat.

They shook their head, a flash of torment in their eyes. "So, several factors led to me taking the leap. I don't trust my employers to be truthful about my family's safety any longer. And the Alpha Blue line is something I cannot be complicit in. Aiding Triton in kidnapping my own kind is reprehensible. Then...there was you."

My heart fluttered, adding to the complex mix of emotions brewing inside me. "The thought of leaving you was breaking me."

They caressed my side with their tentacle, and I shuddered from the contact. They were by my side, escaping with me.

"You two are giving me a toothache," Jaffar called from the front seat.

Ursuline's lips curved in a sexy smirk, and they opened their arm. I leaned in against their side, and their tentacle curled around my waist, keeping me in place. The heat from their body, the scent of brine and currants, and the rise and fall of their chest with their steady breaths all soothed me. I soaked in the feel of them, the fact they were here by my side, when I'd believed it would be an impossibility.

Yet, the news about Alpha Blue and Triton's plans only reaffirmed the plan to leave. That stirring in my gut, the sense of unease had been on target. If I'd stayed, he would've used the connection with Alpha Blue to round up monsters, ones who'd escaped his clutches down below. The thought made me queasy.

"And Jason is going to check on my family," Ursuline murmured. "He leaves for New Atlantis tonight."

"Sofia is okay with harboring us?" I asked, even though I trusted Ursuline to have crossed their Ts.

Jaffar let out a laugh. "Sofia's spent a lifetime getting monsters out of bad situations. Same with Cillian. We all contribute in whatever way we can. And we'd do that and more for Ursuline."

They stilled—I could feel it with how I leaned against them. "I don't need more," they said. "I'm not going to put anyone in danger."

"Would it kill you to accept assistance?" Jaffar said and jerked a thumb back in our direction. "Tell them, Elrich. They've offered pro bono legal help to all of us, have been there for pickups, to transport monsters in need time and again. Yet they think they deserve to live in torment."

Guilt was a hell of a thing, and Ursuline had worn the mantle for a long while.

"I'm just grateful you're here," I said, squeezing their hand again. I basked in their warmth, in the movement of the car as we sped toward a new destination. I should be terrified. I didn't know Sofia's house or where we'd head next or even what we'd do after that, but with Ursuline at my side, I felt invincible. I'd get a job—whatever one would take me—and help as we made ends meet together. As we started a new life far away from here.

That reality sent a silent thrill through me, one I couldn't deny.

As if those once-impossible dreams were now within reach.

Except, we had a massive hurdle before we got there. The Triton family.

"He's not going to let us go quietly, is he?" I murmured, the realization crashing down.

Ursuline let out a bitter laugh. "Oh, never. Frederick Triton will chase us down to every corner of the world. He doesn't like to let possessions out of his grasp."

My stomach dropped. And yet, despite the reality that the Triton family would continue to haunt us, I wouldn't be by myself. And that fact settled something deep inside me, offered a resolve I'd been searching for my entire life. "What can we do?"

Ursuline chewed on their lower lip. "I'm still searching for some answers on that."

"You know you won't be alone," Jaffar offered from the front seat. "And we've all got connections."

"You more than others," Ursuline commented. "This one is deep in the politics of Peregrine City." They separated our hands and beckoned me in. I scooted in and pressed my body against theirs. The contact soothed me at once, and by the time they started carding their fingers through my hair, the relief rushed through me so hard I was shaky.

I should've known more about who ran Peregrine City, but my entire life had been about following orders. Trying to appease parents who'd never approved of anything I did. However, Ursuline had connections to a whole other world than what I'd grown up in, and one that seemed infinitely more interesting to me. Ursuline's fingertips strummed out a melody on my scalp, competent and relaxing at the same time. Fuck, how were they here with me?

The reality still hadn't settled in, even as we zipped through familiar streets of the city. We'd gotten far enough from the Triton manor that I didn't fear immediate pursuit, but my pulse hadn't calmed.

"What will you do about your apartment?" I asked. Surely Frederick knew where Ursuline lived. He'd send men there the moment he discovered they'd abandoned their position.

That they'd run off with me.

"Already in progress," they said. "Charles and Theo are moving my belongings over to Cillian's for the time being. Bastard has plenty of room."

"You planned for everything, didn't you?" I breathed out. At least they wouldn't have their space overturned, lose all they had.

Their lips curled into a smirk. "I never planned for you, sunshine. You were the curveball in this, the impetus of my escape."

My chest squeezed tight. As much as I'd feel guilty if anything happened to their family because of this, I couldn't be upset that they'd left. They'd been trapped for so long that they hadn't known anything else. Ursuline had sacrificed everything and deserved a chance at happiness.

And I selfishly didn't want to be apart from them either.

We drove past the bright lights of Haven Diner, and I half expected Jaffar to pull in there, even though that wasn't where Sofia lived. Still, the place was so unabashedly her from the brief interactions I'd had that I associated it with her on instinct.

"Can you drive around the manor afterward?" Ursuline asked Jaffar. "Update me on where he's dispatched his people?"

The comment sent a shiver down my spine. Here I sat, basking in safety, but Ursuline was in attack mode. Maybe this was why my parents viewed me as worthless.

Except when I was with Ursuline, I didn't feel that way.

For those incandescent moments, I was useful. Wanted. Desired.

I didn't regret leaving Arielle or the Triton family behind in the slightest. After seeing her lack of care, the slip behind the mask, I couldn't view her in the same light. Couldn't pretend she was the person I'd first thought her to be. And the more I learned about the Tritons...a shiver rolled through me.

"You okay?" Ursuline asked, tender concern reflecting in their eyes.

I swallowed hard. "Just...the escape settling in."

Their lips thinned into a hard line. "I won't let anyone harm you. We'll find a way to survive, Elrich."

The unspoken hovered in the air between us. Even if we had to run forever.

My parents wouldn't let this drop, and unless Ursuline found a loophole, a way out of their contract, neither would Frederick.

"Okay, kids," Jaffar said, pulling to a stop in front of a massive two-story house. "This is where I let you off." It wasn't a mansion like the one we'd left but still carved a unique space in the neighborhood. The deep purple clapboard siding, the black roof, the wide arched windows that glowed with a hazy, homey light created a remarkable sight, a place as unique and inviting as Haven.

"Kids, indeed," Ursuline murmured, arching their brow. I didn't know how long cecaelia lived for, but I had the feeling it was longer than a human. Yet Jaffar being a vampire meant he could've been around for far longer. The questions I had about his kind multiplied. Why was there so little information accessible on monsterkind?

Maybe for safety. We hadn't made society welcome for them when the Awakening happened. Instead, Human First had emerged and other monster hate groups, and humans had stuck to their kind while monsters tightened their communities in response.

"Thank you," Ursuline said, reaching up and squeezing his shoulder. "I'll remember this."

Jaffar nodded and cast a glance back. "You don't owe me shit, Urs. See you at the next game night."

My chest clenched at the casual camaraderie. At the deep connections they'd forged with so many people. I'd always wished for long-lasting friendships, relationships that would withstand storms, but time after time they'd been stolen from me, until I'd all but given up.

Ursuline pushed the door open and glided out, and I scooted behind them, tugging my bag along with me. The second I stepped outside and settled on the solid ground of the sidewalk, the crisp air greeted my nose, threaded with the scent of decaying leaves. The scent of change, of endings and beginnings.

"Follow me," Ursuline said as they led the way down a winding walkway leading to the front door, a deep black with a silver knocker. Once we got close enough, I noticed silver markings carved into the surface of the door.

Ursuline tracked my gaze. "Protection spells. You don't think a witch of this caliber would leave her home unguarded, do you?"

"Truthfully, I don't know much about Sofia at all," I admitted, shifting the strap on my shoulder.

The door opened, and the witch herself stood in the frame. Her crimson lips curled into a grin. Her dark waves flowed over her shoulders, and she tilted her head to the side. "You're about to find out much more."

Heat flushed through me. Had she overheard? She couldn't read minds, could she? When it came to witches and their types of magic, my knowledge was dodgy at best.

Sofia's eyes crinkled at the edges. "In case you're wondering, mind reading isn't in my wheelhouse. You just have a very expressive face. Come in, both of you."

"Thanks, Sof," Ursuline said, their voice low, throaty. They placed their hand on my lower back and guided me inside.

I wasn't sure what to expect of Sofia's house, maybe the same cinnamon scent as Haven, but their place held a lot less of the bright colors that the diner did. The entryway had black accents, but the lavender walls complemented them well, and the décor was muted rather than extravagant. Since I'd grown so used to massive displays of wealth, of foyers filled with gilded nonsense, this simplicity settled in my veins.

"I'm sure the two of you could use a cup of tea and a seat," Sofia said, striding down the main hallway. A soft glow came from the end of the hall, and the closer we got, the more I could see her kitchen, which was clearly the prized area of the house. This also had homey, rustic vibes, so different from the presentation at Haven. The spacious wooden countertops, the massive amount of matching wooden cabinets spanning the room, the large double oven and the racks and racks of carefully labeled spices and herbs created an impressive kitchen. With the myriad of wooden spoons, canisters, and jars, this room wouldn't fit in with the luxurious sterility of the places I'd grown up with, and I loved that even more.

The scents of the spices lingered here, some still drying in their hanging places on the higher cabinets, and I drew in a deep inhale, trying to calm myself.

"Here," Sofia said, pulling out seats by the kitchen island. "I'll make the two of you tea."

"My usual?" Ursuline asked. They glanced to me. "What type do you need now?"

"Herbal," I said. "I'm good with anything."

"I've got your number," Sofia said, sashaying over to her electric kettle. Her skirts swept back and forth against the floor, fluid and billowing, the opposite of her black lace-lined top that hugged her lithe form. She was impressive and gorgeous, and Gretel was a lucky woman. However, I felt just as lucky to be here with Ursuline.

I sat down on the seat, finding my footing in this unfamiliar place. Everything was unfamiliar, and now I didn't have a permanent spot to rest my head. Would Ursuline and I be on the run like this for the rest of our lives? My stomach churned at the possibility.

Ursuline sank into the seat beside me, and then their palm rested on my thigh. The touch quieted the anxiety brewing in my brain, and I let out a long, low breath. Their eyes searched mine, as if to ask if I was okay, and I didn't try to force a smile back. No, I gave a small shrug, to which they nodded.

"Here," Sofia said, sweeping back in our direction, this time with two steaming mugs. "This should help settle you."

She placed a black ceramic mug in front of me, and I drank in the fumes, all floral and delicious. I picked out lavender notes, but I wasn't sure what else was in the tea. I blew on the surface and then took the first sip. The tea scorched me slightly, but I savored the flowery sweet taste, letting it linger on my tongue.

Ursuline clutched their mug in both hands, but they didn't try to sip. No, instead they zeroed in on Sofia. "We won't bother you for long."

"You'll never be a bother, Ursuline," Sofia said. "And if you think Frederick scares me, you've sorely mistaken my abilities."

Ursuline's lips pressed tight together before they spoke. "You don't know what he's capable of. It's…Those of us from New Atlantis don't talk about it much, but there's a reason none of us go back home."

"You forget how many walk through my doors at Haven," Sofia said, her dark eyes holding an understanding there. "I'm aware of Frederick's sins. And I've got enough connections to bury him."

"It hurts to hope," they admitted, their voice a whisper.

I placed my hand overtop the one they left on my thigh and gave them a squeeze. Ursuline offered me a grateful look, and my heart traveled right out of my chest. In that moment, it belonged to them.

"Thankfully, I've got that in abundance," I offered. My folks had tried for years to stamp my dreams out of me, and sometimes I had grown bleak, but the moment my parched soul sucked down even a single drop of hope, it blossomed at once.

"He's good for you, Ursuline," Sofia commented as they brought their own mug of tea to the island and sank into a seat. "The two of you are a beautiful contrast."

And yet, part of me understood them on a deeper note than I had anyone else. For as different as we were, we'd both been trapped. We'd both craved depth—in the sea, in the people surrounding us. We both understood how the arts could transform. With Ursuline, I never thought they viewed my painting as frivolous or a stupid hobby like so many others in my life. And in turn, their musical ability thrilled me, their soft smiles they saved for few, the cleverness and tenacity they'd used to survive all these years.

"He's remarkable," they said, their gaze locking with mine. My eyes heated at the comment, at the regard they gifted me. No one ever treated me like that. Like I mattered.

I sucked a swig of my tea to try to hide my blush, but I swallowed too fast and spluttered on it.

Sofia let out a laugh, the sound tinkling and elegant. "And it seems you're good for him as well."

"When's Gretel get home?" Ursuline asked, taking a sip of their tea.

"Not for another few hours," Sofia said. "She's working later at Haven tonight. In the interim, have your tea, then crash in the guest bedroom. Find a way to relax a little. I'll continue digging into the Triton family."

I swallowed hard, my throat tight. When I'd been drawn into this mess in the first place, I'd felt so hopeless, so helpless. I didn't have a community, just a family who didn't want me and a revolving door of other individuals. This support Ursuline had from so many—a deep envy and admiration bloomed in my chest.

They placed a hand on my thigh again, their palm warm from clutching the mug. "For now, let's settle with the tea."

***

In the hours after we'd arrived, Ursuline and I hadn't done much beyond drink the tea, stare out the window, and discuss random topics, none having to do with the overwhelming life change hanging over our heads.

Whenever I looked out the window, I half expected someone to be staring back at me. While Frederick didn't have an army, I had the feeling he had more at his command than the guards who'd milled around the mansion. Right now, all I saw was the streetlamp flickering outside and the occasional passersby focused on their destination, not peering in trying to find escapees.

"Come on," Ursuline said, weaving their hand through mine. "Vigilance is good, but rest is better. Sofia set up a guest room for us."

They led the way up the steps, which made discordant creaks underneath the weight of their tentacles as they climbed the length. My heart thundered. I was in a strange house, on the run, and yet I felt safer here than I had at the Triton Manor. Safer here than in my childhood home.

Sofia's guest bedroom featured two cozy lamps that cast gentle amber beams and a massive bed with a gray comforter and fluffy pillows. The nightstand was a rustic dark brown, same as the bookshelves, which were filled with myriad of leatherbound tomes. The art on the walls featured gorgeous blooms in different arrays and patterns, the artist employing meticulous brushwork. I wandered closer to one of the frames and noticed that in the flowers themselves, there seemed to be markings like the ones on the door.

"Witch paintings aren't just pretty to look at," Ursuline said as they sank onto the mattress. "Sofia's collection is a treasury of spells too."

I let out a low whistle. "How come I never knew about this?"

"Your kind doesn't like learning about monsters," Ursuline said. "They prefer us to stay in our spaces, in our own communities."

Guilt throbbed through me. They weren't wrong. My parents were perfect examples of the ignorance humans employed, acting as if they were the only species that mattered. "We're clearly missing out."

"Come here," they said, leaning back in the bed and patting the spot next to them. Heat flooded through me at the sight of them in the bed, along with a bone-deep ache. Every stolen moment with them, every time we'd fucked, all I'd wanted to do was curl up by their side afterward. To spend the night with them, in their arms.

We could never have done that while keeping things secret in Triton's manor.

Yet here, we were...free.

A jittery rush of adrenaline shot through me, and I almost tripped over myself on the way to them. I toed out of my shoes and slipped onto the bed. A gravity hummed in the air, as if Ursuline understood the depth and meaning behind this moment as well. As if they'd been craving the same this whole time.

I didn't even bother stripping out of my clothes. The exhaustion crept in like a misty fog, rolling in with enough intensity to smother. I settled next to Ursuline, and they didn't hesitate. They slid their arm around my shoulders and drew me in. I'd checked my cage, which still fit snugly around my cock, and Ursuline's hand wandered and gave me a light squeeze there. The possessiveness in the motion sent a hot spike of lust through me, even though exhaustion won out.

My cheek pressed against their chest, and I let out a shuddery sigh. Their scent of brine and currants wrapped around me, a comfort that I succumbed to, their natural warmth almost as intense as the cups of tea we'd had earlier.

"Did Sofia spike our tea?" I asked, my brows drawing together.

"Define spike," Ursuline responded, a laugh exploding from them with a rumble in their chest I could feel. "She wouldn't give you any drugs without consent, sunshine. But she chose an herbal for you that's known to soothe."

I cuddled into their side a little more, soaking in every second of this. "Can we sleep like this?"

"What, upright?" they teased, slumped against the backboard of the bed.

"No, together," I murmured, my heart thumping hard.

"Of course," Ursuline said, their tone hushed. "It's something I didn't think we'd ever get."

I swallowed hard, and tears stung my eyes. I was so incandescently happy, but this sense of doom filtered in like blackened fog. As if this was a temporary gift before our bliss was stolen away. As if we'd dared the fates too much.

And I'd learned far more than I could bear over the past few weeks. Enough that I'd run from Triton's manor instead of following the trajectory laid out for me.

Enough that Ursuline had done the same.

However, it was still to be seen whether or not rattling the snake's den would prove our undoing.

Chapter 25

I blinked my eyes open, darkness surrounding me. Warmth did as well, a foreign sensation. Those muscular arms wrapped around me, and those tentacles rested across and between my thighs. I'd never experienced this sort of bliss before, the sense of calm, of quiet without the ache of loneliness. In this moment, a completeness drifted over me, and I didn't want it to end.

"Awake?" Ursuline's voice was husky and low. I twitched in surprise, and a laugh rumbled through their chest. "I've been drifting in and out, but I'm...vigilant."

"Worried, you mean," I said, pushing up to sit so I could see them better. Their tentacles tangled with my legs, the contact enough right now. Ursuline propped themself up on their elbow, and their serious gaze confirmed my concern. "Are we safe here?"

"Sofia's competent," they said and then let out a sigh. "But I don't believe we're truly safe anywhere. We both breached contracts—yours a social promise, mine in writing. And Frederick's type of revenge..." They shuddered.

"Explain it to me," I asked, my fists tightening on the sheets. Ursuline's lips flattened, and I had the feeling they would try to spare me. "Please don't leave me in the dark. I've lived there long enough."

Ursuline pushed up to sitting as well, and they sank against the headboard. Tension simmered in the air between us. "There's a reason I took the contract on the surface. My middle sibling, Jaris. They'd caught Frederick's attention back then. They were bright, gorgeous, snagged everyone's eye, but his was dangerous. However, they'd received a job at the castle, and we needed the money. I wasn't comfortable with them going, but Mom and Dad supported their choice—we were barely able to scrape for food."

They paused for a moment, and I clutched the sheets a little tighter. My stomach churned with unease at where this story might be going.

"He...forced himself on them," Ursuline choked out, venom flashing in their eyes. "After that, Jaris left their employment at the castle. All that brightness, that beauty, had been smothered out, leaving them like a ghost wading through the house. Mom and Dad didn't know what to do. And Frederick wasn't satisfied with breaking them once, no, he showed up on our doorstep, prepared to drag them back to the castle. So I offered a trade—my sibling's safety, my family's well-being in exchange for servitude."

"He never..." Bile rose in my throat, and a cold sweat broke over me.

Ursuline shook their head. "Physical blows during his tantrums early on, but once I formed my safety nets here in Peregrine City, he knew better than to lay a hand on me. Triton had his sights set on others. I was forbidden to return home, but my family has maintained steady communications with the surface ever since to ensure their safety, that the Tritons have been upholding their end of the bargain."

I swallowed hard. Fuck. The horrors their family had been through, what their sibling had experienced... Frederick had always made me uneasy, a darkness to him that I hadn't been comfortable with, but I never could've imagined the lows he'd gone to. And his family all surrounded him and supported him. Did they know the terrible things he'd done?

"Except now I'm wondering whether he did hold up his end of the bargain," Ursuline said through gritted teeth. "If he hasn't..." They didn't complete the sentence, just cast their gaze downward.

I reached over and placed my hand over theirs, squeezing tight. "You did everything you could for them. No one can take that away from you."

Their dark eyes glittered like shattered shards, but they looked up at me. The haunted expression punched me square in the chest. I couldn't imagine the pain they'd endured, the agony of being apart from their family, knowing the horror their sibling had suffered. Having to work for the monster who'd broken them.

"You're the strongest person I know," I murmured, the truth slipping out of me. "But you've got to be carrying the heaviest weight too."

They swallowed hard, the sound clicking in the air. "You're the first who's made it feel less heavy."

My brows drew together. "Me? I haven't done anything." Instead, they'd constantly been doing things for me—pulling me out of bad situations, offering company and compassion when I needed those the most.

They leaned in and brushed a kiss to my cheek. A shiver raced through me.

"You don't see how bright you shine," they said. "Your acceptance, your unerring kindness. The creativity that explodes from you. There's a purity to you that's almost painful, a beauty I didn't think still existed in this ugly world."

My eyes heated, and a tear slipped out. No one had ever made me feel this valuable, made me see myself differently. Only Ursuline.

"Is that why...sunshine?" I asked. The nickname filled me with warmth every time they used it.

"Even back then, I knew I wanted to be around you," they said. "I just didn't realize how much you'd transform my life."

"Same," I murmured, my cheeks flushing.

A headlight passed by the window, causing the beam to filter through the blinds into the room. I wrinkled my nose. Who was driving around at this hour?

When I glanced back to Ursuline, they were tuned in on the window.

"Is something wrong?" I asked.

They squeezed my hand and then pushed up from the bed to glide over to the window. They peered through the blinds, the silence spreading between us with a percolating tension. I was well aware they hadn't said Sofia's was safe. We were tucked away with somewhere to sleep and amongst people who wouldn't hurt us, but...

The beam filtered through the blinds again, and Ursuline let out a low curse.

"There's a car circling the street. Same one, and guaranteed it's about to make another loop." Ursuline slid back and forth, the closest thing to a pace I'd seen from them. Their shoulders were tense, their chin lifted as if prepared for battle.

"Not a late Drivr ride looking for their pickup?" I said, even though the idea sounded ridiculous to my own ears.

Ursuline let out a hiss of a sigh. "I should've known this would be too visible a place. As much as the house itself is protected, we need somewhere more formidable to disappear for a while."

"I'm assuming you know a spot?" I asked, pushing up from the bed. Jitters rushed through me, waking me up better than if I'd chugged caffeine. How Ursuline remained calm now while I prepared to hide under the bed mystified me, but I was grateful for their endless well of competence.

"The Spires," they said. "It was the next stop on our tour, just a day or two early." Their brow furrowed. "I should've known Frederick wouldn't wait around."

I placed a hand on their arm. "The fact we escaped the manor itself is nothing short of a miracle. We'll do what we can to keep moving forward."

"Our escape was only because they underestimated you," Ursuline said. "Grab your things." They jerked their chin in the direction of my duffle, which still lay on the floor. "I'll nab my bag."

"You brought a bag here?" I asked. I didn't remember them toting one with them when they picked me up.

"Dropped it off this morning," they said with a half smile. "I've had getaway plans in place for a long, long while."

I swallowed hard, the reality of who they worked for crashing in. "I understand why." I pushed up from the bed and slipped on the pants and shirt I'd been wearing, then popped on socks and shoes. Next, I slung my bag over my shoulder, a sense of unease percolating inside me. I'd figured we'd at least have until morning, but apparently Ursuline had been telling the truth about Frederick's relentlessness.

The headlights shone through the blinds again, and I peeked out. Same car as before. My chest sank. "How will we get out? They'll just follow us wherever we go."

Ursuline let out a low hum as they buttoned up a tunic. "You're not wrong. I'll have to discuss with Sofia and Gretel."

Even something as simple as that—acknowledgement of my suggestions, my concerns—reaffirmed they were the person for me. I'd never met anyone like Ursuline in my life, and if anyone was worth a little risk, they were. "We'd better move fast."

Already, the need to run itched at my legs, and I couldn't imagine sitting back while Triton's guards circled around us. These were guards I'd tried to get to know during my stint there, even though, unlike the staff, they'd remained aloof and distant.

For good reason, I supposed.

I followed Ursuline out of the room, and we stepped into the midnight corridor, the shadows crawling at this time of night. The air prickled, a cool quality to it, and I suppressed a shiver. Ursuline walked right up to a closed door and knocked. Rustling sounded from inside, and a second later, it creaked open. Sofia wore a pale-purple negligee that didn't leave a lot to the imagination. The woman was stunning, all sinuous curves and a lethal grace. Even the way she leaned against the doorframe was effortlessly sensual.

"They're here already?" Sofia asked, her sharp voice signifying that she was alert.

"Fuck," Gretel's muffled voice came from inside. Then she slipped her arms around Sofia's waist and rested her chin on her wife's shoulder. Unlike Sofia, she wore a tank top and boxer shorts. "He moves fast."

"You're not kidding," Ursuline murmured. "How do we want to make this getaway? He's got a guy circling the neighborhood."

"Asshole," Gretel cursed, her eyes flashing.

"Elrich pointed out that hopping in the car is exactly what they want," Ursuline said. "It'll tip them off to where we're heading next too."

Sofia nodded. "That's why we'll act like you're in the car—meanwhile, you'll be heading to the light rail."

"To Cillian's," Ursuline confirmed, and my pulse fluttered with nerves. I'd only ever heard of the Spires, as my parents refused to go to a demon-owned casino. They gambled at Spectacle instead. Yet the reputation of the Spires was spoken of in whispers throughout the city. And the owner happened to be one of Ursuline's closest friends.

Gretel slipped back into the room, and when she stepped up again, she donned all black. "I'll drive." She pressed a kiss to her wife's cheek. "You hold down the house."

Sofia sighed and patted the circlet on Gretel's wrist. "Be safe. Keep me updated."

"Always, love," Gretel said before striding past her and down the hall. She didn't bother glancing back to us. "Move quickly. We'll act like we're loading you into the back seat, and then you'll slip out the other side. The alley behind the house stretches down to one of the main streets. Stick to the shadows until you get to the light rail station."

Goose bumps prickled along my exposed skin as we hurried down the stairs and up to the foyer. I'd gone from ambling through my days in a watercolor state to...this. The shadows were sharp, the urgency sharper. The front door loomed ominously, the knowledge of what awaited us heavy in the air.

The second we stepped out into the front yard, we'd be exposed. What if they weren't simply tailing us? What if they had orders to take us at gunpoint? Or worse, eliminate us on sight? Bile rose in my throat, and sweat burst on my palms. Ursuline placed a hand on my shoulder and squeezed, the slight touch bolstering me.

Then Gretel opened the door.

The night held an aching sort of quiet, loaded with tension. Apart from the distant sounds of traffic from the city, this street lay silent, as if a spell had been cast over the place. The car from before wasn't prowling down the asphalt, but it'd only be a matter of time. And we needed them to see us get into the car—to make sure they followed.

My gut churned. "Are you sure you're okay with this?" I asked Gretel. I hated the idea of putting her in danger.

She let out a sharp laugh. "I was born a hunter. I was in more dangerous situations than this at the ripe age of five. Now, let's go." Well, that explained all the lethality that surrounded Gretel. I'd never encountered a hunter myself, but I knew of them, given they often ran in Human First circles. Families who swore to eradicate monsterkind, to hunt them down and destroy. Clearly, she'd left that life behind.

I cast another glance to the end of the street, but no cars emerged. My heart thudded in double time. We began to walk to the black sedan parked behind Sofia's car in the driveway. The quiet crawled under my skin, the tension unbearable. Everything looked inky black. How was I supposed to fumble my way unnoticed in all that mess? How was I supposed to find a clear path without tripping over a root or falling on my face? Ursuline glided beside me, emanating a gunpowder calm—steady but on the precipice of action.

"I'll give the signal to climb in," Gretel said. "Watch through the windows."

My palms had turned into a sweaty mess, and my limbs were shaky with adrenaline. Gretel hopped into the driver's seat, and the car engine thrummed to life. Ursuline cracked the passenger's side door open at the ready. Where would we go? What if the driver caught sight of us? The questions multiplied with each passing second, threatening to bury me under the load.

The first flash of a headlight sliced through the surrounding night.

Gretel gave a thumbs-up.

Go time.

"Come on," Ursuline said. "Follow my lead. I won't let you fall behind."

I cast a single glance back. The same car that had been circling the past fifteen to thirty minutes started the next round, moving at a crawl. A riotous shiver ran down my spine. The darkness from the tinted windows glared back at me, as if they could see right through our flimsy attempt.

As if they'd keep chasing us no matter what.

Ursuline hopped into the car, and I snapped back into motion.

I launched myself into the car, slamming the door shut behind me.

"Hurry," Gretel hissed.

Ursuline cracked the opposite door open, and already, they slid out that door, hunched over and out of sight.

I scooted along the back seat, my legs trembling as I tried to ignore the headlights flooding the area from the oncoming car. If we didn't get out in time, it'd spot us. This escape attempt would be over before it began.

I almost tumbled headfirst out of the car, but I managed to hit the ground. Then I turned around and eased the door closed. Ursuline grabbed my arm and yanked me forward. A bush ahead was the closest thing to hide behind, and we crouched as we slipped over to the scraggly branches.

Gretel didn't wait. She backed out of the driveway, even with the oncoming car approaching.

I peered from between the branches of the bush, which pricked at my skin. The car slowed, obviously waiting for her to go.

Like I'd expected, Frederick's men would trail her.

"Come on," Ursuline murmured, tugging at my arm. "No waiting to watch."

They slipped around the side of the building to the alley that Sofia had mentioned. Back here smelled like rotting trash from the dumpsters and mildewing leaves, but the alley was narrow, and the close-together houses loomed, keeping us out of sight from the main street. Exactly the cover we needed right now. I tried to listen for the sound of tires, for any hint that Gretel was okay, but all I could hear was the increased *thump, thump, thump* of my heart.

Ursuline prowled ahead of me, moving with a purpose that helped center me. I might not know these streets, but they did, and we weren't rushing into the abyss with no plan. Instead, we had a place to go and people in our corner. Ursuline might think we'd never stop being chased by Triton, but I had hope.

We just had to make it to the Spires.

The leaves crunched under my feet as I followed Ursuline, who somehow slunk quietly, even with their mess of tentacles. Every time we passed a sliver between houses that gave a glimpse of the main road, a shiver coursed through me, the feeling of being exposed hanging over me like an errant cloud.

I opened my mouth, questions wanting to spill from my lips, but then I shut it again.

The wind whistling through the alley held the crisp coolness of night and carried the scents of the city with it—metal and asphalt, along with an undefinable sweetness I'd never been able to place. I drank it down for courage, choked on it as I strode into the unknown.

For as long as I'd daydreamed of running off on my own, the reality was terrifying.

The end of the alleyway loomed up ahead, getting larger by the moment, and a fresh, cold sweat broke out on my temple. At least back here we weren't visible to many, but once we reached the main streets, we'd be on clear display. Anyone driving by could spot us.

"How far is the light rail?" I asked.

"Five-minute walk," Ursuline responded, keeping their tone low. "Don't stray from me."

I wouldn't. Not for a fucking second. While this situation terrified me, what scared me worse was being separated from them.

The closer we got to the main road, the more adrenaline pumped through my system. While I might recognize the car that Gretel hopefully led on a merry chase, how many others prowled out there looking for us? At the moment, every car held an enemy inside. No one could be trusted.

We reached the end, and the sounds of the street flooded over me, the thrum of traffic louder here. Even this late at night, several cars zipped down the street, their headlights slicing through the dark. My heart thrummed. Ursuline peered out and looked both ways. Then they jerked their head to the left and slipped out onto the sidewalk.

Right. I sucked in a breath and stepped out too.

My skin prickled at once, with an awareness that hadn't been there when I'd walked through the city before. Granted, I'd never been hunted down by an ex-future-father-in-law.

"Keep your eyes peeled for any cars slowing down," Ursuline said as they glided forward. "If they're Triton's men and get close enough, they could drag you into the car."

I shivered and scrubbed at my arm. The bag over my shoulder weighed heavily at my side, thumping against my thigh as we strode along. A few cars whizzed by, their headlights near blinding, but I didn't dare pause to scrutinize them too heavily. My pulse increased with each one that passed. They were moving fast enough and zipping by, not seeming to pay attention to Ursuline and me.

"How far are we?" I asked.

They figured out what I asked at once. "The station's a few blocks away. From there, we're a few stops from Casino Alley."

I swallowed hard. I should be able to process how far that was, but right now I summoned every ounce of mettle just to put one foot in front of the other. We reached a light, and I jammed my hands into my pockets to stop fidgeting. The cars whirred past us, none of them giving a moment's pause, but I scanned them regardless, every shadowy face in the driver's seat a potential threat.

The pedestrian light blinked on, and we set off like a gunshot. I kept pace with Ursuline and tried to suck in deep breaths to calm my system. The effort didn't work. The cars that whizzed by opposite us set my nerves on edge, the space around us far too open. I'd rather slink through the shadows to get there, but we had to reach the station and fast.

I hoped Gretel was okay.

"One more block, sunshine," Ursuline said, their reassurance coming at the perfect time. Renewed urgency flooded through me, and we strode to the right, past a set of storefronts with their neons lit and a steady stream of customers flowing up and down the sidewalk, even at this time of night. Here, we could mingle with pedestrians a bit better. Here, we'd stand a chance at hiding from whoever Frederick had sent to prowl the streets. I had no idea what power was at his command, but he had an in with Alpha Blue, and that meant he was downright dangerous.

At the end of the block, I spotted the sign for the subway, the arrow pointing down where steps would lead us to salvation. We just had to get there.

A sedan began to slow down nearby, coasting along the edge of the road, as if they planned on trying to park. Ursuline's shoulders tightened, and they quickened their pace.

A few people jostled around me, obscuring the car from view for a moment, and my heart rate shot up. I surged forward, trying to move as fast as possible without drawing attention.

When I glanced back again, the car was parked, and the doors cracked open. The men who emerged were dressed all in black, wearing typical bodyguard attire. Fuck. Cold rushed through me.

"Get to the station," Ursuline said. "Run."

They surged ahead, their tentacles whipping around them in their mad dash. I didn't hesitate. I lunged forward. My feet thumped against the pavement, the force resonating all the way up my shins.

The sign for the subway awaited up ahead, close and too far at the same time. Fuck. Fuck. Fuck.

Sweat trickled down my back as I raced forward, ignoring the shouts around me as I shoved past people who didn't dodge out of the way fast enough. We were drawing attention to ourselves at this point, but if we didn't get to the station quick, we never would.

If I tuned out the honks from the street, the shouts from passersby, the thrum of the city, I could hear the thump of quickened footsteps, just like ours. Ice rushed through me.

The steps to the subway loomed in front of me, a dark descent.

I plunged down them.

Ursuline burst ahead the slightest bit, but they kept glancing back, to meet my gaze, to make sure I was still there. The fact they watched out for me, even now, made my chest squeeze tight.

Ursuline flung the door open, and I jumped through before it shut behind me. Down here, the sounds echoed, especially the rattling of the subway cars. How often did the subway come? I should be embarrassed I'd never taken it before, but when we traveled around the city, it was always by car or personal driver.

Ursuline slowed as we closed in on the platform, and I followed suit. They reached out and offered a hand, which I took, even though my palm was slick with sweat. I cast a glance back to the door. No one had plunged through it yet, but the tension hummed in the air, the understanding that at any moment Frederick's men could be upon us.

From the end of the tunnel, the headlights flashed our way from the subway car, and my pulse sped.

Almost there.

It zipped forward in a cacophony of clanks and squeals, and then it came to a halt right in front of us.

The subway doors slid open.

"This way," Ursuline said, tugging me onto the subway car with them. We didn't wait by the entrance—no, we walked another car down and then stood in the center, grabbing onto the pole. I squinted as I tried to catch sight of the platform we'd just exited.

Two men dressed in black emerged at the base of the stairs.

Oh, fuck.

The subway's doors clicked shut, and it surged forward. The breath sagged out of me, and I watched through the windows as they raced in our direction. However, we'd already started chugging away.

"Well, that was lucky," Ursuline murmured, their shoulders rising and falling from the exertion. "Saved by the subway."

A hysterical laugh bubbled out of me, and their eyes crinkled with a soft smile.

We zipped into the darkness of the tunnel, and I leaned against the pole, clutching it tight. The air-conditioning in the car caused the sweat on my skin to dry with a tacky sort of feeling.

"And how many stops away?" I asked.

"Three," Ursuline said, not taking their eyes away from the doors. "We'll remain vigilant."

I didn't know how much more vigilance my heart could take.

The subway zipped forward at top speed, and while a few people sat in the seats lining the car, it was far emptier than during the day.

"You sure you don't miss the quiet?" I asked, trying for a joke. Still, a part of me wondered if they regretted their choice to come along with me.

"That place was louder than you realized," they responded, the sobering look in their eyes conveying everything I needed to know. That they'd been haunted there for years, so much so that even being hunted like this could be worth it for a taste of freedom. "Besides," they said, their gaze skimming up and down my body. "Once we settle at the Spires, I'm looking forward to a different sort of loud."

Their tentacle curled around my leg, creeping up my thigh, and heat rushed through me. In our rush from the Triton Manor, arriving at Sofia's, and this escape, I'd almost forgotten I was still caged for Ursuline. Still unable to come, and after this long without being able to masturbate, my balls positively ached.

I licked my lips and looked up at them. The feral expression on their features had my heart fluttering, my pulse pounding in a far better way. I'd been too exhausted when we'd arrived at Sofia's, but if we made it to the Spires...

We had to accomplish that first, though.

The subway screeched to a halt. I swayed with the motion, and my body tensed as I watched who hopped on. Just an older man who used a cane and a few minotaurs who lumbered on board.

Then the doors shut, and the subway took off again. I exhaled, not realizing I'd been holding my breath the entire time.

"I'll protect you," Ursuline said, their voice the same level of calm they'd been throughout. I'd wondered how they could remain that way through all this chaos, but after hearing what they'd gone through, I could understand a little more. They'd been dragged through fire and survived.

"When can I do something for you?" I asked, more of a pout in my voice than I wanted.

Ursuline arched a brow, and a wicked grin split their lips. My cheeks flushed at the implication from the gesture alone, and their tentacle brushed against the inside of my thigh again. Fuck.

The subway stopped again for a moment, but the doors didn't open. A second later, we were off.

The next stop was ours. My heart accelerated a little faster. I wasn't sure how far a walk the Spires was from the station, but at least we'd thrown off Triton's men for the moment. Gretel would hopefully lead them on a chase through the city, far away from our direction.

"You ready?" Ursuline asked. Their reassurances, their check-ins meant the world to me right now, because I held on by a thread.

I bobbed my head and tugged the strap of my bag, the weight dragging down my shoulder. Insane to think the contents of my life were packed into such a small thing right now. I chewed on my lower lip, my legs humming with the need to move, even though I needed to rest badly too.

The subway began to slow.

Ursuline made the first strides toward the door, and I set into motion as well. My veins lit on fire again, my skin feeling exposed as we waited to reach the stop. No one paid us any mind, but it felt like they watched us regardless. The crawling sensation would be rough to shed.

The subway came to a firm stop, and the doors slid open.

Ursuline and I lunged through the exit.

When we stepped out, Casino Alley's flashing neons and dark alleys created a barrage of noise and chaos. The subway zipped off behind us, and the air *whooshed* around us in its wake. Dry leaves skittered by, circling around my feet.

The Spires loomed over all of it, a dark, craggy silhouette against the skyline.

To many it might be ominous, but to us? It spelled salvation.

Ursuline extended their hand, and I rested mine in it. The squeeze of our palms bolstered me like nothing else.

"Let me introduce you to the 'Beast' of the underworld," Ursuline said, flashing me a wicked grin. "If we'll be safe anywhere, it's here."

Together, we set off to safety.

Chapter 26

Going up in a private elevator was a new experience, and the older woman who escorted us seemed formidable at first, her silver hair in a tight bun, but then she cracked a joke or two with Ursuline. We'd been shown to a room and given the time and space to settle in and catch some rest. Amelia, the older woman, had told us what time breakfast was in the morning and then let us be.

We'd promptly passed out.

When I woke up in the foreign bed, my muscles were screaming. The only solace was the fact that Ursuline was wrapped around me like they'd been when we were in Sofia's house. If I could sleep like this with them every night, I wouldn't want for anything more. Something as simple as their companionship filled in the cracks in my psyche like nothing ever had. Not even art. The need for touch had been an active *thump, thump, thump* in the background of my entire life.

For a while, I lay there, staring at the ceiling.

Had Gretel made it safely? What was Frederick doing now that we'd given him the slip? How were my parents reacting to their business deal falling through?

The carousel of thoughts was dizzying, and my fingers itched with the longing to paint, to sketch, to get these messy emotions out on paper or canvas in whatever way possible.

Ursuline's arms clutched me tight, a solidness I clung to. The feel of us touching skin to skin like this sent a shiver down my spine. This sort of comfort had always been so out of reach for me, and despite the danger we were in, I couldn't help but bask in this moment. Their body was so intensely warm, and their tentacles encircled my legs, the extra contact making my skin sensitized. My trapped cock throbbed in the cage, and I let out a low groan. My balls ached at this point, so heavy, and we hadn't even discussed when I'd be set free.

Truth be told, I'd had more important things on my mind.

However, now that I was lying in bed with them, with no immediate plan, I couldn't help but fantasize about their tentacles spearing into me. I longed for the moment they released me from the cage and I could unload everything that was pent up now.

Ursuline shifted, a soft murmur coming from them, and one of their tentacles roamed a bit higher up my leg. My whole body flushed at the attention, and I chewed on my lower lip to suppress a moan. I hadn't even looked around the room yet or examined my surroundings, but something about the sinful way they stroked higher and higher up my thigh had me reeling. Pre-cum gushed from my cock, trapped in the tiny metal cage.

Their tentacle slid against my taint, and I whimpered. The sensation felt so strong, so intense, I almost grew lightheaded.

"Missed hearing that sound," Ursuline murmured, clearly awake. However, their arms remained around me, just the way I wanted it. "You've been such a good boy for me, Elrich. I'll make sure to reward you tonight."

My mouth went dry. By reward, did they mean...?

Ursuline nipped at my ear, and I didn't need to turn around to sense the wicked smile on their lips. Before I could ask, they stroked against my taint again, and I trembled. The pleasure that shot through me was wild, the area so much more sensitive after the time I'd spent with my cock caged up. I swallowed hard, trying to keep from being too loud as they continued to tease me there.

"You're going to look so pretty coming undone on my mating tentacles tonight," they said, their breath a hot puff against my ear. "And since you've been so good for me, I'll let you sink your cock into my hole to release."

That answered my question. Heat roared through me, and I detonated.

"Maybe I'll even fuck you into it," they teased. "Just control your thrusts with mine."

My jaw dropped, and I salivated with want. The imagery that sprang forward in my brain had me burning up inside, and the neediness that had been dormant for a while now returned with more force than before.

Ursuline pressed their lips against my neck, then they sank their teeth into the tender spot between my neck and shoulder, and a soft moan escaped me.

"I want that so badly," I confessed. "Just to be surrounded by you."

Three little words rested on my tongue, ones that had become clearer and clearer through every moment we'd been together. Maybe tonight I'd be brave enough to confess what their sacrifice meant to me. The fact they'd chosen to come along...my heart thumped harder. Maybe they felt the same way.

The tender look in their eyes, how they protected my body and my heart...I'd never experienced care like that, and I imagined that was what love felt like. The true kind. The sort I'd always dreamed of but wasn't sure I'd ever find.

"I'll give you everything, sunshine," they said, a gravity to their words that sent a sharp shard of longing through me. Ursuline wasn't just steady and steadfast in a way I craved, so different from my daydreams and wandering mind. No, they were a warrior, a survivor. They'd clawed out of hell in New Atlantis and survived living with their sibling's aggressor for years.

They'd had to remain hard and stalwart against the cruelty of the world for so long.

My heart fluttered as understanding settled inside me.

They called me sunshine.

Maybe I did have my place in this relationship, to coax the hope back out of hiding for them. To offer a softness that had never been bled out of me, no matter how much my parents wished it.

"I want you to have all of me too," I admitted, my voice hushed in the awe of the realization. After so many years of feeling worthless, of viewing every attribute of mine as a flaw, they brought me back to life.

"I didn't think I could have that," Ursuline said, their voice hoarse. The quiet descended between us, and they withdrew their teasing tentacle. "I'm still not sure if I can."

Anger flared within me that Frederick had broken them down this badly. I circled around to face them and rested my hand on their hip. "Right here and now, you do," I said, jutting my chin forward. "For as long as we can make it. And that's all that matters. Every moment we can get."

Ursuline's throat bobbed with their swallow, and they stared up, avoiding my gaze. Their eyes were glossy, and my heart squeezed tight.

"He may have ruined a lot, but he doesn't own you," I reasserted. "No matter what the contract says."

"If I could find a way to keep my family safe and be free," they said. "Fuck, if they even are safe. My entire world is flipped upside down. And I can't rest knowing Frederick will try to sink his claws into you too. He can't have you. He can't. I need to stop him—no matter what," they growled.

I ran my fingertips along their chin, my chest tight. "He can't have you either. Do it for both of us. Do it for your family. Do it for everything he's done to the monsters in New Atlantis."

Because if anyone could think of a clever way out of this, Ursuline could.

My stomach rumbled, and a slight grin stretched their lips. "Well, while I'm searching for a path out of this mess, why don't we start with breakfast?"

"I wouldn't be sad," I said, my heart thumping hard. "I wouldn't mind exploring the place too."

"Just stay out of the West Wing," Ursuline said. "Cillian prefers his privacy, and you'd probably get too much of an eyeful of him and Beau."

"Beau?" I asked as I slipped out of the bed. At once, I began the search for clothes in my bag and then changed into loose gray pants and a linen shirt.

"Cillian's partner," Ursuline said, a note of warmth in their tone. "He found him about a year ago, and I've never seen him happier."

When I glanced back to them, the longing in their gaze hit me full force. Did they want that too? As badly as I did?

Ursuline tossed on a tunic, wove a comb through their hair, and then brought toiletries to the bathroom. We both made quick work of cleaning up for the day, and completing this mundane task side by side sent a silent thrill through me. Who knew this was what I'd been searching for my entire life?

Ursuline stepped out first, and I was happy to follow. This place was one of their safe havens, though I'd come to realize that even when they weren't comfortable, they commanded a room regardless. That sort of surety and bravery drew me in every time.

"They'll have food in the dining hall around now," Ursuline said. "I texted Amelia that we were up, and they aren't flooded with guests here at the moment."

"This isn't a hotel, though," I said, my brows drawing together in confusion.

"No, but monsters who need help often take some time up here getting back on their feet. He's made this place a sanctuary, a refuge."

I blinked, surprise flooding through me. Far too often, I was reminded of the ignorance I'd grown up around. The way the society that raised me discarded monsterkind, how they churned out lie after lie to keep us separate from them.

"That's pretty amazing," I said, taking in the midnight tones of the hallway. Even though it had to be daytime, there was a quiet, subterranean feel here, as if we strode through a cave. I could never live somewhere like this—at least not long term. I needed people, the sunlight, the ocean breeze to survive.

Voices came from farther down the hall where an open doorway beckoned. The scent of sweet syrup wafted our way, and my stomach rumbled again. Ursuline's lips twitched in amusement, and they reached out to offer a hand. I laced my fingers in theirs, the gesture socking me right in the chest. We were heading to meet their friends, and they weren't trying to hide the connection between us.

When we stepped into view, I paused at the entrance. The room was huge, a full-on dining hall filled with plenty of long tables. A chandelier dangled overhead, glittering and casting shards of light across the floor, and the place felt even more massive given that only two of the tables had occupants.

"You're up," Amelia said, rising from where she sat next to a hulking red demon in a suit at the head of the table. The man to his right was slender and gorgeous, with golden curls and expressive eyes, and he appeared human, though I was fast learning to never assume. Two other men sat at the other table, one long and gangly, and the other burly and built, and they chatted with someone very familiar.

"Sofia?" I said, thrilled to see her intact.

She glanced to us at once and gifted us with a huge smile, her dark eyes crinkling at the edges. Something inside me relaxed at once. If Gretel had run into trouble, she wouldn't be this calm or measured.

"Gretel's asleep," she said with a wink. "Spent the night driving, but I figured I'd check in on you this morning. I took my precautions."

"Come, eat," the lanky guy said. "Theo made way too much, as if we expected a horde of people."

"Jaffar was planning on swinging by too," the red demon said. His obsidian horns, broad shoulders, and regal features made him stand out. "He's got a naga he picked up from a bad situation."

"You softie, you," the blond with the curls teased.

"This is Cillian and Beau." Ursuline murmured the introductions. "And Charles and Theo are at the other table. Let's go sit."

With their hand on my back bolstering me, I went over to the open spots at Cillian and Beau's table. We both took our seats, and Amelia dropped empty plates in front of us, along with silverware. The two tables held a veritable feast. There was fruit of every shape and color—some I didn't recognize—toast, eggs, different types of cooked meat, including bacon, and a bread pudding sort of dish.

I didn't wait, snagging a few pieces of fruit for my plate, along with the bread pudding.

"The sweet tooth strikes again," Ursuline murmured, an affectionate grin on their lips. One of their tentacles caressed my leg beneath the table, the touch offering the comfort I needed.

"Where did you come from?" Cillian asked, his voice booming through the place as his golden gaze zeroed in on me.

I paused, a piece of cantaloupe lifted to my lips. Nerves rushed through me. Was this where he interrogated me?

Beau elbowed his partner in the side. "Forgive my rude boyfriend. He's never learned manners during his many years in this dimension."

I bit back a snort. The relaxed exchange took Cillian's intimidating factor down a notch or two. The way they bantered with each other amplified my longing for the same sort of familiar relationship, one filled with a natural ease like that. Except then Cillian returned his gaze to me. Fuck, I hadn't responded. "Also on the run from the Triton family," I commented, then paused. Did I mention I was with Ursuline? Were we together now?

Before, when I was engaged to Arielle, I was too afraid to claim anything, but now a relationship with them was all I wanted.

Ursuline's tentacle curled around my thigh and squeezed. "He's mine."

The words sent a thrill through me, a shot of adrenaline and lust. My balls ached, and my trapped cock served as a reminder of exactly what they said. The confident, fearless way they staked their claim was everything I could've dreamed of, and they'd done so in front of their friends. When I met their eyes, their gaze blazed—with heat, with passion—and I lit up inside.

"Never thought I'd see the day," Cillian said, a wan grin on his lips, his fangs protruding.

Ursuline arched a brow. "The same could be said of you."

"No one is surprised I'm in a relationship," Charles proclaimed. "Probably because I didn't have the Broody Trauma Starter Pack the rest of you lot got."

Beau let out a laugh at that, and I couldn't help my smile. I didn't miss the fact that Ursuline's was due to their upbringing, though. How many other monsters suffered from the way those in power in our society treated them? I swallowed hard, the realization settling into the core of me.

"Eat," Amelia said to me. "I'll make sure my boss stops interrogating you."

I offered a genuine smile and took a bite of the bread pudding. It was caramelly and buttery and perfect, and I tried to stifle a groan, my lashes fluttering. Ursuline's tentacle squeezed my thigh. They leaned in close enough that their lips brushed my ear, and I shivered.

"That groan was filthy," Ursuline whispered. "Save it for later."

Heat roared through me, and I shifted in my seat. Oh damn. After waiting this long, all of a sudden my patience had vanished and I needed them now. I wanted them taking me apart piece by piece, and for whatever time we could claim, I just wanted to be reminded that I belonged to them.

"Are you going to join us for the next game night?" Beau asked, his gaze fixed on me.

I blinked. Ursuline had mentioned them in the past, but I hadn't believed that invitation would ever extend to me. "If we're around. I'm not sure what the plan is with Frederick sending guards to scour the city for us."

"I've reached out to my contacts for any dirt on Frederick," Cillian said.

"I may have an avenue myself if I can get to my files," Ursuline murmured. "Though it's a long shot. And chances are, he's already set my apartment on fire and burned anything that remained."

Sofia shook her head. "I hired my favorite boundary witch to set some wards on your apartment. Until we step foot back in there, he'd have to work hard to find a way inside."

"You're amazing," Ursuline said, their voice thick. "All of you."

"Like you haven't stuck your neck out for us before," Theo said, in a gruff tone. "You did the paperwork pro bono when we were getting Charles out of his situation."

Curiosity piqued in me, but I figured that was a story for another time. I chewed on a different fruit, something dark red and fleshy, and it was so sweet it melted on my tongue. Ever since I'd met Ursuline, I'd been experiencing so much more than the stale upbringing I'd grown up with, so many different cultures that existed outside of the high society I'd been trapped in.

"What's the plan for the rest of the day?" Amelia asked us.

"I'm just here to look pretty," I joked, and a familiar sadness wove through me. Everyone had roles to play, things they were able to do, and as usual, I was useless. Unable to help or pitch in.

"You're far more than pretty," Ursuline said, a dangerous edge to their voice as they caught my gaze. "And I was hoping for your help in contacting Jason, as well as reviewing a couple of photos Gretel sent over of the guys who were following us. Your attention to visual detail will be useful there." They saw right through me, and my eyes stung. I swallowed hard. Somehow, they always made me feel more, when I'd been so used to feeling less.

"We can pitch in with research," Beau offered.

"You were just waiting for the opportunity," Charles teased. "In case you didn't know, he was a librarian."

Beau rolled his eyes, and a lightness spread in me at seeing the way these people cared for each other openly, honestly. How they showed up when it mattered, how they helped without being asked. This warmth was everything I'd always thought would exist in a family, but that had never been my experience.

However, if Ursuline and I could find a way out of Triton's web, and if Ursuline truly wanted me...maybe I could be a part of this too.

My heart twisted with longing—for all of it.

"You started breakfast without me?" a voice called out from the doorway. Jaffar walked inside and extended a head nod at Ursuline and me. His black hair was slicked back, and he wore a pressed suit, as if he was heading to a meeting after this. "Long time no see."

"You're too capricious for us to wait on you," Amelia said. "And we were hungry."

Jaffar snorted and pulled up a seat at the other table. "As long as you saved some blood nectar for me, all is forgiven."

"Of course," Theo said, pushing a glass in his direction. "I made sure it was prepared."

Ursuline wasn't the chattiest of the group—no, they offered wan smirks and casual comments—but I didn't miss their presence by my side for a second. Right now, their lips were pursed, their eyes dancing, and the rumpled silver hair and crooked tunic made me swoon, like I got to glimpse behind the armor. They were all sharp angles—nose, jawline, brows—but a softness emanated from them in those often haunted eyes, a tenderness that I craved. And more than ever, I longed to tell them everything I'd been clutching tight in my heart.

That I'd completely and utterly fallen in love.

Chapter 27

The tension simmered through my body, a constant awareness that had been building all day.

Body, heart, and soul, I belonged to Ursuline, and I wanted them to know that in every damn way. Except we'd been focused on poring through pictures, trying to draw correlations between the Triton family's major holdings, as well as going through the whereabouts of his daughters, to see if any of them were involved. Cillian and the others living up in the Spires went about their business, occasionally poking in to help, but for the most part, Ursuline and I were locked in a study all day.

And they'd teased me throughout.

A brush of their tentacles along my upper thigh. A tight squeeze around my ankle. My trapped cock leaked to the point I'd caused a stain in my underwear, and I was about to have an embarrassing one on the crotch of my pants. Except we'd eaten light fare for dinner with Amelia and Charles, and then Ursuline had declared we were retiring for the night.

Eight at night. Completely normal.

Well, normal if I wanted them to fuck me for hours.

Heat rushed through me, and I squeezed their hand, a reminder that I clutched it as we walked through the hallway in the direction of our temporary abode. As much as I would've preferred to have my own safe spot, in reality I'd never lived in a home I'd felt...well, at home in.

It was the secret dream I'd clutched to my chest for longer than I wanted to admit.

"What do you have in mind tonight?" I asked, my voice coming out breathy and filled with need.

Ursuline cast me a wry glance, then scanned down to my crotch. My balls throbbed in response. "Well, first, I'll be freeing you."

My cock strained against the cage in response. As much as being in the cage had been a constant awareness in the back of my head, part of me had loved being in chastity for Ursuline, having them control my orgasms. I'd loved feeling like their plaything.

We reached the room, and Ursuline opened the door for me. They let go of my hand and guided me inside first, then closed the door shut behind us. The audible click resounded around the room, reminding me of the privacy we had. Despite the fact we were staying in Cillian's fancy upper part of the Spires, he and Beau were a whole wing away from everyone, and Amelia, Charles, and Theo were heading to work down in the casino tonight.

Which meant we'd have the seclusion for Ursuline to take me apart piece by piece.

"Strip down and climb onto the bed for me," Ursuline said, crossing their arms.

I leapt to obey. I kicked my pants off, yanked my shirt overhead, then shunted down my boxer briefs and rid myself of my socks. Within seconds, I stood in the room naked apart from the cage around my cock, and I hopped onto the bed as asked, settling there with my ass on the mattress, my legs spread.

"You're such a good boy," Ursuline purred as their molten gaze skimmed me from head to toe. "You've been so obedient with your cage, never complaining. You deserve everything, Elrich."

I swallowed hard, their praise filling cracks inside me that I hadn't realized were still there. Ones that had formed long ago. Ursuline loomed at the edge of the bed, in their tunic from earlier, and I loved how they towered over me, clothed while I was naked and exposed to them. They made me feel safe in a way I craved, in one I hadn't known I needed.

"You asked for my plan tonight," they said, one of their tentacles reaching up and caressing my calf. I shivered at the lust that coursed through me. "I'm going to eat out your pretty ass until you're sobbing and then pin you down with my tentacles. I'm going to fuck you with my mating tentacles until you're drenched with cum from both holes. Only then will I free you from your cage so you can come inside me."

Heat roared through me, and my legs trembled in anticipation. I wanted that so badly, to be consumed by them in every way possible.

"Please," I gasped out, and Ursuline's smirk and the wicked tilt of their brows wrecked me. My balls ached, and I just wanted to be filled. To be reminded of pleasure and care and...love.

Because while I knew I'd fallen, I couldn't be alone in my feelings.

The tenderness and singular attention Ursuline gave me was unlike anything I'd ever experienced.

"You're so gorgeous, sunshine," they said, sliding off their tunic. The fabric pooled on the floor, and the flat panes of their pale-blue chest, the dips and divots of their abs stood out in the dim lighting here. I salivated, wanting to taste every inch of them. Fuck. Ursuline's brow crooked up. "And desperately needy too. Do you need something to suck on while I eat you out?"

The whimper that escaped me would've been embarrassing if I didn't want it so much.

I leaned back against the bed, settling into the silken sheets, and spread my legs to expose my hole.

Ursuline crawled onto the bed and then pivoted me onto my side. "I'll start this way," they murmured as they settled behind me with their body curved up my back, their tentacles closer to my head. Their hot breath puffed against the sensitive furled skin, and I let out a keening cry.

"So responsive," they murmured as they gripped my thighs tight and spread my cheeks open. One of their mating tentacles slithered up around my shoulder and then the tip brushed against my lower lip. I dropped my jaw on reflex, the saliva producing in anticipation. They let out a warm chuckle and slid the tip in. I wrapped my lips around it and sucked, and euphoria rushed through me fast and fierce. My moan was muffled around their thick length in my mouth.

"Good boy," they purred and then their hands pried my cheeks open, exposing my tight hole. "You're my favorite meal."

With that, they licked the sensitive skin, and I let out a keening cry. Ursuline began to lap and nip at the skin, and pleasure rolled through me in small pulses. I sucked harder on their mating tentacle, just the tip in my mouth. They were clearly using my mouth to warm it, giving me something to suck on.

They licked and nipped at my hole with a voraciousness that rippled through me. My balls ached fiercely, and I writhed on my side, fisting the sheets to have something to hold on to. Their firm grip on my ass cheeks braced me, keeping me pinned in place no matter how much I squirmed. Spit dribbled down my crack, sliding down my cheek to drip onto the mattress as Ursuline dove in again and again with an exquisite hunger. The way they claimed me was unparalleled.

My cock dripped pre-cum, testing the confines of the cage as those waves of bliss traveled through me. I wanted more, yet at the same time I didn't want them to stop. Their tongue, their teeth, their lips threatened to unmake me, my hole relaxing more with every pass. I needed them—both of their tentacles thrusting inside me and filling me up. I'd become addicted to the feeling, to taking them any chance I could get.

And the caging had amplified everything, both physically and emotionally.

I sucked hard on their length in my mouth, and the slick liquid dripped inside me. I swallowed it down, my mind dizzy with lust. My balls ached to the point of madness, to the point I'd explode if Ursuline didn't get inside me and release—something. Gods, I was desperate to feel them inside me, needing that claiming, that reassurance, that no matter what we faced in the future, tonight belonged to us.

Tonight, we could take what we wanted, despite the threats trying to rip us apart.

More saliva dripped down my crack, my hole sloppy with it, but I wanted to be more of a mess. I needed them inside me, claiming me completely.

Ursuline drew back and nipped at my ass cheek, the slight sting sending sparks through me. "Such a delicious hole, sunshine," they said in their darkly beautiful tone. "You're going to take my tentacles so well. Roll onto your back."

They withdrew their tentacle from my mouth, even though I tried to chase it for a moment, and then I took my time rolling onto my back again. My hole tingled from the working over it had received, and I reached down to brush my fingers against my balls. Even the slight touch sent a spike of sheer need through me, my desperation increasing by the second.

"I need you," I begged, my emotions rising to the surface. Somehow, they coaxed them out of me every time, the ones I'd spent years trying to suppress when I was younger, because my parents would be displeased.

"I've got you, sunshine," they said, a tenderness in their dark eyes that made me soar.

I spread my legs open, my back braced against the mattress, and first their tentacles wrapped around my wrists, then my ankles. Ursuline gave the restrained spots a light squeeze, and adrenaline shot through me. I loved when they pinned me down, when they took me mercilessly, when they fucked me until I was sore and dripping with their spend.

They brought the same mating tentacle I'd been sucking on back to my mouth, and I wrapped my lips around it eagerly. The first suck sent a dribble of slick down my throat, and I relished the slightly briny taste, the heavy weight on my tongue, the smoothness there.

Ursuline teased my hole with their other tentacle, brushing the tip against the furled skin, and I shivered. My legs and arms twitched as I writhed in place, but Ursuline's tentacles kept me from moving too far. I loved the slight pushback from them, which created a feedback loop of the possession I craved from them.

"You're such a treasure." Their voice was hushed, reverent, and the awe in their eyes sent a deep shard of emotion through me, almost painful with yearning. I'd spent my whole life feeling worthless, but around Ursuline, I wasn't. They treated me like I had value, and the more time I spent around them, the more I found excitement in creativity and ideas I'd once silenced.

Their mating tentacle breached my hole, just the tip, teasing me there, and I tried to shove downward to take more of them, but with my limbs pinned in place, I couldn't do more than writhe.

They pumped in and out shallowly, more of the slick spurting inside me with every light thrust. I sucked harder on the length in my mouth, trying to draw it deeper too, but they continued to tease. My balls felt so full, so heavy, I thought I'd explode. Ursuline loomed over me, between my spread legs, their hands on my thighs, keeping them pried open. They looked like a dark god this way, their features severe and forbidding even as their actions held gentleness in spades.

"Need more, sunshine?" they teased, a wry twist to their mouth.

I bobbed my head, unable to answer with my mouth full of their length. They slid their mating tentacle deeper into my mouth, and I gagged from the sudden intrusion in my throat. I relaxed it, and a floaty acceptance began to steal over me, like clouds descending from the skies to the earth.

Then, they pushed their mating tentacle deeper inside my hole, stretching me open with ease. After taking both of them the other week, I craved that fullness even more, the need rising with every waking moment. They thrust in to the point I cried out, their thickness filling me up. They moved their length back, and then forward again, the glide smooth with the amount of slick they'd secreted. The bumps and ridges from the suckers created an extra sensation as they fucked into me, and I moaned around their mating tentacle giving the same gentle thrusts deep into my throat.

Tears welled in my eyes, my trapped cock weeping pre-cum. A dribble trickled down my balls, pooling on the mattress beneath me. I craved being a mess for them—of cum, of spit, of their slick.

"Gods, you're still so tight," they groaned out. "Both your holes feel like sin, sunshine. I'll need to work them daily, just fill you up every damn day to keep you ready for me."

I whimpered around their mating tentacle, my throat convulsing. A deep, low chuckle came from them.

"Like that, sunshine? Want to sit under my desk and warm me all day while I'm writing briefs?"

"Mmph," I moaned around their length. Fuck, I loved the idea of being claimed by them like that. As if we had all the time in the world.

"I'd breed this pretty hole all day long," Ursuline murmured, and the hunger in their gaze as they scanned over me was unreal. I preened under their attention, an unabated, unquenchable thrill rising inside me. "Just come inside you over and over until you were a mess."

Fuck, I wanted that. Wanted to feel their slick dripping down my legs.

I tilted my head back in surrender and closed my eyes, the sensations increasing with each stroke, each thrust inside me. The squeeze of their tentacles around my wrists, my ankles, the pressure there, only elevated everything. They thrust in hard again, brushing against my prostate, and the intense flare of pleasure eradicated all other thoughts from my brain.

"Ngh," I gasped out around their thick length, my hips lifting slightly from the bed.

"Oh, sunshine, your sounds create the most beautiful melody," Ursuline said, their low voice gravel and sin. "I'd better play you until we reach a crescendo."

They pumped into me harder and faster, the sloppy sounds echoing in the room as they fucked into my throat and hole in tandem. The light pulsing squeezes of their tentacles around my wrists and ankles brought constant attention there, all while my balls ached and my cock screamed for just a touch, the slightest bit of freedom to spill.

Ursuline raked their fingernails along the insides of my thighs, tracing patterns there, all while they thrust against my prostate over and over, to the point that I sobbed. Tears leaked from my eyes, trailing down my cheeks. They squirted more slick down my throat, and I swallowed it, the salty taste addictive. More of it gushed into my hole and smoothed the glide, creating those squelching sounds that made my cheeks heat.

"Such a sloppy, sweet little hole," Ursuline teased. "Such a perfect boy for me. Does someone need to come?"

I bobbed my head. My balls were so heavy at this point they felt like weights I dragged everywhere, and the neediness had ratcheted up a thousand degrees.

They drew back from my mouth, and I dragged in ragged breaths, my throat a little raw from the way they'd been fucking it. Then, one by one, they released their grip on my limbs, and then slowly pulled out of my hole.

I whimpered. "Please."

Ursuline arched a brow. "Patience, sunshine. If you remember, the lock around your cock needs a key."

My body hummed in anticipation, like someone had jammed electricity through my veins.

They shifted off the bed with a creak and bent over to grab their bag. The lines of their body were so gorgeous, smooth and sinuous, and I bit down on my lower lip, the sharp longing intensifying in my chest. When Ursuline turned around, their expression looked feral, a wildness there that I craved.

"You've earned this," they said as they returned to the bed, a small key glinting in their hand. They reached down and with a small click, opened the cage on my cock. They removed the pieces one by one, careful to not snag anything, and I almost wept from the immediate relief. The pressure that had been there for the past few weeks vanished, even though the ache in my balls was unrelenting.

My cock filled out at once, my erection stiff and desperate. I made a motion to reach for it, but Ursuline fixed me with a look.

"You'll be coming inside me, not by your hand."

Flames roared through me, the heat growing into an inferno. Gods, they were the sexiest creature I'd ever met, and the idea of getting to sink my cock into them...I couldn't even imagine.

Ursuline settled next to me on the bed, lying back to get comfortable and letting their tentacles spread out, some teasing along my side. "You're going to sink into me from on top," they murmured. "And then I'll fill you up with both my tentacles. I want to see your face when you come, sunshine."

I pushed up, my limbs unsteady from the sheer amount of times they'd made me tremble already. This felt momentous in a way I couldn't explain. As if Ursuline offered me a gift they didn't often give others. A zing traveled through my cock in anticipation, at the idea of getting to sink into the hot, wet clench of a hole, and my heart trilled. This wasn't just a casual fuck.

No, this was a coming together, an Ouroboros, where we were buried in each other, twisted together for an eternity. The same way they'd made an indelible mark on my soul.

I settled in front of them and ran my hands down their tentacles. A visible shiver ran through Ursuline. I'd never gotten a chance to play with them before, to tease them like they did me, and I relished the ability now. Even though my cock ached something fierce, I wanted to take my time given the opportunity.

Their mating tentacles had retreated to the privacy beneath the ones they glided around the earth with, and being able to pry open their tentacles sent a dose of lust through me. My knees dug into the mattress, my limbs jittery and trembling as I spread Ursuline open, brushing the tentacles aside to expose the deep gray flesh there. I ran my fingertips across the smooth surface, stopping right by the dark slit in the middle. Fuck. They were so sexy.

Ursuline's breath hitched, and I watched their expression with rapt attention as I teased around the slit, circling there over and over again. My hard cock throbbed with need, but the curiosity had overtaken me. I teased around the edges and then ran my thumb along the slit.

"Oh, fuck," Ursuline moaned, tossing their head back. A silent thrill rose inside me that I got to touch them, to affect them like they did me. "Come on, sunshine. Sink deep into me so I can enter your pretty hole again. My mating tentacles are getting restless."

I swallowed hard at the thought, a wave of lust roaring through me. Gods, they were stunning in every way, all sharp edges and unwavering strength, and I wanted to lose myself with them entirely.

I circled my hand around the base of my cock to bring the tip to their slit. The moment I even brushed against it, a moan exploded from me. Bliss radiated up my spine from the slightest touch. I'd be wrecked once I sank fully inside.

Ursuline reached up and gripped my ass, drawing me into them. Slick, wet heat squeezed my cock tight, and my eyes rolled back in my head. My cock hovered on the precipice of coming already, after being so long in captivity, and a moan exploded out of me. Except this wasn't enough. I needed them filling me up in return. Needed them thrusting inside me, taking me apart.

Ursuline's intelligent eyes landed on me, and a small smile tilted their lips, as if they could read my mind. Their mating tentacles rose up, and one of them slipped around to tease at my hole.

"I've never let anyone enter me before," Ursuline confessed, and my chest squeezed tight. "Only you."

I opened my mouth, awestruck at what a gift they'd given me. No words sufficed, though, so instead I leaned forward and pressed my lips to theirs. They kissed me back at once, and I savored the intensity of the emotions crashing through me, as powerful as the tide. Ursuline had been my savior—from the sea, from my cage. They'd set me free in every way, but with them...I wanted to be captured.

They made me feel cherished, and they inspired me—with their strength, their kindness, their loyalty.

I tried to pour all those emotions into the kiss, needing them to know how deeply my currents ran for them.

When I pulled back, the tenderness in their gaze stroked at my heart.

"Thank you," I murmured. "For trusting me."

"You can thank me by coming for me, sunshine," they responded, their eyes crinkling at the edges. Their emerging playfulness sent a sharp shard of longing through me, at seeing them melt from cold, aloof, and serious to everything they'd tucked deep inside them.

It made me want to work toward melting them each day, for the rest of our lives.

They pried my cheeks open with their grip, and their mating tentacle pushed inside my hole far too easily. The sloppy noise it made when it settled deep made me whimper. Surrounded like this, my cock buried in their heat, and their length buried inside me, I vaulted to unparalleled heights. My body would fall apart at the seams from the sheer tension and need percolating inside me, growing stronger with every second.

"Think you can take the other one?" they asked, a smirk on their lips.

"I need it," I pleaded, not even the slightest bit ashamed. I wanted them splitting me open as I came, longed to feel them stretching me wide. Ursuline's pupils grew darker from lust, and their other mating tentacle brushed at my rim. I widened my stance, which shifted my cock a bit inside them. Pleasure rushed me at once, and I sagged slightly forward.

"Precarious position, isn't it?" they teased.

"Mmhmm," I managed.

Ursuline started to work their other mating tentacle inside me to join the other one, taking their time as they loosened my rim. The stretch burned, but I relished it. I was incinerating from their snug hole clutching my cock tight, my balls poised to burst any second now. I clenched my jaw, trying not to blow before they even sank inside me. It'd be embarrassingly fast.

They pushed in past the rim, and then continued to thrust in a bit deeper, working farther into my hole.

I gripped the sheets tight, keeping myself braced so I didn't get overeager and start pumping inside them. Once I did, I wouldn't last. Ursuline nudged their mating tentacle in far enough that the pressure against the next ring of muscle was enough to deflate my cock slightly. I sucked in a deep breath and then bore down. They slid through the rest of the way, and my whole body vibrated from the tension.

"Oh fuck," I gasped out. "I'm so...full."

"You take me so perfectly," Ursuline murmured, making their tentacles shift just the slightest bit, enough to send sparks up my spine. "Everywhere, sunshine."

I swallowed hard, their praise coating my skin like pure light. "Can I move?"

"Or do you want me to move inside you first?" they asked, arching a brow.

Heat flushed my cheeks. As much as I loved that they'd given me the chance to explore them more, I adored them being in control. I nodded and chewed on my lower lip.

The moment they shifted one tentacle forward and the other back, a shout flew from my lips. The suckers glided along my insides, and my prostate lit up, the strength of the sensation knocking the breath from me. They found a back-and-forth rhythm, slow and steady, and each time they shifted, it jostled my cock inside them. The slight dip in and draw from their hole was enough to send a hot flush through my whole body. I was incinerating.

I was going to come. I was going to come so explosively hard that I wasn't sure I'd even be conscious after.

"I can fuck you into me, sunshine," they teased, the seductive purr of theirs setting my bloodstream aflame.

I bobbed my head, some unintelligible words pouring from my mouth. I kept myself braced as they thrust into me hard with one tentacle, shoving me forward, then they pulled with the other, and I shifted back. My cock moved inside them, the hot, tight squeeze bringing me closer to the edge. Their tentacles grazed across my prostate, over and over and over, and blinding white bliss poured through me with every pass. My eyes started leaking at some point, the tears flowing freely down my cheeks, but I didn't try to fight them. The squelch of their tentacles gliding inside my hole echoed through the room, along with the softer sound as my dick sank into their hole again and again.

I began to shift with the movements too, small pumps of my hips, which brought me so breathlessly close to coming that my balls radiated with the ache in them. My cock throbbed, the need for release a living thing.

They squirted more of their slick inside me from the ends of their tentacles, easing the glide as both of their lengths stretched my hole to the point I wasn't sure I'd be able to take it—and yet I craved the burn all in the same breath. My arms full-on shook at this point, and my thighs quaked, but I continued to pump inside them, every movement bringing me closer to that elusive orgasm.

I buried my head in the crook between their neck and shoulders, nuzzling my face there, and the scent of currants and brine, of sweat and sex, wrapped around me, imprinting on me. Sweat slicked my limbs at this point, dripping down my back and their arms, and their forehead glistened as well. I thrust in again, their velvet grip strangling me, and they fucked into my hole hard with one of their tentacles, the other drawing back. I bit down on my lip to keep from crying out, and my gaze tangled with theirs.

Ursuline's high cheekbones were flushed, their mouth open in pleasure, and their eyes held a soft incandescence that reminded me of the lazy coasting of gulls on a sunlit day at the shore. My heart squeezed tight. They were everything I'd dreamed of in a partner, and three words hovered on my tongue, begging to escape free.

"Think you can come for me, good boy?" Ursuline asked. "You fill me up, and I'll return the favor doubly."

"Yes," I blurted out as I thrust in again. As much as I didn't want this to end, the ache in my balls bordered on painful.

Ursuline reached up and wrapped their hand around my throat, enough that the slight pressure made my mind reel but not enough to cause a problem. The possessiveness of the gesture—fuck, I loved it so much.

"I'm going to take you hard and fast, sunshine," they said. "And you're going to flood me with your cum."

I almost nodded, but they kept their light grip on my throat. They pistoned their tentacles in and out of me, working with a symmetry that sent me reeling, so the flares against my prostate arrived intense, quick, and unceasing. The breath stuck in my throat, my body forgetting how to do basic processes under the onslaught of pleasure that slammed in over and over.

My balls grew so heavy, my cock throbbing, and I was so. Damn. Close.

Ursuline gave my throat the lightest squeeze. "Come for me."

The command lit up my synapses, my balls drew up, and I released.

The cum flooded inside them, and my balls emptied out as my cock sputtered spurt after spurt, as if I couldn't come enough. My length pulsed with each movement, and the orgasm barreled into me with a ferocity that stole my vision. I straight-up blacked out as I coasted on wave after wave of teeth-numbing pleasure.

They didn't stop fucking into me either. No, they continued to work my spasming prostate through the whole thing until I howled, my fingers clutching the sheets with a death grip. Tears flowed down my cheeks, blurring my vision, and I sagged against their chest, as the aftershocks of coming so hard continued to flutter over me.

"So good, sunshine," they groaned out. "I'm so close."

Ursuline's pace picked up, until all I could feel was the thrust of their mating tentacles inside me, the way they dominated me completely. My cheek pressed against their sweat-slicked chest, and my breaths came out ragged as I savored the feeling of still being inside them. The heat was scorching, consuming, even after I was spent.

"So close," Ursuline grunted. Their lengths slid in, sinuous and demanding, and I sobbed, the tears streaming down my cheeks as waves of pleasure crested over me. I clutched the sheets tight, burying my face against their chest to try to muffle my cries.

They let out a harsh, broken noise, and their hole spasmed around my spent cock. Then their tentacles began to pulse.

The cum shot inside me in heavy load after heavy load, until I was full and dripping with it. They continued to pump their lengths inside me through their release, and the sloppy noises echoed through the room as the cum dripped from my hole. Still they continued to unload inside me, until it spilled out more, soaking my thighs, dribbling down my legs. I sank my teeth into their pec, the pleasure so intense it bordered on painful.

Quiet descended between both of us in the wake of our completion.

Slowly, they withdrew one of their tentacles from my hole, but they left the other snug in there, and I nuzzled against their chest. I remained buried inside them too, connected to them as deeply as they were to me.

There was only one other thing that felt close to this—this wild, ferocious, reckless buoyancy.

When I stared at the rise and swell of the sea. The beckoning of the water that was undeniable, a calling to my soul that had been there from the first day I'd set eyes on it.

I see you. I understand you, it had always seemed to say.

And I'd found that in Ursuline.

My chest squeezed tight, and the words leapt to my tongue again. Except this time, I didn't hold them back.

"I love you," I said. I didn't expect to hear the words in return, even though I yearned. But in this moment, I needed them to know this truth of mine.

Ursuline stilled, and I lifted my head from their chest to look up at them. Their jaw had dropped, their dark deep-set eyes wide, and the surprise that painted their features broke my heart.

"You love me?" The hush in their tone told me everything.

I met their gaze. "I've never felt this way before about anyone. And I understand if you don't feel the same, but I needed to tell you tonight."

Ursuline's hands settled on my hips, and they squeezed tight. "What do you think sunshine means, Elrich?"

My brows drew together. "A nickname. I figured it was because I like the sun so much."

They shook their head. "I grew up in the deeps of New Atlantis, and we rarely made trips to the surface. I still remember the first time we traveled above. It wasn't for a vacation or anything enjoyable—no, those sorts of trips were for the wealthy. We were following a school of fish, part of a fisherman's crew that day.

"I'd never experienced the sun on my skin before," they said. "And when I emerged from the sea, I thought I'd caught on fire. The golden rays were so hot, so dazzling, I didn't think they could be real. Years of living in the deeps could never have prepared me for how it swept through me at once, filling me with this foreign sensation—a lightness, like zipping through the water. And when we returned below, I never forgot the sun. It was an elusive, farfetched idea that I'd ever have it in my future, and walking above the sea the way I do, it's one thing I've never taken for granted. I might be more comfortable in the quiet of the dark, in the moonlight, but the sun, it challenges me."

They met my gaze. "It fills me with hope I didn't believe still existed."

My chest squeezed tight as the impact of their words settled inside me.

"I love you, Elrich Durand. You're the sunshine I've spent my life chasing, and I won't let anyone tear us apart, the Triton family be damned."

Tears burned my eyes, and I sucked back a sob. The fierceness in their gaze, the sheer love that poured from them in waves was what I'd dreamed of finding since I was a kid.

"I'll fight for us too," I promised, and then I leaned down to press my lips to theirs.

They kissed me with a fervent passion, one I lost myself in, and our limbs tangled together while we were buried in each other. A few silent tears streamed down my cheeks, the feelings that rose inside me far too massive to contain. Every tender look, every soft "sunshine" clarified in my mind, swirling there like pieces of a puzzle we'd completed together.

One that I'd do anything to protect.

I drew back and rested my cheek on their chest to listen to the steady *thump, thump, thump* of their heart. It beat in time with mine, and I didn't try to move from this spot, holding onto the sanctity of this moment for as long as possible.

Ursuline loved me.

No matter what we faced in the future, we would forever have this time here in the quiet night.

Chapter 28

"Fuck."

Ursuline's voice rang through the room, stirring me from slumber. I rubbed at my bleary eyes, my whole body aching after the intense fuck last night. My cock was hard as a rock, which felt foreign after having it caged up for so long. In a way, I missed being in chastity for them. Maybe we could explore it more if we found our way out of this mess.

They were sitting up beside me, hunched forward, their phone to their ear. Their face looked stricken, concerned. "We'll be there as soon as possible."

Panic shot through me.

"What's going on?" I asked, pushing myself up from the comfort of the mattress. Ursuline radiated a nervous edge, which was unlike them.

"Jason called," they said. "He said he's got urgent information for me. Something he wasn't able to share over the phone."

I placed a hand over theirs and squeezed. Already I sensed what was at the heart of their concern. "About your family."

"If he can't tell me over the phone..." They worried their lower lip. The news couldn't be good. That much was true.

"We've got to go," I said, sliding off the bed. My feet landed on the floor, and I made my way to my bag for a fresh set of clothing, which was limited. "Where does Jason want to meet?"

"Haven's too obvious," Ursuline said. "Guaranteed, Triton will have people lurking nearby. So we agreed upon Starlight Diner in the center of town. It's busy enough that we can use the buffer of the public in our favor."

"And then come straight back here?" I asked, curiosity rising in me. Ursuline's jaw was clenched, their look a bit faraway.

"I'll have to chance my apartment," they murmured. "I need to get a few files from there, and I can't delay any longer. However, I'll make sure you're safe here first."

I crossed my arms and fixed them with a look. "You're not going anywhere without me."

Ursuline glanced up, their wan smile wavering. "Can't be dissuaded?"

"You're stuck with me," I said, confidence building inside me that I hadn't felt with anyone else. In the past with partners, I'd back down, unsure of their true feelings or if they'd find me a bother.

Meanwhile, Ursuline called me "sunshine."

They treated me like I mattered.

I wouldn't leave them to face this by their lonesome.

"Thank you," they said as they slipped on a tunic and then leaned in to press a kiss to my cheekbone. They glided to the attached bathroom, and the water from the faucet sounded a second later. I popped on my boots, my mind whirling with what Jason might tell us. I'd been to the Starlight Diner before with Jason, even though it was in an area my parents didn't approve of me going. Their approval stretched over a few choice sectors on the outskirts of Peregrine City and the mansions of their friends, which was a paltry experience at best.

Ursuline stepped out of the bathroom looking perfectly presentable, their hair slicked back, their tunic neat. All the sharp lines and edges reminded me of the armor they always donned for the outside world.

They'd need it more than ever today.

I slipped into the bathroom and relieved myself, then brushed my teeth. I didn't bother doing anything else, mostly because I'd somehow end up making a mess anyway. When I stepped out, Ursuline waited at the door, humming, humming, humming.

"I let Amelia know we were leaving," they said, a smaller bag slung over their shoulder. "Starlight Diner is a few subway stops from here."

We exited the room in haste, and I didn't even peer through the open doors we passed by, since Ursuline moved with enough rapid purpose that I worried I'd fall behind. They ran a card at the elevator, followed by a thumbprint, and we descended to the lower levels of the Spires. The place sprawled out before us, rich red carpeting, swords on the wall, and deep golden and bronze embellishments that seemed antiquated compared to the jangling slot machines lighting up throughout.

Yet all the flashing lights whirred by in our hurry, until we plunged out of the casino and onto the streets.

The second we stepped outside, my nerves jangled.

I hadn't forgotten the pursuit from the other night, the way Triton's men had hunted us down. And now they could be lurking anywhere in the city, waiting to drag us back to the manor. Or...worse.

My skin prickled despite the bright sunlight beaming down on us, and a shiver ran down my spine as we coasted along the sidewalks, en route to the light rail stop. My heart *thump, thump, thumped* as we passed dozens of people strolling through the city, going about their day. No one paid us any mind, no furtive glances or staggered steps, but I couldn't shake the feeling of being watched, whether it was real or remembered.

"What will we do if the news is bad?" The question slipped out unbidden, even though I handled a live grenade.

Ursuline slowed down the slightest bit, their shoulders hitched. "Keep moving forward. It's all I can do at this point."

I swallowed hard. Their resilience was something I envied, even if I hated their need for it in the first place. "One day, we'll be able to stop."

They glanced back to me, a heartbreaking sadness in their eyes. "That's a beautiful dream."

We halted in front of the light rail, and the subway car came barreling our way with thunderous force. It stopped in an explosion of screeches, and the doors zipped open. I hopped on, and Ursuline followed me, casting a wary glance over their shoulder.

"Are we clear?" I asked as the doors closed.

"Yeah," they said. "I thought I caught some extra stares back there, but no one who boarded with us."

Cold water trickled down my spine. No freedom existed while Frederick pursued us like this. We'd have to fight for it tooth and nail. The subway shot off on the rails, and I clutched the cold metal pole, my mind whirring. From the second I'd woken up today, we'd set into motion, and I'd barely been able to process everything that had shifted last night.

"Are we dating?" I blurted out and then clapped my hand over my mouth. "Shit, that's a terrible question right now."

Ursuline shook their head, a faint grin on their lips. "Not terrible. I'll cling onto any good thing I can." Their tentacle wound around my leg. "And I'm proud to claim you as mine."

My heart thrummed. Despite all the unknowns facing us, how at any minute this temporary bliss could be dashed, I'd take this one beautiful moment.

The subway car screeched to a halt, but Ursuline shook their head. "Next stop."

Once a few people had shuffled off, it zipped forward again in a cacophony of whines and screeching metal.

"Do you miss the paintings you left behind?" Ursuline asked.

I chewed on my lower lip. "A little? They represented pieces of my journey to get here. And I had one very clear source of inspiration." I met their gaze, and their eyes softened.

Ursuline brushed a thumb across my lower lip. "If I have it my way, you'll have the opportunity to create thousands more."

"What does that entail?" I asked, hope stirring inside me. I ached for a future with them, more than I could express.

Before Ursuline could answer, the subway slammed to a halt at our stop, and they let out a sigh. "Let's go. Starlight Diner is a block away from here."

Disappointment thudded in my chest, because once we stepped outside, the cozy bubble of conversation vanished. Nerves returned, along with the awareness that Triton's men would be prowling the city. Waiting for us.

The sign for Starlight Diner stood out at the end of the block, navy blue and white, and the silver accents on the exterior of the building glinted in the sunlight. Ursuline and I walked along at as fast a pace as possible—not that we'd be able to relax even in the diner—but I wasn't sure if the desperation was for cover or answers.

A little bit of both.

A heaviness settled over me, a foreboding I couldn't explain. We were walking into bad news, but the ever-present danger of our current situation rolled in like storm clouds. My phone sat heavily in my pocket, turned off for the moment to avoid tracking. I'd also avoided checking it because I didn't want to see the messages my parents were guaranteed to have sent.

The only thing they cared about was business, and I'd botched their biggest deal.

I stepped in front of the Starlight Diner, and when I opened the door, the casual murmur of conversation mixed with the scent of berries and bread. The interior featured a navy-blue ceiling studded with softly glowing yellow lights, like stars, and the black vinyl booths with their silvery, almost mirror-esque tables created the perfect ambiance.

It didn't take more than a moment to spot Jason in the back, his preferred spot when he was out in public.

He hunched deeper than normal, his tentacles twitching as he stared at the surface of a mug. My heart thumped hard, and I reached over to interlace my fingers with Ursuline's. Whatever he had to tell us, I could guarantee it wouldn't be good.

"Jason," Ursuline announced as we stepped up to the booth.

He looked up at last, his face stricken. "I ordered teas."

I slipped into the seat across from him first and placed my hands around the porcelain mug, clinging to the warmth. The furls of steam tickled my nose.

Ursuline didn't touch their tea. They withdrew their hand from mine and balled theirs into fists, the whites of their knuckles visible. "What is going on?"

Jason's brow line drew together, his black eyes filled with pain. "They're dead," he said without preamble. "You asked me to check on your family when I went down..."

Ursuline's shoulders stiffened. "But I just got a letter a month ago."

Oh no.

The pieces started to click together, far too fast.

Jason shook his head, one of his tentacles twitching. "It wasn't written by them..."

"The Triton family," I completed the sentence, my gut churning with acid. "That was why they were trying to keep you from going below."

"Oh gods," Ursuline choked out, their eyes widening, and their whole body locking up like they were in rigor mortis. Like they'd died a little bit with their family. "Everyone?"

"Mining accident," Jason said. "Your parents and younger sibling got caught. Jaris...didn't want to go on without them."

Oh fuck. Fuck, fuck, fuck. Bile rose in my throat. Ursuline sat beside me unmoving, as their whole world crumpled apart. They'd sacrificed years of their life to servitude under Frederick's hand, and the family had known all along they were stringing Ursuline along.

A newfound rage kindled inside me, one that warred with the anguish that emanated from Ursuline, that dwelled in my chest at everything they'd lost. At the way their loyalty had been betrayed.

"They never said a word," Ursuline whispered, staring at the surface of the table. "Just kept me working like a cog in the machine."

My throat burned, and so did my eyes with tears that begged to unleash. I placed the mug in my hands down, because they were shaking.

Ursuline's family was dead.

All their work, all their effort, all their sacrifice was for nothing.

"Excuse me," they said, and they pushed up from their seat, their tentacles trembling as they glided in the direction of the restrooms.

"I'll be right back," I said to Jason, who nodded somberly. My feet carried me across the tiles after them, whether they wanted company or not. I couldn't abandon them. Not now.

I pushed into the restroom, but they weren't in the main area.

A shuddery sob resounded across the tiles, coming from the large stall in the back. I rushed over and rested my hand on the handle.

Another sob echoed through the room.

"Can I come in?" I asked, adrenaline rocketing through my whole body, like I needed to fight something.

Except the person who'd caused this was the one we ran from.

Ursuline didn't respond, but the lock on the door clicked, and I took that as a cue I was welcome. Ursuline barely had space in the stall as they curled on one side, and I wouldn't be able to squeeze in on the other. Instead, I locked the door then sank onto their lap, slowly, making sure my presence was welcome and not too much.

The visible shudder that ran through Ursuline as I settled there had me tempted to bolt, but then they wrapped their arms around me to clutch me tight. Their face buried into my chest, their nails dug in, and I squeezed them hard, not wanting to let them go.

Another sob escaped them, and my tears began to sting. My heart ached like someone had torn it out of my chest at seeing Ursuline undone like this. At the cruelty that had been inflicted on them for fucking years.

They deserved so much better. They deserved freedom and love and loyalty. They deserved long, passionate nights and gentle, quiet mornings. I wanted to give them all of it.

A few tears slipped down my cheeks as I clutched them tight. Condolences felt paltry in the moment, and I couldn't bring the dead back. All I could do was stay here by their side now. Let them take off the armor they'd donned.

"I should've fucking figured it out," they said, their voice ragged. "The letters the past few years…the frequency. The distant tone. Fuck, everything."

I squeezed them again, as if I could offer them some of my own soul in the process. "They didn't want you to know. They were careful because you're clever, not the opposite."

A wounded sound erupted from Ursuline's throat, the combination of a sob and a howl, and fuck. I couldn't imagine how devastating this news was. Maybe because I'd never had the sort of family they did.

However, I did understand how it felt to be betrayed. How it felt to be used, just an object for an endgame you weren't even a part of.

And the Triton family was responsible.

My gut churned. Arielle had been aware. She'd smiled and laughed and acted carefree, all while knowing they kept Ursuline here unfairly. Knowing they should be free.

"I didn't think…" they said, a slight tinge of horror in their voice. "When I said my goodbye before coming to the surface, it was never supposed to be the final one."

Oh gods. My eyes watered anew, and I shut them as hot tears streamed down my cheeks. My chest ached. They'd lost everything. Everything they'd sacrificed all these years had been for…nothing.

I wasn't sure how long we sat here in the quiet of the bathroom, holding each other like life preservers in a storm. Time melted away, until all that existed was the heat of their skin, their heavy breaths, and the press of their body. The reminder that we were here, and we were alive.

Jason was probably still waiting for us out in the diner, but I didn't feel the need to rush back to him. If anyone would understand the weight of the news Jason had delivered, he would. And he wasn't someone who had an issue with sitting in the quiet either. I refused to budge while Ursuline needed me. They'd been alone up here for so long, working for that horrific family, but they weren't on their own any longer.

For as long as we had, I'd be by their side.

"Shit, I thought I could handle myself better," they muttered, swiping at their eyes.

I pressed a kiss on their forehead. "You haven't managed to out cry me, so I think you're fine."

Ursuline's lips twitched the slightest bit, and I internally cheered at the win. Their expression was haunted, from the ghosts they hadn't realized were following them around all this time, but the reflexes of their humor still existed.

"We should get up," they said. "I just left Jason out there, and we can't stay in one place for too long."

I tilted my head to the side. "Are you sure? Take whatever time you need. Jason probably sketched out a whole new piece on the napkins, and no one has entered this bathroom since we've been in it."

Ursuline offered a strained smile, more of their lips pressing together in a tight line. They weren't okay, but they pushed forward regardless, doing what needed to be done. I leaned in and squeezed them tight once more. Their scent was sharp, currants and brine, and I soaked it in, the feel of them, how they were here and real, even though they'd just shattered to pieces.

"I'll be by your side no matter what," I murmured into their ear.

They squeezed me back. "That's the only reason I'm still fighting."

I swallowed hard, my eyes burning again. Fuck.

My mind spun with the news dropped into our lap, even though I'd had a sneaking suspicion ever since I'd overheard the conversation between Arielle and her mother. The more stories that stacked up about the Triton family, the more I was grateful I'd run, even if I wasn't sure where my destination would be.

I pushed up off my spot on their lap first, my legs creaking with the motion. Then we made our way to the sinks. Ursuline splashed water on their face, but I didn't bother. I'd never been good at donning a mask anyway.

I strode out of the bathroom first and spotted Jason in the same booth we'd left him. He hunched forward, his pencil in hand and his gaze intent on the table. When I got closer, as I'd expected, he was sketching out a piece on the napkins.

"Hey," I said, grabbing his attention. "Sorry we were in there so long."

Jason nodded. "I never wanted to bring that news."

"I'm glad you did," Ursuline said from behind me, their voice somehow sturdy. "I now know that the contract between me and the Triton family is void. I'll take any bargaining chip I can get."

"The server cleared your cups, but I can ask them to bring more," Jason offered, though he squinted at Ursuline. "Except you're heading out."

I shook my head, warmth flowing through me. Jason was as blunt and insightful as usual. "I'll message you when we get to safety."

"Do so," Jason said with a firm nod.

"Thank you," Ursuline said. "For finding out."

Jason nodded, but I didn't expect more of a response. With that, Ursuline took the lead out of the Starlight Diner. The moment we stepped back into the sunlight, my skin prickled. A sense of alertness pumped through my veins, probably because Triton's men could be prowling anywhere out here. The streets were busy, filled with cars bustling by and people on a stroll or brisk walk.

"Where is your apartment?" I asked as we stepped onto the sidewalk.

"I live about ten minutes from here," Ursuline said. "A little spot in the arts district."

My chest squeezed. Of course that was where they'd be—the exact area of the city I'd always wanted to live in. Everything about the way we came together, how we infused into each other's lives, felt a bit fated.

A shadow from the alley to my right drew my attention.

Too late.

One moment, Ursuline was walking by my side. The next, three men dressed in black with masks over their faces surrounded them. Their eyes widened, and they twisted around. The second they saw the men in the nondescript uniforms, they froze. My gaze snagged on the Alpha Blue symbols on their shoulders.

A scream tried to rip past my lips, but it wouldn't emerge.

"Get the Liquidium Industries file," Ursuline shouted, snagging my attention. "Get Sofia."

The men snagged Ursuline, dragging them back into the alley, and my whole body rocketed into panic. Yet my limbs wouldn't move. All I could see was the flash of fear widening their eyes, their arms flying up in defense. The twirl of their tentacles as they tried to fight off these kidnappers. One of the men slammed a fist into their stomach, and another smashed the butt of one of their weapons against their back. Ursuline's jaw dropped, and a howl emerged from them, one that made my cells vibrate with panic.

My mind spun, my legs begged to run, my insides rioted as wave after wave of panic crashed over me. One moment, Ursuline was struggling against their grip as they yanked them deeper into the shadows. The next, they'd vanished around the corner.

Gone.

I stood there, frozen, as my partner, *my soulmate*, was dragged away.

Chapter 29

My hands trembled as I dialed Sofia's number.

Gone. Ursuline was gone.

They told me to get to their apartment, but I'd never even been there. I didn't have their address. Fuck, they were *gone*. Agony ripped through my chest as the pale sunlight beat down on me, too alien and foreign to process in the wake of what had occurred. I stumbled back a step and sagged against the brick building behind me, my knees barely keeping me upright.

I couldn't breathe. I couldn't *breathe*.

Ursuline's presence, the calm, enduring one that had given me so much strength, was gone, and I didn't know what I'd do. This entire time, I'd been following their cues, following their plans, their way out. My arms trembled.

A sense of uselessness washed over me like a tidal wave, reinforced by the constant comments from my parents. I wasn't able to do anything. I should've fought for the person I loved. I should've thrown myself into the fight, tried to kick one of those men off, but instead I'd stood there frozen, watching as they'd been hauled away.

My chest tangled in knots.

I managed to press call, and the phone began to ring.

"Hello?" Sofia's voice came across crisp and concerned.

"They took Ursuline," I choked out, those trembles radiating through my body. "Just snatched them away."

"Who did?" Sofia's tone grew dark and dangerous, and I was grateful it wasn't aimed at me.

"Alpha Blue," I said. "I...I don't even know where they live." Heat burned in my eyes, and the first few tears slipped down my cheeks. "We were heading to their apartment. They told me to get the file... They were here, we were going there, and now..."

"Fuck," Sofia spat. "Cillian will have to handle Alpha Blue. He's got a few connections he can strong-arm. But if they told you to get a file from their apartment, that's what we should do."

"We?" My heart thudded a little faster.

"You didn't think I'd leave you to handle this by your lonesome, did you? I'll text you their address, and we'll meet there."

Words wouldn't emerge now either, even though the gratefulness washed through me so fast and fierce it was dizzying.

Except shame followed on its heels. Yet again, I wasn't doing anything on my own. I wasn't taking action, just waiting to be told what to do. My guts twisted to pieces.

There isn't a competent bone in your body.

My father's voice echoed over and over again. I clutched the phone a little tighter.

"Stay safe, and stay alert," Sofia said, then hung up.

I gripped the phone still, staring blankly at the street ahead. My phone buzzed a moment later, and I glanced at the screen. The address was there waiting for me, so I punched it into the GPS.

A ten-minute walk, as promised.

Except I didn't have Ursuline by my side. My brain screamed in panic, the sound growing louder and louder inside me by the second. Ursuline should've been here with me. They should've been by my side.

We should've been together.

My body numbed, even as I forced myself forward.

I didn't question why Alpha Blue had targeted them and not me. Alpha Blue went after monsterkind.

And now that Ursuline was on the run from the Triton family, they'd been easier pickings. Bile churned in my gut. I continued onward, even though I could barely feel the ground beneath me as if my limbs were detached from my body. Nothing connected, not while my heart was being carried away by those specters who'd swarmed in from the shadows and stole Ursuline.

I needed to get to the apartment, though. For them. So I scanned the streets as I went, slowing before any alleyway that emerged, in case others were lying in wait for me. My jaw clenched so hard I was surprised my teeth didn't chip, yet I continued to stride forward, down one block and then another.

Ursuline was with Alpha Blue. The bile rose in my throat as I passed by building after building, house after house. The hum of traffic to my right was ever-present, and even though I floated through like a husk, I didn't stop the scan of my surroundings.

Maybe this was how Ursuline would have kept going forward too. One step after another despite the agony that coursed through me. If something happened to them... Bile rose in my throat. All too fast, my mind spiraled down dark paths. If they were tossed in a threadbare cell. Beaten, battered, worse...

If they weren't around, only a charred future remained for me.

A shudder rolled through my body, and my eyes ached, even though no tears emerged for once.

I glanced at the GPS on my phone. A minute away. My heart thumped hard. The idea of going into their apartment without them felt sacrosanct. How would I even get inside? Ursuline hadn't given me a key. Hell, we'd only just agreed to be in a relationship.

And already, the glimmer of hope had been shattered.

Monsters didn't escape from Alpha Blue. No, they vanished, and they were either dragged off to cells to rot or were banished to monster colonies. Knowing how Frederick operated, Ursuline would be sent below to New Atlantis to work in the orichalcum mines. If I didn't stop this, somehow, they'd never escape the monster that had plagued them their whole life. Panic gripped my chest.

If they ended up below, I couldn't reach them.

While there was underwater transport to and from New Atlantis, I could guarantee Frederick wouldn't be letting me aboard any time soon, and he controlled a large portion of the city.

If I didn't get Ursuline free, and fast, I might never get the chance.

Pressure seeped into my bones.

I stopped in front of a three-story home with a steep gabled roof and decorative purple trim against the black clapboard exterior. It reminded me in a way of Sofia's place, unique and definitively them. Ursuline had made it sound like they lived in an apartment, but the building before me looked like a singular house.

I stepped up the walkway, my skin prickling as if I were being watched. Ever since I left Triton Manor, I couldn't shake the feeling. Chances were, I'd have to wait for Sofia to get here to do anything. Not only did she have a barrier spell cast, but I also didn't have a key or lockpicking skills.

All I had was a directive to nab the Liquidium Industries folders.

When I reached the door, a sense of...something wrong...settled inside me.

Maybe I should try the knob, just in case. Standing out here in front of Ursuline's apartment was like asking to be caught. And this time I'd be by myself, left to my own devices.

I reached for the knob and twisted.

Unlocked.

My brows drew together. Had Sofia somehow gotten here before me? A lingering burnt sugar smell hinted of the perimeter spell that they'd set in place, and yet when I tried to step inside, my foot settled onto the ground.

The inside of the house looked similar to the exterior, and the deep scent of currant lingered through the entryway. A sharp shard of longing pierced my chest.

This couldn't be the end for us. Not when we'd only just begun.

Rustling sounded from up the steps. I sucked in a shaky breath. The art on the walls snagged my attention as I ascended the staircase, moody and atmospheric pieces, which fit them perfectly. Even from here, the imprints of Ursuline on this place made me twist to knots inside. In a way, this felt like a fugue state, as if they'd reappear at any moment. They'd been right by my side less than an hour ago, and I couldn't fathom what would happen if Cillian didn't have enough sway to track them down. To free them.

How would this situation be for people who had no one at all? Like Jason, and others who'd escaped bad situations and were trying to survive? Fuck. My mind dizzied as I reached the top of the staircase, and I clenched my jaw hard, attempting to shut out the conflicting thoughts and worries.

More of the rustling came from one of the rooms to the right, so I followed it, making sure to approach quietly. While the only logical explanation was Sofia, given the boundary being down, I wasn't in a safe situation, by any means. Each wooden floorboard tried to creak, so I slowed my paces, focusing on my breathing, on each forward footstep.

A low curse sounded from the room, freezing me in place.

That didn't sound like Sofia.

Sweat prickled on my palms as I continued to approach. Fuck, what if the noise came from one of Frederick's men? What if they'd somehow made it through? Ursuline and I could be locked away in separate prisons and never be able to reach each other. Adrenaline pulsed through my veins, cold and icy. The temptation to turn around and run back down the stairs and out the door flooded through me in a real way.

Except Ursuline needed me to do this.

I might be a failure in everything else in my life, but I couldn't fail them here.

I reached into my pocket, wishing I had more than a wallet with a bottle opener attachment, my phone, a few pens. Something I could defend myself with. My mouth dried as I reached the doorframe.

Then I peered inside.

Back turned, a man rifled through one of the massive filing cabinets in this room, which looked like an office. The broad shoulders, the thick, silver hair fired signal flares. He didn't need to face me for me to know who this was.

Frederick Triton in the flesh.

The very man I was running from.

I backed up a pace on instinct, but my heel snagged on a nail sticking out of the floorboard. My arms shot out as I wobbled, and a slight, sharp breath escaped me.

"Who's there?" Frederick whirled around, his eyes flashing. When his gaze landed on me, they darkened. "Elrich Durand. Thought they'd captured you too."

Ice rushed through me in a fierce torrent. Fuck, fuck, fuck.

This was the exact last person I wanted to see.

"Ursuline sent you here, didn't they?" he said, his eyes narrowing. He took one step forward, looming over me even from the other end of the room. If he closed the distance, I wouldn't stand a chance. "Their documents won't do much good if they're burnt to ash."

That was when I noticed the container of accelerant on the floor.

My throat tightened. Of course he'd be trying to tie up loose ends. One thing those in society knew how to do was to keep the skeletons in their closets hidden, at all costs.

With Ursuline disappeared and their house incinerated, Frederick could slip out of any repercussions.

"You should've just married my daughter, Elrich," Frederick said. "Not that you've got anything going on upstairs, but you would've been provided for. Could've still lived your own life." He took another step forward, the floorboard creaking under his weight. "Now I can't let you leave alive."

A chill spread all the way through my body. Frederick would get away with it too. Just like he'd gotten away with so many crimes before. With horrifying things. This wasn't a man before me but a waking nightmare, one that had ruined countless lives.

One that had destroyed Ursuline's family.

"Your parents won't be looking for you," he said, reaching into his pocket. "And you'll have tragically died in a mysterious fire at your lover's house. The cops won't waste a second glance at the report."

The truth of what he said stabbed me right in the chest. Because at the end of the day, the person who'd come to mean the most to me, the one who viewed me as valuable, had just been dragged away by Alpha Blue. Rage kindled inside me, starting with a spark, a flicker of the starter to dry wood. It spread, those flames licking up my insides, the heat building, building, building.

Frederick Triton had so much blood on his hands.

And unlike with Alpha Blue, where I'd been frozen, in shock from the suddenness of Ursuline's abduction, here and now, I burned.

I burned for every sea monster who'd lost their life in the mines.

I burned for Ursuline's sibling, who Frederick had assaulted. For their family, who he hadn't protected.

I burned for Ursuline, for every loss, every ounce of pain he'd inflicted on them, both physically and emotionally.

A quick scan of the room gave me two things—a black, pointed paperweight on the desk to the right and to the left a bookcase filled with heavy tomes. Either could work to bludgeon, but I'd have to move faster than Triton.

Frederick stepped forward another pace, and my guts clenched.

I couldn't run from here. Not now.

"Well, well, I was wondering who'd broken through the boundary spell." Sofia's voice sounded behind me.

Relief slammed into me fast and fierce. Sofia had arrived.

"Now, what would you be doing rummaging around Ursuline's apartment?" Sofia said in mock surprise. She stood beside me and tapped her finger against her chin. "Seems an odd thing for an ex-employer to do."

"Sofia, stay out of this," Frederick growled. "They're my contracted employee, and I'm going through documents that belong to me."

"Because clearly you need accelerant to search for some documents," Sofia said, arching a brow. "Your arguments are getting flimsier by the day."

Frederick's face turned purple with anger. "Your status won't protect you."

"Nor will yours," Sofia said, her voice dark and low, a menace there that would've struck terror into me if she weren't on my side. "Elrich, find the documents. I'll handle him."

"What good will your boundary spells do here?" Frederick said, taking another step forward. His hands neared his pockets, a few handles sticking out. "You're out of weapons."

Sofia tutted at him. "You should know better than to trust the rumors, Frederick." With that, she lifted her hand, and electricity crackled in the center of her palm.

His attention switched to her, and I darted to the left. He reached out with a swipe, but his focus remained front and center on Sofia. I looped around him to rush up to the filing cabinets he'd been rummaging through.

I yanked open the top filing cabinet, the sour stench of the accelerant tingling my nose. Frederick had splattered it over the surfaces of the cabinets, and all it would take was a match to set these ablaze.

"You wouldn't unleash that in here," Frederick growled at Sofia.

"Try me," she challenged.

Fuck, fuck, fuck. The folders were...oh, thank the gods, they were alphabetized. My fingers shook as I flipped through A names then checked the back of the stack, only to E. Godsdamn.

I tugged open the drawer beneath it, this one starting at F. I flipped to the end—K.

A sharp crackling noise lit the air, along with a flash.

"Fuck," Frederick cursed, mere feet away. Far too close for my liking. My arms trembled, but I didn't dare look behind me.

I had one task. I was damn well going to complete it.

I bent forward and dragged the bottom drawer open. The L files. My hands shook so badly at this point I could barely filter through. I just grabbed a huge section of the files and yanked them out. The ones remaining started at M, so I could only hope Liquidium Industries had been filed here.

Before I could rise to my feet, all of a sudden, an arm wrapped around my neck and dragged me upright.

Frederick. He'd closed the space between us.

"Try and aim at me now, Sofia," he growled, and he jerked me in front of him, the pressure on my windpipe making my breaths shudder. The files dropped out of my hand, and I tried to swallow but couldn't. Frederick drew a blade from his side, the glint of the metal clear in the short space between us. The stench of him, brine and sweat and burnt...something made me want to gag.

Frederick slid the blade right under my chin, a mere inch above his meaty arm.

I balled my hands into fists. Fuck.

Sofia stood before us, the lightning crackling in her palms. Her brows drew together, and her eyes calculated.

"I'll slit his throat right now," Frederick said. "He's worth nothing."

Sofia's expression darkened. "Now that's where you're wrong."

Her words burrowed inside me, trailing deeper, deeper, deeper, until the spark settled on the pile of my self-esteem that had crumbled to nothing over the years. But in this moment, this second, the spark dropped there and ignited the whole damn thing.

I was tired of feeling helpless. Time to fight, damn the consequences.

A glint caught my eye right beside me. Frederick loomed from behind, and his pendant dangled forward.

Cerulean, shifting, and full of magic.

I had one shot.

I reached for it, wrapped my fingers around the pendant, and yanked.

Frederick let out a curse, and the knife jostled against my throat, a light sting blooming as the blade kissed my skin. The chain of the pendant snapped, my fist tight around the stone.

Lightning sparked and sizzled by our feet, and Frederick barked another curse. This time, his grip around me loosened. I raked my nails at the arm holding the knife, then stomped down on his other foot, and he yanked it back, the blade avoiding my skin by a mere inch.

I launched myself toward Sofia. She was the safest place to be.

Sofia all but pushed me behind her as she positioned herself in front of me.

Frederick glanced between us, wild-eyed, and he reached into his pocket. "Fine. We'll start this instead."

In three deft motions, he pulled out a lighter, flicked the flame on, and dropped it onto the filing cabinet. Covered in accelerant.

Flames burst forth, fierce and furious, devouring the vast amount of paper in the room. This place was a tinderbox.

Frederick charged past us, shoving in the process. My heart hammered hard. He couldn't get away. Not after setting Ursuline's house ablaze. Not after hurting so many people. I clutched the pendant hard and raced after him.

I wasn't sure what I could do—weaponless and weak—but I had to try.

Heat bloomed inside the office, the flames spreading across every surface.

"Out," Sofia called. "Stop him."

I didn't bother turning back, just raced after him, the floorboards thumping with the force of my movements. Frederick moved liquid-fast, already at the bottom of the staircase. Once he burst out the doors, how would I get him? Guaranteed, his men were waiting to back him up.

I had to stop him.

I squeezed the pendant still in my hand.

Maybe...

When I reached the last stair, I whipped around the foyer, looking for something. Anything.

Frederick tossed the door open, and he'd already taken the first step out, the sun blaring in.

A heavy-looking bust was wedged in the corner on a side table, some ornate, gorgeous obsidian piece.

I dropped the pendant to the ground, snagged the bust, and brought it crashing down on the crystal.

A crunch sounded from underneath, echoing through the air.

Frederick shouted outside. I didn't bother checking the pendant and bolted for the door.

Sofia rushed down the steps, and behind her, smoke roiled from the second floor. The heat had spread here, and we needed to get out.

When I got to the doorway, I clutched the frame.

Frederick wasn't running away now. No, he lay on the sidewalk, a bright green mermaid tail extending out in place of his legs.

A bark of a laugh escaped from Sofia.

Already, three men in black emerged from cars, and they circled around him. Two guys lifted him from the ground, and they shifted him toward one of the cars. Frederick cursed up a storm, his face purple with rage. With him flopping around on the concrete, it was hard to view him as the towering threat from mere moments before.

"Fuck, should we pursue?" I asked, my throat dry.

Sofia lifted her phone. "This is better than stopping him. Already snapped a few shots. We need to get out of here, though. The whole house is about to go up in flames."

"Should we call the authorities?" I asked, chewing on my lower lip.

"Once we're in the car and on our way," she said. "Follow me."

My chest clenched tight. Fuck. Ursuline had asked me to do one thing, and I'd fucked up. When I glanced back at the staircase, it was so full of smoke there was no way I'd get back up there. I was going to be sick.

"What are you waiting for?" Sofia asked, standing a few feet away from me, heading toward her car.

"The files," I murmured, taking the first steps to follow her.

"You mean these?" Sofia said, lifting up a handful of manila folders. "I grabbed the ones on Liquidium before we left."

Relief slammed into me, followed by embarrassment. I scrubbed at my chest as I matched Sofia's pace. "I should've figured to do that."

She shook her head. "None of that pitying shit. You thought fast—snagged the pendant in the first place, then you broke through Frederick's veil of being human. Wonder how Alpha Blue and the Human First assholes will take to learning they've been rubbing elbows with a monster."

A hysterical laugh bubbled up inside me, exploding out. Out of anyone, I knew intimately how well that would go over.

Sofia unlocked her small purple sedan and slipped into the driver's seat. I hopped into the passenger's side, casting one more glance at Ursuline's apartment, now brimming with smoke. Any moment now, the fire engines would be arriving, and we wanted to be gone beforehand.

"Where to now?" I asked, my heart thumping hard.

A grin stretched Sofia's lips. "We're going to jailbreak Ursuline."

Chapter 30

It would've been far too easy for Cillian to make a few phone calls, threaten a few people, and have them return Ursuline. Of course things didn't work out that way. Yet I couldn't help wishing we could've solved this situation simply.

Instead, we headed to an all-too-familiar place.

One that made my gut churn.

"Who knew your family had such strong ties to Alpha Blue," Sofia mused as she headed down the winding back road in a direction I'd driven for years.

All those years, and I'd never realized we kept a holding cell for them on our grounds. I'd explored, sure, but there were areas I'd never bothered with, stretches of the woods too dense to wander on the massive expanse of what we owned.

"I sure as fuck didn't," I murmured, bile rising inside me. Not that the discovery surprised me, given the way my parents had always easily disappeared any problems, but the disappointment slammed into me regardless.

"I assumed," Sofia said. "You don't strike me as the type who'd tolerate that."

I chewed on my lower lip. Maybe I'd remained too blind for too long. Too busy trying to please my parents rather than fighting against the crimes they stacked up. In a way, I could understand Arielle turning a blind eye to her father's atrocities. The alternative was a hell of a lot scarier.

"I won't," I promised Sofia, since I couldn't speak to the past. "My parents were talented at keeping our lives compartmentalized. Yet I should've looked closer. Should've realized what they'd been involved in."

"Suddenly makes sense why Frederick wanted an arranged marriage with your family in the first place," Sofia drawled.

That, I had figured out, even if I hadn't realized my family had an Alpha Blue holding house on their property. I'd spent so much time trying to leave the place that I hadn't wanted to explore it. And when I was younger, my tutors and nannies had kept a close rein on me, so I hadn't been free to wander through the grounds.

The nearer we got to my parents' house, the more my chest tightened. The weight of those memories grew heavier and heavier, until it threatened to crush me. Yet Cillian had gotten intel that they'd shifted Ursuline to the holding cell there, and the next step would be taking them back down to New Atlantis.

Where I'd be unable to do a damn thing.

"Mal arrived ahead of time," Sofia commented. "So the guards at the back entrance should be dealt with."

I swallowed hard. I didn't want to know what "dealt with" meant. "Should I be carrying any weapons?"

Sofia arched a brow and passed me a glance. "Not unless you're trained in them. I've got a few spelled flash-bangs to use in a pinch, which I'll pass on to you."

A little relief fluttered through me, as I didn't feel confident with anything sharp or dangerous.

The gates to the Durand family manor rose into view, and my chest constricted. My parents hadn't tried to contact me once after they'd sold me off. Once I'd left, I hadn't checked. I didn't want to witness their disappointment.

We bypassed them, heading for the entrance that staff used, less ostentatious and more economical, just a pair of black iron gates with zero flourishes.

"Ready?" Sofia asked. My whole body hummed. The alternate option—being away from Ursuline permanently—wasn't one I could consider. My heart twisted hard at the thought of them, how they'd be suffering in a cell, alone, after finding out about the death of their family.

"Yeah," I murmured, my voice low.

We entered through the gates. True to expectation, they were empty of the normal guards. To the right led to the manor, but instead, Sofia jerked the car to the left, down a dirt path that wound its way into the woods.

"How many are in there?" I asked, my heart thumping hard.

"Threadbare operation," Sofia said. "And I called in reinforcements. As long as Frederick didn't sound the alarm..."

The shadows descended over us from the thick surrounding forest, and the coolness settled beneath my skin. Dread rose up inside me upon our approach. Seeing an area so foreign amid something I'd grown up with cast such a dissonance to my whole upbringing.

At the end of the winding pathway, swathed by darkness, was a small hut.

I could barely process that this had been here the entire time.

"When we head in, stay back," Sofia said, slowing down outside the building. I didn't spot any other vehicles, which meant the Alpha Blue stationed in there had most likely been dropped off. "I'll stun the guards."

I nodded, the words drying on my tongue. Once she shut off the engine, tension hummed in its wake.

We exited the car in silence, and the shadows settled over me at once, the air crisp out here. I'd lost all sense of time today, disoriented like I'd been tumbling in a dryer. Sofia pressed a magic-based flash-bang grenade into each of my hands, and I gripped them tight, my palms slick with sweat. She didn't say a word, but I assumed we were past the time of talking.

The hut was simple, with a black clapboard roof and spartan white exterior. The door had black bars over the front, as did the windows, making it clear this was a prison not a cottage. How many people were inside there? Alpha Blue was always armed to the teeth, and I'd what, sparkle them to distraction? My throat was dry, and my limbs trembled as we approached.

Sofia tested the knob, and it jiggled. A slow smile rolled to her lips.

Then she flung the door open and marched inside.

Panic flooded through my veins as I raced in after her, then skidded to a halt.

Three men in all black surrounded another guy in the center of the room. Their guns were trained on him. On closer glance, the black horns, the dark scale patterning along the side of his face signaled he wasn't quite human. Along both sides were jail cells, a pale seafoam-green color, and I couldn't help but scan them. A familiar figure stood behind them to the left, clutching the bars.

Ursuline.

Their dark eyes locked in on me, widening in surprise. My heart cracked open at the sight of them.

They were alive.

They were here, and they were alive, and our window hadn't closed yet.

"Sorry, Sofia, I got caught," the monster in the middle of the room called out. All attention diverted to us as Sofia continued her march toward the Alpha Blue guards. The monster shrugged, his hands slightly lifted, but I caught the glint in his gaze, the hint of a grin.

Hope bubbled up inside me.

"Mal," she said. "Just the dragon-in-distress I was looking for."

"What are you talking about?" one of the guards called out as he rushed toward Sofia.

"I don't think it's a good idea to leave me alone." Mal's voice grew deeper, darker. "You never know what a dragon will get up to." A wicked grin split his lips, and the air hummed. His whole body began to shift into an orange-red, like he immolated from the inside out.

"Fuck," the guy next to him yelped. "He's on fire!"

"Go, get Ursuline out," Sofia commanded me.

I didn't need to be told twice. I raced up to the bars holding Ursuline back, and at the first brush of my hands against theirs, a sob welled up in my throat.

"You came for me," Ursuline murmured, wonder shining in their eyes. For a moment, all that existed was us—the air thick with tension, the joy rising within me fast and fierce.

"I always will," I promised, meaning those words with every ounce of my soul. When I'd been stuck at the manor, they'd sacrificed everything to get me out. And there wasn't a future I wanted more than the one with them by my side. "Now, how do I free you?"

"The lock is there," Ursuline said, caressing the large lock keeping the cell shut with a tentacle. "The keys are with the asshole over by Mal."

The guard they gestured to had backed away a few paces, as Mal turned himself into a bonfire, the flames licking up around him. My stomach churned. Out of one fire and into another.

The guard's keys jangled at his side. I squeezed the grenade in my hand. I had to try.

I raced up to him.

He whirled around right as I reached for the key loop on his belt. My hands dropped to the loop, and he dipped down to his other side—for his pistol.

I yanked for the loop at the same time I tugged at the pin for the flash-bang grenade—and then shoved it right into him.

His boot thudded into my chest, and I staggered away. The keys clattered to the ground, right as the flash-bang exploded.

I slammed down to the floor, winging my arm over my face. A crack sounded in the air, and light flared, along with another flash that sizzled around me. Sparks zapped at my skin, and I cursed. White spots filled my eyes, and I blinked as I fumbled forward, hoping to land on the keys.

Any moment, more Alpha Blue could be arriving, and we'd be fucked. We needed to get out, and soon.

My hand landed on cool metal, and I yanked it.

Just as it tugged in the opposite direction.

"Fuck," I swore, trying to tighten my grip, even as I squinted and blinked. Trying to get my vision back again.

"Get off," the man growled, but a second later a thump sounded, and the tug went lax. I teetered backwards, the keys in hand as I caught a flimsy glimpse of a man on the ground and Sofia looming overhead. Lightning crackled around her like a living entity.

I scrambled backwards on the floor, the keys jangling in my grip, until I hit the bars with a thump.

"Good job, sunshine," Ursuline said, their voice so steady and tender. My heart squeezed tight. Fuck, I hadn't been sure I'd ever hear them call me that again. Their tentacle slipped around the key loop, and seconds later they were undoing the lock to their cell.

It opened, and I pushed myself up to crash into their arms. They squeezed me tight to their chest, and I sucked in a shuddering inhale. The warmth of them surrounding me, the scent of currants, of the sea, the way their presence quieted something inside me—Ursuline was all I wanted. Their tentacle curled around my thigh, and I clutched them a little tighter, as if we could merge into one.

"Sorry to cut this reunion short, but we need to jet," Mal called over.

I stepped back at once. Right. In the middle of an Alpha Blue holding cell.

Sofia and Mal stood upright, but I noticed the three Alpha Blue guards did not. They lay on the floor, and despite their all-black attire, I caught the dampness on a shirt here, an uncomfortable twist of a limb there.

"Only one of them is dead. The other two are incapacitated," Sofia said. "Whether they survive or not will depend on timing. But they're not our problem."

"We need to get out," Ursuline said, grabbing my hand and gliding toward the entrance. I stumbled at first but then hastened to catch up. Mal and Sofia barely breathed hard after taking out three Alpha Blue guards, and an air of deadliness simmered around them. They'd handled these armed, trained men with ease. My stomach roiled at the awkward placement of one guy's neck, his eyes vacant. The sight imprinted on my brain as I rushed past.

When we broke into the cool forest air, all four of us headed toward Sofia's car at a record pace. My shoes kicked up dirt, my steps springing off the loam. Unlike on the way here, I claimed the back seat with Ursuline, while Sofia hopped into the driver's side and Mal in the passenger's.

"Let's get the hell out of here." She turned the engine on and circled around down the path.

All it took was one glance at the road ahead of us to see the obvious problem.

Two Alpha Blue vans rolled our way.

Oh fuck. I clutched Ursuline's hand, and they exchanged a worried glance with me. My heart thudded hard. No matter what happened, the fact we'd reunited, the fact I'd found them—it mattered.

The tension in the car skyrocketed as the vans barreled toward us.

"What can we do?" I asked. "If you can pivot around them, we can try the main entrance." If any of the people I knew were manning it, I could probably sway them to let us go. Maybe.

"You ready?" Sofia asked, glancing at Mal.

"Of course," he said, flashing a charming grin. "Happy to oblige."

With that, Mal cracked open the car door, while we were moving, and he rolled out.

A shout of surprise lodged in my throat.

One second a scaled dragonkin tumbled onto the ground, and the next he began to expand. His tail extended, his body grew larger, more dragonlike, and his face transformed into a maw. Massive wings expanded from his back with a powerful flap, and he rose above the car. I plastered my face to the window, just to catch a glimpse of the magnificent black dragon that now hovered above our car.

I'd never seen one up close before, and the sight knocked the breath from my lungs. All black shining scales, deep obsidian claws, and the same clever eyes that belonged to the man who'd been sitting in the car. His legs and arms were poised as he sailed on his wings above us, the wicked arch of them mesmerizing.

The Alpha Blue vans slowed down. They must've caught sight of him.

Except he didn't shrink back from them in the slightest. No, Mal opened his mouth, and a stream of fire descended upon the vans.

My heart raced.

"Well, damn," Sofia cursed as she turned the wheel hard to the left, taking us off the path. Sticks crunched under the tires, and we bumped over rocks as she zoomed us around the Alpha Blue vans.

"If they made it in through the side, that means their sentries are back in action," Ursuline warned.

"Main entrance," Sofia said. "Think you can help us out, Elrich?"

"What about Mal?" I asked, twisting around. He released another torrent of flame, a bright orange and gold stream.

"He'll be flying off," Sofia said. "He was just buying us a few minutes."

I swallowed hard, my throat impossibly dry. "I can try at the gates."

Ursuline squeezed my hand, and their eyes met mine. "Thank you." The seriousness there settled on me like a weighted blanket, offering a security I craved right now, even though the panic threatened to carry me away.

Sofia turned right at the fork in the road onto a pathway I knew by heart, one I'd traveled a thousand times over. Approaching it from this foreign place, after living outside of here...my head buzzed like I'd stirred a hornet's nest. And the guards stood at the gates, Michel and

Jeremy, guys I'd waved hi to for years, given a smile and a greeting on a regular basis.

We'd already left a trail of bodies. My gut churned. I couldn't stomach more—not them.

Sofia slowed upon her approach, and Michel lifted his walkie-talkie to his mouth, seemingly in discussion. Had Alpha Blue alerted them? Had these men known about the holding cell my parents had on their property? They had to. My insides curdled.

She rolled down the window and hung halfway out. "Just heading out."

Jeremy strode over, dressed in his black turtleneck, black exercise pants. His head was shaved, and a glower twisted his features. "How did you get in?"

"The other entrance," Sofia said, eyebrow arched in challenge.

"I've been told to hold you here," Jeremy responded.

I pushed up between the seats. When his gaze landed on me, his brows rose.

"Elrich?" he asked, glancing between me, Sofia, and Ursuline. "What are you doing here?"

"The short version is that my parents sold me, I escaped, and I'm trying to live my life," I stated.

Michel stepped around next to Jeremy. "Technically, he's one of the people we listen to."

"Was," Jeremy clarified, but then he frowned again and cast a look in the direction of the manor. My heart hammered hard. Then he heaved out a sigh. "But it's good enough for me."

A grin ripped across my face. "Thank you."

I wanted to believe in the good in people, that not all of them would disappoint, and little moments like these—they helped.

"Oh, fuck," Michel swore.

I twisted to follow his gaze. Another car rolled up behind us, but it wasn't Alpha Blue. My gut sank.

For me, it was worse.

"Who's there?" Sofia asked, looking to me.

Ursuline squeezed my hand again. "Want me to come out with you?"

I shook my head. "I'll take care of this on my own." My legs trembled at the thought, but I forced myself out of the car, even though I fumbled with the handle a few times. Sweat already burst onto my palms.

Already waiting for me were two people I hadn't seen since my engagement party.

Angus and Mina Durand. The parents who might've wanted a son, but they'd never wanted me.

"What is this?" My father's voice was thunderous. "I got reports that someone had broken through the gate into the..."

"Alpha Blue's containment unit?" I asked, my voice sharp. The disgust welled in me, giving me power I'd never held before when facing them. While I had known they were problematic, I hadn't realized the depths of their complicity. "They were holding my partner hostage," I said. "And we grabbed them, so now we're leaving."

"We had an arrangement with Frederick, to try to salvage some of the deal after your failure," Angus said, arms crossed, looming over me like he always had. Except this time his posturing didn't shrink me down the way it used to. Because after witnessing the strength of my lover, I could see how weak this man truly was. With all of Angus's posturing, he was terrified to step an inch outside the rigid society he'd been born into. He was fragile glass, one bat away from shattering.

"Oh?" I challenged back. "Didn't think you made deals with monsterkind."

Trying to plead with him for my sake would get me nowhere. But I was well aware of one thing he cared about.

Appearance.

"What are you talking about?" he asked, his voice sharp.

"Sofia, the pictures?" I called to the car, and she tugged her phone out fast, flipped through, then leaned out to pass it to me. I showed the screen to my father, of Frederick being carried away, his mermaid tail fully showing. "Those are going to hit the nearest news cycle the second we send them in. If I were you, I'd get away from the blast zone as fast as possible. But if you don't let us go, I'll make damn sure to expose the deals you made with him. We'll see how your business fares after a blow like that."

"Elrich," Mina chided, even though the reprimand was hollow and empty. My father gaped, opening his mouth and closing it like a fish.

I stood there with the phone in hand, clutching it tighter. My heart reeled from the confrontation, but a buoyancy rose inside me as well, a groundswell of energy that had been building, building, building all these years. I'd spent so long cowed by them, but no more.

I was free.

My father's face turned purple as he processed, and I waited, hands balled into fists. Would he...? I resisted the urge to chew the inside of my mouth or glance to the car, facing him this time. Not backing down.

"Let them out," my father snapped, then he turned on his heel and stormed to his car. Mina glanced between us, her eyes wide with shock. "Come on," he barked at her, before he hopped back into his vehicle.

Michel passed me a broad smile and pressed the button to open the gates.

My heart thumped hard. I'd done it.

I'd stood up to them.

I swallowed, my throat dry, and I headed back to Sofia's car. Once I slid into the seat, Ursuline captured my face in their hands, and they crashed down on me with a bruising kiss. I savored every second of it, the endorphins pumping hard through my veins, the exuberant joy rising like a tide to the point it overwhelmed me.

Sofia glanced back at both of us and winked. "Let's get the hell out of here."

With that, we drove through the gate and out...into our freedom.

Chapter 31

Three days of waking up beside Ursuline, and they weren't enough. I didn't know if I'd ever get enough. I rolled over in bed, reaching out for them...except their side of the bed was empty. The sheets were cold.

I blinked and then rubbed my eyes before pushing myself upright. The room was the same one we'd been staying in at the Spires all week, a safe haven while we figured our situation out. In the days that followed after we escaped my parents' manor, Sofia had forwarded the photos to the news outlets. Articles were plastered everywhere with Frederick Triton's image in true mermaid form. Some tried to argue it must be altered, but others began to put the pieces together about how he'd managed to control the orichalcum trade this way, and then the stories spiraled from there.

Except his retreating to New Atlantis wasn't good enough. He'd ruined so many lives down below, and knowing he'd continue to do so made my chest ache.

A cough sounded at the doorway.

Ursuline leaned against the frame, taking up the whole space. They wore a loose black tunic with a low V that exposed a good amount of their chiseled chest. Their silver hair was slicked back, the strands tamed, and a lazy smile tilted their lips. Fuck, the sight of them knocked the breath from my lungs. Their dark eyes held a voracious hunger as they scanned me over, and when they glided forward on their tentacles, I squirmed in place. My cock was still hard from waking up, and the sight of them turned me on effortlessly.

"Where did you go?" I asked.

"I was working on finishing touches," Ursuline said, sweeping in. They plunked down next to me on the mattress and leaned in. I met their lips at once, savoring the sweetness of their kiss, how it made my whole body wake up. Gods, I loved them with everything in me, and I could barely believe they loved me in return.

Ursuline wove their fingers through my hair and tugged. They drew back, tenderness in their gaze that traveled straight to my heart. "You're perfect, sunshine."

"Mm, I'm a bit rumpled is what I am," I murmured, heat rising to my cheeks.

"Perfect," they insisted, and the emphasis filled me with warmth. "And all mine."

"Is that a hint you want to start chastity again?" I asked, shifting on the mattress. My cock ached at the thought. "Because I wouldn't be opposed."

Ursuline's eyes danced with wickedness. "Tonight, I'm going to fuck you until you're screaming, make you come so many times you forget your name. And after that, I'll lock up your pretty cock."

Flames rushed through me in a fast, fierce torrent. "Please."

"But we've got something important to do first," they said, their voice growing serious. My chest sank. I knew what awaited us, and while it was necessary, that didn't mean the nerves hadn't swept in.

"I'm coming with you," I said, pushing out of bed. Ursuline watched as I slipped on underwear, loose black pants, a gauzy gray shirt, socks, and then dragged black shoes on. "Are you sure you don't need more time?"

Ursuline's lips formed a thin line. They hadn't broken down, even though mention of their family caused a storm to cross their face. Yet pain emanated from them in interspersions. It wasn't constant—probably because they'd been separate from them for so long—but every so often a song would play, or they'd stop on the page of a book, or a comment would be made in passing that held memories.

And those caused them to recoil, for their expression to darken, for them to retreat into themself. Yet, I had the sense the dam was waiting to break. And when it did, I'd be there.

"More time gives Frederick the ability to escape," Ursuline said. "I need him to understand he made a mistake in crossing me. That the power he wielded is gone."

I swallowed but nodded. "Will anyone be joining us?"

Ursuline shook their head. "Just you and me. How we started this, and how we'll end it."

My chest squeezed tight. We could do this. As much as Triton was a scary bastard, so was Ursuline.

And they'd done their homework.

"What do you need to get?" I asked, popping into the attached bathroom to brush my teeth and piss. I ran a brush through my hair, but it always had a sort of windswept look.

"I've got it all right here," Ursuline said by the door to the bathroom. One glance in the mirror and I could see the suitcase held up by one of their tentacles. "Once I got the information to the proper channels, it was easy to set things in motion."

I shook my head. Ursuline had tried to explain their plan to me several times, but the legalese made my ears leak. "Well then, let's get on the road."

We exited the room and zipped down the elevator, stopping at the parking garage level. Cillian had a host of cars there, and he was letting us borrow a sleek purple one for the time being. As much as I appreciated the safe place and generosity, part of me couldn't wait until Ursuline and I could set out into the world and start to carve our own future.

My mind whirred with the options ahead of me, so different from the cattle chute I'd been stuck in my entire life.

We exited the parking garage and set off into the streets of Peregrine City, the skyscrapers looming around us. The colors and sights of the city burst all around, from the massive wing sculpture in the center of Argyle Park to the multicolored overhangs on everything from restaurants to divination centers.

"Now that you're no longer employed by the Tritons, what do you want to do?" I asked, curiosity sneaking in.

Ursuline glanced to me, their one hand on the steering wheel. "I've known that for years. I'm going to start up a non-profit law firm to help monsterkind."

My chest squeezed tight. As if I couldn't love them more.

"I'm not the only one who's free, though," they commented. "What do you want, Elrich?"

Gods, what a question. "To paint sounds trivial, doesn't it?" I murmured, staring out the window as the buildings flashed by. "Yet that's what I've longed to do my whole life."

"With talent like yours, it's not trivial," Ursuline said. "I'd love nothing more than our future home to be filled with your art."

My heart thudded hard, my mind soaring with possibilities. My fingers itched to grab a paintbrush and find a canvas. Yet we had an important task to complete, one that would secure the future we were speaking of.

Already we'd reached the edges of Peregrine City, those familiar back roads leading to Triton Manor. I'd thought once I left that prison I'd never return, but today was worth the trip.

Ursuline's knuckles whitened as they clutched the steering wheel a little tighter the closer we got. I wasn't the only one affected. I reached over and stroked one of their tentacles. They passed me a grateful smile, and my heart bloomed with fresh warmth. They were everything I'd wanted in a partner, and a future with them? Fuck, I'd never longed for anything more.

We reached the winding driveway for Triton Manor, and the air in the car tensed. We slowed our approach as we rolled down the long path, heading toward the mansion by the sea, the one that had such a twisted hold on me. Despite the days of confinement, how trapped I'd felt there, I'd also always remember it.

For it was there I'd met Ursuline.

It was there I had fallen in love.

We had been a bloom poking through the cracks in the concrete, something beautiful in spite of all the ugliness surrounding it.

When Ursuline pulled to a park in front of the main entrance, they heaved a shaky breath.

I placed a hand over theirs. "We've got this. You did your research, and Frederick doesn't deserve to escape, not after everything he's done."

Ursuline bobbed their head in a nod. They traced the side of my face, the touch feather-light. "Thank you for doing this with me."

"You're stuck with me," I said, a grin rising to my lips. "Even though I'll warn you, I'm needy."

"Maybe I love that about you," Ursuline said as they cracked the car door open. "Maybe I love everything about you, Elrich Durand."

With that, they snagged their briefcase from the back seat and exited the car, and I took my cue and did the same. Each step toward the front door echoed, and despite the bright sunlight beaming down on us, I couldn't help the chill that raced down my spine. When I'd first come to this place with my parents, I'd had no idea what awaited me.

However, the trials and tribulations had led me to being here, with the love of my life.

Ursuline lifted their fist and knocked. We waited, a hum in the air between us that all but vibrated.

Then the door creaked open.

Ernest, the butler, stepped into view. When his gaze landed on us, he paled. "What are you doing here?"

"I've got a legal summons for Frederick Triton," Ursuline said, cracking open the briefcase. "If you wouldn't mind fetching him."

"Right away," Ernest said as he rushed from the entrance like his tailcoats had caught on fire.

"Who's here?" a familiar voice sounded, and I chewed on the inside of my cheek until I tasted blood.

Arielle peeked out the doorway. Her face grew tight and angry, the most I'd ever seen from her in my entire stay at Triton Manor. "Haven't you both done enough?"

"Did you know?" I asked, the question one that had lingered with me. "What your father was doing?"

Arielle glared at me, hatred shining in those eyes that were once always light and carefree. "Don't be naïve, Elrich."

Her response settled in my gut. The comment was so similar to things my parents had said my entire life, how I'd missed so much of what was going on around me because my head was in the clouds.

"You'd better get used to figuring your own life out, navigating situations yourself," Ursuline said, their tone sharp. "Your father can't evade his crimes forever."

Arielle opened her mouth, but before she could say anything, a looming shadow drew our attention.

Frederick Triton strode forward, looking like he'd bring lightning down from the heavens to strike us where we stood. Today he was on two legs, a different pendant around his neck. But the slip with the old one had cost him his reputation.

"Is it wise to show up at my doorstep, given you're in breach of your contract?" Frederick rumbled, casting a dark glare in our direction.

Ursuline stared him down. "You'll find, given my family was not protected, that I'm not in breach in the slightest. That agreement ended the second they passed. Funny how long it took for the news to travel to me."

Frederick glared back at them, brimming with unspent violence. "Go, Arielle," he said. "I'll deal with this trash." She shook her head and slipped away as quickly as she'd arrived. Frederick crossed his arms. "Have you returned back to your apartment?"

"Heard it's a bit too crispy for that," Ursuline responded coolly. "Though I'd rather live there than where you'll be headed."

"Ernest mentioned a summons," Frederick said.

"Right," Ursuline said, passing over the file that they'd pulled from their briefcase. "A certain business, Liquidium Industries, is under the spotlight right now. And there are a host of angry businesses who've been fooled by the shell corporation for years. If you follow the financial trail, it sure looks like Triton Industries has been receiving undisclosed payments from the company for as many years."

"Get out," Triton growled, his face darkening. "Get out of my sight."

Ursuline stared back at him. "You've been evading justice for too long. Harming anyone who got in your way, taking anything you wanted—even people, monsters. No more. Hiding away in New Atlantis won't save you now. Some of the companies you screwed over reside down there as well. So have a nice life, Frederick. I'll see you in court."

With that, Ursuline turned and glided away. I set into motion after them at once, my skin prickling from the weight of Triton's glare. He didn't budge from the entryway, simply stood there glowering as he held the documents in hand that would seal his fate. Ursuline was a talented lawyer, hence why he'd kept them on for years, and they'd made sure he wouldn't be able to wiggle out of escaping the punishment he deserved.

I reached out for Ursuline's hand, and they took mine at once, their slender fingers weaving with mine. Together, we strode away from the Triton Manor, connected, united. We weren't racing away in fear any longer, and with Triton dealt with, we were no longer on the run.

We could finally start walking toward the future.

Chapter 32

I hadn't been to the Sentient Sea in some time.

The moment I stepped out of the car and into the bright sunlight, those warm beams filtered down onto my skin. Except our trip wasn't a casual or easy thing, despite the salt-soaked breeze swirling around me, the sky an aching sort of blue. When we'd left Triton Manor, Ursuline had one stop they wanted to make.

One they'd needed to ever since the meeting with Jason.

We'd made it to the beach, to the sea. We might not be down below in New Atlantis, but this connection to the water mattered.

Breakneck Beach was the place where Ursuline had first saved me, and they'd continued to do so the more we got to know each other. Except I was able to save them too. I'd spent my life feeling useless, like I didn't matter. Like I'd never be enough for anyone—certainly not my parents.

Yet Ursuline had effortlessly made me feel loved. They'd built me up brick by brick, and I'd begun to discover what I was capable of in the process.

They clutched my hand a little tighter as we headed toward the sand dunes. The sea roared in the distance, the steady thrum of the waves quieting my soul. After facing off against Frederick, this was needed.

My feet hit the sand, the warmed granules a caress, and ahead of me, the water sparkled under the bright midday sun. A few seagulls circled overhead and cawed, and smatterings of seaweed and shells decorated the shoreline. In the distance a few krakens swam out in the deep, and some mermaids splashed around, but they kept to themselves. I found a dry spot farther up and kicked off my shoes, my socks, and rolled up my pants. Ursuline waited for me, quietly, patiently, though I could feel the unspoken hum of tension coming from them.

At facing the sea.

Together, we walked down the shore, to where the waves rolled up. The first foamy lap of water made me shiver, and I reached out a hand for them, needing the connection. They intertwined their hands with mine for a moment, and we both stared out at the brine before us.

"How does it feel?" I asked. "Being free."

Ursuline squeezed my hand tighter. "I'm not sure."

"You can go back to New Atlantis now," I murmured, even though the thought of them heading somewhere I couldn't tread caused my chest to squeeze tight.

"What's left for me there but ruin?" They let go of my hand and waded into the water, just enough that it lapped against their tentacles. Their chest caved in, their head tipped down, and their shoulders began to shake. "He destroyed every last gasp of light down below."

I took one slow step after another to stand beside them, the waves swilling around my ankles. Ursuline's whole body shook, and it wasn't until I reached their side that I caught the glimmer of tears streaking down their face. I reached out but hesitated, not sure if this moment was too fragile, as if one touch might shatter it.

I lowered my hand and stood there with them, staring out at the sea, as if it might hold answers. Of why this much pain existed in the world. Of why horrors happened to innocents. Of why the rich and powerful were determined to cause destruction.

The red streaks on a canvas bloomed in my mind, and I itched to paint this agony. To cast it out from my heart, from my soul, and into art that might stand a chance of lasting beyond me.

I wasn't sure if minutes passed or longer, but Ursuline's tears slowed. They wiped their eyes, and then they slipped their arm around my shoulders. I leaned in.

"Thank you," they said.

"You don't need to thank me for loving you," I responded softly. The steady *thump, thump, thump* of their heart mirrored the same flow of the waves to the shore, undulating and constant. It grounded me in the moment, where I was here at the Sentient Sea with the monster I loved.

With the only one who'd ever spoken to my soul.

"I have no need to go back below," Ursuline murmured and pressed a kiss to the top of my head. "Once I found sunshine, I never wanted to return to the deep."

Their words etched into me, and my heart soared.

"So what's next?" I asked, but whether I referred to today or more, I wasn't sure.

Ursuline glanced at me with a soft, incandescent smile. "Well, this evening is game night at the Spires, so we couldn't miss that. Tomorrow, though, I think I'm going to start looking at homes for sale in Peregrine City. What do you say? Want to start a life with me?"

My eyes burned, and my throat tightened. "I can't wait."

***

Ursuline had mentioned game nights at the Spires before, but I'd been thinking about the casino itself. I'd figured it was flash, competition, where Ursuline and their friends all got together and gambled. But when I stepped into the dining hall on the upper floors where we'd been staying, the realization of what this was descended. This was a family gathering.

Sofia and Cillian chatted with each other at one of the tables, while Gretel and Amelia started to set out the cards for what looked to be a game of Sparks. Jaffar sat at the other long table, his long black waves pulled back today in a low ponytail. Mal sat beside him, and his bright purple lipstick and eyeshadow made the black scale accents along his features pop. Opposite them was a woman with wild brown hair and eyes that almost glowed, along with Charles and Theo, who I'd gotten to know well over our week here.

"Now we can get started," Amelia said, glancing up to us. "Who's ready for some Sparks?"

"I'm ready for some food," Charles said. "Did anyone place the pizza order yet?"

"I have it handled," Cillian responded. "Food should be here shortly."

"I'm over playing Sparks," Mal called out. "When can we bring a different game to the table?"

"Why do you think I sat here?" Jaffar commented with a smirk.

"Come sit down," Beau offered us, pointing to the spots at their table that were still open. So many of these people had become friends in such a short time. The shift made me realize how few of them I'd had before, how isolated I'd been.

"I'll always play a few rounds of Sparks," Ursuline said with a wan smile. They kept their hand on my lower back as they guided me over to the table, and I soaked in every bit of contact I could.

Today had been emotional, life-changing, and a revelation.

And tonight, we could celebrate our freedom with the people who'd helped us earn it.

"Did the Alpha Blue guys give you any difficulty?" I called over to Mal from our table.

Mal let out a bark of a laugh. "They're underequipped to deal with dragons. I flew off right after the first blast while they floundered."

"And you delivered the final blow to Triton?" Sofia asked Ursuline.

Ursuline nodded. "Now I'm done with that family for good."

"Fuck yeah," Charles called. "Bring out the champagne."

"Luckily I thought ahead," Beau said as he pulled a few bottles from a small cooler he had by his chair. "We already planned on celebrating."

"Tonight is also an official welcome to Elrich," Gretel said, and heat rose to my cheeks at being acknowledged like that. "We're happy to have you here."

Charles let out a hoot, and the wild-haired girl at the other table howled.

My heart thrummed. I'd never found this sort of acceptance before, this warmth. One of Ursuline's tentacles wrapped around my thigh and squeezed tight, and a shiver ran down my spine. This was what I'd spent a lifetime looking for, something I believed I'd never truly find. The love and support of a partner who understood me better than anyone, who brightened my world, and the warmth and belonging of a family.

"Get on my lap," Sofia said to Gretel, who arched a brow.

"Ugh, you two are nauseatingly cute," Amelia grumbled.

"Don't be jealous, Ames," Beau teased. "You could find yourself someone if you'd pull away from work once in a while." Cillian let out a rich, rumbling laugh.

"So, is anyone here good at Sparks?" I asked. I was a mediocre player, but I enjoyed the game.

Charles groaned from the other table. "They'll all start grandstanding now."

"Maybe if you were better at Sparks, you'd like it," Amelia called over.

"Who wants champagne?" Beau asked, and he popped the cork. The hiss echoed through the room.

"Me," I volunteered, raising my hand. "We've got a lot to celebrate."

Ursuline leaned in and pressed a kiss to my temple, the casual motion making my heart careen. "And tonight we'll continue the celebration."

Heat roared through me at what we'd discussed before, and already the anticipation rose within me for those private moments later with them, where they'd make me come undone at their hands, their tentacles, their mouth.

But right now, I basked in the moment. We were sitting among friends and celebrating. No more running, nothing keeping us apart. No more having my path dictated for me. I was with Ursuline, the one who quieted my soul, who made me feel complete in a way I'd craved my entire life. And we were with our family, one that would fight to protect each other.

Finally, I could chase the life I'd always dreamed of.

Epilogue

One Year Later...

Nerves filtered through me, a slow and steady hum that had increased with each passing hour.

"You'll do amazing," Ursuline murmured, pressing a kiss to the back of my neck.

I shifted, uncomfortable in the formalwear I'd donned, even though I'd chosen a pale-green linen suit and an off-white tee underneath. I'd been scrubbing away at the paint stains on my fingers all week, hoping to be presentable for today, and I'd done my best to style my hair. Ursuline looked formidably fine in their black tunic and silver choker, their hair carefully styled and liner making their eyes pop.

Their tentacle curled around my wrist and squeezed, and I took solace in it as we stepped into view of Landmark Gallery. It was a large building in the middle of the city, and the lights glowed from inside, beckoning us.

Tonight, it'd be the space hosting my first gallery showing.

The past year with Ursuline had been beyond my wildest fantasies. We'd found ourselves a new house in the city, similar to their old one. Ours was only a few streets down from Sofia and Gretel's, so we'd started to spend more and more time with them, the occasional catch-up over tea or dinners. Plus, game nights at the Spires were consistent and endlessly entertaining. The three-level house with its ornate carvings and wooden detailwork had ensnared my attention, and we'd set up an office for Ursuline's new business, a non-profit law firm. That had taken off at once, and given their connections, there was no shortage of work for them to get involved in. Pride thrummed inside me every time they came home and shared their cases with me.

And we'd converted the top room of the house into my studio.

I'd spent so many hours there, painting after painting pouring out of me. My muse had no shortage of subjects, whether it was the monster who made me scream in bed every night or the trials and tribulations we'd faced to find this peace.

And Jason had not only brought over my paintings that had resided at his place, but he'd made the initial contact with Landmark Gallery to set up this exhibition tonight. Now that I was my own man, separate from the Durand family, I was free to pursue the career as an artist I'd always longed for.

And my parents hadn't made a peep. They were too happy to keep their distance, especially with how the Triton kingdom had toppled.

The Human First members of society had blacklisted the Triton family at once upon discovering they were merfolk, but the Liquidium Industries scandal was what buried Frederick. Many of the companies who'd worked with him above and below had fallen prey to the shell corporation owned by Triton Industries, and Frederick and his family had been skimming off the top of it for a long, long while, living large on those funds.

He'd been prosecuted among his peers, found guilty, and faced jail time, and it couldn't have happened to a better person.

"Are you ready?" Ursuline asked, offering an arm.

I accepted their arm, the touch grounding me at once. Their quiet presence had been a touchstone for me from the moment we'd met, and I could barely believe some days that I'd get to keep them for the rest of my life.

We walked up the pathway, the spotlights casting plenty of visibility. When I reached the door, I hesitated. This was every secret dream I'd held. Of my art making it out into the world. Of a partner who lifted me up rather than tearing me down. Of a freedom that surged through my veins more with every passing day.

I stepped inside, along with Ursuline.

Relaxed music filtered into the foyer, setting up the ambiance for the building, and a gorgon in a flowing red dress approached, her bright-lipped smile engaging.

"Elrich Durand," she said. "Pleased to meet you. Follow me into the main gallery space, and we can get you set up for the showing."

"Thank you," I said, my voice a little hushed. This place was elegant, like the buildings I'd circulated through growing up, but from the gorgon in front of me alone, I could already see the difference.

I followed her in through the ornate green doors, which she latched open, and the sight before me caused my breath to snag.

The room itself was beautiful—crystal chandeliers, sweeping staircases leading to the second floor, and a black and white checkerboard floor. The walls were a dusky blue, the trim powder white, and the ceilings vaulted.

And adorning the walls in every direction was piece after framed piece of my artwork.

"I'll let you wander for a moment. Soak it in," the gorgon woman said, flashing another grin before she hustled back to the foyer.

I could barely move, frozen in place. The pieces that spanned before me were of darkened hallways, bloodied seas, of tentacles and motion, of love and light—unending light.

They were the quiet of velvet night and the bright sunshine that pierced through darkened clouds.

They were the story of Ursuline and me, of how fate had pushed us together. How we'd found each other, and how we'd fought for our freedom and didn't let go.

"I'm so proud of you," Ursuline said, their lips brushing against my ear. "See how you light up a room, sunshine?"

Heat prickled my eyes, and I had to swallow down a sob. The immense love that swelled within me was unparalleled. Each painting formed a tapestry of us, and seeing them all displayed at once overwhelmed me in the best way.

"I love you," I murmured. "As long as we're together, I'll never run out of inspiration. You bring color and depth to my life."

Ursuline pressed another kiss to my temple, and their tentacle squeezed around my ankle. "I love you too, Elrich. You're a gift I'll never stop appreciating. And no one will ever tear us apart."

They brought their arm around my shoulders, and I leaned into their warmth, into the solace I found in them. Heat spread from my chest outward, to my fingers, my toes, until my whole body was suffused with it.

I'd spent so long confined, same as them, but now a brilliant and meandering road sprawled out before me, filled with mysteries and grief and beauty and love so sharp it hurt. And with Ursuline by my side, this path was one I couldn't wait to travel.

Afterword

Thank you for reading Elrich and Ursuline's, the continuation of the Monstrous Cravings series!

While the first book in the series was more faithful to the fairytale, this was where I started veering off course, especially because I'm getting deeper into the world. The familiar thread through all my books though have to do with found family, and that's not changing in the slightest. I love the vibe of the Little Mermaid, and I hope this story captured that sense of yearning and a lead with big dreams—even if it's Elrich and not the usual mermaid.

The next fairytale we're diving into is Aladdin, and wow, it's getting darker. Aladdin and Jaffar's dynamic is fascinating and so different from the first two books because Aladdin's perspective comes from a much different part of Peregrine City, and his experiences shade that. I love how each bit of the series brings in new areas of Peregrine City and the universe itself too. And of course, there'll be more interludes at Haven Diner to enjoy!

If you enjoyed the book, leave a review. Kind words are what us authors survive on, and I can tell you personally I treasure each and every one.

Have you checked out the start of the Monstrous Cravings series, the origin of Gretel and Sofia's relationship? Check out the Lure of the Witch for free!

Want the latest updates on my books? Best way is to join my reader group, Katherine McIntyre's Mayhem, or my newsletter!

Also by

Ready for the next Monstrous Cravings book? The Aladdin Retelling, The Adder and the Ally is coming...

Aladdin's drawn the eye of a dangerous man, right as he's playing a dangerous game, but their illicit entanglement could bring down an entire city...

Also by

Want hurt/comfort romances featuring a geeky, queer found family?
Read across the rainbow with the Dungeons and Dating series!

Strength Check (Dungeons and Dating #1)
Wisdom Check (Dungeons and Dating #2)
Intelligence Check (Dungeons and Dating #3)
Constitution Check (Dungeons and Dating #4)
Dexterity Check (Dungeons and Dating #5)
Charisma Check (Dungeons and Dating #6)

Or if you want your hurt/comfort romances kinkier, check out the
Leather and Lattes series!

Immersion Play (Leather and Lattes #1)
Extraction Play (Leather and Lattes #2)
Percolation Play (Leather and Lattes #3)
Filtration Play (Leather and Lattes #4)
Concentration Play (Leather and Lattes #5)

Also by

If you're looking for light kink, high heat, and low angst, dip your toes into my other universe...Hot Under the Collar, filled with geeks, bears, and blue collar workers.

Sweat Connection (Hot Under the Collar #1)
Hot Conduit (Hot Under the Collar #2)
Joint Penetration (Hot Under the Collar #3)

And if you enjoyed the folks in Hot Under the Collar, then you'll love the spinoff into Ollie's family with The Brannon Boys!

Heat Transfer (Brannon Boys #1)
Bond Strength (Brannon Boys #2)
Direct Nailing (Brannon Boys #3)

Want even more in this universe? Join us for the tattoo shop found family at Alchemy Ink!

Open Liner (Alchemy Ink #1)
Stroke Frequency (Alchemy Ink #2)

About the Author

Katherine McIntyre is a feisty chick with a big attitude despite her short stature. She writes stories featuring snarky women, ragtag crews, and men with bad attitudes—high chance for a passionate speech thrown into the mix. As a genderqueer geek who's always stepped to her own beat, she's made it her mission to write stories that represent the broad spectrum of people out there. Easily distracted by cats and sugar.

www.ingramcontent.com/pod-product-compliance
Lightning Source LLC
LaVergne TN
LVHW091705070526
838199LV00050B/2290